It's the...

Gentle Breeze

...that Guides us

A Novel by

Marianne A. McDonald

When he was present, she had no eyes for anyone else. Everything he did was right. Everything he said was clever. If their evenings at the park were concluded with cards, he cheated himself and all the rest of the party to get her a good hand. If dancing formed the amusement of the night, they were partners for half the time; and when obliged to separate for a couple of dances, were careful to stand together, and scarcely spoke a word to anybody else. Such conduct made them, of course, most exceedingly laughed at; but ridicule could not shame, and seemed hardly to provoke them...

This was the season of happiness to Marianne.

From Sense and Sensibility by Jane Austen

From Embrace: a collection of poetry and prose in celebration of love by Robert Frederick Ltd.

DEDICATION

To my husband Robert McDonald
Thank you for all your love and support
throughout our years together.

And to our children:
I thank each of you for your love,
guidance and friendship.

I love you.

ACKNOWLEDGMENTS

Thank you goes to my husband who has helped me through every stage of this process. From being my first reader, my editor, my counselor on occasion, and my loving and supportive spouse.
I wish to thank my daughter, Danyelle, for all her help and support over the years and for her unending encouragement which has been invaluable.
Thank you also, to all my family and friends who have supported me.

CHAPTER ONE

"Sergeant, don't you think that Rayburn has been punished enough? He's been carrying that NBC mask for a week now." Private Thomas asked.

"Punishment would be making him wear it, this is corrective training." SSG Carl Reynolds answered. "What do you think Specialist Rayburn?"

"Hooah, Sergeant!"

"Do you think that I have been too hard on you?" Carl asked.

"No, Sergeant."

"Educate our private on the merits of corrective training and speaking of corrective training, make sure he did all of his pushups for the day. He's your responsibility; I expect Private PT failure, to become Private PT Stud." Carl winked.

Carl pulled his head cover out from his side pocket and snapped it open. "See you tomorrow - I have an important appointment with my wife."

"Hooah, Sergeant!"

Behind him, he could hear the others singing "brown, chicken, brown, cow." One yelled "That's right, get some."

Carl pretended not to hear them. "Remember 60 minutes. That means 50 minutes for all of you who can't count. Don't any of you be late to formation." He yelled loud enough for the whole room to hear.

"Hooah!" They all yelled.

"That includes you, Peters. *Better late than never* is not the motto of the United States Army."

They all laughed.

Carl heard the others begin teasing Peters by quoting some of his more outlandish excuses.

He exited the secured building and hopped into the driver's seat. It was 100 degrees in his POV. He rolled down the windows and blasted the AC on high. If he were quick, he could get through the gate before the cannon went off. He didn't mind getting out of his car, to stand at attention, and salute the flag. He just didn't want to do it today. He wanted to get home as fast as he could. He had to finish packing and wanted to spend as much time with the kids and Rebecca that he could.

He hated and loved the short ride home. He hated the other drivers. They were a menace. Imagine taking drivers under the age of 25 from all 50 states and some from other countries and putting them in high speed vehicles. The result is an unskilled version of the Indy 500. On terrible days, it is a smashup derby gone wrong. To prove his point, a prominently placed board at the post's main entrance counted the days since the last vehicular fatality. The part he loved about the drive home was arriving to find Rebecca in the front yard looking sweaty and beautiful working at weeding the flower beds. But he equally loved greeting her as she worked at the kitchen sink making their dinner. If he were sneaky enough, he could catch a glimpse of her singing and dancing before she realized he was watching her and became self-conscience. He loved to view the sway of her hips to the music, his body reacted, sometimes violently.

He pulled the car into the driveway to find Danny playing in the yard. "Hey Soldier!" Carl yelled toward his son.

"Hi Dad." Danny answered as he kicked the soccer ball.

Carl intercepted it and kicked it back. "Playing all by yourself?" Carl asked and then saw the angel wing laying on the ground. "Uh-oh, You tell Mom about that?" His son looked at the ground.

"No." Danny said quietly.

"You know what this means, Right." Carl scooped his son up into the air, "The treatment." Carl play bit Danny's abdomen, careful not to drop him as his seven year old squirmed in his arms.

"Dad! No, Stop Dad." He laughed.

He flipped him over his shoulder and swung him down to the ground. Tickling him, he teased. "You going to fix that angel?"

"Yup." He laughed. "Yup, I'm going to fix it." He managed to squeak out between laughs.

Carl picked Danny up by his feet and lifted him up and down. "I don't see any change falling out of those pockets of yours." He flipped him over and placed him on the ground feet first.

"Do that again, Dad, Again... Please." Danny pulled on his dad's hand.

"No." He picked him up. "We have to go get the superglue and fix that wing."

He took his dad's ID tags off his neck and placed them over his own head and let them fall against his stomach. "Okay."

Inside the girls were sorting through old books on the living room floor. "What are you girls up to?" He gently touched Karen's hair as he maneuvered over piles of books and toys that the girls were sorting through.

"Figuring out what we no longer want so we can take it to the Donation Center." Rachel answered.

In the kitchen, Rebecca washed a dish, occasionally, glancing into the backyard. Carl placed his hands on her hips taking a good long look at the view. Then he firmly placed himself up against her and wrapped one arm around her waist as he brushed her long hair away from her neck. He pressed his lips against her fragile neck and kissed it long and soft as he worked his way down toward her shoulder.

"Mmm. That feels nice." Rebecca responded. She loved the feel of him against her. He was the perfect combination of strength and gentleness.

Funny how both of those together; combusted her insides into an instant desire that had to be squelched, and until it was, she wriggled with need. She felt his hand roam to places that made her hurt. "Your being bad." She said and smiled.

"Not as bad as I want to be." He answered. "What are you staring at?"

"I think I'll miss that tree the most." She turned to face Carl, feeling his tight forearms and moving up to his rock hard biceps. Rebecca reached her hands up under his camouflage top to feel his equally hard abdomen. She then investigated a little further. He was hard everywhere.

Carl grinned. He was about to dive into his wife's breasts when he heard "Dad" called out from five feet behind him. "Yeah Buddy." Carl answered and then whispered into her ear, "We'll play later."

"You promise." Rebecca replied.

Carl cleared his throat. "Yup." he replied and straightened his uniform top to cover the remaining hard parts of his body.

"I got it." Danny answered.

"Don't open it, It'll hurt you." Carl reached for the tube of superglue, with Danny in tow they were on a mission to repair Rebecca's statue.

They returned to the kitchen with satisfied looks on their faces that she immediately interpreted as "mission accomplished."

Rebecca filled five plates and set each in its proper place. With Carl at the head of the table, they all sat down to eat, It was a ruckus with all three children vying loudly for their fathers attention. By now, Carl had dumped his dust cover boots by the front door, and his cover sat on the table beside it, with his car keys and driving glasses resting inside. Later tonight a heavy laden duffle and rucksack will also be waiting by the door, but for now he was all theirs. Before the kids go to bed, each will have danced with their Dad to their own special songs. They will have played "Kung Fu Theater" by gang karate chopping him, and he will have asked each of them to help Mom out while he is away. Promising each one that he'll be back home as soon as he can.

She knew the alert would come around 3:00am. She also knew that Carl would forfeit all sleep tonight to be with her. She enjoyed a glass of wine while she watched him pack. It will be the last one that she'll have until he returns. It was an unspoken rule between them that she never drank when he was gone, being she was their children's sole parent while he was away.

He placed his bag against the door. "You drunk enough to dance for me tonight?" He asked her.

"No, I don't think so." Rebecca replied.

Carl placed a handmade advent calendar on the refrigerator and grabbed the bottle of wine. Then he took her hand and pulled her up off the couch and slapped her butt hard as she led the way toward their bedroom. He closed their door behind them, but didn't get two paces into the room before he turned her around and gave her a long hard kiss. "I love you."

"I love you, too." Rebecca replied. She let her hands roam, enjoying the feel of his hard chest under his brown military tee-shirt. She gripped his biceps, feeling them contract into stone hard muscles, when he used them to lift her up off the ground. On the bed, he came down forcefully against her. She felt every muscle in his body, and it excited her more than what she knew he would do next. She reached for his belt and tugged it loose, reaching under to find him ready. He refused to enter her and instead made her lay back. Determined, he took his time, like this would be the last time he would ever make love to her. "Are you okay?" She asked. He nodded that he was.

He visually absorbed every detail. The curve of her hips, the sharp contour the outline of her body made, winding up to her waist and back out again at her breast. He soaked in the soft silky feel of her skin, the sexy pink of her nipples. He wanted this image to last him 30 long days away from her. Did she understand that 30 days to a soldier felt like 6 months? "You're so beautiful, I want to memorize every inch of you." She smiled at him in response. He knew she was indulging him. She didn't realize how difficult it was for him to be away from her. Even so, she was sweet and patient with him, he wanted this memory to be for both of them. He gently lay down next to her and softly touched her until he saw her back arch. When he heard her breath begin to hyperventilate, he tasted her sweetness until he felt her quiver. He did that all again. Then waited for her to beg him to enter her.

Rebecca felt a shutter down her body then she heard her own breath beginning to clip. She felt his mouth sucking gently at her breast and his magical touch building the tension in her body all over again. When she couldn't take anymore, she cried-out, "Please. please, Carl." She wanted to feel his weight, the strength of his muscles against her and inside her. "I want you." Carl finally entered her. She felt his hand grasp the side of her face, and she opened her eyes to see his green eyes staring intently into hers. She felt him move deeper. In response, she wrapped her legs tight around his thighs to help pull him to her harder, deeper. She felt every inch of him, grabbed the back of his head and felt the smooth stubble of his crew cut. She drifted to her husband's moans and felt a surge of butterflies in her stomach when she felt her body sharply embrace his, then she felt hers suddenly burst. A minute later she heard him moan louder and felt him spasm inside her.

He drank his bottle of water, and she sipped the wine that he passed to her, then she lay in his arms a long while. Both of them silently absorbing the reality that, by morning, he would be gone. "I'm Sorry." Carl broke their silence. "I tried to get out of this."

"It's okay." She answered. "We'll finish everything. It'll be okay. Does GDL know that you'll be unreachable?"

"Yes, I talked to Brian this morning. He assured me the job is still there for me and that I can complete the final paperwork when we arrive."

"Good." Rebecca climbed on top of Carl. "Tell me one thing that I don't know."

"Like what?" Carl looked into her dark brown eyes. He said intently, "I hate leaving you."

"Tell me something." He returned.

She smiled, leaned in close and memorized his green eyes. "I'm just with you for the sex." She put her lips to his and drew him into a long hot kiss.

"Are You." He grinned. "I think you'll regret that statement." He flipped her with ease and immediately felt the result of her teasing.

She never heard him leave, but his side of the bed was empty. She reached over and felt his empty space, flat and cold, and told herself that 30 days weren't all that long. The truth was; she already missed him. The evidence of his departure was obvious; his hygiene products were gone from the bathroom, as were his bags, boots, and hat. The only thing that he left was the calendar that he made for the kids. It was pinned center mass on the refrigerator with two bright smiley faced magnets.

Rebecca made a short pot of coffee. She heard a child stirring down the hall, then heard the bathroom toilet flush and the sink turn on. She yelled to the other two children and heard Danny's foot prints run to the front door, he opened it and looked outside. Then he let out a deep sigh as he looked down and closed the door. "He'll be back before you know it, sweetie." Rebecca called to him. Rachel pulled out some cereal bowls, and Karen rubbed her eyes as she entered the kitchen. All three kids looked at the calendar. Rachel explained to Danny that they were to open only one flap each day to read their dad's notes. They let Danny open the first. Rachel read it to him: Day 1: Super Dad Flies. The depiction of their Dad was as a small drawing of a soldier with a cape flying in the shape of a plane. The arms outstretched with a capital D on the chest.

Danny ran back to his room. He emerged wearing his power rangers pajamas and the super hero cape from his last Halloween costume tied around his neck. "I'm ready to go with Dad."

Everyone laughed.

"Tell you what, we can't do that, but we can have a movie marathon and make a cake." Rebecca told them.

They all yelled, "Yay!" Rebecca included.

CHAPTER TWO

God, she hated this.

Rebecca stood in front of the picture window. Like she had for the last six months, staring vacantly at the gravel drive, waiting, hoping, praying that Carl would come walking up it dressed in his smelly fatigues, dragging his dust covered combat boots through the dirt as he lugged his heavy gear on his back. She longed to rush out the door; meeting his dirty camouflaged face with a big kiss and unburden him of his long carried load. Tomorrow, she wouldn't be here if he did.

She had always liked moving to new places. It made her feel strong and adventurous to pick-up and move the way they did every year or two. She loved her life and everything about it. She loved the sounds of cadence in the morning and reveille when she went to sleep. She loved the feeling of safety and comfort emitted by the presence of soldiers in uniforms and heavy combat boots. She loved the constant visual reminder of their environment by seeing the high and tight haircuts that Carl and every other soldier sported. She especially loved the patriotic feeling of being a part of this unique community. She knew that it all eventually had to end, but she never expected it to end like this.

After fourteen-years as a military spouse, there were only two things she never got used to; one was sleeping alone and the other was moving day. She should be used to both. Today marked their ninth move, much more than that if you counted all the hotels they have lived in while they were between houses. She waited anxiously for the movers to arrive;

strangers who will sift through, sort, and pack all her personal belongings. She wondered if they felt as uncomfortable as she did. The worst part was when they first arrived and she felt their eyes visually scanning her house and all her possessions. They never failed to mention the boxes she had packed herself. It made her feel like she had somehow offended them by doing this. Then came the uncomfortable questions. What was in it? Was anything breakable? Did she understand that if anything were damaged that they wouldn't be responsible because she'd packed it herself? Frankly, the few items that she packed were probably the only objects she could expect to reach their destination undamaged. This was why she and Carl didn't bother to own anything that they would care two cents about if it broke.

Rebecca wrapped her arms tight around herself as she saw the large truck pull up into the gravel driveway. A pickup pulled in behind it, and she watched as two men jumped down from the truck and three more poured out from the front of the pickup. She greeted them with a half smile and shook each one's hand. Then she accompanied the leader of them through the house as he assessed her life. When they reached her bedroom, he pointed to the boxes on the floor. He started to give her the speech that she's heard eight times before, but for some unknown reason when he looked up at her he stopped talking and instead nodded with a small frown. He then marked the boxes on the inventory sheet. Rebecca signed where he marked the form with big black X's. She was grateful that he didn't insist on repacking them, or knowing what was in them. It's nothing big, just the stuff you don't want others to see and touch. Like undergarments, lingerie and the type of self-help books that she didn't want everyone to know she owned. Not that she's ashamed. She just didn't want everyone thinking that they're oversexed, even if it is true. They're worth the embarrassment though. Those books helped her to keep their marriage intact; especially during years two and five.

Rebecca saw one of the guys turn sideways to carry a box out of the house. It made her chuckle remembering a previous move they had made. She'll never forget Carl's reaction when he answered the doorbell. He went to open the door, and all he saw was darkness. A huge Samoan man was blocking all the bright Hawaiian sunshine from shining through the door. She laughed as she remembered her husband coming over to tell her, "This man is huge. I could see no sunlight from behind him. He is so big." She'll never forget his expression of awe with just a slight bit of fear.

However, this huge man was the most gentle of the movers she had experienced. He was friendly and considerate, and she even remembered his bewildered question about her beheaded statue of Mary. She recalled telling him, "No, it's not normal to have Mary's with their heads broken off," explaining to him that it is a Catholic statue. It was her mother's, and although her husband had knocked it over and broke it, she hadn't had the heart to throw it away. It had been on her family's mantle since she could remember. As a child, her and her sister's job was to keep fresh flowers in a small glass, in front of Mary.

The Hawaiian man had made that move a little easier, and he didn't react defensively when she had boxes of personal items packed ahead of time.

"Ma'am, Do you want this packed with the kitchen dishes or somewhere else? The moving kid was holding something up for her to see.

"Yes, Please. With the dishes is fine." Rebecca answered.

It was the Mary statue. She always had it sitting on the kitchen windowsill, which was how Carl had knocked it over several times while he was washing dishes. Except now it was no longer beheaded. When they had moved to Tennessee, Carl had fixed it one summer while she was gone. So now it had a dented nose from always falling off Mary's balancing shoulders, but she was whole again thanks to Carl and some super glue. Now that she thought about it, the angel in the front yard had fallen over and become beheaded and de-winged, and Carl had fixed it with super glue also. Geez, was God trying to tell her something? It was no mystery how they became broken. Her husband broke Mary, and her seven-year old son kicked a soccer ball into the angel more than once. Forget it. She couldn't make sense out of anything right now, least of all God.

Psychology degree or not, she could not rationalize her way through what was happening to her life right now. Could anyone make sense out of this? No one could. Well yeah, the government could, but they're not talking. How could a soldier go away on a routine training mission and disappear? It's inconceivable, and it was not as if Carl were a Special Forces soldier or something equally dangerous. He was a regular soldier like any of thousands. How was she supposed to react to this information? What should she do? Should she pretend that he's still off in the field and wait for him to come home? Or should she accept that he is gone and not coming back? What should she tell the kids? No one knows where daddy is! But then, she can't help wondering, did he leave her - or is there something the government isn't telling her? Rebecca knows in her heart that he wouldn't leave her by choice. This is crazy. So what should she do? How should she respond to something like this? She just feels numb.

What would the "psych-me" tell someone in my position, Rebecca wondered, to be honest she didn't know. Would she feel good about advising someone to grieve and move on? Or would she worry about giving someone the will to go on hoping for their loved one's safe return, which might turn out fruitless?

"Ma'am, Ma'am, We're going to take our lunch break. We'll be back in an hour." The mover told her.

"Okay. I'll see you then, thanks." She waved to the guy.

The strange thing is this move that she and the children were making. She's unsure how to feel about it. She knew enough about the military, to know that it wouldn't pay her without a reason. They sent a man from the Criminal Investigation Division (CID) to tell her that they were searching the country for Carl, sure that he would turn up AWOL. They said the government would keep her and the kids provided for until they found him. It was six months before they came back and last month they decided to pay her Carl's life insurance, but they could not list him as anything except missing. The man then told her that as long as she didn't go public with this incident, they would continue to have Carl's pay sent to her while they left the investigation open a little longer. She looked at this man and he looked at her and smiled.

It was at that moment that a memory flooded back to her of the time when her husband was in combat. She had moved back to Fort Knox. Standing there with her eighteen month old daughter at her side and her newborn daughter in her hands, the Lieutenant asked Rebecca why she had moved back when the other wives were moving away. She told him that her husband would come home soon, and she wanted his home to be ready for him. That Lieutenant had looked at her the very same way as this man did, and he smiled too. Two and half months later Carl and the rest of his unit got off the bus that brought them home. Rebecca, the kids, and his home were there waiting for him. Later, the Lieutenant told Carl that she was a rock, and she never understood what he had meant. Rebecca thought it was a failing on her part that she didn't somehow love him enough to fall apart. Carl told her it was the highest compliment. Now she understood; that was the Lieutenant's way of saying that she too was a soldier, a boulder of strength and faith.

"Hello, Mrs. Reynolds. We're back, we don't have to much more to finish packing. We should be done by 5 o'clock."

The moving guy stared at her. "That's great." She watched as he and his co-workers came through the door with fast-food drinks in their hands. One carried in a boom box with them.

"Do you mind if we listen to some music?" One of them asked.

"No, I don't mind." She said as she went to gather her and the kids' luggage to put in the car.

It's unnerving not knowing what has happened or if he'll walk through the door tomorrow. What makes her angry is that she never felt that Carl should have had to go on that last training exercise. He only had two months left and then he was going to exit the military and they were moving on. We were moving on; Rebecca thought, moving on to a world with no more deployments, no more packing and unpacking and no more fear of war. He already even had a job lined up as a civilian. Everything was set. Except now, 'we' was gone and the only one moving on was her.

Her final decision to leave had more to do with where they were living than with moving on. She thought it was probably difficult to understand, if you haven't lived in a military town, because then you wouldn't understand how it is a special breed, all its own. The people that live there are all a kinship of sorts, either you're active duty or retired military or a relative of either. It's a bond that everyone shares. Few people have extended family living nearby. Your family becomes the unit your spouse is assigned to and if you're lucky you make friends with a few couples. Your children grow up with their children and your kids hardly ever get to know their own grandparents and cousins. It is the bond of the marriage that makes the family and the couples joined that makes life comfortable and supportive. When that link is severed, it leaves you feeling more alone than anyone can imagine.

Rebecca never knew how hard it would be in a military town

without her husband. Things that seemed small before were huge now. Like the Black Hawk and Chinook helicopters; she would swear she sees more of them fly by than she sees cardinals. The camouflage uniforms; never did she notice before how overwhelming they could be. Even worse, she finds she looks at each one to see if it is Carl. What upsets her more is she has noticed the children doing it too. This town, where she was once so happy, is now making her feel as though she is going insane. She decided that if she is going to feel alone, then at least she could do so in a place where she and the kids wouldn't be looking out the window and through crowds to search for her husband and their father. So she put their house on the market and made the choice to move, just as they had planned. And if the day came where he would walk off that bus, his family and his new home would be there waiting for him.

God, he hoped she was all right. How he had stumbled himself into this shit he didn't know, but he knew he wanted out. He just hoped the kids and Rebecca were okay. He never even thought about his predicament. He only insisted that they not tell Rebecca that he was dead. He hoped they hadn't, because he knew she loved him, but she was also a strong woman. Carl knew she would do what was best for the family and move on with their lives. There was no way he was willing to lose her over some stupid, coincidental mistake. He had stumbled into something big, and he didn't even know what it was. Now they think he is some sort of genius. I'm good at my job, but I'm not that good, Carl thought. He even told them so, but they wouldn't believe him. Those CID idiots said to him, "Who gets out at fourteen years? You must know something or have some plan." "Yeah," he told them; "It's called staying alive. This military has gone to shit, and I don't want to be involved with the next war." He knew that was stupid; only a fool would talk like that to the people who have the power to hurt him. But he'd had it, "It" meaning short-timer's disease. The point where you have so little time left in the service that you can't take the Yes Sir, No Sir, and the Yes Ma'am, No Ma'am even a minute longer. He also knew that he needed to straighten his head out, and quick, because these were people who could make him disappear for real, if they wanted to. The problem is, somebody else screwed up, not him. That computer program shouldn't have been that easy for him to get by. No one was talking, but he knew someone had messed up badly. The real point is that he knew he could probably figure out how to do it again. But the question was, did they know this and would that ensure that Carl never sees Rebecca again?

***

The movers left an hour ago and the only thing left for Rebecca to do was to finish cleaning and leave the keys on the stove for the realtor. She knew the kids, especially Rachel, were going to be sad to leave. They all were, she thought. But Rachel was the oldest child, and she had the most to leave behind. She was a big girl now, in middle school. She was also popular, not only with the other kids, but with the teachers. This will be hard on her. On the other hand, Danny, our seven-year-old, only knows this home. At least Rachel and Karen can remember other homes that they have lived in with their father. Rebecca had known the day was coming when they would put their house up for sale. She just thought it would be under happier circumstances and not due to anything like this.

This was the house they lived in the longest of Carl's military career. They fixed it up a lot since they had bought it, spending more than they planned, and Rebecca had finally finished decorating it the way she had envisioned it. "Rachel, do you remember the horrible blue color that we painted over in the back bedroom?"

"Oh, I know." Rachel said, "It was so bright that we couldn't even sleep in it, it was so bad."

"Yeah, she shook her head, it took your Dad and me three coats of primer to put paint on without that blue bleeding through. The kitchen wallpaper was as old as the house." Rebecca continued. "But it looks pretty now." She looked at the cream walls with the ivy border. "I'm sure that it will sell quickly." But she'll miss their yard and her beautiful shade trees in the back. She checked the thermostat and placed the keys on the stove. She then called the kids to come and look at the backyard one last time, and they circled the house once full around and said goodbye to their little brick ranch in Tennessee.

When they reached the hotel, Danny was already asleep, and that was all Rebecca and the girls wanted to do too. She ordered dinner in and plopped herself on the bed to call her mother and let her know they would be on their way in the morning. Then she hoped that her energy wouldn't give out before dinner arrived, and she could grab a shower. When the kids were all fed and settled into bed, she climbed into bed herself and wondered what she should do next. Agonizing over her choices, she fell off to sleep.

She woke when she heard a thump outside their hotel room door and jumped from the startle it gave her. It was 1:00 am and it didn't surprise her that a casual thud in the night would wake her. She never did sleep well when Carl was in the field. Why would these months without him make her any different? She decided to take just one sleep aid tablet. That way she wouldn't go into hibernation, but it would at least calm her nerves enough to sleep. She knew she had a long day ahead of her tomorrow, and she couldn't afford to fall asleep at the wheel. Her Mom's house was all the way up in Connecticut. That was a long way from Tennessee, especially by herself with three children. Maybe she'll stop for the night tomorrow instead of trying to make the trip in one-shot.

Her mind wandered to when she and Carl would drive home from Kentucky when Carl was just a private. They couldn't afford hotel rooms back then. So instead, they would leave at midnight and drive the trip while the girls slept. She could remember one trip where they went home for Thanksgiving. By the time they reached Pennsylvania, forget it, they were in a blizzard. Rebecca remembered praying on her rosary beads the whole way. She realized now that they never again traveled in the winter. She yawned. Besides, they left for Hawaii shortly after that. The last thing Rebecca could recall was seeing 2:00am on the hotel alarm clock.

Carl watched as a man entered his room, which he prefers to call his cell. What else would anyone call a place where they're kept against their will, even if it were nicer than any barracks room he'd ever seen. Although, he is free to come and go to a certain extent, anyone who keeps him from his family is a jailer in his mind. The man was dressed in his Army Dress

Blue Uniform with ribbons covering his chest. He read the resume displayed across the Major's dark blue uniform jacket, noticing that he had several overseas ribbons, campaign ribbons, Expert Infantry Rifleman, Airborne and Air Assault badges, Three Bronze Stars and a Silver Star. Carl was impressed and he took it as a good sign that he entered his room with his full uniform on, Since wearing it implied that he had no reason to hide his identity from Carl. He couldn't say that about the other man.

With him was a man about Carl's age dressed in civilian clothes. "Good morning, Sergeant Reynolds. I am Major Taylor." He gestured to the other man, "This is Lieutenant Jordan." He said loudly.

Carl noticed that it was just like an officer to enter like a tornado and to talk like one too. Some things never changed.

"Today is a Special Day! Can you guess why that is?" The man barked, "Because it's moving day! No, Sergeant Reynolds it's not your moving day. It's your family's."

Carl's throat fell into the pit of his stomach, but his temper was steadily climbing.

"No, Sergeant. Don't get upset. This is good news. Actually, your wife waited longer than most wives do. Simpler problems usually send them running home to Daddy." He smiled. "We were really starting to get nervous. We thought we were going to have to do some coaxing." He held up his fingers an inch apart. "In truth; we did do a little something to get her to move. We gave her your life insurance." He said with a slight grin.

Oh shit, Carl can feel the blood rushing to his face, They've told her I'm dead. Those Bastards!

"Relax Sergeant, We didn't tell her you are dead. We've kept our side of this bargain." He crossed his arms in smug victory. "But we did give her the means to leave, and it's free, on the house as they say. It's a sound investment though because you're going to save us a lot more money than the 300 grand we gave to your wife and kids. What are their names again?" He tapped the table to jar his memory. "Oh Yes, that's right, Rachel, Karen and Danny. You know, that expression on your face leads me to believe that you question my integrity." The Major paused.

"Well Sir." Carl said, "I can't say that I have a reason to trust anyone around here." Then Carl stood and looked Major Taylor in the eye, "I know I didn't do anything to deserve the treatment the Army is giving me. All I did was my job and a simple harmless favor to a colonel. And this is the thanks I get?"

The Major hesitated and then he softened his tone slightly as he said, "You know, Sergeant Reynolds, sometimes we have reasons for the things that we do." The Major had to feel bad for the situation this soldier was in. He knew the Sergeant was a good soldier too. The Military was losing too many good soldiers these last few years. But after all, they did pride themselves on being an all-volunteer Army and this man didn't exactly feel like a volunteer right now. Major Taylor walked over to SSG Reynolds home away from home's kitchenette and asked if he could have a cup of his coffee. Carl told him to help himself. The Major then asked Carl and Lieutenant Jordan if they would like some also. He grabbed three cups and the pot of coffee and carried it to the table in the corner of the room as the other two men joined him. Then Major Taylor continued, "Sergeant Reynolds, just because I come off as a heartless, hard ass doesn't mean I don't have good intentions. You know as well as I do, the attitude comes with the job. It's unfortunate that your wife didn't understand that; I heard that she would have been a good officer."

Carl considered ignoring the Major's last statement, but he couldn't let it pass. "She understood it just fine. That 'attitude' you talk about didn't sit well with her."

"Ah, Yes." said Major Taylor. "She was a psychology major; wasn't she, Lieutenant Jordan?"

Carl looked at LT Jordan seated next to him. He thought that he recognized him when he came in with the Major. Now, he placed him as one of the cadets at the Reserve Officers Training Corps battalion, Rebecca was with. If he remembered right, this guy was a Sergeant and a Ranger before he became an officer through the Army's Green to Gold program.

Lieutenant Jordan answered the Major. "Yes, Sir. I believe she was, Sir."

"Sergeant Reynolds, Do you recognize Lieutenant Jordan?"

"Yes Sir, I know who he is, but for the record my wife's problem wasn't that she was a psychology major. She just didn't feel a job was worth becoming a different person for." Carl barked back. How rude, he though this man was, to talk to him about Rebecca as if he knew her.

"Sergeant, unfortunately, not all officers view diverse personalities as an asset the way I do. If she could have played the game a little better, she would have been a valuable member to this military."

Carl couldn't argue with his viewpoint. He unfolded his arms from against his chest.

"I agree with you, Sir." The Lieutenant said, "But everyone could see how the camp had broken her spirit. No one blamed her for her choice; after all. Still, it was a damn shame though." said Lieutenant Jordan.

Carl didn't like the familiarity with which Jordan spoke about his wife.

The Major agreed with the Lieutenant. "It is a shame when the military loses good soldiers, which brings us back to you Sergeant Reynolds." The Major warmed his coffee and held up the pot in offering to the others. "I suppose you'd like to finally know what this is about."

Did that understatement need a response, Carl didn't think so. He thought about Hooah, but that seemed inappropriate. He didn't trust that any response would come out without sarcasm, so instead, Carl just waited for Major Taylor to continue.

"You see, as hard as it is for you to believe right now, we have had you and your family's best interest in mind by holding you here. I know seven months sitting idle has been difficult, Your reputation at your current duty station speaks for itself. I also know what type of husband and father you are, which has made this time especially hard for you. Sergeant, my intention, is not to sit here and blow smoke up your ass. I just mean to let you know that I understand what a hardship this experience has been for you." He paused, "Which is why, what I have to tell you, is unfortunately only going to increase your pain and I wish to apologize to you in advance." God, he hated this part of his job. Fortunately it didn't happen too often. This was only the third time in his career something of this nature had taken place, innocent people caught up in something they had no idea existed. The thing is, he read this soldier's record and knew he had opportunities to join programs in the Army that require top secret security clearances. He declined them and the risks involved with them. He also knew he did it because he valued his family more than the prestige of his job. So how do you tell a man that you don't know how long it will be before he can see his family again? The Major sat there staring at Carl trying to figure out what words to use to break the bad news.

Oh God, Why is he hesitating so long to say whatever it is he has to say. Carl's mind started racing through options. It must be Rebecca and the kids. Something bad must have happened to them. Carl wished he would just spit it out, yet he didn't want to hear it either. The silence is overwhelming him. He can feel the acid climbing up his throat. He swallowed hard to force it back down.

The Major stared at Sergeant Reynolds. Watching as his face became red and then white, he recognized that he had better put this man out of his agony soon. He just wasn't sure where to start.

Lieutenant Jordan could feel the thickness in the silent air. "Major Taylor, would you like me to make a fresh pot of coffee."

Oh lord, I'm getting soft in my old age. "Thank you Lieutenant Jordan, could you also find us something light to have with it, some muffins or donuts maybe." The Major gave him a look of gratitude. Just then it came to him; the Major knew what the Sergeant's face was telling him. He thought his family was gone. "No, Sergeant Reynolds your family is fine, I promise you that. We're keeping an eye on them, and I assure you they'll be protected." Oh lord, this poor guy. Actually; that news was easier to give. You just spit it out, and it's over with. There isn't much you can do when one's loved one is dead, except to tell them and apologize. Then leave them to deal with it. That sounds heartless, but what's done is done and you can't change it. Whereas, news like this is a matter of where to begin, and with helping them to accept it; so everyone can get on with their jobs.

Carl's stomach left his throat and returned to its rightful place when Lieutenant Jordan returned with a plate filled with both doughnuts and muffins. The sight of it made the acid, in his stomach, reach once more for his Adam's apple. Carl swallowed hard, commanding his stomach to obey orders.

The Major noticed color returning to Sergeant Reynolds' face. He was grateful for Lieutenant Jordan's return, so they could get this finished.

Lieutenant Jordan refilled everyone's cups and then took his seat once more.

Major Taylor began again, "I've decided it may be easier for all of us if you tell us what you think has happened Sergeant Reynolds and then we can fill you in on the details of the situation and then the operation plan." The Major took his coffee black and took a sugary doughnut to combat the bitterness. "Please Sergeant, help yourself" the Major insisted.

Carl added three heaped spoons of sugar and one-third cup cream to his two-third cup coffee. Then he hoped his stomach would hold as he reached for a sugar coated vanilla cream filled doughnut. The Lieutenant Added only a spoon of sugar to his black coffee and took a blueberry muffin. Carl surveyed their actions and thought of Rebecca. He could hear her now telling him, "If food described a man's personality then the three of them wouldn't be hard to figure out." Carl looked at the two men in front of him. He chuckled to himself and thought she would have been right too. He took a sip of his coffee to choke down his sugar and then said to the men sitting across from him. "Sir, there isn't much for me to say to you, but I'll tell you what I can."

Carl explained to them how he didn't have much time left in the Army, but how he hadn't had a choice about going to the unit's rotation at the National Training Center. This was because they still had not received a replacement for him at the unit yet. Both he and his wife weren't happy about it because it would only give him about three weeks when he got back to do all his out processing from the Army. But of course they had no choice but to 'Suck it up and Drive on.' They were screwed, but capable of dealing with it, and moving forward. A regular occurrence in the military. He told them how the training exercise was routine, the only event out of the ordinary; which was common practice, was that he extended his services as the brigade computer expert to Colonel Dobson at his request. It was no big deal, officers always asked for help with their computers; to fix their e-mail, get rid of viruses, you name it. He was experiencing a problem getting into one of his program files. It was locked, and/or he couldn't remember his password or it wasn't working. Carl explained that he found a backdoor into it and helped him to setup a new password. "That's it" Carl said, "Your men came for me and I've been here since."

The Major thought about what to ask him. To help clear up his own suspicions, he asked him about Colonel Dobson's involvement. "Is that all that was exchanged between you and Colonel Dobson?"

"What specifically are you asking me, Sir?" Carl didn't like the predicament he was in, but he felt the Colonel was a good man, and he didn't want to harpoon him.

The Major looked into the Sergeant's eyes and hoped his own men were as dedicated to him as this Sergeant was to Colonel Dobson. He smiled with pride at the soldier across from him, "Sergeant Reynolds, I admire your loyalty to Colonel Dobson and I want to assure you that I feel he has been nothing but forthright with everyone involved. He also deeply regrets having gotten you into this situation, yet, not surprisingly he also takes pride in the fact that his soldier accomplished such a feat. All I'm asking you to do is to verify Colonel Dobson's account of what happened."

Carl doesn't want to betray the Colonel, yet he also feels that the Major is telling him the truth. Hesitantly, Carl says, damn his body felt twisted, he didn't want to be suckered into ruining a man's career. He finally let it out. "The Colonel told me the file was Top Secret. Immediately, I informed him that I did not possess a Top Secret Security Clearance. When he asked if I could fix it without having to see the contents of the file, I told him I could and neither of us thought that it was worth worrying about. Carl paused, "It took me awhile, but once I got in, it was an easy fix and then we both went on our way, back to work as normal. I didn't see what was in the file, and Colonel Dobson covered both our asses by staying with me the entire time to verify the files integrity was never compromised."

"Thank you, Sergeant. That is exactly what Colonel Dobson told us. Just so you know the Colonel's part in all this was investigated. Although no one can be certain, we are confident the Colonel had no ulterior motives in asking for your assistance. He was locked out, and we understand that it happens to the best of us." The Major stood up. He asked if anyone else needed to pee, and get some more coffee. Because when he came back, it would be time for him to fill Carl in on the significance of what he has done.

The two men nodded to the Major in agreement.

Lieutenant Jordan took quick leave for the door, "Twenty minutes,

Sir." He did not wish to be alone with Sergeant Reynolds, it was better for them to avoid any discussion about what his evolvement in this was going to entail. He knew the man wouldn't be pleased, and he rather the Major was the one who told him. He hoped the news would be less alienating that way. He sympathized with the Sergeant, knowing fully-well, if the tables were turned he wouldn't like it one bit. He rushed out the door when the Major replied. "Yes, Lieutenant Jordan, Twenty minutes should be fine."

They all split up and went their separate ways so each could stretch and get a break from the others.

As Carl stood to stretch and go use his own private bathroom, he noticed how drained he felt, but he also felt relieved that he will finally get some answers for his captivity. He thought about what the Major had said when he entered his four star cell this morning, Moving Day, and he wondered where his family was right now or where they were going.

CHAPTER THREE

Rebecca woke up and reached for the hotel alarm clock. 7:00am, at least she managed to get some sleep. She knew they needed to get up and out on the road soon if she wanted to make the most of the daylight. February's days are short, and she'll lose an hour when she crosses the central and eastern timeline. "Kids, wake-up!" She yelled. "Come-on guys, It's time to get going." Rebecca announced.

"Oh, What time is it?" Karen complained as she stretched and then rolled her body into a blanket cocoon. Rachel was already up getting her toiletries, and was headed for the bathroom. "Karen, it seems dark in here with the curtains closed, but it is ten after seven, we need to get on the road. I also told your Grandma that we were leaving early." Rebecca knew mentioning Grandma would perk her middle child up, Although Karen didn't see her often, there was a special bond between her mother and Karen. She contributes it to when Carl deployed to combat. She had been pregnant with Karen, and she moved home for the help with Rachel. Complications arose that put Rebecca in the hospital for a long time. So Karen's first few months home her grandma and aunt took care of her. When Rebecca was better and ready to go back to Ft. Knox, it devastated her Mom and Sister. Rebecca was grateful for their support, but she felt bad for their pain too. She was right; Karen immediately stopped complaining and got ready to go. "Thank you Karen, Don't forget to take your Dramamine. You can always go back to sleep in the car if you like." Poor Karen, she was always getting carsick. She'll need to make sure her daughter eats something before they leave.

All this commotion never even fazed the boy, "Danny! Danny, Get up Kido! We need to go." Rebecca coaxed him to hear her. "Danny, You need to get up Now!" This boy always does one of two things; he either doesn't want to get up or he gets up hours before everyone else. Rebecca thought of Carl and knew if he were here right now, he would play-yell, "Get up Private, No one authorized you to sleep past the rest of us." Danny would be up. Somewhere along the way, Carl would 'Drop him' to do push-ups, for any silly reason, going too slow or not having his shoes on yet.

Dad to them is the fun one, he plays with them and makes everyone laugh, But he's also their tutor, and most importantly he is their healer. He pulls out loose teeth, mends wounds and gives the most hugs. Rebecca is the practical caregiver. She makes their meals, gets them up for school and takes them to dentist appointments. She guesses she's fun too, but not in the Dad way. She's the type of Mom who dresses mostly in jeans and the artistic colors of red and black; she cranks up the radio overly loud in the car and sings just about as loudly. She's more serious than Carl. He's the kind of person who can break a silence or dead moment by quoting some strange line from a movie or song. You never know when he'll blurt out some Cadence or lyric. She thinks sometimes he does it just to mess with her. He'll sing one line and then go about his day, while she ends up singing it for hours.

"Mom." Rachel said, "I'm done in the bathroom."

"Kids." Rebecca said to the younger two. "Go use the bathroom and make sure you brush your teeth well."

"So, Mom." Rachel asked, "What's the plan?"

Rebecca tied her boot. "I haven't decided what the plan is yet, not any further than visiting Grandma and then Grammie. But, while we're there we'll weigh out all our options."

"That sounds like a plan, Mom." Rachel said, sounding like a young adult from the confidence with which she spoke.

Danny was busy giving mock Karate chops to his sisters and said, "I'm down with that."

Everyone laughed including Danny and Rebecca asked where he

learned that line. Danny told her 'Nickelodeon' and produced a cartoon laugh. Rebecca said, "Well, it will be nice to see Grandma and Grammie again, don't you think?"

It's been two years since they've seen them. Karen hugged her toddler blanket that her Grandma gave her when she was two. She still calls it, Yellowy, she does one of her silly voices and says with a bright sunshiny smile, "Mmm, Grandma." And with that, they leave the hotel and take the turn for the I-24 freeway.

As she made the turn toward the ramp, Rebecca thought she recognized the car in the gas station. Well that's no surprise; she reminded herself that everyone drives cars that look the same. But, as she sat at the light waiting to take the ramp, she couldn't help feeling that the man with the baseball cap seemed too familiar. You're being silly. She scolded herself. We've lived here a longtime, and so he probably is someone she has seen before.

❈❈❈

The three men returned from their break and prepared to sit down and resume their conversation. They were interrupted by a loud knock at the door. They all turned to see a young soldier standing at attention in the doorway. "Yes, Corporal." the Major addressed him.

"Excuse me, Sir. I'm sorry to interrupt you, but you just received an updated correspondence from field team one."

The Major rose from his chair, "Thank you, Corporal." As he exited the room he called to them, "Excuse me, Sergeant, Lieutenant, I hope to be only one minute."

Carl sat there looking at Lieutenant Jordan slightly baffled by what he has to do with all this. He knew Jordan and Rebecca had something of a distant friendship and that he had been supportive to her in ROTC. Rebecca even told him once how bad she felt to have an attraction to this man. She felt like it was a betrayal to him in some way. He had told her she was silly to feel that way because he understood that it was part of nature. Men, he thought, are attracted to almost every woman they meet. He told her that he felt good that she loved him and their marriage so much that she resisted the pull of that attraction. He had admired her honesty and loved her for her vulnerability.

Lieutenant Jordan hoped the Sergeant wouldn't ask him any questions and thought that perhaps a little small talk might keep the opportunity from presenting itself. "Sergeant Reynolds, have you kept up with current events in the news?" the Lieutenant asked.

"I haven't much else to do lately, except read and watch television." Carl said, "So, yes, I have."

"What do you think about our new President?" Jordan jested with him.

Carl asked, "Sir, are you trying to ask me a loaded question?"

He laughed and said, "No, actually I was just trying to make small talk to kill-time."

"In that case, Carl said, I'd say the time is coming for a rematch. Get your Dress Blues ready Sir. You may be in for some bright shiny new metals." The Sergeant only half joked.

Lieutenant Jordan laughed, and thought that he and Rebecca obviously have been together a long time because that was pretty much something she would have said too. Smiling, the Lieutenant responded, "If I were a gambling man, I'd agree with you. You're probably right."

Carl said, "There's not a lot to that gamble."

Jordan retorted, "No, maybe not."

A silence fell back between them as the Lieutenant glanced at the door hoping the Major would come back into the room.

Carl sat wondering about that strange conversation the Lieutenant and he just had. "Did what we just talk about have anything to do with my situation?"

"Sergeant Reynolds. If it were, it wouldn't be my place to discuss it."

Carl gave him a knowing nod and thought it didn't hurt to ask. Then he went ahead and asked what he really wanted to know, "Lieutenant Jordan, have you seen Rebecca?"

Jordan thought if Major Taylor doesn't get here soon he's going to go get him himself. Then he looked into Sergeant Reynolds' eyes and told him, "I haven't seen her up close, only from a distance."

"You've been surveilling her?" Carl asked.

"Yes, I was assigned to one of the teams."

In through the door came Major Taylor.

"Sorry I kept you both so long."

He sat back down. Carl had a strange feeling. He sensed that Lieutenant Jordan wasn't telling him something.

Lieutenant Jordan asked to be excused for a moment to arrange for lunch to be ordered and sent down from the cafeteria to the secured area in which Reynolds was being kept for his own safety.

Jordan remembered the last time he did see Rebecca up close. She was at the university, and they met on the sidewalk. She seemed so happy to be graduating, and she spoke about Carl getting out and their move. She really seemed happy, and now he felt bad for the both of them. He knew that his new assignment wouldn't be a hardship like the one Sergeant Reynolds has been given. When he returned to Reynolds' room, the Major and Sergeant were still in the throngs of small talk and hadn't gotten back to business yet.

"Here you are Lieutenant. Now we can get back to where we left off." Major Taylor said. "I believe we said that I would now fill you in Sergeant Reynolds." As the men prepared themselves some more coffee, Major Taylor thought maybe he should buy stock in coffee, being how drinking it was a requirement to being a soldier. When a good workday starts sometime around 4:30am and ends at 6:00 p.m., but the other half of the time it is a round the clock event; it doesn't take long before every soldier is a coffee drinker. He made a mental note to himself to consider buying stocks in the coffee industry, and he resumed his discussion with the Sergeant. "Almost seven months ago, you did a small favor for Colonel Dobson, as soon as my office caught wind of it, you became my sole assignment."

Carl already didn't like the sound of this. Corporals are assigned one soldier, not Majors.

Major Taylor said, "Your simple favor has caught the attention of many people in high places." Which was how he got this gift of a headache; his superior, Brigadier General Harding, recommended him for this mission and he knew what a gift it was. If he and the Sergeant could pull off this mission, then he knew it guaranteed his instant promotion to Lieutenant Colonel and likely the next star placed on General Harding's shoulder. "Simply put; Sergeant Reynolds, your innocent fix was nothing less than the complete sabotage of the work of our best programmers. They're still, six months later trying to figure out how you did it. They insist that they're program is impenetrable and that whatever it is you managed to do was just some type of fluke."

Carl asked, "Is that why the people here have been referring to me as "The Genius?"

The Major chuckled, "Yes, but "Genius" is the code name for the mission we've been tasked." "Operation Genius" Everyone has been ordered not to use your real name. So you are being called "The Genius." "I'll be getting to all that soon." The Major continued. What happened six months ago, he explained to Sergeant Reynolds is that his men grabbed him and brought him here for safekeeping. The quicker that they moved and covered everything up the safer he and his family would be. "You see." said Major Taylor, "We may no longer be in a Cold War, but our enemies are still very real." "In all actuality," the major explained that the opening up of international relations around the world has made the security of national secrets and government agents even more difficult to protect. With all the unrestricted casual comings and goings of people in and out of the country, it has become much more difficult to keep track of known spies and harder still to recognize new ones. "The most difficult thing to control, the Major explained, has been the movement of terrorists groups, and they are of course the most dangerous of our enemies to watch out against. Since they act out of hatred and anger and feel they have little to lose." All of these enemies, he thought, and he hadn't even mentioned the various radical militias in our own country. "In essence, Sergeant Reynolds, with so many potential enemies out there just waiting to grab you, it left us little choice." said the Major.

Carl couldn't think about anything except, Oh shit. I'm really screwed, aren't I. "Sir, what is it that you are telling me, Exactly?"

"You no longer exist." Major Taylor answered.

Half panic stricken, and half television comedian, Carl exclaimed, "What? So who am I, The Invisible Man."

The Major and the Lieutenant looked at each other and laughed. Then Major Taylor said, "As a matter of fact, at this moment you are."

Carl's thoughts whirled. "What the hell does that mean?" Could things get any worse than this? He asked himself. Then he silently thought; Don't answer that.

❈❈❈❈

Rebecca and the kids had been on the road since about 7:45, and it was now 11:45. Four hours went pretty quick when Danny and Karen were sleeping. It had been rather peaceful, since she didn't have to listen to those two squabble about Danny putting his stinky feet on Karen or that he was kicking her or playing his headphones too loudly. Rachel had been keeping her company. Changing CD's for Rebecca when she got tired of the one she was listening to and looking up mileage on the atlas as they went. Rachel was also reading one of her books, which relieved Rebecca from feeling she had to make conversation with her daughter. She just wasn't up to it and preferred to sing and let her thoughts drift about her family and Carl. She would have liked to think about their future, but all she could do was think about times from they're past. She thought about the first date she and Carl went on and how they almost never did.

She was nineteen. Carl and she had worked together for a couple of years. But he had been dating a girl for a long time. Rebecca had been attracted to Carl since the day she met him, and in the time they worked together she managed to learn a lot about him. So she was shocked, when one of their co-workers had told her that Carl and his girlfriend had broken up. Rebecca couldn't believe it; she thought for sure they would get married. They had been together so long. She was also surprised to be told, "It had been awhile and where had she been?" She had been around; she thought, but she also had been seeing someone and working two jobs. Her other work was scheduled according to project demands, and for the past few months the demands had been high. Consequently, she had been working 55 to 60 hours at that job and then working 20 hours here at night. Projects had slowed down at her daytime job, and during the busy time, Rebecca and the guy she was seeing had stopped dating.

To her luck, she finally had the opportunity she was waiting for; the chance to date Carl. There was no way she was going to sit by and wait, hoping that he'd ask her out. Five minutes after she heard the news, Rebecca went up to Carl and asked him out. Carl was a popular person at work and so he was always going out with friends somewhere. When she asked him to go out with her, he had quickly told her, "I can't" and rushed off to continue working. In shock, Rebecca stood there, not because he said no to her, but because she had turned people down before and knew the routine. He hadn't even given her a letdown line of any kind. About forty seconds later, Carl came running back to where she was standing, still a bit dazed and he stumbled his way through an explanation. He hadn't realized she was asking him out. Asking him out on a date that is and that he would love to go out with her. Except that he already had plans for Saturday night, but he would call her. Carl called her the very next day to say he had Monday off and since she did too, if she weren't scheduled at her other job then they could go do something then. This story had been told to their children many times. Carl told them how daddy was so dense that he didn't even realize that mom had been asking him out, how he almost lost his chance with her.

Rebecca looked down at the dash. The gas gauge showed less than a quarter of a tank of fuel left. The next blue road sign said that there was a fairly large town up ahead because there were at least five restaurants and three gas stations.

Rebecca spoke in a slightly raised voice. "Guys, wake-up, it's time to get some lunch, and I need to get gas."

Danny made a loud "pherrtt" sound.

Rachel said, "Eww!, Dang, Danny, Mom didn't mean that kind of gas."

Karen said, "yuck."

Everyone pee-you'd and gagged as they rolled down the windows. Danny sat there laughing and trying to produce another.

Rebecca told them all to get their shoes and jackets on as she pulled into the exit lane. "What do you kids want for lunch?" she asked and listed all the places she saw on the road sign. Except the Taco restaurant, because the sign said it was two miles down the road and out of our way she thought. She pulled into the nearest gas station and told Danny to hurry up with his shoes. "You guys decide where we should go for lunch and lock the doors." She pumped the gas. Then went inside to grab a twice the caffeine, double sugar drink and a king size almond chocolate bar that she knew she would need in about two more hours on the road. She also grabbed some snacks for the kids and paid the station attendant. Rebecca looked at the man and his wife across the way in the pumping station and thought they seemed like the couple pumping gas behind the man in the baseball cap back in Tennessee. She looked at their license plate and noted it was from Virginia. She also noted that they would be reaching the Virginia border within an hour. This seals it, she thought, this proved she had paranoia. She got into the car, and her and the kids picked a restaurant for lunch. As they were preparing to leave, Rebecca left a tip on the table for the waitress and noticed the same couple from the gas station. Stop being paranoid, she told herself. Then she even forced herself to smile and say hello to the couple as she left.

Turning back onto interstate 40, she switched the radio back on and asked Rachel to find a country CD to listen to. As she and the kids got themselves resettled for another long stint of driving, Rebecca's mind wandered back to Carl and their first date.

Their first date was on August 12th. She never knew why she had remembered that date, but had never done so for any others. Even their Wedding Anniversary was notoriously forgotten by both her and Carl. They were oftentimes reminded, only because her mom would call and wish them a Happy Day. But, she had waited two long years for that date on Aug 12th and she assumed that was the reason she had remembered it. That and the fact it was the most memorable date she had ever had. Not necessarily because of what they did. But rather for the emotional energy shared between them. They had spent an incredible day together, going to the beach and then to dinner. They took a walk in a park and then went to a late drive-in movie. It had been the longest first date she had ever been on and also the most romantic. She had to smile when she remembered the tiny little pink and black polka dot bikini she had borrowed from her sister, intent on making a strong impression on Carl. They had shared more information about themselves then she thought possible in one day. She had also been very impressed that this man never once attempted to kiss her or touch her once the whole day, except for the time he took her hand to help her wade across a river in the park so that they could sit and talk on the other side.

Before dating him, Rebecca knew Carl was the one for her. By the end of their first date, she had been convinced. After that first date, they never missed a single day without seeing each other, at two months they were living together and by six months they were engaged. She felt it qualified as a whirlwind romance, maybe not fairytale. They had had their ups and downs as all relationships do, but in many ways it had been magical.

"Mom, what does the word exacerbate mean?" Rachel interrupted Rebecca's thoughts and asked her.

"Well, I guess I would describe it as, to make worse. If you have a problem, something that would exacerbate it. Would inflate it and make it worse." "Does that make sense and fit your sentence?" Rebecca asked her daughter.

"Yeah, Rachel said, It fits. Thanks."

If they were home she would make her look it up, but even still, sometimes using it in a sentence helps to explain large words better then the Dictionary. She always made her look it up anyway. Exacerbate, Rebecca thought about its meaning and thought that perhaps her own thoughts could be doing the same thing to her problems.

She glimpsed the mountain line of the Appalachians before her and looked briefly at the farms cut into the hillsides on either side of the freeway. They looked so inviting and peaceful. She wondered if the snow would last much longer and envisioned the hillsides as she remembered them two years ago. Beautiful, rich green pastures with purple thistles engulfing the fences lining the interstate. Looking at them from a distance, the thistles appeared to be beautiful flowers and not the glass-sharp weeds that they actually were. She thought how bizarre it was that something so beautiful from a distance could be very painful up close.

Rebecca wondered if they grew there naturally or were planted by the farmers. She presumed they probably weren't intentionally planted. But she recognized that either way, by nature, or the farmer's hands, the message was the same. The thistles said to onlookers, stay back and enjoy the illusion from where you are. Dare to get too close and it will hurt you to see that life is hard for everyone. Regardless of how beautiful the scenery may be.

But that was the harshness of the hot, sun blasting summer she convinced herself. Rebecca also remembered the tender warmth and hopefulness of spring. Drive through these mountains then and you'll see these fences all covered over in the delicious scent of honeysuckle vines. That smell was always irresistible to her. Honeysuckle and Lilacs reminded her of childhood. Some of her favorite memories were of playing under the huge lilac tree in their yard and picking blackberries in the giant patch where all the honeysuckle grew. This was all up in Connecticut, but her family didn't live in that home anymore, even if they could; it wouldn't be the same anymore. What was woods and small neighboring farms are now highways, stores and an overgrown city.

Rebecca believed that was why she enjoyed their time in Tennessee so much. It felt more like her childhood home, and that was how she wanted her own children to grow up. She stared at the white lines painted on the road's black asphalt and realized that at least she knew what she wanted for her kids and what she didn't. That was a start, Rebecca told herself.

Carl sat and listened to the Major discuss what took place during the last six months. He was told that he was being held in the lowest levels of a secure facility in Northern Virginia. The Major explained. "We pulled you out quickly because we were unsure if Colonel Dobson were a spy. At that moment we decided it was better to protect our investment rather than risk losing it. We found out that none of our enemies knew who you were yet because it was taking them too long to find your family." It was then that they realized they needed to keep everyone in Carl's section from talking about him. So, they ordered everyone to remain silent and immediately put them all 'on orders' redistributing them to assignments around the world to distance them from one another and that duty station. "Though they hadn't found your family yet." he said. "There were a few known enemy agents snooping around some of your co-workers." Which is why he and his office decided it would be safer for everyone, if they played into our enemies belief that The United States will stop at nothing to maintain their secrets and the safety of it's country. "So." He said, "We leaked out that you were to be snubbed out for the countries good and we staged your assassination. Of course, we were unable to recover your body from the helicopter wreck in the Gulf of Mexico."

Carl felt an eerie chill run down his arm as he thought how efficient they were. He wasn't sure if this were good or bad.

"Down the road in Arlington Cemetery, we put a marker on your behalf. There wouldn't have been a body to put there, but now no one expects that there should be either."

The Major told Carl all of this with an expression of pride in a job well done. And Carl could appreciate the complicated nature of the task accomplished, but this was after all, his life they were dismantling.

Major Taylor looked at Carl and saw a shade of green, seaweed creep across his face, and he immediately wiped the enthusiasm from his own. "Sergeant Reynolds, I really am sorry, but there was no other alternative."

"No Sir." Carl said, "This is what you do, don't apologize for being good at it. I'm grateful to you, really." Carl wasn't sure how convincing he sounded, but in a way he was grateful, what if they hadn't grabbed him first, where could he be right now, if they hadn't. He didn't even want to contemplate that idea. "Sir." Carl began, "I don't mean to sound unthankful when I ask this, but did anyone stop to think that what I did any computer hacker could have done just as easily?"

"Actually, Sergeant Reynolds." The Major answered with marked enthusiasm, "That is an excellent question and yes we did." "But we also came to the conclusion that if they could why hadn't some little punk done so already." He said. "Then it also occurred to us that it wasn't relevant because if it we're us, and we already know other groups are much more desperate than us, we would have kidnapped you. However, in this case you are already in the employment of our government and it can be cleanly called protection instead." The major was quick to inform the Sergeant.

Just then, they were interrupted once again by the corporal standing in the doorway. Carl looked at his watch and noticed the time had flown by without his even noticing. It was 12:00 noon, the corporal was there to announce that lunch had arrived from the cafeteria. "Would you like me to bring it in Sir?" he asked the Major.

Major Taylor responded, "Yes, Please." When the corporal was done, the Major dismissed him to go and take lunch himself.

Carl concluded that the corporal was the Major's personal assistant judging by the mornings and this noon's performance. Carl also noted what food had been ordered and was grateful to Lieutenant Jordan for his discretion. The Lieutenant had ordered a light meal of soup and a plate of six or so ham and cheese sandwiches placed in the center of the table. In addition to this, he had ordered a platter of desserts, which the corporal had placed on the counter near the coffee maker. It didn't escape him that Lieutenant Jordan had carefully ordered lunch. The layout allowed someone, such as Carl, to eat as little as they liked, while allowing the others to eat a full meal without any uncomfortable looks or questions from the others, namely Major Taylor. Now Carl had a small glimpse into why Rebecca had liked this guy.

Carl was reminded how when he was at work, time would fly by fast, and the day would be over before he even had a chance to look at his watch. Many times he never even had the time to eat lunch. However, for the last six months he marked the day's progression by the meals he ate. They ate lunch quietly with only a few remarks here and there by either the Lieutenant or the Major.

Then they took a break for an hour. The Major explained he had to check up on things and e-mails to reply. He also sent the Lieutenant off on some errand to complete. He told Carl, "You may want to use this time to pack your belongings, we have a flight to take later this evening." Carl thought, at least he said, 'we' and not 'you'. There is some hope to think it's not a trip to the Gulf of Mexico. Yeah, Carl sighed, you keep telling yourself that.

CHAPTER FOUR

Rebecca managed to drive another hour before she felt the need to start inhaling the caffeine she bought earlier. It was now 3:00 p.m. according to her watch, but she knew it was actually 4:00 p.m. here in Virginia. She wasn't sure where the timeline was, but she knew she had crossed it some time ago. As she looked in the rearview mirror, she could see the sky was a beautiful shade of pink and was aware that the sun was going to be down soon. She asked Rachel to look up where they were on the map; so she could find a suitable place to pull over for the night. They saw a sign for the next small town and Rachel located it.

"We're about half way between Lexington and Staunton." Rachel pointed half way up the western border of the Virginia map.

"How many more miles do you think it is, sweetie?"

"Umm, I think about fifteen miles." She told her Mom.

"That's not very far, we'll see if they have a hotel or two and some food places too." She told Rachel. "What's the next big town?"

"Harrisonburg." Rachel replied.

"It's not too late yet. If we need to, we can go on further and stop there."

Rachel went back to her reading.

Rebecca noticed in the rearview mirror that Danny and Karen were both awake. Karen was busy drawing, and Danny was looking at magazines. She caught another glimpse of the sun setting sky and thought how amazing it looked with purple starting to join in with the pink on the horizon. As she was returning her gaze back to the road ahead of her, she caught a darting movement from the corner of her eye. Rebecca recognized it immediately.

"SHIT, don't do it, don't." But she wasn't that lucky.

The Deer ran straight out in front of her car. She had no choice, but to slam on the brakes. She tried to veer the car toward the shoulder of the road. Thankfully, when they stopped, they were safely on the shoulder of the highway. Rebecca realized that the kids were still screaming. She checked to make sure everyone was all right, "It's okay." Rebecca said, "We're safe." When they stopped screaming, she took a minute to let her own racing heart slow down before she got out to check the damage. They were lucky, she thought, when she saw how minimal the damage was. The car had a small dent and a broken headlight on the driver's side. She figured she must have run over something because a tire was deflating, and it wasn't something the emergency can of fix-a-flat could repair. Rebecca went to dig out the spare tire from the trunk, when she saw a car pulled over on the shoulder driving toward her, in reverse. when it stopped, the passenger side window rolled down and a woman leaned out and asked Rebecca if she were in need of any assistance. Rebecca looked up to smile and say No thank you, when she immediately recognized the gray haired woman from the restaurant. Rebecca hesitated. Then she smiled and said hello. By this time, the woman's husband had gotten out and started to assess her car's situation. The woman got out as well, and introduced herself as Anne and her husband as Frank; they were the Henrys she told her.

"We saw the deer bolt out in front of your car." She continued, Looking into the car at the kids, she asked if everyone were alright.

"Yes, thank you." Rebecca answered. "Did you see what happened to the deer?"

Anne looked at Rebecca and thought how kind of her to care about the deer. Frank then told her, "The deer kept running, but judging by the size of him and the small amount of damage to your car, I'd say it probably only has a large bruise. That and he's minus a tail." Frank held up a white deer's tail. He chuckled, "It's better than his life."

Rebecca couldn't decide if she were sad for the animal or if it were funny. "Well, at least I have proof for insurance purposes."

The man smiled, pointing at her, "Good one. But seriously, I'd also have to say you're out of luck when it comes to your tires. That is unless you carry two spares. Your back right one has a cut in it also."

Rebecca went to look at it. "I didn't see that one when I walked around." She told them.

"Easy enough to miss." The man said to her, "See the cut on this one isn't quite as large as the driver side, but by the time you got the spare put on that side, I'd bet you this one would be flat too."

Rebecca's expression deflated as surely and quickly as her tires.

Anne said, "Well, I guess it's good that we stopped and checked on you then. Nowadays we don't usually stop to help. But we thought that we recognized you from the restaurant earlier today, and we couldn't stand it if we heard something bad had happened." Anne gave her a warm; yet, you know what I mean expression.

Frank said, "We don't have one of those cell phone contraptions, but we do happen to have a regular phone at our house up the road. You're welcome to use it and call for a tow."

Rebecca thought this went against her instinct and better judgment, but she didn't have a lot of choices in the matter. She could sit and wait in the car with the kids or she and the kids could go to their home and call for help. However, the thought of fifteen miles either way, with nothing in between, helped her to make up her mind. "It was very kind of you to stop." Rebecca looked at the car and sighed. "Thank you, the use of your phone would be very helpful." She went to the shoulder sidecar door and opened it to tell the kids to make sure they were prepared to get out.

Rachel had already made them get their shoes on, and Rebecca was relieved she had thought ahead. Rebecca explained to the kids that they needed to get a tow truck to bring the car to a garage. "Hurry." She told them, "This couple has offered to bring us to their phone."

The kids piled out the side door. Rebecca introduced the children to the Henrys. "This is Rachel, Karen and Danny." she said.

"And you are?" Anne asked.

"Oh, I'm so sorry, My name is Rebecca Reynolds." She told the kind faced older couple standing there looking at her.

Anne checked her watch, smiled at the children and then at her husband. Rebecca remarked on how dark it had gotten. Frank went to his SUV and pulled out one of those bright orange emergency signs to place on Rebecca's car.

Rachel said, "It is very nice to meet you, Mrs. Henry."

At least someone had managed to remember their manners Rebecca thought, flustered as she watched the darkening sky and looked at the tall, crowded pines on either side of the highway.

"What a pretty young lady you are, and so polite. Please call me; Anne, and this is my husband, Frank."

Rebecca grabbed her purse and began to lock the doors.

Frank suggested, "It may be a good idea if everyone grabs their overnight bags, just in case. Things can be a bit slower on this side of Virginia." the man told them. "You just never know if a storm might blow through here. But what I fear, he said to Rebecca, Is that we may not find a garage open tonight."

"People just aren't in much of a hurry here." Anne added, "Garages don't need to stay open late anymore with all the new automated gas pumps out now." She smiled at Rebecca, "But we'll go make a few calls and see, okay."

Everyone grabbed their overnight bags and climbed into the Henry's truck. Anne and Frank were quite the talkers and they had explained to her and the kids that they owned a small farm not far from where they were now. The kids asked them if they owned animals. "Yes, do you like animals?" Frank asked looking into the rear view mirror at Danny. Then he asked the girls what type of animals they thought they might like. Frank had told them they had just about a little of everything on their farm.

Rachel asked, "Do you have horses, Mr. Frank?"

He laughed, and told her yes, they had two and their son had more than they did.

"You have a son!" Danny asked, "How old is he?"

"Our children are all grown up, But David built a house not far from us and he took over our families cattle farm a few years back." Anne explained.

Frank said a little excitedly, "If the car doesn't get fixed until tomorrow then maybe in the morning I can take you kids to see David's farm."

The kids all shouted, "Can we Mom!"

Rebecca and the Henry's couldn't help laughing; the kids were so excited.

Rebecca told them "We'll see." And felt sort of excited too.

She always wanted to see one of the farms that she looked at from the highway. She then remembered her thoughts about the thistles, realizing that she liked the dream and hoped it wasn't going to be crushed.

The girls both asked if they would be able to see David's horses too and Anne told them "Of course." Frank then explained to the children that if they truly wanted to experience a farm they had to get up at five in the morning and view it in the rush of feeding and milking and tending to the animals. That way they could feel the dark and cold of the morning and see the sun rise. "If you're up to it, maybe we'll be lucky enough to see a good clear sunrise." Frank continued and told them, "If that pink sky we saw earlier means anything then we just may have a nice one too."

Rachel told Frank about the saying grandpa taught mom and she taught them. As her daughter told them the saying, Rebecca thought it to herself. "Red skies at night, sailors delight; Red skies in morning, sailors heed warning."

"Well," Frank said, "If it works for sailors, maybe it will work for us too." As they turned right, into the long dirt drive that led to the Henry's farmhouse, Rebecca thought how wrong she was about the farmers planting thistle to keep others away. Even in the dead of winter, she didn't think she could see a more welcoming sight.

❄❄❄

Carl thought about this morning and remembered what the Major had said. Moving Day. He told him his family was moving, not him. That was a lie, and he wondered how many other things he said that were also lies. There wasn't much point in worrying about it. His hands were tied, and the best he could do was whatever they wanted. All he wanted was to get back to his family. He promised Rebecca before leaving for Saudi, to do whatever it took to come back home to her and he kept that promise ever since. He thought about her beautiful paleface, dark eyes and long jet-black hair, and he told himself. "Whatever it takes Rebecca, I'll come home to you." He pulled out his wallet and looked at the picture he had of his wife and their three children; the four most precious things in his life. A single, tear began to well in the corner of his eye, Carl wiped it away. He knew it would be a longtime before he would see them and hold them again. If it took them six months to set up whatever plan they had concocted, then Carl knew it was a sure indication that this was going to be a long endeavor. Carl finished packing his belongings and was curious where they were flying to tonight. He flicked on the television set and caught the weather. There was a blizzard or a 'north easterner', as the weatherman called it, expected to hit sometime late tonight. Carl thought about Rebecca and the kids but then reassured himself that Rebecca was sensible, she would stop at a hotel long before it was supposed to hit. He flicked off the television and lay down on his bed for the half-hour he had left of his break.

Carl dreamed he was driving their car and his family were all there with him. He felt warm and comfortable. The next thing he knew he and Rebecca were at a beach. She was standing in the water with the waves splashing her thighs and her hair blowing in the wind. He could see the shape of her hips and the dramatic incline of the curve leading to her waist. She turned and smiled at him as she tried to brush her hair back away from her face. When her hair flipped around, it flew in the wind like a flag on a pole before a storm. She waved for him to come into the water with her. With her back to the water, a large wave came crashing cold against her and she let out a scream and began laughing. She caught sight of something and leaned over to pick it up. She was the most incredible sight he had ever seen. He tried to see what it was she picked up and thought it was probably a shell, but then he caught a glimmer of gold. When he looked back up at her, she wasn't twenty years old anymore, but was even more beautiful and womanly then he remembered. She was smiling at him, but there were tears welling up in her eyes and silently rolling down her face. He woke to the wet feel of tears trailing down his neck. He wiped them and thought, "Don't cry, I'm still here. I love you, always remember that, I love you."

Carl looked at the clock and saw that it said 4:00 pm. He could hear the Major and the Lieutenant talking in the hall. Jordan was speaking: "Team one saw the accident and was forced to keep going. They pulled off at the next exit and are circling back now. Team two was following the operatives and saw them pull over to help them. They decided to pull off the exit and wait to see what happens there."

The Major told Jordan: "Don't tell either team to move in. This is perfect, I know the old couple. They've been inactive since the early eighties. They're also riding both sides of the fence. I don't think they're in any trouble with them. Tell both teams to maintain their distance, just sit back and observe. And for crying out loud- tell them not to blow it this time!"

"Yes Sir." Jordan said bolting down the hallway.

The Major entered Carl's room. "Sorry to keep you waiting so long, Sergeant Reynolds, I had some things come up that couldn't be delayed."

"Sir." Carl asked, "Was that conversation about my family?"

"Yes, Sergeant, It was, but don't worry, everyone is fine, and no one has any reason to hurt your family. They are just trying to find out information about you. We already cleaned up all the physical evidence, they're in no danger. Besides I know the couple, they were recruited from East Germany in the sixties, they're strictly information people."

Carl couldn't believe what he had gotten himself into, But worse, was that his family was now caught up in too. He just hoped this wasn't another one of the Majors lies.

"Are you all packed, Sergeant. We have an earlier flight to catch because of the impending weather. I'll have to catch you up on business in the plane." The Major called for the Corporal to come help fetch Sergeant Reynolds' duffle bag to place with the rest of the baggage. The corporal carried out the bag and returned with a black suitcase. "I sent the Lieutenant out this afternoon to get you some civilian clothing. I hope his and your taste are the same because we'll be going to the West Coast and we need to blend in with the general population." He instructed the boy to leave the second suitcase and close the door. "You and I are headed to our country's best covert intelligence facility, Sergeant, and we're going to work with its top personnel." The Major was excited. "Do you know how we won the war against Germany?" The Major asked him.

Carl told him yes he did. "It was our ability to break their codes, but they couldn't break ours because we used a Native American Language."

"Yes," said the Major. "But now it has come down to computer languages and programs, Sergeant, and it's our turn to break the code."

Carl couldn't help but to feel a little excited too. Working on a secret mission with the top people in the country sounded like a "James Bond" movie, and he was in it.

"I'll meet you down the hall in twenty minutes." Said the Major.

Carl opened the black suitcases and found four suits and a stack of shirts, ties and everything else he could possibly need. He picked out the dark brown suit and debated over the shirts and ties, finally selecting the olive drab shirt and hunter green multi design tie. He finished the outfit off with dark brown shoes and socks.

He turned to look in the mirror. So much for change, Carl thought, as he saw the reflection of himself in corporate army camouflage. At least it felt comfortable. He could try colors another time he told himself. Rebecca would like it anyhow. Carl turned, picked up the suitcase and the trench coat the Lieutenant had bought for him and left his cell without once looking back.

Riding up the long dirt drive, Rebecca could see two hundred yards from the house a beautiful stone fence lining either side of the road. Anchored in the stone fence was an elaborate yet aged, wrought iron arbor that said Henry at the arch. On it, she could see hibernating rose vines that extended down the rock walls. The land was covered with white snow, and the farm's landscaping was accented with very discreet lighting coming from only a few lamps hanging from the telephone poles lining the long drive. Red barns and out buildings were set back a distance from the house, each with a lamp that hung over the buildings large doors. The white farmhouse gave telltale signs of someone being home. When Anne cranked the window down, the air carried in the scent of wood smoke. The porch light was on, and she noticed one or two lights on inside, as well. Rebecca thought she couldn't even imagine the beauty of this place during the other seasons of the year.

Anne called out in a happily surprised voice; "Look! David must be here. The fire is going. How sweet of him." She said to no one in particular.

The truck came to a stop. Frank opened his door and told Anne that he was going to check on the animals. He invited the children to tagalong.

"He's as excited as a small child." Anne told Rebecca, "Frank knows that if David is here he would have already cared for the animals." Anne smiled as she watched the bounce in her husband's step, leading the children to the barn. "Look!" Anne pointed in Frank and the children's direction to show Rebecca. "I can't remember the last time he had that kind of enthusiasm in his step." Then she added, "We don't get to see our grandchildren very often."

Rebecca looked at her kids running to keep up with Frank's heels and then looked back to find Anne grinning. She thought these people seemed very nice, and she finally allowed her guard to come down. After all, she told herself; they were the ones bringing strangers into their home. Rebecca told the small woman, "The kids are thrilled. This is very special for them. We've never visited a farm or seen animals up close. But, Also." she said, "My kids no longer have any grandfathers of their own, my Dad passed away when Danny was two years old." She paused, "My husband's father hasn't been around since he was a boy."

Anne looked at Rebecca, "I'm so sorry, Dear." She answered.

Rebecca could feel that she had really meant it.

Anne led Rebecca into the white wooden farmhouse. The women deposited the few bags they had carried in with them at the foot of the stairs and Anne told her that the men could bring in the rest. Rebecca hated to ask, but she really needed to borrow a restroom. She had been trying to wait until she and the kids got to a hotel, but they hadn't made it that far. A little embarrassed she asked, "Is there a restroom I may borrow?"

"Of course." Anne told her. "It's down there." She pointed down the hall, "Across from the kitchen. Please, help yourself," Anne said, "Actually, I'm going to do the same. Traveling can be such heck."

As she made her way down the hall, she could see inside the kitchen and noticed it smelled good. She knew some type of roast or something was in the oven because the scent had filled the kitchen and was spilling out into the hallway. She glimpsed inside, but seeing no one, she turned toward the adjacent door, fumbled around for the light switch and closed the door behind her.

David stood up with the retrieved pot in his hand and his jaw dropped as he saw a strange dark haired woman standing in his parent's hallway. Was he imagining this or did his mother make good on her word? Wow, he thought. She's probably about his own age and her shape didn't hurt the eyes either, he told himself. Before their trip to Nashville, his parents had been complaining to him that he needed to find himself a nice girl. "Two years is long enough", they had told him, "It was time to move on with his life. It was too short to waste." they had insisted. When his mother left, she told him if he didn't find himself someone then she would revert to the Old World ways and find a girl for him herself. "Whoa, I thought she was only kidding." He said aloud to himself.

His mom came down the hall and into the kitchen half shouting. "David, It's so nice of you to make a fire and what is this, you made dinner too. You're so good to us." she told her son as she gave him a hello hug. Then she lowered her voice just a little and said, "You won't believe what we brought home with us."

David smiled at her and said, "I saw." He giggled slightly, "You did

45

Good, Boy, you really keep your word. Don't you." He chuckled to see his Mother's face blush.

Anne laughed, waving her hand as if to mock a slap at her son. "Don't be silly, David." She tapped his thick arm with her thin, frail hand and asked if he had spoken to Rebecca.

"No. I only saw her go into the restroom."

Just then, Rebecca came out from the bathroom and joined Anne and her son in the kitchen. She presumed the man standing behind the island was David and said "Hello". Anne introduced Rebecca to her son and he asked the women how they had met. Anne told him about the deer and the car and how Frank was outside in the barn showing the kids the animals. She reassured Rebecca that she'd have Frank make the call to the local garage. Anne then excused herself to go and check on Frank and the kids, remarking to David, how she hoped Frank hadn't been overzealous and was showing them how to shoe a horse or something.

David laughed and teased her, "You married him, now run and save those kids before Dad has them milking cows and roping steer out there." He flashed Rebecca a smile. When she went to follow Anne, he informed her that it was okay to stay there with him. "I don't make it a habit of biting guests in my parent's home." He winked. "Would you like to take a seat, I can get you a hot tea or a soda if you prefer."

"Thank you." Rebecca sat down at a stool on her side of the island. "Tea would be nice."

David looked into her face and noticed her eyes were dark; they almost matched her jet-black hair. Too bad, he thought; that she wasn't here for the reason his mom had threatened.

"Your Dad promised that we could go visit your farm."

David noticed his heart lurch when she told him this, "When are you coming?"

"Frank insisted that the only time to get a proper feel for a farm is at 5:00am." Rebecca answered.

He listened to her words carefully. She said it in an innocent matter-of-fact manner, with no hint of sarcastic or demeaning intention he noted to himself. His wife had hated the farm, and she was always sarcastic even before she ever saw it. "Dad's absolutely right." David smiled at her.

"Well then." She cheerfully continued, "We'll be there bright and early, maybe not wide awake though." She smiled at him and casually sneaked one of the carrots he was chopping for a salad.

Rebecca noted that she liked it here. So far, everyone was very comfortable to be around, and she had to admit she was also grateful not to be in a hotel, the four of them alone. Rebecca asked if she could help and he told her thanks, but that he was almost done.

David smiled when she took another carrot and thought how he liked her comfortable nature. She felt familiar for a stranger. The kettle whistled, and he asked if she liked cream and sugar as he retrieved them from their places.

She asked about his farm and he told her it was just under, two thousand acres. He had 500 head of cattle, most raised for beef, but he also had dairy cows. He had six horses of his own, but his friends and the men who worked for him, stabled their horses there too.

She asked if he had any sheep dogs and he laughed and told her he had no sheep, but he did have five dogs that worked the farm. As he finished making their meal, David took his teacup and leaned his sore back forward, resting his elbows on the counter. He sipped his tea and asked if she liked Roast with Potatoes, then laughed and told her he hoped she wasn't a vegetarian.

She wasn't, but she didn't know if she would have had the heart to tell him if she were, not with his being a cattle Rancher and all. "No, It smells wonderful, we've eaten a lot of fast food lately."

David told her to hold the thank you until after she had tasted it, because he had only recently begun learning how to cook. He looked down into his teacup, "Only since my divorce." He took a sip and looked back up at her. "I figured I better learn because the frozen dinners were killing me."

She smiled. "I'll bet." She agreed with him and then she told him she was sorry about his divorce. "Not that it is my place to talk about with you, But for what it's worth, I can see that it has been painful for you and I'm sorry."

He had hoped by now; it wasn't so obvious, "Thank you."

They sat companionably for a moment drinking their teas. David thought that for the first time, since his divorce two years ago, he was doing all right. "Well dinner is ready, we better go drag your kids away from the animals and my Dad with them." Right when he said this the entire gang came charging in through the back door.

"MOM!" All three kids yelled and began talking all at once. Karen said, "They have everything. Cows and sheep." "And horses and chickens and goats." Rachel added. Danny said, "They have gooses and dogs and cats too." Rachel told her, "You have to come and see them, Mom." They were so excited, and she did want to see them too.

David told her, "Dad's barns look like they're straight from Noah's Ark."

Rebecca calmed the kids down and introduced them to David.

"Mr. Frank says we're going to go and see your farm." Danny looked up at David.

"You are! I heard that too." He squatted down to Danny's height. "We better eat then, so you guys can get cleaned up and hit your sacks, 5:00am comes pretty quick." he told the children.

Karen asked if he had lots of animals too, as David led them to the bathroom to clean up for dinner. "Yes and No." he said. "I have a lot of cattle."

"And horses." Rachel added. "Mr. Frank said you have horses too."

"Yes," he told the children. "I have about thirty horses on my farm, but only six of them are mine."

Karen asked, "Who do the other horses belong to?"

"My partners own some; the people who work for me have a couple, and the rest are boarders." David planted a washcloth on Danny's face. "What animal have you been putting your face all over."

All three kids laughed. Rachel told David, "Every one that would let him."

By the time David finished helping the kids clean up, Anne and Rebecca had set the dinner table and were in the process of carrying out the food. Rebecca thanked him for helping the kids, and he responded with "No problem."

"This looks really good, David." Anne told her son as she carried out the main dish, "And you even made gravy, I am really impressed." Anne placed it on the table and watched her son with Rebecca's children as he helped them take seats at the table. Getting Danny a small pillow to sit on so he could reach the table properly. She hadn't seen him look this happy in a long time, and her heart broke for him.

Frank returned from the other room and announced, "Rebecca, I took the liberty of leaving a message on Jerry Cauldwell's answering machine. In the morning, he should get it and pick up your car." He said to her with a sense of accomplishment.

"Thank you very much." Rebecca said to the older man taking his place at the head of the table.

Anne sat next to her husband and David sat at the other end with Rebecca next to him and the children placed in between all the adults. Frank gave the thanks for their meal and everyone dug in and filled their plates. David told Rebecca not to expect the car to get picked up any time before 9:00 am.

Frank laughed and said, "Only if Jerry makes it home early from the tavern tonight." Anne shushed him and gave him a stern look. Frank added seriously, "But Jerry's an excellent mechanic." Frank turned the conversation to the children, "What do you think of our animals?"

They all said how wonderful they were and the kids told Rebecca "Mom, the cat is pregnant." Rachel said, "Dang, that cat is so large it can't move, you should see her mom."

"Sugar is due any time now." Anne said.

"Most of the females are pregnant." Frank added.

Karen giggled, "You missed it, Mom. Danny was petting one of the sheep, leaning against her when all of a sudden this kick jolted out of the side of her and knocked him down."

Danny was laughing.

"That's how he got dirt all over himself," she said to David.

The kids were so grateful to be having a real meal that there wasn't a scrap left on their plates by the end of dinner. When the kids were done eating, Anne said she would show the kids where their room was and get them started with baths. As they all ran off, Frank yelled to the kids, "Hurry and get to sleep."

The kids said to Anne "It's only 7:00pm."

Then Frank finished, "4:30am comes really fast."

"DANG," said Rachel.

Rebecca had gone with Anne and the kids upstairs. There were four bedrooms. The one the kids were put in had a bunk bed on one side and another twin bed on the opposite wall. The walls were covered with flowered wallpaper in the shapes of daisies and carnations and over the windows hung yellow Pricilla curtains. The girls looked at the room and couldn't contain their delight. They told Miss Anne how pretty the room was and she told them that her youngest daughter had picked this paper when she was in high school. She lived out in California now with her husband and their daughter. She told them they had the beds put in here for when their grandchildren did get a chance to visit.

The room next to this one she led Rebecca to. Its walls were papered with beautiful pink roses and had a white and ivy background. She told her this one was once her and Frank's room, but when the boys both moved out they moved into the larger bedroom.

Opening their door, she showed her their room, it was papered with a very delicate blue forget-me-not flowered design all on a white satin background. There was a white wrought iron bed covered with a pale blue chenille bedspread, and it had a pile of assorted blue print pillows. She told Rebecca that she had the bed redone a few years back; it had been her mother's. Rebecca told Anne how lovely she thought her home was. Anne thanked her and then she showed her the spare room she used for sewing. Anne told Rebecca to go and visit with her husband and David, she could check on the children and see that they were all settled in.

Rebecca thanked her and popped in on the kids and reminded them about being on their best behavior, and quietly said, "You remember what we discussed, before we left Tennessee?"

"Yes, Mom." They whispered, "We remember."

"I know that it is hard on all of us, but we promised the men, remember."

Rachel said, "We know, Mom. We won't talk about Dad."

Rebecca gave them all a hug and told them she would give Grandma a call to let her know what has happened. Before she left she said, "Get ready for bed and go straight to sleep, we have an exciting and busy day planned for tomorrow."

When Rebecca returned to the dining room, she saw that the men were finished with their meal. She overheard Frank saying, "The kids are great." When she entered; David pushed his plate forward, "Dad was telling me how great your kids were with the animals."

The thin man with salt and pepper hair explained, "I was showing them how to groom." Frank's face turned bright red and he burst out laughing, "When one of the goats shit on Danny's boot." He hooted. By the time he got the whole story out, all three of them were laughing. "We were all sort of dumb founded, Anne and I weren't sure if Danny was going to get upset." "That's when, your oldest saved the moment by saying," he talked like Rachel, "Dang, Danny, now you smell like you belong in a barn." "Then all three kids broke out laughing and Anne and I did too." "Your kids are really good natured Rebecca." Frank complimented them. "And their funny too."

They all talked a little about the kids. It was an easy and safe subject. Rebecca appreciated that.

"Well, Thank you for dinner it was very good." Rebecca told David.

"You're welcome, now you can give me a hand." He told her.

"Sure, now you want my help. Once the fun part is over." She kidded him.

"Actually, This is the fun part. After we finish cleaning up we get to take a walk down to the pig pen and feed them some of the scraps."

"Really?" she questioned.

He nodded to her.

"That could be fun, maybe."

"I assure you." David told her, "This chore was one of my highlights as a teenager."

Rebecca highly doubted that, but she gave him the benefit of the doubt.

They cleared off the table, and he showed her which scraps to save for the pigs. Then they put the rest away in the refrigerator or the trash can. David dumped the rest of the salad in with the scraps.

Rebecca said, "Wait. That was perfectly good for another day."

"Don't be greedy." He handed her one of the carrots, "The pigs need to eat too."

David grabbed two coats off the back door and handed Rebecca one of his mother's thick winter coats. Explaining to her that the fashionable one he saw her with earlier would probably cause her to freeze to death. He grabbed the pail of scraps, and being a gentleman, he held the back door open for Rebecca.

Stepping out into the night air, they noticed the temperature had dropped significantly from a few hours earlier. With the pail swaying back and forth, they made their way up the long trek toward the barn.

※ ※ ※

Carl left the cell behind him, and he thought "good riddance." He was ready to get on with things. The sooner he got whatever this was done. The sooner he could get home to his family. So, he looked at this new move of his as a positive step toward the process of getting home and decided to take that optimism with him. "Do whatever you have to do," he told himself.

The Major met him in the lounge down the hall, and he was now dressed in civilian clothing too. He was wearing a gray suit and Carl thought how glad he was that he chose the dark brown. He also noticed the corporal come in to take his suitcase, and he was wearing a navy blue suit himself. Carl felt as if he were in some old rerun of "Drag Net" and all they were missing were the bad hats. He passed it off as his getting used to the new uniform. intellectually, He knew it was around 6:45pm. but after living under these florescent lights for the last six months, it could be 3:00am for all he actually knew.

The Major told him to wait there while he finished up some last arrangements. When he returned he was ready to leave and God-forbid Carl chuckled to himself, the man was wearing one of the bad hats. That clinched it. Now he knew he was participating in an outdated television program.

The Major said, "Time to go."

Sergeant Reynolds stood up and barked "Yes Sir."

"You can drop the Sir." He told Carl. "From now on, its first name basis only and we're no longer military." "You can call me Randy, Carl" and pointing to his assistant he said, "This is Matt."

Carl nodded to Matt and then to Randy in understanding and they left the basement and headed toward civilization.

On the elevator, Carl watched as the numbered lights rose to 1, and continued to follow it as it dinged upward. He realized that they were climbing to the roof. The door opened and a tall, wiry man greeted them and told Randy that everything was already aboard. When he stepped through the doorway leading out to the roof, Carl saw a helicopter waiting for them. The three men climbed aboard the bird and the man from the roof told them all to have a good flight and slammed the door behind them. Carl listened to the thwacking of the blades as he watched the wind propelling the man running to reenter the building.

About fifteen minutes later, they landed at a small airport, where another man greeted them. He passed along information to Randy about the pilot being caught in traffic, and that he expected to be here within ten minutes. He then said the jet was already fueled, and it was ready for them to board if they wished to wait for the pilot there. Randy thanked him and apologized for the short notice. The man assured him it hadn't been a problem, what so ever. He explained that he would have the bags transferred to the jet and then he spoke to all the men, wishing them an enjoyable flight. Randy thanked the man again, and Carl noticed him hand the guy a tip for his trouble.

Carl looked around the airfield and saw that there were a lot of private jets, a few private helicopters and a large group of planes at the far end of the airport that he thought were Cessna's. He assumed everything was privately owned because many of them had names on the side. Similar to what one would see on boats in a harbor, he thought. But, he added to his conclusion that harbors were a lot more pleasing to look at and figured that was because there is more activity in a harbor. There were seagulls flying around and diving in the air. Plus as you look out to the expanse of the ocean beyond the harbor, there are so many creatures to imagine below its surface. Carl could hear the seagulls in his mind now and hear the water lapping up against the boats. This airport was the opposite; it was lonely. The tarmac was flat and hard and on the last day of February it felt cold.

"Carl!" Randy called out, "Let's go get settled on the plane."

Carl thought about the James Bond films he had watched as a kid and thought, This is where the plane would have an enemy spy or a bomb on it. He turned and looked at the man in his late forties and said, "Bond, James Bond" then he dropped the voice and finished, "Okay Randy, Lead the way."

The other two men laughed. "Yeah, Right," Randy replied, "Smart Ass." Then Randy joked, "Matt, I think he really means you!"

"Everyone knows," Matt said, "That it's the side kick who ends up biting the bullet, And that's you, Randy."

"But," Randy replied, "It's the insignificant No name who takes it in the first act and that can only be you, Kiddo!"

The three men laughed, and all headed toward the jet. Carl reminded himself silently, But I'm Bond and no matter how banged up he gets, Bond always gets the bad guy and the girl by the end. He aimed to keep it that way.

As they climbed the stairs leading into the plane, they all felt the pressure had been slightly lifted off their backs, and each was grateful for that relief. The jet was rather nice Carl thought. Instead of rows of seats, the plane was designed like a living room, except it also had a medium sized conference table in the center. He was just thrilled that it was comfortable, and they didn't have to share it with anyone the whole trip across country.

The pilot arrived about ten minutes later than he had expected. He apologized and told them rush hour traffic had been hell to get through. Randy and the pilot shook hands and exchanged "How have you been." Carl realized that they knew each other pretty well. "We'll be up in the air just as soon as I get it cleared with the tower." He told them. Within minutes, they were up, and charging through the darkening sky toward the West Coast.

Matt got up and resumed the role for which he was hired. He offered to make coffee and to check out what food was on board in its small galley. Randy then pulled out his briefcase and spread stacks of paperwork across the table they were sitting around. Carl could see the words Operation Genius across the top of one stack of documents. The gray haired man across from him yelled back to Matt and asked him to put a short shot of brandy in his coffee if there were any. "Okay." He yelled back. Carl could hear casualness in the exchange between the men and figured they must have been working together for some time now. Randy finished taking out his stack of files and decided there was no time like the present, to get his new soldier acquainted with his life, since there was no saying how long they would be working together. He liked screwing with people's minds he admitted to himself and so he looked straight at Carl and said, "Matt your mother and brother are expecting us around 10:00 pm. You may need to let them know we could be late." "Okay." The boy replied. Randy laughed to himself as he watched Carl lift his eyebrows in complete confusion. "We have what appears to be a long assignment ahead of us." He told Carl. "So I thought we'd make things easier and drop all pretenses now. Matt is my stepson. My wife and our younger son live up in Washington State."

Carl thought that the boy was very professional when they were in the facility and he was impressed. Carl said so to Randy, "I would never have guessed that you were related, but I did catch that you had worked together for awhile."

"Well, He's a good kid, I tried to get him to go to college, but he wanted to join instead."

Carl told him there is always time for him to go to college later.

Randy looked down towards the stacks of papers and answered "We'll see."

Matt brought out the coffee and a plate of turkey sandwiches. "Kenny must have stocked up the galley. I found these cold cuts and some chips." He said. "I also found a frozen Lasagna and garlic bread."

Randy replied, "It sounds like Carrie called him with instructions." He told Carl that Carrie was his wife, and their other son's name was Joey. He was seventeen and was a high school football star with big plans of going pro.

Matt placed the sandwiches on the table and told them it was a snack to tide everyone over until the lasagna was done. "But if you would like I can get the chips too." Matt asked the men.

They both thanked him and told him the sandwiches were fine without chips. Matt took one of the sandwiches and went to turn on the Television. "Look." He said, "Kenny left some new DVD's too." He explained that Kenny was his Uncle, his mother's youngest brother. He worked in the families' East Coast office. His other Uncle lived with his family in the United Kingdom, mainly in London he told Carl.

Randy looked around the jet and decided he could use a real drink instead of the little bit of brandy in his coffee.

He drank a short glass of whiskey Matt found in the galley. He stared around at the object, which represented the family he had married into. He hated the way it made him feel he wasn't good enough for Carrie. Randy then proceeded to tell Carl how his wife came from money and so the plane they were in now, was part of her father's corporate fleet. His father-in-law was about money, he told Carl, but there was also nothing better than having a soldier for a son-in-law. "After all", He said, "It proved they were true blue-blooded Americans." Randy was accepted into the family. However, Carrie's father would have preferred he was a man of higher rank and was politically powerful. Carrie, on the other hand, was glad he wasn't in the game. It was something she grew up doing. Being forced to perform as the daughter of a wealthy business tycoon became something she resented. She married the first time for her father and it ended miserably. But their marriage was for love according to Carrie. Randy spoke with the two men who would be his companions for only god knew how long and spilled his life story to whomever was listening. "But now, I'll finally get what I should have had all along." Randy remarked.

Carl could feel the pain pouring out of this man sitting beside him. The irony didn't escape Carl. Randy gave up respect for the love of his life. If he had fallen in love with any other woman; then he would have naturally had the respect and admiration of her family, just for being an honorable man. Now he was hoping to earn some respect from his father-in-law by becoming a hero. Carl didn't know if he should tell him what he thought or just keep it to himself. He decided that the best thing to do was to say something because he knew what people say and what they actually mean are not always the same thing. "Sir, my world is a lot smaller than yours, but judging by this boy here, he pointed to Matt watching the movie his uncle left for him, I'd say the odds are good that your everything Carrie and your sons need." Carl continued, "After everything has been said and done, Matt chose you over his own father and his Grandfather." Randy thought about what he had said to him, and he looked at his son. The man returned his gaze to Carl and said "Your right, sometimes it's hard to see the road through the windshield when so much shit and mud has been flung up against it, But you're absolutely right, Thank you, Carl."

Carl thought that he might have caught the glimmer of a tear welling up in the Majors eye. He turned from Carl for a second and then turned back and looked down at the paperwork in front of him and exclaimed, "Let's get started on this then." He picked up a packet in front of him.

CHAPTER FIVE

The walk to the Barn was farther than Rebecca thought it would be. She listened to the gravel crunch under their boots. Then off in the distance she heard an owl hoot. It was cold outside, but it was also a nice night. Rebecca saw that the sky was very clear, and the stars were bright. It reminded her of cool fall evenings sitting under the stars next to a campfire and making s'mores. She thought the clear sky meant that they would be fine as far as the weather went and she said this to David.

He held his own thought about the subject to himself and felt it wasn't worth her getting worried over. But, he knew the weather in the mountains could change in an instant.

"Is this what you meant earlier? That it was nice being a teen and walking with your girlfriends under the stars to go feed the pigs." Rebecca looked up into the sky and thought how romantic it must have been to be young and in love. "It must have been very romantic?"

David chuckled and said, "Yeah, It was romantic. I suppose."

"What was that chuckle for?"

"Well," he said, "All I seem to remember is the lust, but, now that I think about it, it was very romantic."

"Yeah." she said, "I remember that too, teenage lust that is."

"No, not you, a nice girl like you?" He teased her, and she knew he was enjoying himself.

They finally came to a building set way back from the house, where David stopped and opened a side door to the barn. He walked in, and she stayed at the door. Switching on a light, he told her to come in out of the cold. As he emptied the pail, the pigs came squealing for it. She smiled when she saw the pigs come running around a wooden wall and charge for the feed trough.

Then she turned to David and responded to his kidding. "You don't even know the first thing about me!"

He stood there staring at her with her hands on her hips, and he said, "Are you trying to say that you have fooled my family into believing that you're a nice girl?"

She thought about how to answer that and said with a slight cringe, "Well, Yeah, ah, I guess so."

Whew, he thought, now I know I'm going to like this girl. Climbing up to the loft David told her, "You're going to have to prove it to me before I'll believe that."

"Now wait a minute. I'm not that kind of girl, well maybe I was once. But... she said, strong and loud; so he could hear her. I'm not, NOW."

He leaned over the loft's edge, "Well you've already started convincing me, I'm impressed, your mind is in the gutter or should I say the Loft." He teased her. "Rebecca get your cute little butt up here. I want to show you something." he said.

"I'll Bet!" she said.

"Impressed again." He yelled down, "And bring that flashlight with you."

"A man who likes the lights on." She said to herself.

He heard that and thought that if she didn't shut up she very well might find out just what she was doing to him. His pants felt strategically tight.

She climbed the ladder to the top and didn't know how to get up on the landing. David took the flashlight and took her hand to help her the rest of the way. She noticed a sweet and slightly damp smell of hay and they sat down in a pile of loose straw and leaned their backs against some bails. Then the light switched on, and David was pointing to names with hearts around them carved into the beams and ceiling.

Rebecca melted a little and thought how sweet. But, she couldn't resist teasing him and so she said in a jesting tone, "Is this your families version of notches on the bed post."

"No- smart ass." He quipped back at her, "This is the family romances you spoke of on the walk up here." "You see that one. That was my first sweetheart." She saw a heart with David -N- Tammy in the middle. "We dated for about six months in ninth grade." Then he told her about a couple of others he had dated and some of the girlfriends and boyfriends his siblings had as teenagers. She could almost image what it was like to grow up here. He told her about his first kiss with Tammy and that the first heartbreak he experienced was when she decided to breakup with him to date a tenth grader. He also told her, about his junior and senior long romance with Samantha. How he gave her a promise ring when he left for boot camp, but then returned to find she had changed her mind, went off to college and met someone new.

They sat there in the dark looking at spotlights on hearts while this man spilled his. Then Rebecca asked which one was his ex-wife. David switched the light on and off, on and off a couple of times and then turned it back on so he could see Rebecca's face. He told her she wasn't one of his childhood sweethearts. He also told her he had been in the Navy for ten years and that he met her when he was stationed at Norfolk. Their marriage had worked fine while he was in the service, but when he got out to move back home their relationship died. "She didn't like it in the mountains." David added, "The lifestyle wasn't to her liking either." Since then, she had remarried, and the kids, his son Ryan, who was ten and his daughter Jessica, aged eight were both with their Mom.

She told him she was sorry. Then Rebecca softly said, "It must be very difficult without your children."

He looked up and saw her face was a little rosy on her checks and nose. Her eyes penetrated his as he thought he felt lightning strike his chest. She was so beautiful; He thought as he watched her tuck a strand of black hair behind her ear. It fell back in front of her eyes, and she moved it again.

She shivered and thought, "What am I doing here, this was really stupid." She yelled internally. "You're not a sixteen year old anymore." She reminded herself. Her hair slipped from behind her ear, and David gently replaced it for her. "Why did he have to be so wonderful, she thought, and God, he's so sexy."

He saw her shiver and decided he had kept her out here too long, she was freezing. He reached out to her and pulled her closer to him. "Are you cold?" David asked Rebecca as he wrapped his arms around her. She could smell a bit of wood smoke on his shirt and a slight scent of grain. The warm, sweet yet musky, male aroma of him hit her hard. Rebecca's head began to spin, and she thought she was about to faint, then realized, that she was drunk from the intensity of the moment or more accurately the man.

He thought, if he didn't get them out of here quickly then he was going to do something he would regret.

He had unzipped his coat, and she could feel his body, so hot, up against her. It had been so long since she had felt this type of warmth.

He looked down, to see her face flush. He brought the palm of his hand to the side of her face. Looking into her eyes, they both felt a rush of heat slam into their bodies as David leaned toward Rebecca.

In a moment that felt like an eternity his mouth came down on hers. She felt the warm moist passion of his lips against hers as his tongue twirled with her own. She felt an explosion of reaction within her as she felt his engorged massive body press down against her. He had both hands on her face and was kissing her again. When suddenly, a hurricane wind of ice came rushing at them.

David rushed to re-latch the barn window and thanked the weather for helping him to regain some self-control. When he took his seat next to her again, he noticed Rebecca's face turned away from him. She seemed to be crying. He obviously upset her. David felt like an overzealous idiot. He immediately wished he hadn't been so stupid.

"Are you okay?" He asked Rebecca, as he carefully slid her hair back behind her ear with his fingers.

"Yes, Rebecca said. I'm fine."

"I'm so sorry, Rebecca. I didn't-"

"It's alright, David." Rebecca cut his words off, "Really. It's not, your fault."

She couldn't handle the intense guilt she felt for betraying Carl. These damn tears, she couldn't control them either. "Suck it up and drive on, her thoughts yelled at herself, Your freaking his man out, stop crying." But, they wouldn't stop and she knew they couldn't since they were the first she had allowed herself to have.

"Rebecca you're a beautiful woman, David said, But, to be honest I'm glad that wind blew in when it did." She sat listening as he continued. "I would love to make love to you, he took her face in his hands, But, if and when I do, I want it to be after I know who you are and I want it to feel good." He elaborated, "In my bed with warm blankets and candles."

She looked at him with tears still coming down her face.

He released her face, "I apologize if I offend you when I say this, but I don't think I believe you when you say you're fine."

Rebecca spoke through muddled sobs, "I really am fine." She insisted.

"I don't believe you." He said again. "But what's worse, he told her, Is that I'm scared that if we leave here now with this feeling between us, then I'm afraid tomorrow we won't be able to look at each other."

Then he took her face in his hands again, "I want you to look at me as much as I want to enjoy looking at you." He gently kissed her this time. When he was done he said "By the way it's snowing like hell outside, we better get back to the house."

"Shit." She said, "My car!"

"It will be fine, he smiled, besides there's nothing we can do about it, so why bother worrying." "Rebecca," David asked as he helped her down off the ladder. "Would you please tell me what is wrong." He looked at her face and restrained himself from kissing her again. "Hard to do, he told himself, when she felt so damn good." Her mouth felt soft like silk, and she tasted of sweet honey. "What was that smell?" She reminded him of spring, was it the smell honeysuckle or was it Gardenia? Whatever it was, it was mixed with some incredibly sexy scent that was all her own. David told her, "I think we both are wounded souls in need of some mending." "You've been nice enough to listen to my battle scars, I'd really like to listen to yours."

She looked at this man in front of her and didn't know what to say. She didn't want to say no, yet she didn't know what she could say in explanation.

David saw her hesitation and quickly responded, "I promise to keep my lips off you, the next time we kiss, it will be because you kissed me." And he pulled the muzzle of his parka up over his mouth to prove it.

Rebecca smiled and told him all right as long as he got her indoors and made her another cup of tea.

"Deal." David called out as and he grabbed her hand entwining their fingers and placed it inside his coat pocket. Then he rushed them back toward the house.

The snow on the ground had already reached a foot high. The wind was gusting so hard that she thought that if David weren't holding on to her, she might literally blow away. By the time they reached the back door her face felt like a sheet of ice and she was grateful for the blast of warmth that hit her when she entered the kitchen. Anne had baked something while they were gone. it smelled like fresh bread, but also banana bread or muffins, she wasn't quite sure.

"What is that smell? It's delicious smelling, but I can't place it." Rebecca questioned.

"My mother probably made a few baked goods for the next day or two."

Anne heard them come in and came to see what her son had been up to. "Hi you two, where have you been David?" "I was starting to get a bit worried. The weather is getting so bad out there." She finished, but not without letting her son know she was concerned in more ways than one.

"Mom, I wouldn't let anything happen to your beautiful guest, We're big people too."

She gave him a look only a mother could give and prayed her son wasn't setting himself up for another heartbreak.

"Mom, Rebecca, was asking what the wonderful smell was." David changed the topic before his mother said something embarrassing in front of Rebecca. His parents held nothing back, and that could be a burden as well as a blessing. It's how he learned to be open and honest, but not everyone was like his family.

"Yes, Rebecca elaborated, but I couldn't place it. I thought maybe bread of some kind."

Anne told her that her nose was right. She had made bread, but she had also made some muffins and strudel. She explained that they had a generator for the necessary things, but for the heat and cooking they used the wood stove and fireplaces when the power went out. She feared that they would lose it sometime tonight, by the looks of the storm that was blowing out there.

"Speaking of power, David said to Rebecca, If you have someone you need to call. You better get it done soon. Just in case."

"Oh my goodness, I forgot to call my mother." Rebecca cried out. "She'll kill me for making her worried sick."

"As any good mother should." Anne said in response. The clock on the wall said 10:00pm. "There is a phone in the other room by the chair, if you would like to use that one." The kind woman pointed her to the burgundy recliner in the living room.

"Thank you," Rebecca dialed the operator and called her mother collect.

"Hello." She heard on the other end.

"Hi Mom, We're safe. We did have a small problem, but everything is fine."

She told her mom all about the accident and the people they were staying with and told her that she was sorry for calling so late. Her mother wanted to know where they were exactly, and the phone number she could reach her at. When Rebecca asked for this information, she lost the phone. Anne took it and talked away to her mother and told the whole

64

story again, her version of it anyhow. Rebecca wondered if all mothers were this way because she wasn't like this, yet anyway. She made a mental note, to ask David if his mother were German because hers was, maybe that was the connection to their mothering. When Anne was done talking, she handed the phone back to Rebecca. At which time, her mother then told her that she would talk to her in a day or two depending on the situation with the car and the weather. Her mother cheerfully and contentedly hung up the phone.

Rebecca was flabbergasted. Her mother was always worried when they hung up the phone. She actually sounded calm and relieved. But what blew Rebecca away was how these two mothers had planned out her itinerary for her. They made not one consultation with her at all.

That was easy she thought.

She felt slightly uneasy, but she couldn't decide what there was to be upset about. So she dropped it.

When she returned to the kitchen, Rebecca overheard Anne and David talking. It was Anne's voice she could hear, "She's German. I could tell."

David saw Rebecca return. "Here she is, I'll ask her." "Mom was wondering."

"Not wondering at all David." Anne corrected. "I was telling you."

David asked. "Is your Mom German?"

"Yes, she is."

Anne smiled and now thought she knew why Rebecca and her children seemed to fit in her home as if they were family. She patted David's hand and said, "I was right, Goodnight."

"Goodnight." They replied.

David was getting the teakettle off the stove when his father came into the kitchen. He told Rebecca that Anne wanted him to let her know that she left long underwear on her bed and to be sure she used them, or she would catch her death. Then he asked David if he would check on the animals and make sure they were warmly bedded and shut up tight for the night.

He put his hand on Rebecca's shoulder. "You'll help him won't you dear?"

Rebecca smiled and told him, "Of course." Though she doubted how much help she would be to a grown man who was raised caring for animals.

David just laughed and said you might want to get that underwear on before we venture out to the barns.

She looked at him to try and gauge whether he was joking or not.

He said, "No really, It would be a good idea."

She explained that she would check on the kids at the same time, and David said he would check the fires and the wood stove.

As Rebecca looked into the sunshiny room her kids were in, she saw Rachel stirring. She stood there and waited to see if she would wake enough to talk to her.

"Mom, are you okay?"

"Yes, I came to see if you guys were doing okay yourself."

"We're good, Mr. Frank read to us before bed." "I think the Henry's are really nice." She told her mom half-groggy.

"Sweetie, it's snowing pretty hard and I'm going out with David to check on the animals."

"Okay Mom" Rachel said and rolled over to go back to sleep.

She went to her rose-papered room and put on the thermals that Anne had left for her, and then she added the heaviest sweater she owned.

He was filling a thermos with hot water and decided to add hot cocoa and cream instead of tea. He knew what his parents were up to; he wasn't born into this family yesterday. They were big believers in faith and what he sometimes termed, superstition. They think Rebecca's being German is some kind of fate. So now they're sending them out into the cold to bond. It couldn't hurt to check on the animals, but he knows they are fine. He wouldn't mind getting her alone so he can find out what is wrong with her. "There you are." He greeted Rebecca as she entered the kitchen, "I hope you like hot chocolate because tea didn't seem hearty enough and I thought we'd bring some of mom's banana nut bread too."

"Umm, I think you read my mind." she replied.

"Here, he said, can you carry some of these blankets I picked up from the mud room."

"Are these for the animals?"

"Maybe, if they need them. We'll have to wait and see."

When they went out the door, she noticed that the snow was now half way up to her knees. The wind had died down some, but the snow was still falling just as heavy as it was when they had come inside. David told her they would check the larger animals first. That was the horses and cows mainly. Then they went and put more straw down in the smaller animal's pens.

"What is this?" She asked David, "Is it what it looks like?"

"Yes, actually it's an old coal stove that we sometimes use for wood." He explained that a long time ago it was used for farm hands to keep warm, "Would you like to put a little fire on and have our bread and hot cocoa?"

It sounded like a rather nice idea and so she answered, "Only if it's not too much trouble."

He smiled and told himself that was a code phrase for Yes. Then he felt hopeful and made himself busy setting the fire.

She watched him as he worked. He was tall, and he was very strong. She assumed this was from working with his animals. David's hair was black with just a hint of gray mixed into his temples. It wasn't the stubble style of a military cut, yet it wasn't long either, it was a clean cut, but long enough to have some wave to it. His eyes were the color of a clear blue ocean, and there was a sparkle in them that made you believe he was holding back some secret. Yet they were gentle, and he seemed to carry a smile with him everywhere. He wore blue jeans and a plaid navy blue shirt. When they entered the barn he had removed his coat and instead, replaced it with a gray pullover sweater.

David smiled because he knew she was watching him and that pleased him to no end. To have a beautiful woman like her stare at him was a major confidence builder, he wouldn't deny that to anyone. Her sitting there viewing him made him self-conscience enough to use his muscles, but be careful not to flex them and have her think him arrogant.

The stove was set in an area that had a small clearing around it, and he made sure to keep it clear as he brought over some pitchforks filled with fresh straw. He made a pile for them to sit on then he instructed her to take one of the blankets they brought and lay it across the mound. David and Rebecca then shut off the lights so the animals could get some rest and they sat and had their late night snack in the flickering light of the open wood stove.

When they finished eating, Rebecca asked him, "David was this a set up?"

"Yup." He laughed. "How could you tell?"

"I don't know, the animals just didn't feel very cold to me." She concluded.

He explained. "It did get cold tonight, but they keep each other warm." "Are you cold?" He asked her.

"Not too bad." She replied.

They took the extra blankets and wrapped up in them as he tried to convince her to tell him about herself.

"What do you want to know?" She squirmed.

"Why you're so sad."

Rebecca sat for a few moments and then explained to him that she wasn't sure if she were ready to talk about that right now.

So he said to her that it was okay with him if she started someplace else. But he wanted to know something about her life.

She thought everything about her was in some way wrapped up in

Carl, and she didn't know where to begin. So she decided to start all the way from the beginning.

⁂

The plane bounced all of a sudden and all three men scrambled to grab their cups so that Randy's paperwork wouldn't get covered in coffee and whiskey. He had filled Carl in about where they were going and why.

As Carl understood this, they were headed to a compound located in the mountains of Washington. It was a jointly owned facility, partly government, but mostly Industrial Corporation. It was the brainchild of "Douglas Defense Advancement Solutions" Randy's Father-in-law's corporation.

A few select companies, Randy explained, decided to join forces so that technological advances could be made quicker. "Some of the top scientific and technology minds are working together at "Tech Park". The government provides a cover up of the facility and security from outside forces and the companies give the government first dibs on the newly invented wonders they've created.

"What are the companies gaining from this deal?" Carl asked.

"By cover up, I mean off the books." Randy explained. "No records, translates into No knowledge of its existence anywhere, which in turn translates into..."

"I got you, No taxes." Carl said.

"Exactly, Do you have any idea how much money this saves." Randy shuddered from the thought.

"A fleet of Jets?" Carl joked.

Randy exaggerated his wide-eyed expression and said, "Much, much more than that."

Carl believed him, but he just couldn't begin to conceive what that must mean.

Randy picked up a folder and opened it for Carl. Inside he pulled out a large diagram of Tech Park and a couple of Ariel photos along with a few standard shots.

Carl's ability to comprehend became much clearer. "How do you cover that up?" Carl wanted to know.

He explained how the Ariel shots were designed to look as if it were an elite resort. If anyone gets curious enough to drive all the way into the mountains and find it, the gates are secured. Picking up a picture, he passed it to Carl. It was of an incredible entrance that said, "Peak View Resort. That was my idea, and I also came up with the brochure." Randy told him as he handed it to Carl. Of course, he told him the only way to get it is to call our office, but only a few people have ever tried that hard.

Carl looked at the brochure in his hand and said "Haven't I heard of this place before." He looked at the prices on it and laughed.

Randy said the prices were placed there to discourage the people who were determined to find the place. For average people, those prices were enough to stop their inquiries. Famous people, on the other hand; have more money than the average person, and they have agents who call to arrange for their getaways. Agents working for rich people are persistent, but of course we're always booked solid.

Eventually, Some famous actresses and musicians started lying and telling how wonderful it was there, Matt said as he talked like one of the over privileged, "How everyone and anyone who can afford such a luxury simply must experience it." He batted his eyelashes; "It's just heaven."

They all laughed.

"But seriously, Randy continued, A lot of people put a ton of hard work into designing this place, and there are some wonderful features to enjoy when people are not busy working."

"If you have to be away from home Carl, Matt quipped in, this place is the bomb."

Carl looked at the pictures of his new home away from home and was determined he would much rather be home with Rebecca and the kids. But if he had to be somewhere, this was much better than being in his little cell.

"Carl." Randy handed him a folder. "I've put together a packet for you. It contains maps of the compound." In it, he explained all the areas that were off limits to him and all the places he was free to explore. There were also lists of activities that were planned on different weekends throughout the next year. "All employees are given this packet, he told Carl, Your welcome to attend any functions listed or not any of them at all, if you like." He then showed him the building in which they would be working and asked if he had any questions.

Carl shook his head back and forth and told Randy. "Not at the moment."

"You've got a lot to look through there, I'll let you do that and then you can feel free to ask me any questions later." He stood to go stretch and use the bathroom. "Oh, and Carl there are just two things we require of you." First, Randy told him, was that they expect him not to attempt to leave the compound. They have worked too hard to protect him already, and they don't wish to be his jailer. "Secondly, You are required to have a bodyguard." Randy finished and walked out of the cabin to go relieve his bladder and call Lieutenant Jordan, whom he temporarily left in charge of his three surveillance teams.

Carl sat and looked at his file full of diagrams, lists, schedules and maps. He was impressed with how authentic the facility appeared to be a resort. After glancing through the diagram closer and reading the itinerary for employee entertainment, Carl came to the conclusion that it wasn't an appearance at all. This place really was a resort. The place had everything, a movie theater, pool, game rooms and a gym. It also had stables and game fields of all types. A conference and banquet hall was in one of the main service buildings. He even noticed one of the events listed for employee entertainment this past February was: A day of skiing and snowboarding with dinner and a movie to end the evening. Carl couldn't believe it. He said out loud. "I've been kidnapped and taken to Disney World!"

"No doubt, But not bad, Huh." Matt said.

Carl was clueless in how to respond to the prospect of a

spontaneous vacation. He sort of felt bad for Rebecca. There she was, wondering if he was even still alive and here he was getting ready to go live a life of leisure. He looked at his watch and wondered where she was and whom she was with. It was 11:30pm, back east and he thought she could be sleeping, but not likely, Rebecca never slept well when he wasn't with her.

Matt finished watching one of his movies, and he came over to sit with Carl. "We should be landing soon." He told the Thirty-Something year-old man across from him. He knew he couldn't empathize with this guy's feelings. He hasn't had any really deep relationships with any girls, but he still wouldn't like to be forced to do things he didn't want. Even still, he thought, when it came down to it, Carl was getting a really Sweet Deal. He thought about some of the people he knew that worked at the facility and chuckled, thinking there was one bodyguard in particular that he wouldn't mind being protected by. Then he wondered if she still worked there. The last time Matt recalled seeing her was about a year ago. Matt remembered this guy was married, and he asked him, "What is your wife like?"

Carl looked up from his paperwork and stared at the young kid across the table from him.

"I'm sorry." The boy said. "I shouldn't have asked you that, I was just curious."

Carl was surprised, "No." He told Matt. "It's okay, you're just the first person to ask me about her."

"You're kidding." The boy replied.

"No I'm not, actually everyone I've spoken to seems to think everything they need to know about Rebecca and me can be found in some file or other." He answered. "What exactly would you like to know about her?"

"I don't know." "What does she look like?" Matt wondered.

Carl pulled out his wallet and produced a picture of his wife and kids and handed it to Matt.

"Wow, you're a lucky man." "You have a nice looking family, Carl."

"Thank you." Carl responded.

"How long have you two been together?" Matt asked.

"Fifteen years, but we've been married for fourteen." Carl thought, How do I describe Rebecca. He realized; she was a contradiction. "Matt, My wife, is a contradiction. She is very smart and intuitive, but yet the next thing you know she is the silliest and ditziest woman in the world. She's creative and sews and does all kinds of traditional womanly things, yet she is a very liberal minded woman. She loves to be sexy and feminine, but she also loves to get down in the mud with the guys. Her feet are always freezing cold, but let me tell you, the rest of her burns hot. What can I say, she's the woman I want in my bed for the rest of my life, if you understand my meaning."

Matt looked down at the picture of Carl's wife and said, "Yeah, I think I do in more ways than one." Then he handed the picture of Carl's family back to him. "I hope I find someone like that for myself someday."

Carl smiled at the young man and gently said, "You will. Someday, she'll just be there, and you'll know that she's the one."

Randy had been standing in the doorway behind them and had listened to their conversation. He knew he was guilty of the crime Carl spoke about. He too had read this man's file and assumed to know what he and his wife were all about. He felt some shame in that knowledge. Especially after Carl had listened to him speak about his own marriage. The man had even given careful consideration to what I told him and offered advice, he thought to himself. Randy felt bad. He knew the conversation Carl and Matt had could never have taken place between him and Carl. Randy thought he learned something about Carl today. Carl was a good man and Randy vowed to himself that no matter what happened, he was going to get this man home safely to his family. To seal his vow, Randy chased down a shot of whisky and tore his shirt pocket. Then he went and rejoined the others in the cabin.

"Dad?" Matt asked. "Are you okay?"

"Of course, Randy said, Why do you ask?"

Matt pointed at Randy's shirt pocket.

"Oh that, Randy exclaimed. That's nothing, I snagged it on the bathroom door."

Matt said, "Tomorrow I'll have one of the crew fix the door."

"Thank you Matt, but that won't be necessary, it was only me being clumsy."

Matt nodded that he understood and hoped his father hadn't had too much to drink or his mother was going to kill him for not watching how much he'd had. It wasn't like Randy to drink too much; Matt thought, particularly when he was working.

The pilot came over a speaker and told them he was beginning their descent toward the airport and for safety reasons he would appreciate it if they would remain seated for the duration of their flight.

Randy gathered up all his paperwork and placed it back in his briefcase. Then he told Carl that he would hold onto his packet until they were safely on the compound.

Carl handed it to him, glad to be relieved of the responsibility of any haphazard release of information about this extravagant setup he was being brought to, he knew his pocketbook couldn't handle that kind of dock in pay.

Ten minutes later they had arrived safely on the ground in another small airport. Carl told himself, Only now they were somewhere in the State of Washington. They rushed from the jet and fought the wind while they boarded another helicopter, which took them on a twenty-minute flight through the dark.

"It's too bad that it is dark out, Matt told Carl. You should see this scenery we're flying through." "It's absolutely beautiful."

"Have you been to Washington before Carl?" Randy asked. "No, Carl told them, but I've heard the mountains are spectacular."

Matt said, "Wait until you wake up in the morning, the view of Mt Rainier is an inspiring sight."

"I can't wait." Carl responded.

When they landed it was too dark to see anything, except the lights on the helicopter pad and a bright overhead light, guiding them to the side of a building. Carl could tell there was a marked drop in the temperature from the East Coast. A man came out through the door, and he had a boy with him. The man shook Randy's hand, and the boy hugged him. Matt and the boy grabbed their suitcases from inside the helicopter and Randy escorted Carl into the building.

"Carl, this is Paul." The men shook hands. "He is in charge of security here at the facility." Randy thanked him for staying late to greet them, he appreciated it.

"Not a problem, Sir." Paul smiled." My pleasure, It's been a while since we have seen you. Are you doing well?"

"Yes, Thank you. How have you been?" Randy asked distractedly.

"Good Sir." Said the pleasant man, "I can't complain about anything except maybe this cold weather."

Carl thought how this man really seemed genuinely glad to see Randy. They watched Randy searching the doorways leading to the great room in which they were standing.

"Excuse me, Paul, Have you seen my wife?" Randy's raised voice echoed slightly off the walls. Before Paul could reply, they heard the force of clicking heels sounding off the walls of a nearby hallway.

A woman yelled. "Hear I am Randy." She entered the room. "I'm sorry I wasn't there to greet you. I was in the ladies room when I heard the helicopter." She walked straight up to her husband, placed her hand to his heart she gave him a quick kiss. She noticed the torn shirt and she smiled up at her husband, but said nothing. She turned to Carl and gave him her hand in greeting.

Randy introduced them and then excused himself to go find his sons. From the door, the man with grayer hair than was usual for his age yelled at the two boys. "Knock it off and get in here." He yelled. "Get those suitcases out of the snow, Joey." Then he turned and jokingly said. "They're sending me to an early grave, Carrie."

She smiled at her middle aged husband. "Hush, Randy, let them be young while they can still get away with it." Just then, they entered the building and Matt was completely covered in snow. Carrie gasped, and

Paul belched out laughing. Randy shook his head and Carl just smiled and enjoyed watching this family unfold. Joey insisted that Matt tackled him first. Carrie said to Matt, "So why doesn't Joey have any snow on him." Joey beamed with pride while his older brother cringed. Matt said a little sheepishly, "Because I'm the only one who hit the ground." Carrie pretended to be really mad, but everyone knew she wasn't. "Your father, told me you two are sending him to an early grave." She barked at them. The boys both stood there looking pathetic. As the snow began to drip off Matt's suit, a puddle began forming at his feet. Carrie started to chuckle, and she told him to go get changed. "You look like a drowned rat, and don't forget to clean up this puddle." She screeched. Then she turned to Carl and whispered to him. "If you don't yell at them, then they forget that you love them." As the boys started to rush off, Randy grabbed Joey by his shirt collar and introduced him to Carl. Then he told his seventeen-year-old son, "Since you're so strong why don't you carry Carl's bags for me and we'll show him to his quarters."

Carl turned to the woman next to him. She was tall for a woman even without the heels. She had short blond hair and wore a hot pink dress suit. Carrie accented it with lots of bold jewelry, and she had long hot pink nails to match. She appeared to be an aggressively charming, yet likeable woman. Carl also thought, those were necessary traits judging by what he had been told about her life. She was nothing even close to his type of woman, but he liked her. He could see how Randy would be in love with her. "It was nice meeting you, Mrs. Taylor." Carl extended his hand to her once again.

"Please, don't be so formal, call me Carrie, besides you'll see me around here often enough." Then she gave him a friendly wink and a pat on his hand as she flashed him a warm motherly smile.

Randy smiled at her and gave her a gesture to hold on a minute. He took his briefcase, and Joey with Carl's bags and the two of them led Carl to a two story stone and beam building. It was located about the length of a football field away from the building they had just left. The rustically elaborate building contained six apartments. Randy explained to Carl that the first floor housed four one-bedroom apartments. Then he led him to the second floor and opened the door to one of the two bedroom dwellings. When they entered the place, Randy noticed that Carrie had given it some personal touches. Things like throw rugs and blankets. Some needle point pillows he remembered her making herself. Randy noticed that Carrie and Joey went out and bought a component stereo and a DVD player and installed it for Carl. But he was really touched when he saw that Joey gave him some of his and Matt's old CDs carefully chosen for Carl's age group. There piled next to the CD's was a stack of slightly older movies too, with a couple of new releases carefully placed on top. Joey looked at his Dad and Randy gave him a grateful smile.

Carl was happily surprised to find that the place didn't feel like a hotel. It was wall to wall carpeted with accent rugs casually placed throughout. The furniture was plush and overstuffed, and he even had throw blankets and pillows. There was just about everything he could need there and he knew Carrie must have done this for him, but also for her husband.

"Carrie and Joey added the touches and stocked up the shelves." The man in his late forties told him.

Carl thanked Joey and the boy shyly told him he was welcome. "Please thank your mother for me." He said he would.

Randy opened his briefcase and pulled out Carl's packet and laid it on the kitchen table. Then he told Carl that Matt would be by tomorrow around 9:00am to pick him up for work. "In the morning I'll introduce you to our mission, and everyone we'll be working with."

Carl told Randy he would be ready and thanked him for everything his family had done for him. Then before the man left Carl asked what the large box next to the living room couch contained.

Randy said, "That's a surprise, you'll have to open it to find out."

Then he and Joey left. Walking back to the main building, Randy put his arm around his son and told him what a nice thing he did for Carl.

"It wasn't much, Dad." Joey said.

"I know son, but it was to Carl." He paused. "And to me."

When he saw his wife standing in the great room waiting for him, Randy thought that his heart was going to burst he loved her so much. He went to Carrie, put his arms around her and said, "THANKYOU."

She touched his shirt and asked him. "To whom did you make a vow to?"

He told her, "To myself- And to Carl."

He knew she understood, and he kissed her to say, "Hello, I love you and Thanks." All at once. Then he took his family home for a well needed rest.

CHAPTER SIX

Rebecca tried to think about where on the time line of her life she should begin. She took the last sip of her hot chocolate and put the cup down. When she looked over at David, she noticed him watching her. He was lying on his side with his head propped up with his hand and forearm and waiting patiently for her to begin. She thought it was safe to start with her basic factual background. She took in a deep breath and then she began.

David enjoyed watching and listening to her as she sat there cocoon-like in the blankets. She was telling him about her childhood. She had explained to him that she was the youngest of six children and that she grew up in Connecticut. He knew that her father was French and that her mother was German. She never knew her Dad's parents, but her mother's passed away when she was in her early twenties. They lived next door to her grandparent's for most of her childhood, she told him, so she knew them pretty well. David wondered if his children would ever be able to say they knew his parent's well. Rebecca told David that her grandparent's had owned a small farm. She described riding on the old red tractor with her grandfather as he plowed the fields. Holding on tight to the back of his seat as the tractor bumped up and down. Listening to the blades dig into the ground and turn over the dirt with a loud scraping sound as the metal hit against rocks along the way. She talked of watching as her Grandfather's neck and shoulders turned redder from the sun as each daylight turned to dusk. Her father spent his days working in the green houses. He would mix together varying types and amounts of soils like it were some special recipe, for all she knew maybe it was. Then he would carefully select seeds and plant and water them in the small miserably hot greenhouse. He grew vegetables and flowers, and when they were large enough he moved them into the large greenhouse and then planted some more. On the weekends, the entire family would come to her grandparent's farm. All her Aunts, Uncles and cousins, would help to plant the seedlings that her father helped grow in the greenhouses. Then by the end of the day after everyone had been burnt by the sun and were covered in sweat and dirt, they would all enjoy a good picnic. As the grownups sat in the evening and talked while smoking cigarettes and enjoying a beer or two, Rebecca, her siblings and cousins would play king of the hill on the huge mounds of potting soil and manure. They would squirm and wrestle to see who could fight their way to the top and maintain their status as king. Rebecca recalled that, on some weekends, they would plant seeds directly into the ground. As the plants grew taller, the weekends evening entertainment for her and her childhood playmates would turn into flashlight Hide and Seek in the cornfields.

She could still feel her fear of garter snakes as she remembered them slithering through the cornfields. Rebecca could see the farm clearly in her mind as she described all this to David. The small red farmhouse with pink, wild rose bushes along the side. The long dirt drive with all the cars parked up into the yard. The hot greenhouses with the large industrial fans sounding like a hurricane which produced the only air bearable enough to breathe. But most of all she pictured her family exactly as she remembered them during the happiest period of her life.

"I haven't talked about that time of my life in a long time." "Those are my favorite memories" she told him. Rebecca told David about the wreaths of daisies her sister would make for her to wear on her head. Also, how Rebecca drove her sister crazy by following her everywhere. David watched her talk about being a child and he saw the happy glazed over look in her eyes as she spoke. Rebecca said. "I was probably the dirtiest child in the neighborhood." "I remember hardly ever wearing shoes." "I walked bare foot everywhere." The only time that she recalled definitely putting on shoes was when she entered the enormous world of blackberry picking. "The bushes were huge, way over my head and full of sharp thorns", she said, "not to mention my fear of the snakes." Her body shuttered from that thought. She chuckled, and David asked, "What's so funny?" "I can't believe I wanted to be around my brothers and cousins so much that I was willing to go snake hunting with them." She shook her head in disbelief. "And of course they always tortured me with those nasty slithering things once they caught them." Rebecca thought about being little and envisioned her dirty feet and ankles. Wiggling her toes under the blankets, she recalled her sneakers, the red Keds that her mom bought at the beginning of the school year. They would always be a little too small by the time summer came. She saw in her mind; the flat, rubber soled, dirty canvas shoes with holes at the toes where her big toe would stick out.

As he listened to her, he thought they shared a lot of similarities while growing up. They both came from large families that shared a similar heritage, and they both grew up working the soil. He thought people like us may not come from lots of money. But, he had always felt rich with love and family and he bet Rebecca had too. David said, "It sounds like we're more similar than either of us expected." "When I was little." he told her. "I let my older sisters dress me up like a girl to play house."

She smiled. "The girls do that to Danny too, makeup and all." Then they both giggled as they thought of her seven year old son with a buzz cut wearing pink blush and eye shadow."

A terrifying sight they both agreed.

David told Rebecca how he never knew his grandparents or really any of his extended family. "They all lived in the Russian occupied, West Germany, By the time the wall came down everyone had passed away except for my grandma and a few distant relatives." "She died about two years after the wall crumbled, But Mom and Dad did get to go visit her at least."

"I'm so sorry," Rebecca told David.

"Don't be sorry, Rebecca, he told her, I'm grateful to have been born an American. My parent's always told us how lucky we were that they were allowed to move to the United States." They had told David and his siblings how hard it was to live in Germany after the war. They were only small children when it ended, but the devastation of the war lasted a long time, splitting up families in the process. David wanted to change the subject. That one was too sad to talk about, and he didn't want to ruin her cheerful mood. As he thought about what to ask Rebecca next, she flopped backward against the straw next to him and brought her hand out from under the blankets to cover her mouth as she yawned.

That was when David noticed the golden rings on Rebecca's left hand. He felt his heart drop to the floor, and he feared his mouth had too. After her yawn, Rebecca flipped her wrist to see what time it was, 1:00am,she yawned again. David yelled at himself, 'How stupid could you be.' His mind raced. How could he have not thought to look earlier for a wedding ring? She had gloves on in the Loft he thought and she kept her hands in the pockets of her sweater or wrapped in the blankets. David decided to stop fooling himself. "She never hid her hands from me." he told himself. He knew that it was he who chose not to notice them and more importantly not to know that she was married.

Rebecca looked over at him, "What's wrong?"

David did not know what to say to her. "Nothing is wrong." It was him who had been too blinded by her to notice she was married. David pointed at her wedding rings.

"Yes." Rebecca was confused, and she defensively thought, she hadn't kept the fact that she was married a secret.

He said. "For some reason I never noticed them until now."

Rebecca exclaimed "Oh." But she said nothing else. A couple of seconds later she felt anger rising in her and before she knew it she became outright pissed off. "Really, David. She yelled loud enough that one of the horses stomped below them, and let out a snort." I have three kids, didn't you think it was likely that I was also married, Come on." Get a clue, she wanted to yell at him, but then she felt a tear run down her face. Why does his accusation make me feel so damn guilty, she demanded to know, especially when she knew she had done nothing wrong.

He said softly, "I think I thought that you had been married like me, but I wasn't thinking that you were married." David noticed that she was crying again and wondered if this had something to do with why she was so upset earlier. "Rebecca." He apologized. "If I hadn't been so thick headed earlier; I would not have kissed you." "You've done nothing wrong. It's all my fault."

She rolled away from him because she didn't want him to watch her crying. Then it occurred to him that maybe there was something wrong with her marriage. "Is there something wrong between you and your husband?" He waited. She said nothing. "He's obviously not with you, so where is he?" David wanted to know.

Rebecca answered in a light whisper. "I don't know."

David couldn't believe it; the bastard walked out on her. Who in his right mind would walk out on a beautiful woman and their children. What a Moron and a jerk. "I'm sorry, Rebecca." David said. As they lay there, he put his arms around her and let her cry.

David had offered her comfort and she accepted it as she let herself pour out all her sorrow, pain and fear until she was exhausted.

Then they both drifted off to sleep.

Carl walked through his new residence and took note of the little details Carrie added for his comfort. They weren't much different from the things Rebecca would have picked given an unlimited pocketbook. Her choices were very down to earth and homey. The basics of the apartment were all neutral browns and beige. Like Rebecca; Carrie had chosen burgundy and a variety of greens to accent the place. The back of the couch had a fluffy angora throw in hunter green. There was also a knit throw with a forest scene on a corner chair near the fireplace. The mantle had brass candlesticks and an ornate figurine of an angel. Carl picked it up and looked at the bottom. He saw a plaque, which read limited edition, 01, and an artist's signature. He didn't recognize the name, but that meant nothing, because he wouldn't have recognized anything that came from the local hallmark store either. Home decorating wasn't his thing, but he still appreciated looking at it. "Now, he thought, Let me loose in any electronics store and I'm in heaven." Rebecca always complained that he could spend a week straight in their local "Electronics Emporium" if she'd let him.

In one corner of the living room stood a small table with two winged back chairs. A Tiffany lamp hung above the set. As Carl approached the little table, he noticed it had a drawer on either side and he opened one. Inside Carl found a chess set made of pewter. Each piece was unique. They were designed as mystical creatures. One set had pawns of fairy's and the other was gnomes. Carl sat down and pulled out the pieces. They were very pretty, and he knew how much his wife would have loved to see them. Carl placed them on the inlaid board. The rooks were castles and the knights were dragons on one side with unicorns on the other. He pulled out the drawer further and found the bishops were wizards and the kings and queens were taller fairy's with more elaborate wings for the one side and the other side had jeweled, medieval period humans to go with the gnomes. Carl put them all back in their drawer and then looked into the smaller one on the other side of the table. Inside he found black and white backgammon pieces and small leather cups with dice, he closed it back into place. Then he leaned down under the table to see if it contained a backgammon board. He found nothing and told himself he'd figure it out another time.

Carl went into the kitchen and found all the cabinets stocked with food, dishes and glasses. He went to the refrigerator and took out a soda and ice for one of the glasses and went to investigate the rest of his new apartment. Every room had a special feature added by Carrie. Carl thought of only one object that he would possibly need that wasn't already here. There was everything except a computer.

He went to sit down in the living room, and he noticed the box sitting there, waiting for him. He was avoiding the thing, unsure if he really wanted to know what was in it. Carl looked at the markings on the box and saw that it came from Nashville and had today's date on it.

He went to the kitchen to get a knife, and when he returned he noticed a box built into the wall next to the fireplace. He opened it and found chopped wood and a group of paper logs. Carl looked at his watch and read the outside package of one of the logs. It said it would burn for at least two hours. Carl decided he could stay awake that long, so he picked up a lighter and watched as it began to burn on each end. Taking a sip of his drink, he looked through the stack of CD's, then picked one and turned the stereo on low.

Staring at the box, he took a deep breath and cut it open. Opening the flaps, Carl found the box filled with all his families photographs. On top was a framed photo of his and Rebecca's ten-year reaffirmation ceremony. The second one he picked up was of one on the same day with their children. Carl sat and looked through the pictures and all the photo albums. Remembering all these moments, he decided he's had a good life up to this point and hoped Rebecca felt the same. Wrapped up at the bottom of the box, there was a family photo taken one year ago, a mock antique photo of Carl's family taken during a reunion. It was set in the old southern belle style, and he recalled how much fun it had been at the boardwalk that day. All of them in the photo had bathing suits on under the fake clothing. Carl went to the fireplace and replaced the woodland picture hanging there with the one of his family. Then he strategically placed all the pewter picture frames around his new apartment. He noticed the coffee table lifted up to hold blankets and such. He took out the blanket and pillow Carrie placed in there and put all the albums in it and closed it back up. Then he put the photo of himself and Rebecca on the top and stared at it until he fell asleep.

He dreamt of making love to his wife and of sitting on the beach watching the Porpoises glide up and out of the water in the distance. Then he reached a heavy sleep and dreamt no further.

❊❊❊

Rebecca awoke to a gust of wind as David opened the barn door to the world outside. "Rebecca." He called out. "Come here and look at this." Rebecca stood and wrapped a blanket around her as she approached the door. She leaned around the corner of it to see what David was staring at and was amazed by the incredible vision nature had bestowed upon them. With all its fury, Mother Nature had given birth to the storm of a lifetime.

David gazed at it. "I haven't seen anything like this since I was a little boy."

Rebecca agreed and told him the same went for her. When she was about four years old she remembered a similar storm, but this one beat it. She looked down at her feet and noticed that the snow outside came up to the middle of her thigh. "How deep would you say the snow is?" She asked. "Three feet?"

"At Least." David said. "Probably more."

But what caught their eyes and mesmerized them was the inch and a half of thick ice covering all the snow. It made the entire landscape look as if it were covered in glitter. It reminded Rebecca of a particular crystal snow globe she saw in a store once.

David said it was good that they started that fire last night, if they were lucky it helped to melt some of the snow off the barn roof. He said he needed to start it back up again before the weight of that ice broke through somewhere. David did that as Rebecca stood there staring at the snow outside. a few minutes later she heard a loud crack and then an even louder crash. She jumped and turned to check on David.

"Don't Worry. That was only some tree limbs and a tree falling in the woods behind the barns." He told her. He got a good fire going in the old coal stove. Then he explained to her that when the sun came up fully they'd be lucky if it melted some of the ice from the trees. "That might save us from a huge mess to clean up later." He told her. "Or else we'll be all set on firewood for many years."

"David, How are we going to get over to the house?" She asked, more puzzled than concerned.

He lifted Rebecca up and placed her on top of the ice and held on. Rebecca held her breath and then within ten seconds she shifted her weight slightly on one foot and down through the ice she went. David caught her and said, "If it can't hold you, then it won't hold me either." He asked her to take his coat and then he grabbed her, and carried her as a husband carries his bride, and they made their way slowly toward the house.

"HERE THEY COME!" Danny called out, looking out the back door window. Everyone came running to see. They watched the couple as David slowly lifted each leg forward, crashing them down through the ice as he carried Rebecca toward the house. "Their laughing," Karen said. "It does look fun," said Rachel. "Not for David." Danny returned.

Frank thought otherwise. But he didn't say so. "We haven't needed snow shoes for over twenty years." Frank said to no one in particular. "Danny, Do you want to help me look for some in the attic after breakfast?"

"Okay." he said.

"Can I come too?" Karen asked.

"Of course you can." Frank told her as he opened the back door and asked them how they made out last night.

Anne thought she caught a slight blush on their faces when Frank asked them that question.

When they stepped inside the kitchen, they could feel the warmth and smell of wood smoke mixed with frying bacon. Rebecca hugged her kids and asked if they slept all right. They all exaggerated and told her how much like "rocks" they had slept. In response, Rachel asked Rebecca a little sarcastically how she had slept.

Frank tried to smooth that one over by thanking them for watching the barn and animals last night. They both nodded to him, and Danny broke into the conversation by asking where they slept. Rebecca told him they brought blankets and slept on the hay. "I want to do that too" he told them.

They noticed that Frank and Anne had a portable radio on and David asked if there were any news. Frank told them that there was power outages all up the eastern seaboard, from parts of North Carolina all the way to Maine. "The weatherman announced that this is the worst storm to hit since 1974." Frank told them. Rebecca said she could remember that storm. She told them she was little, but that she couldn't forget walking on top of the ice, everyone sleeping in the living room with sleeping bags and that they didn't have power for a week. "Cool," the kids said excitedly. "All the roads were legally closed to all cars." Rebecca told her kids. Frank said. "Well it's happening again." He told them all the roads in the state were closed to tire vehicles.

Anne was cooking pancakes on the wood stove in the corner of the kitchen. David went over to his mother and asked if everything went all right in the house last night. She explained that they ended up losing the power shortly after they went to the barn, but that Frank filled and started the generators, so the refrigerators and freezers were fine. She told him that she found his cell phone over next to Frank's computer in the living room. She used it to call his men and check on things over there.

"I forgot I brought it here with me." David told her. He wasn't worried about his farm. He knew his men would take care of everything.

David thanked her anyway and told her he would call them again in a little while, to give them an update of his return home. David knew that the guys were probably a little ticked off because he never came back last night. But when he brought his four little reasons home later, he knew they would forgive him.

Anne asked who wanted eggs and who wanted pancakes, and they all prepared to have breakfast. The children were sent upstairs to get dressed while Anne finished making the food. Rebecca watched the thin gray haired woman flip a pancake.

"Anne, Is there something I can help you with?" Rebecca asked.

Anne thanked her and asked if she could get some fruit out and cut it up for a small platter and then place some of the baked goods on the breakfast table. David helped Rebecca and then they both set the table.

Frank kept himself busy listening to the weather updates and jotting down which roads the state official said were closed to all traffic except for emergency purposes. Frank got it all down on paper and then turned off the radio to conserve the batteries.

Rebecca questioned. "I thought all roads were closed and no vehicles were allowed."

"They don't want people attempting to use regular cars and trucks because they'll just get stuck and need to be rescued, but a lot of folks have snow mobiles and they can use them on the town roads." David explained to her.

Frank added. "They don't want anyone on the highways and principal throughways if at all possible. Road crews are going to be busy clearing them and they don't want any accidents to take place."

"Mostly." David told her. "They don't want anyone to get plowed into snow banks and get buried."

This snowstorm was more severe than Rebecca had realized, and she was really grateful the Henry's had brought her and the children to their home. What would it have been like in a hotel with no power and no way to get food and heat? She didn't even want to consider the horror of that prospect. Rebecca was worried about her mother and asked if Frank had heard any news from outside the state.

"I only heard that North Carolina had it the easiest and that the storm hit harder as it went up the East Coast." Frank explained the rest of what little news he knew.

David saw the concern on Rebecca's face and realized she was worried about her mother. "Would you like to try calling your mom on my cell phone?"

"Are you sure, it should probably be used only for emergency, don't you think?" Rebecca asked.

"One phone call won't hurt, besides, he told her, worrying about your mom is a small emergency." Rebecca smiled at David and thanked him for the use of his phone. They went to use it.

Frank asked Anne after they left the room, "Did you find anything?"

"No, not yet." Anne whispered. They could hear the kids returning from upstairs. Stopping their conversation as they listened to the kids come stomping their way back into the kitchen. "Well, you all look nice, Anne told them. "But do you have sweaters."

"We left them on the couch, Rachel told her, Mom always says not to dress warm in the house or we'll be cold when we go out."

"That is very true." She smiled at the children. Then she made a note to herself to find long underwear for the kids in the dresser upstairs that she kept for her own grandchildren.

David and Rebecca returned to the kitchen. Rebecca was once again cheerful. She told her children, and The Henrys that her mother was well. She was staying with her Aunt Beverly. All her sisters and brothers were safely camping out with each other or other friends or family. Her mom said that she heard another storm could be on the way later tonight.

Frank turned the radio back on to wait for another weather report. When he pushed the button a beep, beep, beep came blaring through the radio. The national weather service was issuing an emergency storm warning for the entire Eastern United States. A massive Arctic cold front was expected to continue in a southeasterly direction and to meet up with a large band of precipitation moving towards us off the coast of Florida. "All listening areas should expect heavy snow showers and icefall to continue today from 1:00pm through 3:00am Eastern Standard Time. Please be advised this storm is expected to exhibit severe icy conditions. It will likely produce gusts up to and/or exceeding 60 miles per hour. The national weather service advises all listeners to take immediate action to seek proper shelter. Please remain tuned to this frequency for further directions, and more specific information regarding your regional area. Thank you. Beep..." The local weather channel came on. They told the local forecast, repeating exactly, what the National Weather Service had all ready said. They followed with specific instructions for all pedestrians and drivers of tracked vehicles to be off the roads by 2:00pm. They were told that the storm was expected to begin hitting their area around 4:00pm. Frank was about to shut off the radio when another announcer came on the air and told everyone listening that the Central and Midwestern states had already begun preparing emergency supplies to be delivered to the East Coast by noon tomorrow. He then said everyone was to get what supplies they would need for the next 36 hours and find a warm, safe place for the night. Their station would announce the nearest appointed supply stations around the local area sometime tomorrow. Frank shut off the radio.

Anne had all ready begun feeding the kids breakfast as she said, "Well, before you run off, get some food in you and then I'll get the kids ready for when you all return." On that note everyone ate and then, Anne brought the kids upstairs to look for the warmest clothing she could find and get them prepared to go to David's House. "Why are we going to David's house?" Rachel wanted to know. "Because, Anne said, David's home is much newer and stronger than this one and it doesn't have as many trees around it that can fall on it." "What about the animals?" Karen wanted to know. We'll milk the cow and feed them all before we leave." She told them. Downstairs David and Frank were making plans and Rebecca made lists of everything they were to try and find while they were in town. Gas, Batteries and Bottled Water were the highest on their list. When they had finished making their plans, Frank went to tell Anne that they were leaving. "Are you going to be able to walk through that snow like David did?" Frank yelled out. "Danny, Karen? Do you want to help me find those snow shoes."

All three of the children went upstairs to find them. Rachel looked around and saw trunks of old photos and clothing, and there were old desks and chairs and boxes filled with shoes and books. Then Danny noticed an old long sled. "What is that?" he asked. "That's called a toboggan," Frank told them. The kids and I used to go sledding on it together when they were little. "We'll take that down with us, once we find the shoes." Karen said. "There's a whole box of shoes over here." "We aren't looking for that kind of shoes." Rachel told her. She knew the type Mr. Frank was looking for because she read all the "Little House" books a few years ago. She told her siblings. "They are sort of made out of basket wicker, and they looked more like Tennis rackets." "Are those them?" Karen asked her. Frank said, "Yes, those are the snow shoes." There were three adult size and four child sized. But Frank told them that only two of each size were still useful. The others were rotted. Then he told them to look through that box of shoes to see if there were any of his children's old boots. They found six pair of boots and each child left the attic with one that fit. Down stairs they carried all their treasures and Frank said to Anne, "Look, I told you these old things would come in handy one day!" She said, "Of course it took thirty years for that to happen." And she hugged her husband and then felt the children's toes to make sure the boots were not too small. "Good find, Kids." Anne said looking at all three of them in their knee high rubber boots with lamb wool lining that folded down along the top outside edge. Then Anne kissed Frank goodbye and told him to be careful and try not to take too long. "Come on kids, help me get all the things we'll need together, before Frank, David and your mom get back." They ran off up the stairs and found Rebecca in her room getting money from her purse. Rebecca could have sworn she hadn't left her purse unzipped yesterday, and her wallet wasn't in it the way she usually placed it. Rebecca dismissed it as something that went unnoticed yesterday during the jumble of the accident.

Oh no, she thought, my car is probably really a mess now. "I hope no one hit it on the side of the road last night." "Hit what, Mom?" Karen asked, as they came in to say goodbye to their mother. "Nothing for you to worry about." She gave them all hugs and told them to be careful if they went outside with Anne and to make sure they helped her. "Bye," they all yelled.

Downstairs David was waiting for Rebecca and making a quick phone call to his men. He told them the plan, and that they would be there this afternoon. Kevin told him that he already had Mark and Tommy moving the fire wood onto the porch and that Daniel called earlier to say that He, Pam and the kids would be there soon. He had a cargo net in one hand and an empty gas can in the other. Rebecca noticed that on his feet were snowshoes. "Where are mine?" David told her only two pair were in working condition and so she would have to settle for a chariot. He opened the door, and there was the toboggan. David lifted her up, and Rebecca sat down on the sled then scooted herself away from the door so that David could step up onto the ice.

Outside the window, Danny looked out and saw his mother being pulled by David toward the furthest barn to the right. "Miss Anne," he asked, "What's in that barn?" They all looked out the window, and Anne told them, "Their headed toward the equipment barn." Smiling she thought they looked straight out of a Norman Rockwell portrait. Then they saw Frank and David pull the snowmobiles out and hook up a ski bladed cart to one and the toboggan to the other. They all watched as the men considered the toboggan for a moment and guessed they figured it was worth a try; because the next they saw from the window was all three adults peeling away on the machines. "WOW" The kids all yelled. That looks fun, one of them said, and another said. "I want to try that too." Anne told them they would all get their chance, "That's how we're going to get to David's house." Anne looked at her watch and read 8:30am.

Carl awoke in a strange darkened room. He pushed the button on his watch, and the green glowing light showed him the time was 5:30 am. He looked around the room and remembered where he was. The last thing he recalled last night was sitting on a shore in the warm sunshine with Rebecca and feeling how wonderful it was to hold her. Now, he felt cold and wished he were still dreaming. He wrapped the blanket around him and rose from the couch to go find the thermostat and raised it a couple of degrees. Then he went to the kitchen and made a pot of coffee.

He returned to the living room and turned on the television. The early news had just started, and they were talking about the winter storm that had hit the East Coast late last night. Carl could feel himself starting to panic. His family was out somewhere in this mess without him, and he felt complete anger and helplessness over not being with them. Carl picked up the phone, and a young man answered it. "Good morning, Sir. Is there something I can do for you?" the person asked Carl.

"I need to get hold of Randy Taylor." He told the guy on the line.

"I'm not authorized to let you make phone calls outside of the facility, but I can take a message and get it to Mr. Taylor for you." He told Carl.

"No thanks." Carl replied.

The young man then told him that Mr. Taylor was expected in within the next couple of hours, and he would let him know that he wished to speak with him.

"Thank You." said Carl. Then he hung up the phone.

Carl watched the telecast from Seattle as they described the four feet of snow and ice that came down on the Eastern United States. They showed footage of the people braving the already fallen snow, in preparation for another impending storm expected to hit them later that day. Carl was now pacing the room and he went over to the curtained glass door and opened them. The sun was starting to come up, and Carl could see in the distance Mt. Rainier to the southwest. He watched as some deer ran off into the woods 100 yards away and following them, darted, what he thought was a large cat. It had all happened so fast. He wasn't sure if he saw it correctly. Then a small deer came flying back around and the large cat caught it and carried it away. Carl stood there surprised by what he witnessed and stared at the trail of blood in the snow that led into the woods beyond.

The television became louder, distracting him, as the telecast broke off and a commercial came on. He hated how advertisers did that. He assumed that they designed commercials to be louder, so that people leaving the room to get food or go to the bathroom could still hear the ads. He left to go get his coffee still waiting for him in the kitchen. As he filled his cup, the phone rang. Catching a glimpse of the wall clock he read 6:00am. Carl answered it. "Carl, This is Randy. When I called to check on things, Mike informed me that you tried to call." He didn't give Carl a chance to speak but kept right on talking. "I imagine you must have caught the news already, I spoke with Jordan last night and he said he had to pull the teams off and sent them to a local hotel. The last they knew everything was going fine with everyone. Don't worry about them,

Carl. They're safe." He continued, "We haven't discussed this yet, but this is now Jordan's job, the teams were going to be removed soon anyway and he was to be left as the only surveillance.

"Why?" Carl asked.

"Because Rebecca was getting very suspicious." Randy told him.

"No!" said Carl. "Of all people, Why Jordan?"

"Because she knows him and already trusts him, it made perfect sense to me." said the man who had planned out everything.

"Why haven't you just brought my family here, like you did me?" Carl asked the man who was destroying his life.

"Carl, If you ever want to have a regular life again, then you'll have to trust me. I'll see you at nine." That was all he said, and then he hung up the phone.

Carl heard a buzzing sound, and he placed his receiver back down on the phone. Taking his coffee to the living room, he decided to see if there were any new information being put out on the local news and when he saw none he switched it to the cable news channel. They were showing the areas that had been hit the hardest and then they switched to Georgia and the local people there preparing for the snow.

Carl switched off the television and went to grab a shower. Then he shaved and took some time to arrange his new clothing in his drawers and closet. He returned to the kitchen dressed in his black suit and went to fix another cup of coffee. He had struggled with which shirt and tie to wear, he finally settled on the gray shirt with the maroon striped tie. He looked into the mirror in the entryway to see if it were straight. He decided to go find something to eat when his doorbell rang.

Carl opened his door to find Matt standing there. He looked at his watch. "You're a little early, aren't you?"

"I'm sorry, I can come back later." Matt told Carl.

"No, come on in, I was going to eat something. Did you eat yet?"

Matt told him that he had coffee and nothing else. Carl offered him a bagel and some yogurt or fruit, and they both went to the living room to eat while watching television. Matt told him he liked his place and asked about people in the photos. Carl told him who everyone was and then he asked if Matt knew how the table worked.

"Oh. Mom, gave you this." He was surprised. "This was my father's set."

Carl felt funny. It was obviously a family heirloom, and he shouldn't have been given it to use.

Matt continued, "My mom is so sentimental." She thought that I would want it because it was his." Matt continued as he fiddled with the table's edge, "But something doesn't have sentimental value if you have no memories attached to it, don't you think."

He pushed two of the decorated brass buttons that were spaced along the edges of the table, except these two had a place in the center that was plain where all the others had colored stones. The buttons released the table's top and revealed a second board underneath. It was the backgammon board, all black and white triangles with a gray marble center and edging. In the very middle were the initials CR with the bottom half of the C being the curve to the R. He pointed to the initials and told him that his father's name is Charles Ruthford. "Hey, Matt said, Those are your initials too."

Carl looked at his watch and noticed it was only 8:20am. "Do you want to play a game." He asked the boy. "I don't know how." Matt said. Carl was surprised, though he supposed he shouldn't have been, since he just told him he hadn't any memories of playing with it. Carl offered to teach him. So, Matt reattached the board, and they pulled out the pieces. Carl realized what he hadn't noticed last night. The pieces hadn't been removed from their places in a very long time.

The first thing he had Matt do was to pick a side and then he showed him how to set the board up. By the time they had to leave, Carl had explained to Matt how all the pieces moved. Then they had both made a couple of opening moves and left the game table set as it was to go meet Randy.

CHAPTER SEVEN

By 9:00am they made it to the outskirts of town and the first place they stopped at was Jerry Cauldwell's service station. The line was about thirty people long, and it took them 45 minutes to get to the pumps. The fuel pumps were full service today, being run by Jerry and a couple of high school kids that were in his employ. David said. "Hi," to the boys and Jerry came over to David and Frank.

"Frank, I got your message last night and went ahead and picked up that car for you, she's parked in back under about three feet of snow."

Rebecca's face lit up, and Frank thanked him for seeing to it right away.

"Well, the snow was coming down pretty hard and I didn't want to risk someone hitting it."

"Thank you." Rebecca said.

David introduced Rebecca to Jerry and then he asked David if he didn't mind taking a can of fuel to his sister on his way home. Then he handed him sixty dollars, "And if you have enough room, could you get anything else you think she'll need."

"Sure." David told him. "How about your parents?"

"They're staying at Jenny's with her."

The boy was finished filling the Henry's cans, and Jerry ran to get a large container for them to take to Jenny.

"Where are you staying tonight Jerry?" Frank asked when the boy his son's age returned.

"Bobby's putting together a sleep in at the tavern tonight, Only a few of the guys and their girls."

"Have fun." David said.

"Don't stay out here working too long after the snow starts." Frank warned him.

"I won't." He told them. "Thanks again, David."

They waved to him and went on to their next destination.

David and Rebecca climbed on the snow mobile and David told her that Jenny has a young baby, and they should remember to get her some diapers and wipes and some jarred food. As he revved the engine to take off she nodded her head to him. Five minutes later they were in town, and they noticed that only a few of the mom and pop stores were open for business. Frank and David needed to get oil for the snowmobiles since they hadn't used them in a couple years. They got some at Drake's hardware store, where David decided to buy chain saw oil too.

Then they went down to the local grocery and dept store and found that they were closed, and no one was allowed inside except for employees. Both of the managers had set up a system where the employees took your list if you had special needs and they went in and got the items. Otherwise; they had all the emergency items located outside the stores front entrances. The managers asked everyone to take only what they needed. They placed a donation can over to the side and paid little attention to it except to empty it every once in a while. The line for both stores was long, and half way through the line David noticed that it was 11:00am.

Rebecca watched as people made their way slowly to the front of the line. She was touched by this community of people. Especially by the manager, who made sure that everyone had at least the minimum supplies needed to get through the storm, regardless of whether or not they could donate any money. There was a young mother, with her toddler seated on a sled in line ahead of them. Rebecca watched the man go to the donation can and take out money. He handed her the stack of currency and told her to go over to the hardware store. He was told they still had a few heaters left. One of the high school kids told her he could go get some fuel for her and drop it by her house on his way home. She thanked the manager and the boy. Then she pulled her son cushioned between two supply bags down the half plowed and trodden road. He then took out his cell phone and called the store ahead of her to make sure they saved her one. "She's walking so it will take her about twenty minutes to get from here over to your place, Yes it's for Sandi Carter, Thanks Hal. Bye."

It was 11:30am by the time it was their turn at the grocery store, and across the street they could see that Frank was almost to the front of his line too. Rebecca handed the girl a list of baby items and they got enough water and canned food for themselves and Jenny's family for two days. Then they picked up two packages of lighters and a box of candles. David shook hands with the manager, and they made small talk for a few minutes. Tim asked who the woman was with him. He told him the story and then they talked about the coming storm. David told Tim that he was taking things over to Jenny for Jerry. Tim left and then he came back with two bags. He told him one was for Rebecca's kids, and the other was a bag of things to send to his kids and Jenny. The girl came out with the things on their list and Rebecca looked into the bag to see what was there. She found everything, plus a bottle of baby medicine. The girl told her, "I babysit my niece a lot, and she never fails to get a fever." "Thank you." Rebecca smiled at the girl. She didn't think to ask for something like that. It had been a while since her children were that little. David put a stack of bills in the donation can and they waved goodbye to Tim.

As they left he told her he went to high school with Tim and he and Jenny were now separated. "I feel bad for the guy, he's made some mistakes but he really loves Jenny." He looked in the bag and found a large cranberry candle, the last box of "D" batteries the store had, baby formula and a little flashlight shaped like a frog which turned on when you opened its mouth. Inside the other bag; he found the makings for s'mores; chocolate bars, marshmallows and graham crackers. At the bottom was a deck of playing cards.

They crossed the street to where Frank was waiting for them at the snowmobiles. "They didn't have any sleeping bags or batteries." Frank told the two as they packed up the toboggan.

"Do you think that will hold?" David asked the others.

"We'll take it slow and find out." Frank told his son.

"You know who may have some of those things." David said excitedly, "The Wilson's, Jamie opened up a sporting goods store behind his parents Corner Market." "I'll bet few people thought to go there. It hasn't been open for long." David told them.

"When did Jamie get out of the service?" his Dad asked.

David said. "Around nine months ago."

Frank looked at his watch and told them it was noon. "We're supposed to be off the roads by 2:00, do you think we can make it all the way there and get back to your house by then?"

David told him that he thought they could make it. "The Corner Market is closer to my house then yours. We can drop off this stuff then hit Jenny's house on the way to yours."

"Do we really need to get sleeping bags?" Rebecca asked them.

"I guess we can make do without them." David told her. "But, we should really try to get some batteries."

Frank added. "If we get as much snow and ice as we did last night then probably half the trees in the state will fall."

What a mess, Rebecca thought, but this wasn't as scary to her as preparing for a Hurricane. Or maybe she just felt safe with these two men. She wasn't sure which it was.

Frank finished, "There's no saying how long it might take to get all the trees cleared and the power back up and running."

They all got back on their snowmobiles, and Frank took off slowly. David went to start the engine as Rebecca told him she was sorry that her and the kids have imposed on his family at such a bad time. David turned to face Rebecca. "Don't be silly, you haven't imposed at all, It just so happens that you were invited during a disaster." He smiled at her, "That only makes your company even nicer for my family." She smiled. "Knowing my parents, they'll probably take pictures and video the whole time. That way they can keep the memories of you, your kids and the big storm, in their photo album forever."

"Come on you two, we're wasting time." Frank yelled back to them.

David roared the engine, and they took off across town toward the market and David's home.

David believed what he told Rebecca. But what he didn't tell her was how nice it felt taking care of a family again, even if it was not his own. He told himself he didn't know this woman very well, but he still couldn't help feeling that he wouldn't mind her and her kids being in his life. He liked what he did know about her. Plus, her kids seemed wonderful. David drove the machine down the snow packed, bumpy, trodden road, Rebecca put her arms around him and held on tight. He knew she was a little scared on the snowmobile, but he enjoyed her arms around him anyway. "Keep an eye on the stuff." He yelled to her and she yelled back. "Okay."

❊❊❊

Carl and Matt left the stone and timber building that he now called home and went off down the road on a golf cart.

"What's with the golf cart?" Carl asked him.

He explained that the majority of the places they go to on the compound are within walking distance, but right now it is sort of cold to walk. "However, driving a car feels ridiculous." said Matt.

Carl sat and looked at the incredible view before him. All around them was a big beautiful forest, and in the distance he could now see Mt Rainier clearly. The sunshine was making it sort of glow from all the snow on it. It was cold, but Carl had noticed, there hadn't been any fresh snowfall in a while. Carl thought about his family. He knew Rebecca would be okay; she was always the one who prepared their family for storms. He assumed she must still be with that couple Randy spoke of last night. He needed to find an opportunity to pull Randy aside to inquire after Rebecca and the kids. Simply being told their safe wasn't good enough.

100

"So, what do you think so far about our place here?" Matt asked, interrupting Carl's thoughts.

"I think it's very pretty, but I was shocked by the wildlife this morning."

"What do you mean?" Matt asked him.

"The cougars, I watched as one caught and carried away a deer this morning." He told the boy.

"You're kidding, I've never seen anything like that before." Matt was envious." I'll let Paul know what you saw."

"Why?" Carl asked confused.

"That cougar is either recklessly brave or desperately hungry; either way it's a danger." Matt explained. "It should never have come so close to the compound."

A few minutes later they arrived at the building where they were expected to meet Randy. It was a large building that had three floors, and it was built from logs and fieldstone on the outside, but once you went past the lobby it looked and felt like an office building. Matt led Carl down a hall and into a large conference room. Inside this room was a big conference table, but instead of there being stuffy boardroom type surroundings, there was a room full of people with their jackets removed, all working on computers inside a brightly lit room. The entire circumference had computers lining the walls, and the centerpiece wall had a huge flat monitor screen so everyone in the room could read off it when needed. Talking to a man across the room, Randy waved to them to come over to where he was, "Good morning," he greeted the guys as they approached him.

Then Randy clapped his hands really loud, and everyone immediately stopped what they were doing. They all looked at Randy and then at Carl and Matt standing next to him. Everyone picked up pads of paper and folders, and they all made their way to the conference table at the center of the room. Matt and Carl took a seat too. As everyone waited for Randy to begin, a young girl carrying a stack of papers began handing them out as she made her way around the table. When Carl was handed his, he noticed the familiar "Operation Genius" across the top and he read the synopsis below it, which stated their mission statement. It simply said. "Mission Statement: Gather intelligence to prevent World War III."

Randy dispensed with the military lingo and pro-to-calls to make it civilian friendly. Carl was happy because he was tired of the formality of the military and he just wanted Randy to cut to the chase. Randy told this group of very intelligent, but short attention spanned people, the gist of the problem they faced and then introduced Carl to the rest of the group. Then he dismissed them all so they could get back to work.

Carl was amazed by the seemingly cool and unconcerned response these people had to Major Taylor's explanation of their job descriptions. He thought it must be because he was the one expected to play the role of Superhero, that everyone else appeared to be so calm and collected, unfazed at all really.

"Seriously, Randy. You must be joking. This really is straight out of some 007 movie." Carl told him, as he wondered if he had been kidnapped by a crazy man.

Randy said to Carl. "How do you think they come up with the subject matter for all those movies, Carl. Government and politics is a whole lot scarier than any made-up movie." He finished.

"Well, except maybe "The Exorcist."" said Matt.

"Very funny Matt, now get with the program." Randy raised his voice.

"So, let me get this straight." Carl wanted to reconfirm all he had learned from Randy. "You're telling me. The man you work for, General Harding, discovered that another general, named Davis, is plotting to start World War III."

Randy nodded his head.

"And he has been staging the war by creating small international incidences to help him justify going to the president with a proposed plan to start a major war."

Randy again nodded his head.

"You want to locate files of his covert operations so that you and

General Harding can prove this entire fabrication has been created by General Davis." "Why would Davis want to do this?" Carl asked Randy.

"Davis has rambled for years about how our economic system has been waning because we haven't had any Major Wars to stimulate growth and lower population rates. But the real push for him now is that he hasn't received his mark in our countries history books, and he faces mandatory retirement next year." Randy explained.

Carl said, "But we somehow know that he plans to start the air invasion by July 1st, and the land invasion by July 4th."

Randy told him. "General Harding was good-friends with Davis, they went to West Point together. Harding was offered second in command of the armed forces if he went along with him. He declined the position, and General Davis doesn't know that he has been trying to find information to destroy him. Harding is a good man, and he can't sit by and watch as hundreds or thousands of innocent, young service men and women are killed needlessly."

Carl felt the concern in Randy's voice. He listened to him discuss what they have done already and what they need to try. "We think that General Davis has removed the files, but we're not sure, we have been breaking into some covert ops files, but we don't think we've found anything that is illegitimate. Of course the more delicate the information is the more difficult it has been to break in."

"So, Carl said, you want me to break into top security systems and then try to recover documents that may no longer exist."

"So, Randy asked, do you think you can do it?"

"Yeah, I think I can probably figure it out."

"But?" Randy asked.

"But with the time constraints. Carl told him. If we break into maybe two files a day and do a thorough search... I don't know how far we'll get with the amount of documents there must be in the programs of the Department of Defense."

Randy said, "You just master doing it first, then he pointed to the other men in the room, then you can teach them."

"What about the security risks involved?" Carl asked him.

Randy told him, "We have no choice, the security of our nation is already at risk."

Carl was afraid Randy was expecting this to be easy. Even if he managed to get into one file, there was no guaranteeing the next would be the same. He looked at the men in this room, and wanted to know what made him different from them. other than, his having a lot less education than the rest of them. "Randy, Why me?"

"Have you ever thought about what a genius is, Randy asked Carl, Every one of these men have been written down somewhere on a piece of paper as an intellectual genius. But a real genius is more than book smart, they can see outside of the box, instead of looking straight at the problem and using some prescribed formula, a genius uses creativity and goes around it instead. With Colonel Dobson, you proved that you see outside of that box, and they only see within their tightly constrained rules. I need you to help them to use their creative instinct again and less of their intellect."

Carl asked Randy, "What exactly do you have them looking for?"

"We've been looking for evidence of covert files, everything he has already done and anything he plans to do." said Randy.

Carl debated for a moment what he would have done if he were the General. Then he thought about what might get him caught if he didn't carefully cover it up. "Those are things that he'll have deleted. We can still keep searching for them. But what we really need to do is to look for phantom files, data that gets written to other files, but fails to be erased later. Things like orders for fuel and weapons or planned troop movements. These may lead to other trails."

Randy smiled, knowing he had this boy for a reason and told Carl he'd get some of the men on it now.

"Oh. And I'll need at least five computers to myself and for every file you want me the crack, I'll need another one as much like it as you can find me, one that I already can get into."

Matt saw to the equipment. He also found himself charged by the rooms renewed energy as the men felt their first glimmer of hope since this project began.

Carl was ready to work.

Back at the house, Anne was starting to worry, It was 12:30 and the men and Rebecca were still not back yet. She hoped they didn't have a mechanical problem with one of the snowmobiles. She and the kids had everything all ready to go and now Anne had them eating lunch, while they waited for the others to arrive. Earlier, She had taken the children outside to the barn to care for the animals and so that chore was done too. It had been fun showing them how to milk the cow. Of course, they all missed the bucket on their first try. However, she was surprised how quickly they had learned to milk Clara. She pointed out to the kids how Martha was preparing to have a calf and then later they would get milk from her also. While they had been busy feeding all the animals, the children had asked her what the noise was they kept hearing. They all went to investigate and found that Betsy had given birth to her little kittens this morning. The kids were really excited but were disappointed that they didn't get to see her give birth. She told them that cats usually like to be alone and run off to hide when they have their kittens. They were concerned about leaving them to go to David's, but she reassured them that their mother would take care of them. "Betsy is a good mother." she had told them.

This morning, she helped the children pick out some warm clothes from the bedroom dresser and she aided them with sorting through their bags. None of the children had any pictures or information about their Dad. She was assigned to find out what he looked like and where he was. If he were even still alive. The only thing she found that proved he ever existed at all, was an old pair of military identification tags attached to a chain. When she touched them, Danny reached out for them and safely put them back in a zippered pocket. She couldn't do this to the children and decided not to ask about their father. That was all the snooping her stomach could handle, so they went out to the barn. Now she had to get a look through Rebecca's bag. The children were done eating their sandwiches with chips and fruit, and they all threw their napkins and apple cores in the trash can.

"It's getting late." Anne told the kids. "Do you think your mom would mind too much if we packed her some things."

Rachel answered. "I don't think mom would mind."

Anne asked the kids to come help her pick out a few things their Mom might be comfortable wearing.

"What size clothing does your mom wear Rachel, do you know?"

Rachel said, "Medium, but she likes sweaters to be big."

"No honey, I mean her pant size." Anne explained.

Rachel went and got Rebecca's overnight bag and brought it into the sewing room.

The closet there stored a bunch of Anne's family's old clothes. Rachel and Karen pulled out all their mother's things. Karen opened her mom's personal hygiene bag and had the compact open and was putting on some of her light colored lipstick. Anne told her she didn't know if Rebecca would be too happy if she went into that. All the kids said. "Mom doesn't care."

"As long as we put it back, so she can find it, when she wants it." Rachel explained.

"Really." Anne was surprised. "But I still think we should put it all back." She told them.

She helped the kids fill it back up. Then looked inside to see what was there. Seeing nothing, Anne closed up the bag. Rachel had Rebecca's blue jeans from yesterday and told Anne size 10. She flipped the pants upside down when she tried to fold them and everything spilled out. Anne said she would help her. She folded the pants and they all picked up the contents; coins, two sets of keys, six dollars and a couple of receipts. Anne was relieved. She found nothing and so she wouldn't have to betray Rebecca's trust.

She hated doing this and was horrified when they were called and given this assignment. Especially, after ten years of receiving none. She thought it was finally over, the terrible price they had to pay to come to the United States. Anne opened the closet and looked through it, "These old pants of Jane's look like they'd fit, would she like these?" She held up two pair of jeans, one black and one red. They all said those are mom's favorite colors. "Good, then they should be fine" Anne smiled as she went back to enjoying her visitors. The kids then picked out a large black oversized turtleneck sweater and a big cream cable knit sweater that had once been David's. Plus Anne found another set of thermal underwear and they packed up her bag and brought it down stairs to put with all the others. Then the four of them brought out a board game and waited for the others to return.

CHAPTER EIGHT

"David!" Rebecca yelled. "We lost something." David beeped the horn to alert his Dad. Then they both stopped and David ran back to get it. They fixed the Toboggan and continued on their way slightly slower this time. By the time, they reached the Corner Market they had lost almost an hour. Frank stayed outside with their things as David and Rebecca went inside to see what was left.

David said hello to Jamie as Rebecca went ahead and started shopping. "You're doing pretty good today, I didn't think that many people would think to come here, he told Jamie, being your place is so new."

"My Luck, Jamie told him as he rang up a customer, is that I mailed out my first box of flyers a couple of weeks ago." "Who's the girl you came in with?" Jamie asked.

"She's a family friend." David replied, being vague. He didn't feel he was good enough friends with Jamie to go into the details.

"Is she married?" He asked.

David felt a little defensive and jokingly asked, "Why, are you interested?"

Jamie laughed, looked over at Rebecca across the room and said, "Who wouldn't be."

"Yeah." David paused. "She's married."

Jamie looked up from the register and said, "Sorry Man."

David asked if he had any batteries left. He told him they had some, and he pointed him in the proper direction.

Rebecca found a small cart and placed in it; three heavy duty cylinder drink coolers, two rolls of olive drab 100 mile an hour tape, three five gallon collapsible water containers, toilet paper, a pack of long metal toasting sticks used for camping and large trash bags. Under all this, she had even more stuff: a few comic books, magazines, a book for Rachel, two romance novels, a hunter's cap, a pack of camouflage, acne pads, paper plates, aluminum foil and two cases of soda. Plus, she picked up, four packages of hotdogs and two loaves of bread. When Rebecca went back to the sporting goods store, she spotted David and a stainless steel coffeepot. "Hi" she said.

David was standing there looking at the batteries trying to decide what size they needed. Still looking at the display case, he asked, "What size do you think?"

"Most portable radios need D's. Old walkmans take double A's and flashlights depend on the type you buy." Rebecca said quickly.

David grabbed two packs of D's and Rebecca took one more.

"I couldn't find any sleeping bags." She told him.

David looked up and saw Rebecca's cart, "Holy crap" David let out, "Do we have enough stuff!" "We've only been here ten minutes, how can you shop that fast?" He asked amazed.

Rebecca said. "I've had a lot of practice."

"What do you have in there?" Curious, David looked though the cart lifting up this and that to see everything inside. "Why do we need all this stuff?" He wanted to know as he pointed to one thing and then another.

Rebecca asked, "First, do you have one of these?" Holding up the coffeepot.

"No." He answered with an incredulous look on his face as she added it to the already heaping pile.

She went to go back toward the market.

"Where are you going?" David asked her.

"To go get some instant creamer for the coffee." She told him in a matter of fact manner.

David laughed at her and said, "Rebecca; I own two hundred dairy cows."

Rebecca turned a little pink.

"You look cute when you're feeling a little silly." He told her. "Now, he said, What's all this for?"

Then Rebecca explained to David. "The water containers are so we can melt snow for washing and flushing the toilets. The soda is to lower the use of bottled water plus kids don't like anything without sugar. The hotdogs and bread are easy to make on a fire, and the metal sticks are a great way to cook them and keep children busy at the same time. The paper plates and aluminum foil are, so we don't have so much clean up to worry about without running water, trust me with that one. Rebecca took in a breath. Have you been in a house with three kids when there is no television, video games or computers? She asked. That's what the comic books and all these things are for, she pointed to the stuff at the bottom of the cart. The coffeepot is because I've never seen a man anyone can live with if he hasn't had a cup of coffee. The trash bags are to help get it all back home and of course for the garbage once we're there. And, Rebecca said as she held up a roll of tape and one of the drink containers. These are how we're going to get all of this to your house.

Rebecca was finished, and it took her only two minutes to explain.

David was impressed. "I think maybe you've done this before."

"Two hurricanes, long car rides and camping trips, not to mention everything else." She answered him. "Do you think we have enough room for it all?" Rebecca asked David.

David said as he picked up a package of large bungee cords. "Six kids. I'll make sure it fits." "There will be six kids?" Rebecca asked.

David confirmed. "There will be six kids to keep entertained."

Rebecca said with a smile on her face. "Six kids can halfway entertain themselves."

Then she ran back and grabbed a container of hand wipes. She returned with them raised for him to see and told him. "But there's more of a mess."

David said, "What are the romance novels for?" Pretending to be hurt, he asked. "Don't you like talking to me."

Rebecca told him she picked up one for herself and one for his mom. "Then we should probably go pick up one for Daniel's wife, Pam, so she doesn't feel left out." Rebecca went and got another.

"Daniel and Pam have three kids around the same ages as yours." David told her when she returned. Then he picked up a hunting hat for Daniel's son too, and a four pack of colored flashlights for the girls and two camouflaged ones for the boys. Just in case, he also got an extra large pack of AA's for when one of the little ones forgets to turn off their flashlight.

They went to the check out, and Jamie began totaling everything up on his calculator and bagging it as he went. "You're a woman after my own heart." Jamie told Rebecca.

"Why do you say that, because of what I bought or how much? Rebecca jokingly wanted to know.

"Both," He smiled, then Jamie pointed to the olive 100mph tape, the metal sticks for cooking, the package of camouflage, the coffee pot and the toilet paper and said those five things are all a soldier or hunter needs to survive in the woods.

David asked. "Jamie, Do you have any more sleeping bags?"

"Feel free to go check in the back storage room. I couldn't tell you." He paused to look at Rebecca, when he picked up the acne pads. "I haven't had a chance to leave the register all day, except for one bathroom break." He told David.

"Rebecca why did you get that?" David asked.

"Aren't you rude." Jamie told David.

"No, wait, she has a specific reason for everything here that she bought." He told Jamie.

Rebecca told them, "I bought that to get the camouflage off Danny's face." "Of course, it doesn't hurt to have some when you may not be showering properly for a while either."

"Double duty, Jamie said, It takes off the paint and prevents breakout."

David went into the back to find the sleeping bags.

"Where are you from?" Jamie asked.

Rebecca told him Tennessee.

Jamie started to sing, "101 patch on my shoulder, Rebecca joined him, Pick up your weapon and follow me...we are the Infantry." Jamie smiled at her and asked how long she's lived there.

"We were there for six years." She told him.

"That is a long time in one place, are you moving now or in limbo?"

She told him sort of both, "Limbo while moving."

"Okay, I get that. Are you going home to visit while your husband is in school or on a short tour?"

"Yeah, Something like that."

He was done tallying her bill. Jamie gave her the total, and she paid.

Rebecca was glad because she didn't want David to come out and pay for her things and she wanted the questions to end. "I don't know what is taking David so long?" She questioned.

"I'm sure it's a mess back there." Jamie told her.

"I'll tell him your outside with Mr. Henry." He waved to David's Dad outside.

Rebecca said thank you and told him to be careful in this weather.

"I will." He told her. "Good luck with that load!"

Rebecca went outside.

"That didn't take long." Frank told her and then he looked at her full cart and said. "Did you buy out the entire store."

"Not bad for twenty minutes, don't you think?" Rebecca asked.

"It looks like you did a good job, but can we fit it all?" Frank asked.

"I hope so, want to come and help me get the stuff we already have packed tighter and put Jenny's stuff all to one side."

Frank helped Rebecca get the supplies in the cart rearranged as David finished up inside.

"Did you find any?" Jamie yelled toward the back.

"Yes." He yelled, but I'm trying to get them from the top corner."

"Sorry, I should have told you the ladder is behind the door."

"Thanks." David yelled back.

Two minutes later he came out with four sleeping bags of all different colors. "There are two more back there if anyone asks." He told Jamie as he searched the store for Rebecca.

"Thanks." He said as he rang up David's bags, "She went outside."

David nodded in response. "Are you all set for the storm then?" Jamie asked.

"We are now, thanks to you and your parent's stores."

"Glad to be of service to you, he handed him a business card and told David to call his cell phone if he needed him to put something aside for him. David tucked it in his wallet.

Jamie then asked him. "How many kids are there?"

"Come again." David asked.

"At the house?" Jamie said.

"We'll have six out at my place." He answered.

"She has six children!" Jamie said shocked.

"No, Daniel's three will be with us too."

"Here," Jamie said, handing David a bag with seven long plastic things in it.

"Let her know I was an M.P. and these are for old time sake. One is for her, Mom's always get left out."

"Thanks. I will." David said. "Be careful tonight." Then he asked, "Are you staying with your parents?"

"No, I was invited out to Bobby's Tavern." Jamie answered him.

"I saw Jerry earlier, He'll be there too. Y'all have a good time, but be careful, okay." He called as he made his way to the door.

"Bye." Jamie said waving a hand at David as he left.

Jamie could see Rebecca outside strapping the containers to the bottom of the toboggan. "Pretty smart girl." He said to himself, as he watched her use the heavy duty, fix-it-all tape that no good soldier goes to the field without.

David came out ten minutes after Rebecca, and she and his Father had already managed to rearrange the cart and empty the toboggan. Rebecca was attaching the canisters to either end of the underneath and placing one in the middle also. She applied strips of tape to the sled, along the length of the board and then taped over that, going around the width of the sled over and over. She repeated another application going lengthwise again. They tested it, bearing some weight on it and decided it was worth the try. "I wanted to keep the cargo net clips from scraping against the ground." She told them.

"Good thinking." Frank said. "Let's see if it works."

They put what they could in a trash bag and taped it to the back seat of Frank's snowmobile. Then they put everything that wasn't too heavy on the Toboggan and strapped it up. Next they secured it again by hooking the bungee cords to the cargo net, then going under the sled, they attached it to the other side of the cargo netting. They closed the lid to the ski cart and taped the two cases of soda to it. The only thing they had left was the last sleeping bag, and they taped that to Rebecca's back with the last of the tape.

"Looks good." said David.

Rebecca replied. "Thanks," She was proud of her contraption.

Frank teased. "What looks good, her job on the toboggan or that protrusion on her back?" He smiled at her. "Good job, Rebecca."

They took off and headed for David's. Rebecca kept an eye on the sled. It was doing well. They were able to ride at a good speed and by 1:30 they were at David's place.

When they drove up to David's house Rebecca noticed it was a large log home. In the front, it had a porch going the length of the house and the side had a slightly smaller attached room with a fieldstone fireplace at the end. Behind the house, was another full-length porch and a distance back was a similar large log building to match. Rebecca could see that it was much bigger than it looked. One of the huge wooden doors was open and inside she could see large farming equipment.

Outside, the house, were three parked snowmobiles. There were two men bringing firewood from the barn up to the house. Rebecca saw stacks of wood against the length of the porch wall, piled from the floor to the ceiling. The men walking toward them dragged wood filled sleds down a path they had created from their trampling. One of the men looked like he was around twenty-three years old and the other was probably only eighteen.

Rebecca surveyed the land again and noticed that the only large trees were back behind the barns, one of which had a corral. The property, she could see was all fenced in and there was another fence surrounding the house, but it was quite a ways out. The pastures in the distance had sectioned off areas, as well. On the side of one barn, she noticed a large tank. It reminded her of the oil tanks her grandparent's home had. "What's that?" She asked David pointing toward it. "That is a gas tank, but right now it probably isn't very full. I usually have it filled in the spring, when I need to use the larger equipment again."

David and Frank started unpacking the supplies and Rebecca helped, as the men pulling wood approached them.

"Hey, you made it." The younger one with corn colored hair said.

"How is everything going with you guys?" David asked.

"Good, all the animals, have been milked and fed, and some more fresh straw was laid down. Kevin is finishing up now." The older one who was lanky and had brown hair told him.

They stacked the wood, as Frank carried in some of the supplies.

"Who's your friend?" The younger one asked David.

"Sorry." He introduced Rebecca to the men.

The young one was Tommy, and the older one was Mark. They all shook hands, and David told them the story about Rebecca, as she carried in the cases of soda. Once inside Frank introduced her to Pam. "Their three kids are around here somewhere." He said.

"They're out in the barns helping Kevin." The woman told them.

Frank said, "Well you'll meet them later, but their names are; Stacy, Kim and Cory, and they are about your kid's ages."

Frank asked Pam what she thought of the snow as she came outside and helped them to bring in the things. David asked her where Daniel was.

"He's finishing up with the horses. He should be here anytime."

David watched the guys finish stacking the wood they had brought over. When he came out of the house he asked them, "I thought, Kevin said that you did that this morning?"

"We started to. But then, Mark said, We had to go get some emergency supplies ourselves!" They laughed as they went to the far end of the porch and lifted up a couple cases of beer and said, "We got wine too."

Everyone laughed at the young boys.

Then Tommy added seriously. "But we also got a couple jugs of water and a container of gas."

Mark told them, "You should have seen the line at "The Last Stop" Convenience Store!"

Everyone believed them.

David told everyone they'd be back soon. "We have to go get Mom and Rebecca's kids."

Tommy asked, "Do you need some help?"

"That would be great, thanks." David answered.

Then Tommy hopped onto David's snowmobile that he and Mark had used earlier. The three machines lurched forward as they all sped off toward Jenny's house before getting Anne and the kids.

Pam and Mark watched from the porch as their friends headed off into the snow dense landscape. They watched the southern sky approaching with a dark mass above. Mark told her, "It looks like it might get here a little sooner than expected." Pam responded by telling him, she would find the kids and that they all would help him to finish carting over, and stacking the wood. Then she took a deep breath and prayed that everyone made it back quickly.

Carl walked over to the coffee maker and refilled his cup. Two men were standing there discussing whether or not they wanted to go see the film at the theater later. "Yeah, Helen, wants to go. She loves all those natural disaster movies." The other man said he'd see how he felt later and he'd ask Abbey if she felt up for it. Carl thought about seeing a movie and then he thought about the natural disaster part. He wasn't sure if he could stomach a disaster movie tonight, not with his nerves on edge about his family stranded in the storm.

Carl stared at the screen in front of him. He was searching through the accessible file to see if there were any hidden data while he waited for Matt to bring him his other four computers. "Sir." A man's voice called to him." Paul would like to talk to you, he's in the hall."

"Thanks Harold." Carl said as he made his way to the door.

"Hello, Sir." Paul started.

Carl interrupted him. "Please, call me Carl."

The man smiled and continued, "Matt told me about that cougar you saw this morning. I'm part Shawnee Indian and I wanted to let you know that my people believe that when you receive a visit such as the one you experienced this morning, what you are really seeing is an ancestor spirit trying to tell you something." Carl listened to the man standing in front of him, something about what he was telling him, hit him in the stomach. Carl had felt there was more to what he saw than just the food chain in action. That experience had left an impression on him, but he didn't understand it. He listened as Paul explained.

"Sometimes the vision is to give you warning about your physical health or maybe about the life path you are choosing, but it could just be a message of some type to you."

"How do I know what it means?" Carl wanted Paul to tell him.

"That is something you have to discover for yourself, contemplate the vision your ancestor gave you. It may take a long time before you understand it. But, if you remain mindful of it, the answer will be there for you when you need it." Paul continued, "But as for the animal itself, it was probably a young adolescent male wandering through, you are unlikely to see him again."

He asked Carl to keep watch for a day or two. To let him know; if he saw it again. He had a friend who was a forest ranger who could try and trap it if they needed him to relocate the animal. Carl thanked Paul and went back to work. He thought about what he had told him about visions. What a sight it was, Carl thought, but he was glad that his family wasn't there to see it. Ancestor spirit or not Rebecca would have been upset. He recalled how she had had a scare at the zoo back home when Danny was two and they hadn't been to the zoo again since. A young cougar had gotten half way out of his cage in an attempt to attack Danny. Rebecca wasn't calm for days after that. Matt came in with the other computers and Carl put aside his thoughts and got back to work.

Anne was really getting concerned. It was now almost two o'clock and still there was no sign of Frank and the kids. She was really starting to fear the worst. Since they had left this morning, Anne had heard at least four crashes from trees falling outside. The last one came from the front yard, and she was afraid it had hit the house. When she went to investigate, she and the kids found the tree down alongside the house. Fortunately, it had only grazed the house on its way toward the ground.

"That was a close one." Rachel had told her.

She thought the kids were starting to get a little nervous when Rachel told her she understood what she had meant about the trees. The kids had really wanted to go back out to see the cats once more, but Anne told them they were all safer where they were, here inside the house. The children hadn't argued with her at all. Now as Anne watched out the window and waited, she suggested to the children that they look through the books in the living room shelves and the games in the upstairs closet to see if there were anything in them that they'd like to take with them. Danny and Karen went to the closet and Anne and Rachel went to look on the shelves.

"You have a lot of books." Rachel told Anne.

"We have been collecting them a long time." Anne picked up "Little Women" and asked if she read it.

Rachel told her she had. Anne thumbed through some of her old romance novels and thought, "No, she's still too young." Anne showed her a few other books, but she had already read those ones too. Then Anne showed Rachel some of her son's old books. "Peter loved to read fantasy and science fiction." "Actually, he still does." Anne told her. "I send him books every year for Christmas." She picked up the J.R.R. Tolkien series and showed them to Rachel.

"I've read "The Hobbit" Rachel said.

"Did you like it?"

"Yes, it was very good." She told Anne.

"How about some of these others, should we take some with us?

They agreed to take the next two in the series with them. At least Anne thought they were the next two. She looked inside to see the printing dates, to place them into publishing order and then they took the two closest to "The Hobbit." Rachel packed them in her bag. Karen and Danny came running down the stairs just as Anne heard the snowmobiles approaching. "Did you find something you might like?" She asked them. They told her "Yes" and put them into their bags.

"They're back now, so we have to hurry and get ready to go." Anne told the kids. Frank walked in the back door and yelled, "We're here!" They all came rushing in. They had Tommy with them. "Hi." David said. "Are you all ready to go?" All four of them said they've been ready a long time. Frank told Anne that they needed to bring things over to Jenny's house, and so they took a little longer than expected.

"So." Anne asked excitedly. "Does that mean that we're not ready to pack up and go?" She questioned.

David said, "Mom, Are you all right?" as Frank went to his wife and hugged her.

"It's been a long day waiting for you." Rachel said.

"And the tree just missed the house, Danny said excitedly."

"What!" All four of them said as they ran to the windows in the front of the house. The kids followed behind them. Frank came back to Anne, and all three of them apologized for taking so long. Anne said that she was starting to worry they got hurt or broke down somewhere. David told her that the lines were really long and that the toboggan held them up, until Rebecca fixed it.

Anne was surprised.

"Yeah." Frank said. "She came up with a good little contraption, come and see it."

"Without it, we wouldn't have been able to get as many supplies as we did." David told Anne and the kids. Then he told them all the places they had been to that day.

"When they got to the house she had a sleeping bag taped to her back." Tommy said.

"That sounds like Mom." Rachel told them.

"Mom can shop!" Karen added.

Then Danny wanted to know if she got anything good.

"You'll just have to wait and see." She told him.

"Cool." He said and knew that she had.

"You'll have to share." She told the kids.

David explained to them that his friends and their children are over at his house too.

Danny said, "Way Cooler." And asked if they could go now.

Rebecca went up stairs to get her purse and came back down and asked Rachel where it was. We packed it in your bag with some clothes Anne gave us to pack for you. Rebecca hugged her daughter and thanked her and Anne too. Then they loaded up as much as they could into the ski cart and Frank helped Anne onto the machine. Danny looked longingly at the snowmobile as he waited for his Mom and David to finish packing. She had told him he was riding with them. Frank sat down on the machine and called to Danny. "Come on sport. Let's go." Then he lifted Danny onto the seat in front of him and yelled. "Rebecca, I'm taking your boy with me." Rebecca popped her head out the door and noticed the wind picking up and Danny's smile on his face, so she told Frank. "Okay." and waved to Danny.

They started on ahead without everyone else because Anne didn't like to go fast. "See you over there." Frank told them as he took off extra carefully for Anne's sake. David told Tommy he might want to get started too. "The wind is starting to pick up and I think that is snowflakes starting to come down." He told him.

Tommy went into the house and grabbed some things to put in the snowmobiles seat compartment and then he let Rebecca know that they were leaving. Karen and Rebecca gave their Mom a wave and a smile. "See you in a little while, Mom." They told her as they got on the large machine. Tommy looked at Rachel on the back of the snowmobile, and thought with one turn, she might fall off the thing. Tommy walked up to her. "Do you mind if I borrow this?" He gently tugged on the scarf around her neck. Rachel's heart raced as he reached the scarf around her waist and told her to scoot up as close to him as she could, after he climbed on between the two girls. He tied the scarf around his own waist pulling her up against his back. "There, he said, Now I won't lose you." He flashed a wide smile at her across his blond haired, blue-eyed boyish face. Tommy showed Karen where in the front to hold on to as he hooked a seat strap across her legs. Then he started the machine and through the roar he yelled to Rachel, "Give me your hands." The boy reached behind to find her hands, and he placed Rachel's arms around his waist. He flashed her another smile and said, "Hold on tight." He waved to David and Rebecca, and they bolted off their spot in a flash.

Rebecca's heart pounded in fear for her girl's lives.

"Don't worry. Tommy grew up riding those, he's a safe driver." Then David placed a hand on Rebecca's shoulder and said, "But, Oh boy, I can feel a heartache coming on now."

"What are you talking about?"

"You didn't see a thirteen year old heart crushing?" He asked her.

"Oh, My God, you're right." She's had little boyfriends before, Rebecca told David, but this is her first real crush." And she thought to herself, Carl's missing it.

"Is Tommy nice. I hope she doesn't get her heart broken."

"Tommy's a good kid." He assured her. "He'll be gentle to her heart."

David noticed the sky darkening and said, "We better hurry!" They finished packing up what was left and then closed up the house.

"Will everything be okay here?" She asked him.

"All we can do is wait and see." They jumped on their snowmobile and headed out down the road. Rebecca looked at her watch and saw that it was now 3:00 PM and yelled, "It's started already." The wind had picked up while they had finished packing. The road had a light coat of new snow covering it, and it was now becoming slick. The snow had changed over to a mixture of snow and ice.

Rebecca pressed her face to David's back to keep the ice from hitting her. She could hear the trees cracking around them from the sudden drop in temperature. The bluster of snow gave David trouble seeing ahead. He couldn't tell if the road were clear. He pulled his slightly grubby John Deer cap down over his eyes to keep the ice from pelting into them. Then suddenly they hit something in the road. It sent one side of the snowmobile up into the air, and David yelled, "LEAN RIGHT!" Rebecca sucked her body up against his and held on even tighter as she leaned a hard right along with him. They managed to keep from tipping over, and David stopped the machine.

"You Okay?" David asked." You did Great."

She was fine, but they both looked back and noticed whatever they had hit had taken one of the canisters off with it. She told him it was great while it worked. Then she said. "It only worked because the roads were packed down so hard earlier."

"With all this new snow, David said, the clips to the netting probably won't snap off anymore." She agreed with him. David pulled out a folded utility knife and cut the canisters off one at a time. They packed the canisters in the load and re-attached the cords across the length securing the load to the sled. Then they drove on.

Five minutes later, David and Rebecca both heard a massive cracking sound. David yelled "To hell with the load, Hold On." He gunned the machine and they barreled down the tree lined road ahead of them. Rebecca buried her head behind his back for a minute and then looked behind them. With a huge vibrating crash, a tree came down, landing across the road thirty feet behind them. Rebecca's whole body jumped as she felt it land against the frozen ground. David never stopped or even slowed down to look. He only wanted to get them back to his home as quickly and safely as possible.

"Oh My God." Rebecca yelled to him. "Did you see that?"

"I felt it." He said. "That's good enough for me."

"A huge two foot thick tree just missed us." She told him.

"By the sound of the thud, I wouldn't be surprised if it were larger." David yelled over the engine as he increased the speed even more. Rebecca held on for dear life as she listened to the sled thudding down hard against the ground as they flew through the creaking trees. David pulled off the road into a clearing and charged up a hillside.

"Where are we going?" Rebecca yelled.

"Short Cut." He yelled back.

CHAPTER NINE

Anne and Frank sat at the kitchen window listening for the latest weather report and waiting for the kids to come up the drive. Danny and Cory stood watching from the back porch door as the guy's put the snowmobiles away in the storage building. Rachel was watching too. She was really watching Tommy the most, as she pretended to be watching for her mother. The men finished up and came back inside. Tommy introduced Rachel to both Mark and Kevin. Then the small boys followed the men, to where they went to hang out with the others in the kitchen.

"Are you waiting for your mother and David?"

"It's taking them a while, don't you think?"

He told her he thought they would be here any minute. But in truth he was a little concerned too. "Where is your sister?" Tommy asked her.

"She's off someplace playing Barbies with Stacey and Kim."

"You don't want to join them?"

Rachel just looked at Tommy.

"Okay, forget I asked that." He said, "But there is no point in sitting here worrying."

He didn't understand. Rachel thought. "My mom is the only

person I really have." She told him.

"Where is your Dad?"

Rachel said nothing and then she said softly "He's gone."

Tommy understood or at least he thought he did. He didn't press the subject any further because he knew how it felt. His own father had left them when he was ten years old. "Hey, he told Rachel. I forgot to bring my things over to the main house, do you want to come with me and see where the guys and I live." He pointed to the equipment building.

"You live with the equipment?" Rachel questioned him.

"Sort of, we live above it."

They put their coats on and Tommy pulled her scarf up over her face and told her it was really windy. "Follow close behind me and I'll block the wind." Rachel nodded in acknowledgement and followed him out the door. Once across the way, Tommy went to the side of the building and opened a regular size door. Inside was a set of stairs walled off from the garage below.

The upstairs was larger than Rachel thought it would be. It was an apartment with a large living room/dining combination and a breakfast bar that separated the kitchen from the open living area. Down a hall to the right was a bathroom, and she could see three bedroom doors that were closed. Tommy led her to the last one on the left.

"This is my room." He told her as he opened the door.

Inside was a twin bed against the right wall. There was a window straight ahead and in front of it was a computer desk. There was also a small entertainment center to the right of the door that was against the wall at the end of his bed. It was covered with CD's and DVD's. In it was a TV with DVD player and from the top Tommy grabbed the Boom box and some of his CD's. Then he went to the far corner of his room and picked up his guitar and handed it to Rachel. He stuffed the CD's and some extra batteries from his desk into a backpack with clothes and took a sleeping bag from his closet. He told her he'd be right back and he went to get things from the bathroom.

Rachel looked at the posters he had hanging in his room. He had many types of musical groups on the wall. Many of them she recognized and many she didn't. He only had a small stack of books on the shelf of his desk. She had read many of them. He came back into the room. "Most of those I read in either Junior High or High School."

"I've read many of these too." Rachel told him.

"Oh yeah." He was surprised. "Which ones?" Tommy was curious to know.

She held up, *Animal Farm, War of the Worlds, Lord of the Flies, A Wrinkle in Time, 1984, Fahrenheit 451* and *The Hobbit*.

"How old are you?" he asked her.

"I'm thirteen, but I'm in ninth grade."

Tommy was impressed he hadn't read most of those books until he was in eleventh grade. He told her he thinks he liked "The Hobbit" the best.

"I have two Tolkien books over in the house." Rachel told him.

"Maybe if we end up snowed in then we can read them together." Tommy said.

Rachel smiled at him. They gathered his things and headed back to the house. As they were going down the stairs, Tommy thought that he could be stranded in a winter storm with a lot worse. She may be young, but she was smart. Also, he thought, she's a very pretty girl for her age. He to admit he was surprised how her smile had affected him.

They stepped outside to find it was snowing really heavy now. Tommy felt pellets of ice hit his face. They stepped back inside and Tommy placed the bag on his back, took the guitar from Rachel and strapped it over the bag. Then he gave her the sleeping bag, and he took the boom box. Tommy told her to cover up her face completely with the scarf. They opened the door and closed it and Tommy took her hand and led her back to the house through the heavy snow and blasting ice. When Rachel and Tommy reached the door, both looked back toward the pastures because they thought they heard a noise in the distance, but then there was nothing.

Entering the house they could hear a ruckus going on inside. Anne was panicking as they came in. Everyone yelled at the kids wanting to know where they had been. But they realized when they saw Tommy's things. Anne raised her voice to Tommy. "Her Mother left the care of her children in mine and Frank's hands." Anne shook him lightly and then hugged him.

"I'm sorry Ma'am, I should have known to tell you where we were headed."

Both the kids said, "We didn't mean to worry you."

Frank put his hands on both of their shoulders and told them, "It's okay kids, we know you didn't. Everyone is just worried about David and Rebecca, that's all." The gray haired man said.

Daniel added, "Everyone needs to just try to calm their selves down and relax."

"I'll relax once my family is all here safely!" Answered Anne.

Pam pulled out the coffeepot Rebecca bought and asked if anyone would like some coffee. She fixed the pot and placed it on David's wood stove along with a teakettle. Pam started to put away the supplies brought from Anne's house, Rachel and Tommy helped her. Everyone else, sat and listened as the radio talked about the disaster this storm was leaving in its path through Georgia, and up through the Carolinas. How cars were buried in snow and power lines were snapping from the ice and freezing cold. Then the Governor came over the radio and explained how everyone needed to get to safety because they didn't want Virginia to have the same problem Georgia had had. He was explaining how many people further south were caught out in the storm and how there was no way anyone could get to these people. He told the citizens of Virginia to take shelter and asked everyone to pray for the residents of Georgia. Then he told them all. "Good Luck and God Bless."

The regular radio announcer came back on the air. He told the story of Georgia; how the people were caught totally unprepared and so an estimated third of the population had been out gathering supplies when the storm hit. The state was completely unable to slow the rate of the road conditions because of their lack of plows and salt. People were trapped in stores, and some were trapped in their vehicles. He repeated the governors warning for everyone to seek immediate shelter. He hoped that everyone had managed to prepare because of the intensity of the approaching storm it would probably be at least a few days before the disaster hit states would receive assistance.

Carl was sitting there in front of his five, new, state of the art computers and was getting nowhere. He had one computer with the accessible file on computer 1, and on computer 5, he had the file he was locked out of. The other three he was using to tweak the files between the two. By weeding out a piece at a time, he hoped he would be able to find a hole somewhere that would either let him in or find a piece that he could get the closed file to accept, and gain entry that way. He had been working on it for almost four hours straight, and he now had a pounding headache. Carl thought he should take a break because staring at the screens was getting him nowhere. He sat there and held his throbbing head.

"Are the screens giving you a headache?" Carl heard a soft voice ask him. He turned around and saw a young woman standing there with a wide smile across her face, and she was extending her hand toward him. He reached for her hand and noticed how small it fit into his own. She felt like soft rose petals, and he thought he caught the light scent of roses too. "My name, is Julie Stevens." She told him and then pointed to the machines behind him.

"Hi, I'm Carl." He looked at the computers and told her. "No. Actually, I'm experiencing more of a brain fog and a hunger headache."

Julie smiled at Carl. "We can go get some lunch if you like."

He looked at her and said. "Okay." Then he noticed that the room was empty. "Where is everyone?" He asked.

"Everyone works here from 8:30 to 5:30 and this section's lunch hour is taken from 12:30 to 1:30. She continued. Most people have probably eaten already and are resting and talking in the lobby."

He noticed that her eyes were a rust brown color, and she had shiny auburn hair. Which she had pulled up, so he wasn't sure of its actual length. She was probably no more than 5'2" in height and Carl doubted if she weighed more than 100 pounds. He couldn't help thinking she was very pretty, and he was very taken with her voice. It was soft and smooth; it was sexy like Rebecca's, but it was a slightly higher pitch. He realized that Julie was still speaking to him.

"I'm sorry I wasn't here to meet you earlier, but this morning I had to fly up from California. I work for Douglas Defense Advancement Solutions (DDAS) down there, and I've worked for Randy once before, a few years ago."

"What do you do?" Carl asked her.

What is the matter with me, Julie thought to herself, as she became flustered. She was not acting like herself this morning. This man had caught her off guard. He was not one of her usual charges. She was used to older men, ones who were old enough to be her father. "I'm sorry, didn't I tell you! I've been assigned to protect you."

Carl was shocked. He never expected a young girl could, never mind would, be assigned to be his bodyguard.

Julie saw the look on Carl's face. "I assure you. I am very well trained to protect my charges and I'm an expert Marksman."

"Charges?" Carl asked.

"Yes, my charge, that being you." Julie told him.

Carl trusted her on the marksmanship, but he could hardly believe that a girl so small could crush a hornet, never mind another person. This was silly, Carl told himself, he didn't need a bodyguard anyway. "So, what are your qualifications? Carl asked in a slightly teasing manner.

"I am qualified as an expert in five weapons, but, she pulled out her 9mm pistol; this is my preference on a daily basis. I am a 3rd degree black belt in Tae-kwon-do. I am trained in urban tactics, and certified in level 2 Combatives and several defense training programs and of course, CPR and First Aide."

"Let's hope you never need to use those last two." Carl joked. He smiled at her and asked where the food was.

She led them down a corridor, and Carl caught the smell of cafeteria food from half way down the hall. "It tastes a lot better than it smells, said Julie to Carl, Also, let's hope that I won't need to use any of my training. Okay." She grabbed his arm, so he would turn her way and they could see each other.

Carl saw the concern in her eyes and thought she must have had something happen before. "Okay, he said, Let's hope that I never have to see you in action."

They smiled at each other and entered the dining hall. It was only about half filled by this time, but Randy was there with Matt. They got their plates and sat down with the two men. Randy asked if Julie's trip went all right. She apologized for being late. She had a job she needed to finish up last night.

"Did William give you a difficult time getting away." Randy asked.

"No more difficult than normal." She said.

"So, everything is good then." Randy asked.

"Yes, I'm all squared away, unpacked and ready to work." The softly-spoken powerhouse told Randy. In a tone that Carl noticed was more solid and professional than how she had spoken to him.

Randy stood. "Good. Carl, with this little lady you're in good hands." Then, he asked how things were going and left.

Matt stayed behind, and asked if they were going to work on their game some more this evening, or if he wanted to play in the morning.

Carl thought about that a second and decided, "An hour in the morning is good for me."

Matt smiled a big wide grin at Carl and told him, "Okay." He happily left to go back to work.

Carl knew his brain was usually fried after work, and he was much more refreshed in the morning. "I'm teaching him how to play chess." Carl informed Julie.

"Oh is that what I saw in the living room, a game in progress."

"What were you doing in my living room!" Carl raised his voice to the girl across from him.

"Didn't they tell you?" She asked.

"Tell me what?" Carl demanded to know.

"The rules for my protecting you."

"No, they didn't." Carl raged.

"I always tell my charges the rules before the company hires me, so they should have told you, in case you chose to decline my services." Julie told him.

"Would you please not call me your charge. It makes me feel like a small school boy." Carl replied.

"What would you prefer I call you?" Julie asked, knowing full well what she would like to call him.

"I don't know, Client maybe, anything that makes me taller than three feet." Carl complained. Damn, she was pretty, she was distracting. An unwanted distraction from his goal; work. Especially now, with her skin glowing an arousing rosy hue.

God she was hot, she was roasting, she wanted to pick something up and fan herself, but she wouldn't give him the satisfaction of knowing he had flustered her. "Anyway, Going back to my rules."

"Don't bother- Besides, I wasn't given the option to decline a bodyguard, Carl explained, it was non-negotiable."

"I see. Well, I'll explain it anyway, It's very simple really, You go nowhere without me and the second bedroom in your apartment is mine."

Carl sat there speechless. He thought, "I've not been allowed to live with my own wife for almost eight months and now I'm being forced to live with a strange, beautiful woman. The only thing he wanted to know was; "Who's perverse idea of torture this was."

Carl returned to work and went to find Randy. He found him in an office next to the large conference room. Carl shut the door behind him, closing Julie out into the hallway. "What's the deal, Randy?" Carl wanted to know.

"What do you mean, Carl?" Randy was perplexed.

"Don't give me that Shit, Randy. You know what I mean."

"Is there a problem with Julie?" he asked.

"You know god damn well that there is. I'm not going to live with her. It's bad enough that I have to have her with me the entire day, I don't need my privacy and personal space invaded too."

"Well, I don't know what to tell you Carl, except get over it. We're not changing the arrangements." Randy leaned back in his chair and told him, "She is our best employee, at what it is she does, and it wasn't easy getting her. So, I suggest to you, that you learn to like her and maybe even try to enjoy her company or else this assignment will be that much harder on you."

Carl was furious, but he knew he had no choice and so he reached for the door handle.

"By the way, my latest update from Jordan is that everything is doing fine on the home front. He says everyone is safe. He had to pull his men out because of the storm, but he should have more news in a couple of days." Randy looked at him firmly. "So Carl, relax and get to work, all we can do is put in a good days work and then wake up and do it again."

Carl felt the blood raised in his face, and he also felt defeated. He opened the door to find Julie standing there waiting for him. He looked at her and could tell she heard the whole thing. "No offense, but this whole set up bothers me." Carl told her.

"None taken." She answered.

Carl went back to his work.

Julie sat and talked with people as she kept her eye on Carl. She didn't want him giving her the slip in rebellion to her having been thrown on him like this. She made a pot of coffee and offered him some, but other than brief niceties, he spoke not a single word to her.

Carl was unsure how he felt about this new situation of his. He just wanted to unlock whatever it is they were looking to find, so he could go home before Jordan stole his wife away from him. I just want my life back, he told himself. He wondered what his kids looked like now. They grew in spurts, and he remembered how sometimes they would look so much bigger after only a month away from them. Eight months can feel like a long time; God Knows it has been for him. He wondered if they gave up on him returning to them. He sat there at the computer screen and felt a lump developing in his throat and all of a sudden he felt tired.

He looked at his watch and noticed it was only going on 2:30pm and he knew he would sleep well tonight if a second wind didn't hit him. He found another piece of data and tried it on his second computer. It worked, now to try it on the others.

Carl grabbed another cup of coffee and when he returned he attempted the last one. He did it- he was in the file, and he yelled to Randy. "Get me the next one!"

All the men were yelling and cheering as someone brought Carl another file as he was getting the old one off his computers.

"So, what does that mean?" Julie questioned.

"Back to the drawing board." He answered.

"Isn't that tedious." She asked.

"It can be, but it's great when you've finally out smarted it, when that epiphany hits you and you know you've cracked it. A lot of times it's not a program or file that is the problem. It's the Data itself, the computer just stores, sorts and retrieves it, which is only numbers and symbols. It doesn't always know that this group of data does or doesn't belong there. All it does is save it and organize it to where it thinks it is supposed to be. Sometimes it is wrong, and then I have to try and figure out what it did wrong. Most times people just wipe out the contaminated files or programs and start over from scratch. You don't want to do that when there is a lot of work that you'll lose, or if you're trying to retrieve lost or removed information." Carl pointed to a spot on the screen, "See this; this looks like it doesn't belong. Here-try that-there." He pointed to something else. Now that Carl got them into the file the man searched it for pieces of lost Data.

"Bingo." the man yelled." everyone came running. "It's an order for twenty tons of fuel to be shipped to an undisclosed location in Honduras."

The two men in charge of making sense of the information that they find pulled out a map and started charting the furthest locations that planes could fly with that amount of fuel. All the other men kept searching through files.

"What we really need is planned vehicle and troop movements." Carl told Randy. "I'll bet the general has had this battle plan all mapped out for years."

Randy asked if anyone ran across old files of battle plans. By this time, everyone had gathered around the table.

"I'll bet money, Carl said, Those might help us to find the pieces to which one of these scenarios he chose."

"Search every file, even if it looks like a recipe or a letter home." Randy ordered, "We may just stumble into something unexpected."

Everyone got back to work, and Carl began work on his next puzzle.

CHAPTER TEN

David drove up over the hillside and Rebecca could see David's house in the far distance. They continued down the hill and were headed toward a road wide path through a section of trees that led to a clearing with David's pastures beyond. As they sped their way toward the opening, David noticed a large rise in the level of snow ahead of them. He tried to stop the machine, but they started to slide because of the fresh ice they were driving on.

"Brace yourself!" He yelled to Rebecca.

"HOW!" She screamed. Rebecca held onto David and closed her eyes.

"WATCH OUT!" He screamed "TREE!"

David had lifted his left leg up, but Rebecca wasn't watching, and it was too late. They slammed sideways into a snow covered fallen tree. David jumped off the snowmobile and pulled it quickly away from the tree.

"OW." Rebecca let out.

David felt the length of her leg from the knee down to the ankle. He didn't feel any brakes.

"Damn, my knee hurts."

"You probably cracked something." David cleared the snow from a section of the tree, as Rebecca tried to stand. "No, Don't do that." he told her. It was too late. She was already standing.

"It only hurts a little, I think I'm fine."

"Stop being brave and sit back down." David told her.

She did as he told her. Then he came over to her and lifted her off the machine and onto the tree. David went to check out the snowmobile.

"So, she asked, What's the damage?"

He told her that the vehicle was fine, no damage at all. "I think your leg took most of the blow." David said.

"Lucky me." Piped Rebecca as she exclaimed, "Wow, that happened fast."

He agreed with her. He looked as best he could through the mess falling down around them, toward his house in the distance.

"It may not seem so by your leg, but we are lucky, he told her, It's getting dark and the house is farther than it looks."

He turned to talk to Rebecca and noticed that her knee had some blood starting to seep through her blue jeans. He crouched down to look at her knee, and she flinched when he touched her. He looked up at her face but didn't see any pain revealed in it. She made that movement again with her hair, the sweeping behind her ear, which made him crazy. He could see her earlobe with a small gold hoop in it. She didn't know how her subtle movements made him want to kiss her.

"I'm sorry about your leg." He said.

"I'm okay, it's only getting a bit swollen." She said.

He told her he would put snow on it, but he feared it would only do more to make her cold then it would to reduce the swelling. She asked him if he had seen that the tree was there or if they skidded on the ice.

He looked back down at the leg and told her, "I saw it only once it was too late."

Rebecca could see he was upset. "No, she told David, Hitting that tree dead on would have been too late."

Rebecca asked if they needed to create a ramp. He told her he thought he could probably lift the front end up and onto the tree and then hopefully they could roll the track over it.

"If I push it from this side do you think you can guide it over the other?" He asked.

She told him she could.

They got the machine over the tree and then guided the sled over next. Then Rebecca climbed back on behind David and again held on for dear life. She was shaking a little and David wasn't sure if Rebecca were cold, in shock, or both. He didn't blame her if she were scared; their crash had rattled him too.

"We only have to get past these trees." David told her. "Then we have a smooth ride home."

She shook her head and said. "Alright."

They all heard the snowmobile coming. Daniel grabbed his coat and asked Kevin to help him get the snowmobile put away. Everyone rushed from the kitchen, where the wall clock read 4:30pm, as they reached the door they all saw David carrying Rebecca up the porch stairs. Rachel and the women gasped when they saw Rebecca's knee covered in blood. As he brought Rebecca through the door, everyone wanted to know what happened and why they had taken so long. Daniel told David they would take care of the machine and supplies. "Thanks" David said to his oldest and best friend.

Inside everyone was asking questions all at once.

"WE"RE OKAY!" David yelled over everyone's voices.

"I'm okay. Only a little banged up. She gave them all a big smile. And the really good news is the snowmobile is fine." Rebecca told them all.

No one thought she was funny, except David.

"Rebecca's leg kept us from hitting a tree." He told them.

"Rebecca tell me you didn't purposely put your leg between the machine and a tree?" Frank asked.

"I wish I were that brave. She told him. I had my eyes closed and didn't see it coming."

Everyone laughed. Daniel and Kevin came in with supplies and wanted to know what was funny. "What did we miss?" Pam and Mark filled them in.

"That took all that time?" Anne wanted to know.

David told them about the incident in the road that took out the sled and the falling of the tree story which made them get off the road and take the short cut, which led them back to the tree.

Everyone was amazed and glad they were okay and the household began to settle down now that David and Rebecca were home. Danny and Cory started to complain that they were hungry, and David asked Rebecca if she knew where the hot dogs were. "I put them in a covered bowl filled with ice on the back porch." She explained from the chair she was sitting in at the table. Anne and Pam were sitting there with her and watching the exchange between these two. David went out and got the bowl. He came back in and told her. "That was a good idea, but why didn't you put it in the refrigerator?" he teased her. She blushed just a tiny bit and David leaned toward her ear and said. "Your looking cute again." Rebecca turned bright red, "I forgot about the generators." She said aloud to whoever was listening.

David called to Tommy and Rachel and asked if they would help all the kids make hot dogs on the living room fire, as he handed them a plate of rinsed hotdogs, a bag of bread, the metal sticks and ketchup and mustard. "Only let them have one. okay? Dinner will be made in a bit." They nodded to David. Then Rachel and Tommy yelled to all the kids. "Come with us if you want a hotdog!" The women saw all the men go running too.

David said, "There, all the children are happy and busy." He pointed to Rebecca's leg, "You ready to go take care of that?"

She nodded and told him "Yes."

Then David came over to her and picked her up.

"I can walk!" Rebecca protested.

"Not until I see what you have there, you won't." David gave her a stern look and then a slight smirk. "Mom, do you know where Rebecca's bag is?" Anne told him it was in the den with all the others.

Pam was surprised. They acted like they've known each other for years. She watched them with interest, and knew she was correct in her judgment. She knew David well. She also knew he had fallen for this stranger. As she watched her husband's best friend carry this girl up the stairs. She called out. "Would you like me to bring up some warm water for you?"

"Thanks, Pam, that would be great." David said as he reached the landing with Rebecca still protesting that she was fine.

Pam waited for them to reach the top stair and she RAN to find Daniel. He was helping the kids cook some hotdogs at the other end of the house. When she reached the doorway, she saw that everyone was gathered around the ceiling high fieldstone fireplace that David and Daniel had helped to build four years ago. As she looked at the group huddled in front of it, she thought to herself, "What a collection, Six kids, seven if you count Tommy, and four men." The men had taken over the roasting of the hotdogs and were behaving more like children then the kids were. They were constantly checking to see if the dogs were done, even though they had barely started. The men were arguing amongst themselves as to what was the best way to roast hotdogs. From how the dog should be placed on the stick, to how close they should put it to the fire. "No Mark, if you put it that close the outside will burn before the inside is warmed." Kevin was reprimanding his friend.

Pam went to her husband and told him to let the kids cook their own hotdogs. He looked up at her confused. She would usually want him to help the kids, he thought. "What's up, Pam?" Daniel asked her. She gave him her "We need to talk, now." look. "What did I do!" He wanted to know.

"Uh-oh" Mark said, "Someone's in trouble!" He teased him.

She pulled Daniel toward the kitchen as she heard Kevin say."I wonder what he did now?"

In the kitchen Daniel said, "Why did you bring me all the way in here, You've never held back from letting me have it in front of the guys before." Daniel stressed the word before sarcastically. Anne was sitting in the kitchen, drinking her tea and crocheting as she listened to the couple. Pam went to put some water on the wood stove. "What are you doing, Pam?" He asked. "You brought me in here to make tea?"

"David needs the water to clean Rebecca's cut." She told him.

"Okay, so what's this about." He wanted her to let him have it, and be finished.

Pam waved her hand at him and said, "Stop. You're not in any trouble. Now listen to me. What do you think of Rebecca?" She asked him.

"I don't know her." Daniel said.

"I understand that, but, What do you THINK OF HER!" Pam asked her husband.

"Pam you're not making any sense."

She interrupted him, "David has fallen for her."

"WHAT!" He exclaimed in disbelief. "He doesn't even know her."

"Daniel, you watch him and you'll see, David is in love with her."

Anne interrupted and told them Rebecca was a nice girl. "She has a kind heart and she's strong spirited and smart. She's the one who fixed the toboggan today." "She bought the supplies and she slept in the BARN last night."

They both said, "She slept in the barn? Why?"

"Frank and I sent them out there." Anne told them.

Pam said, "She and David both slept in the barn, together?" Half questioning and half astonished

"For what reason." Daniel asked.

"We asked them to watch the animals and we wanted to know what kind of person she was."

"And they fell for that!" Pam asked her, disbelieving what she told them.

Anne said to the two best friends her son has ever had. "If you saw the way he looked at her and her children from the first moment he saw them, then you would have done it too."

They both understood. They too. Can't stand to watch David go through another broken heart. "He's not thick enough to endure another disastrous relationship." Daniel said out loud to no one in particular.

Pam looked at Anne and asked. "So, what do you know about her?"

The older woman said, "Not very much, factually, But she seems very nice."

Daniel said, "She's wearing a wedding ring."

"What are you doing looking for rings. Pam teased her husband. You still cruising the market."

Daniel rubbed his wife's back and told her it was just an old habit that never died.

"That old habit, may just become a necessary new habit." Pam said, pretending to be mad at him as she walked away.

Daniel grabbed her waist and tugged her to him. "Get that sexy little butt of yours back over here!" He said as he turned her back around to face him and noticed she was laughing. Then he kissed her and helped her to bring a large pot of hot water upstairs.

They found David and Rebecca in the master bathroom upstairs. When they came in they could see David holding the back of her knee with an old towel as he poured peroxide over the cut. Rebecca was wearing a large terrycloth bathrobe of David's and sitting on the toilet. "Thanks." He told them and then he properly introduced Rebecca to Daniel. Rebecca pulled the robe closed tighter and then shook Daniel's hand. The three of them assessed Rebecca's leg and then decided a few butterfly bandages were probably all that was needed and then they bandaged it well with gauze and secured it.

"It doesn't seem to be bleeding too badly anymore." Pam told Rebecca.

Daniel asked if it hurt to walk on and she told him it didn't hurt too much.

They all agreed that there could be a fracture, but it wasn't bad if there were one. Daniel thanked his friends for their help, and they all left Rebecca so she could change her clothing.

Now that Rebecca had a moment alone she looked at David's bathroom. It was decorated with only the bare minimum. Rugs on the floor in the color of navy blue, a shower curtain with an ocean scene on it, and towels in two colors; navy to match the rugs and tan to match the sand on the curtain. On his sink was an assortment of shaving gear, a deodorant stick and after-shave. The medicine cabinet had a small amount of medicine plus a tooth brush and paste. The hamper was stuffed with laundry, and a couple of towels lay on the floor. Rebecca opened her bag and pulled out the black jeans and the cream sweater that Anne let her borrow and she cleaned up a little with some of the warm water and then changed. Hanging David's robe on the back of the door she opened it to go down stairs.

Stepping out the door Rebecca jumped. David was lying on his bed and waiting for her. He had a pile of clothes next to him. "Do you feel a little better?" he asked her.

"Yes." she said.

"I was waiting, so I could show you around my house." He smiled at her.

"Thanks, I would love it see it. It's very pretty from what I've seen so far." She smiled back.

It took him a year to build. He explained that when he came home, his Dad chose to retire and gave him this land to build his home. He also signed over the farm to him and gave Daniel a couple of acres down the road to build a house on, on the stipulation that they run the place together. This all happened four years ago. Since then he and Daniel had added 300 head of cattle and another large stable near Daniel and Pam's house so that Pam could teach riding lessons and they could profit some from the boarding of City folk's horses.

The upstairs was designed to be three bedrooms with a large bedroom loft overlooking the great room below. But David had the loft set up as an office with a corner desk to one side of the room and a couch along the outside wall at the other side. There was a reading lamp at each end of it. On the walls of the loft, there were pictures of David with other men posing with animals of all types that they had shot. It was very dark in the room, but Rebecca thought one of the images was of a bear. She strained to look closer, it was a bear, and in the picture was David, his Dad, Daniel and someone else.

David saw her looking at it and said, "That's Peter, my younger brother. We took a trip about five years ago to Alaska. I've only, last month finished paying for that Grizzly."

"What do you mean?" she asked.

"I put the taxidermist bill on loan." David explained, "The bear is down stairs."

She tried to see it, but couldn't. She did see a large deer above the fireplace and two smaller ones to each side. "I can only make out some deer." She told him.

"The large one in the middle is a Caribou and the two on the sides are white tail deer." He said.

Rebecca asked if anyone else had shot a grizzly.

He explained that Daniel did, but he decided to have only the head mounted and the paws done too. "My bear was so large that I chose to have the whole thing made into a rug, besides I'll probably never get to go again." David told her.

Rebecca understood what he meant. She was aware that trips to Alaska are expensive, never mind hiring a guide and paying the fees for hunting licenses. "I have a brother-in-law who hunts, she told him. It's very expensive." "I can't wait to see your bear." Rebecca told him.

She couldn't help noticing that except for all his hunting trophies the house was pretty much undecorated. David's bedroom had only bare furniture. His pencil post bed was covered in tan colored bedding, and there was no color to the rooms walls, but there was a fireplace that made the room feel cozy despite its emptiness. It had a few photos on its mantle. He had told her they were of his son and daughter, Ryan and Jessica. She saw that the other was a picture of him and his siblings standing around their seated parents. "It was taken on their Fortieth Wedding Anniversary," he told her. He pointed out his sisters to her. There was Debbie, Melissa, Himself, Peter and Jane in that order.

The other room was similarly bare, but it had a large white iron bed with a pink rose quilt and pillows. At the end of the bed was a white toy box that was open and in it was a bunch of Barbie dolls and with them were clothes and horses and cars.

"Looks like the girls were kept busy earlier." He picked up a Barbie and two dresses and put them back in. "Obviously this is Jessica's room."

Across from her room was another bathroom with pink rugs and towels, but nothing else.

Then there was the loft, which they were leaving now. He left all the doors open so that the warm air would circulate throughout the upper level and then they went down stairs. He showed her the Den, which was below his room and had a fireplace also. It had built in bookshelves, which he said he had made a year ago. There was a couch, and a recliner and a French door that led to the back porch. Next to this, was another room that he made into a bedroom for Ryan, and it opened into the entryway to the house by way of double French doors. Both were now open, and she could see a wooden sleigh bed with a primary colored comforter of red, blue and yellow. She could see a couple of baseball memorabilia posters and framed cards on the walls and the dresser had balls of different sports and a bat and glove. There was a nightstand with some puzzle books on it.

He said, "You saw the entry, and the kitchen and dining room." It was an open concept combo. To the right, was a large wooden dining table and hutch with hunter green accents to match the trim on the kitchen cabinets. To the far wall was a wood stove, and it was very warm in this area of the house. Pam and Anne were in the kitchen. The kids came in, asking for something to drink, Pam gave them two sodas and told them all to share. They ran away yelling Thank You.

"Uh, Uh. Where do you think you're going? Pam asked. No drinks in Uncle David's living room, you know better."

"He let us have hotdogs." They complained.

"Yeah, well that one is on Uncle David." She pointed them to the kitchen counter.

The kids took turns sipping and then went running back to the other room. Anne asked how her leg was and she told her better. Pam told Rebecca that the kids were getting along great and that they were instant friends. David said that he was giving Rebecca a tour of the house and that he would bring her right back in a minute. Pam said, "You be sure to do that, and don't forget to take credit for that fireplace of yours." She yelled as she watched David drag Rebecca away by the hand, caressing the top of it with his thumb.

"This is the best room. This is the one that took a lot of time and effort." David told her. He pointed to the huge beam that was at the top of the roof. "That was brought in and then raised by a crane." He said.

Rebecca was in awe of the Great room and understood why it was called that. The room felt tremendous. It was probably a third the size of the entire house, and the massive Field stone fireplace was the focal point of the room. "It is beautiful." She told him.

"Daniel and I have friends who build homes for a living. They gave us deals on the labor because we worked right along with them and a lot of the easy stuff we did ourselves. Like the hardwood floors and the trim, painting, carpet, tile, fixtures, etc. It was the log kit, the plumbing and electrical that we had the most help with and of course the land was free. The fireplace was the last part we did. A friend of ours named Neal is a Mason, and he helped us."

"Where did you get that thick wood for the mantle?" She asked.

"We cut it down ourselves, Whenever we went hunting we kept a look out for the perfect tree and we finally found it." He pointed to the ten point buck on the left, "It was the same day I bagged that deer."

"Does Daniel and Pam's house look exactly the same." Rebecca asked.

David told her, "They bought a log cabin too, but it is a different style. They wanted a more traditional, four bedroom house, and they opted not to spend the money on the great room. But they have a beautiful fireplace in their house too, just smaller."

"Why did you choose to get the great room." She asked him.

Daniel came over and heard what they were discussing. "The big question, why so much grandeur." He joked.

"Well, I liked it as a show piece for my trophies."

"Yeah, Yeah, Now tell her the real reason." Frank told his son. "Suzanne was a spoiled brat."

"Thanks Dad." David said. "I remember."

The room had tall arched windows on the sides and the living room was sunken. They stepped down into the room. The back wall had more animals on it and some fully stuffed animals on shelves. This was also, where David had weapons hanging: cross bows and shotguns hung up high. There were also glass cases with more guns; knives and arrows locked up in it. The bottom drawers locked also.

"I keep the shells in there." David explained.

"Mom, did you see this?" Karen came running, Pointing her towards the large grizzly lying on the floor. It was beautiful. She couldn't believe how large it was. She touched it, and it's fur felt coarse. But the paws felt a little smoother. She looked into the animals eyes. It made her feel sad. She couldn't quite understand what she was feeling. It didn't feel the same to her as looking into a hoofed, animal's eyes. She looked at the face, and she saw that the mouth had been made to look grimacing, so that the teeth showed. But the rest of it wasn't giving her that impression. She hugged it and felt like crying, but she didn't.

David watched her reaction and told her. "It was a lot more dangerous alive."

Rebecca told him. "I'm sure he was." And she tried to smile at David as she said that.

The evening passed by as the snow and ice fell in pounds and feet outside. Rebecca had helped the women make dinner, and David went to change after showing her his house. Frank pulled out a chessboard in the den and he and the other guys were taking turns playing, but no one could beat Frank. David came back down, and his buddy's all teased him for dressing in nice clothes. Mark asked if he were going out dancing. Kevin told Mark he didn't have his dancing shirt on.

Pam whistled and said. "I can appreciate looking at a fine man looking sharp. I know a few other men around here, who could afford to dress in something other than their work clothes, once in a while." She went to David and told him he looked nice. David asked if they needed any help in the kitchen. She told him they could use help making a salad and his company wouldn't hurt them either. She winked at him. David came in and noticed Rebecca had taken out the bag of things from The Corner Market and the girls were deciding which book each wanted to read first. Anne picked one and Pam said the other one sounded good to her. Rebecca ended up with the one about a Cattle Ranch out in Colorado, which was the one she had wanted. Rebecca was slicing carrots as David read the back of her book sitting on the counter. Then he whispered into her ear. "We can act out that one if you like?"

David was so close to her that she thought she was going to fall from the intoxicating effect he had on her. He was cleaned up and instead of the grainy scent that he wore before, he now smelt of a spicy-sweet, after-shave. He was wearing a pair of snug fitting black jeans and he had on shiny black cowboy boots and a matching belt with a large intricate silver buckle with black onyx stones inlaid. He wore only a white T-shirt, and the heat from him was pouring onto her. The knife in her hand came down against the cutting board, and she barely missed cutting her finger.

David covered her hand with his own, and told her. "I think we may already be started, That's my sweater you're wearing there, too bad it wasn't the only thing." He said with a warm breath to her ear. His hand was large and rough and his arm reaching across her was rippled with muscles from his shoulders all the way to his wrist.

"Be careful, Cowboy. You're talking to a married woman." Rebecca told him as she moved away from him to find her bearings.

The women were doing their best to blend in with the wallpaper, and they likewise were doing their best to catch everything the two of them were saying.

"That reminds me." David said loud enough for everyone to hear. "Jamie gave me something for you." He went to the closet and brought out the thin brown bag with the sticks in it and handed them to her. "He told me to tell you these are for old time sake and let you know he was an MP."

She pulled open the bag and found illumination sticks. She had a big smile on her face and said, "Cool, these are nice ones." He told her one was for her that's why there are seven. "Will you tell him thank you for me?" She asked David.

"He said you would understand what he meant by old times." His statement was clearly a question.

"Yes, I do. Thank You." She left it at that.

"So!" All three of them asked.

"It's nothing, really." She told them. They all stood there and waited for her to continue. She was going to have to tell them who she was; there wasn't any way to avoid it now. She knew she wasn't a creative liar, and Jamie would tell them anyway. "Do you know what these are?" She held up the stick.

Pam said. "I think it lights up."

David said he knew what it was, but he wanted to know how it all related to her.

She ignored David and instead concentrated on what she felt comfortable explaining.

She snapped the glass bulb in the plastic stick, and it began glowing purple. "The military uses these so they can see in the dark. They have them in different sizes, usually from a thicker hanging type to a tiny eraser size. Just small enough so you can mark a location or read a map. On Posts, the children are given these on special days by the Military Police. They drive around and hand them out when the kids are Trick or Treating, and on the Fourth of July they do the same." She thought about Carl, and how he and all soldiers would bring them back from the field as small gifts to their kids upon returning home.

Cory and Danny came into the kitchen. "Wow, what is that?" Cory wanted to know.

Danny asked. "Where did you get those, Mom."

Jamie at the Sporting goods store gave them to you. He was a MP at Fort Campbell.

"Really, Danny said, "Does he know where Dad is!"

"DANNY!" Karen yelled, when she came through the doorway.

Danny started to cry, and Rebecca couldn't believe what she had done to her children. She hugged Danny and told him everything was okay. She said. "Jamie doesn't know daddy or us. He only gave you these to be nice."

She smiled at Karen and told her. "We still should only talk about it with family and friends we can trust. The government doesn't want any more bad publicity right now, not with all the accidents that have happened lately." She calmed her son down, and then gave them all the glow sticks. Then she and David sent them on their way with all the things they had bought them at the store.

Rebecca told them that she knew nothing about her husband, except that they had paid her his life insurance. So, she decided to move away, that is why they are now on their way to her mom's to visit, while she decides where she wants to move to. "I have three months to decide, That's how long the moving company will store our belongings."

Pam was speechless. She had no idea how Rebecca could be handling this so well. She went and got one of the bottles of wine and opened it, "Anyone else?" She poured Anne and Rebecca a large glass and David got a beer.

Daniel came in and said to David. "You didn't offer me one." He was shunned by his friend's in-hospitality. Pam gave him a cold look that said, "Shut up." He looked at the group and sat down.

Rebecca thought how good it felt to be able to talk to others about her problems, even if there weren't much to tell. The wine was doing her leg some good too.

Pam had gulped down her glass of wine and took another. They asked her a couple of questions, and she told them that he was away training and just didn't come home. She told them, "It's been almost eight months."

Pam filled Rebecca's half empty glass.

Daniel said. "I've missed something, haven't I."

They all looked at him sitting there with a lost expression on his face and then they all laughed.

Pam told her husband. "Don't you always, Honey." Pam filled him in as always. Rebecca sat there quietly, swallowing down the wine to numb herself, as she listened to someone else dole out the horrific details of her shattered life.

❈❈❈

Carl was exhausted. He had spent the entire afternoon working on his next file but hadn't gotten far with it. He thought he would be lucky to get this one cracked by tomorrow afternoon. Carl looked around the room and noticed most people had already left for the day. The only people still working were the two men tasked with putting all the pieces together. Some of the other men had found more pieces to their large jig saw puzzle, earlier that day, and the men were trying to decipher them. He spotted Julie sitting by a window looking outside. Carl asked her if she were ready to call it a day. She shook her head in response and asked if he wouldn't mind if they went out this back door instead of the front. Carl told her that would be fine. Julie stood there looking at the woods in the distance.

"Is something wrong?" He wanted to know.

Julie said she wanted to check out the woods behind them. "If I were going to sit and watch this room, I would do so from that section of woods right there." She pointed from where she was standing toward a thick section of evergreen trees.

They told the men they would see them tomorrow and Julie opened the back door. Stepping outside she caught a light scent of tobacco smoke. Julie pushed Carl back into the room before he could step out. She quickly called Paul. "Paul, I need you down here now!" She yelled into the receiver. "Stay here and lock the door." She told Carl.

She opened the door and went outside. Julie ran toward the trees. She doubted that whoever may have been there, would have waited around long enough for her to come back out of the building. She was right. She found a large cigar butt, still smoking, in the snow behind the thick trees. She searched the area and then returned to the building. Paul let her back in and asked what had happened. "Whoever was out there made the mistake of smoking. I caught the scent as soon as I stepped out the door." The auburn haired girl told them. "I didn't expect to find them. We probably startled him as soon as we opened the door."

Paul said that he would see to it that security was doubled and that those trees were cut down. "What are you thinking?" Paul asked the young girl as she was replacing the pistol back into its holster.

"I'm thinking that whoever that was. They have been there a long time judging by the track marks in the area around those trees. Not to mention, the huge pile of cigar butts on the ground. But, whoever they are, they're either, not well trained or they're very sloppy. I don't know which." Julie told them.

Paul explained that he didn't think it was worth going out and tracking him, since it will be dark quickly and he is sure to be long gone before we could even get the dogs. Julie agreed and told him they could wait until tomorrow and check it out then.

"There isn't anything we can do now." Julie looked at Carl. "Carl, are you ready to get some dinner." Julie asked him.

They both told Paul they would see him in the morning. They went down to the cafeteria. but it was already closed.

"Well, we can just go home and I can make something if you like."

151

She told him. She cringed to herself for using the word home.

"We don't seem to have any alternative." Carl said. There wasn't much point in avoiding going back to the apartment, he told himself. They would eventually have no choice, but to end up there anyhow.

Entering the apartment, Carl felt a chill come across him. He flicked the switch on the wall, and the room came into the full glow of artificial light. He went to the glass door and was about to close the curtain when he felt someone or something staring at him. He looked closer and caught the green glow of two eyes looking straight at him. Carl looked into them, and they moved and disappeared.

Julie was in the kitchen banging around pots and pans, evidently, searching for ones that she needed to make dinner.

Carl closed the curtain and made a fire.

He looked at the pictures of his family and tried to ponder the information that Paul gave him earlier that day. But he couldn't make any sense out of what the message could be. Carl thought about the concept of ancestors and the only person he thought would be talking to him from beyond would possibly be his grandmother. He contemplated that possibility, but she would never have been a cougar, the deer maybe, but not the cougar. Then Carl thought what if he were the deer, hunted down and destroyed by the cougar. Maybe that was the message, for him to beware of the cougar. That he, needed to be careful not to go about grazing carelessly, and he had better not make the mistake of letting his guard down.

Carl gave up and decided to see if Julie needed any help in the kitchen. When he entered the room, he saw her at the sink with her back to him. He noticed that she had changed out of her work clothes and was wearing a pair of gray sweat pants and a pink sweater that was either too big or designed to fall slightly off the shoulder. Her hair was swept up still, the way she wore it for work. He looked at her long, pale neck leading down to her bare shoulder in the outfit that hinted at a gentle sexuality. Carl watched as she put down the potato peeler and reached up and rubbed some stress from her neck. Then she pulled out two long pins and all of her hair came tumbling down. Thick reddish brown curls landed at the middle of her back. Carl felt his breath catch as she leaned over to pick up the peels that had fallen to the floor. The sweater she wore fell downward exposing her entire waist and back.

Julie looked up and saw Carl standing there across the room. She smiled and brushed her forehead with the back of her hand as she said, "Hi, is that the smell and crackle of a wood fire coming from the other room."

Carl sucked in a deep breath of needed air and told her. "Yes. I started a fire."

She asked if he were feeling all right and he told her he was fine, and then he asked if she needed any help. She told him everything was set, and dinner would be out of the oven in an hour or so.

Carl decided to change out of his work clothes and found a few sets of casual outfits that Carrie had left in one of the drawers. He put on some comfortable tan khakis and an olive and brown sweater and went back to the living room. When he returned he found that Julie had poured them both a small glass of wine and she was watching the news. He took a seat in a recliner and asked if there were any news about the storm hitting the East Coast. They both listened as the newscaster told them that the entire eastern sea board was currently being pelted with the worst storm system that The United States had had in last seventy years. "Yesterdays totals had beaten the storm of 1974, But with the continued snow fall and the expected ice to follow this current system, it was expected to be worse than the storm of 1940." The man continued to explain that the Eastern residents only saving grace was that compared to the emergency services of 1940, Today's, FEMA has developed quicker disaster reaction plans, made possible because of new technology. The newscaster broke off to another reporter who had researched the disaster of 1940 and compared abilities from then with those of rescue and relief organizations of today. They concluded that although this storm has the potential to be worse than storms in the past. The modern technology of the day would likely prevent many of the fatalities that would have been expected in previous times. Assistance and recovery times have been charted out and are estimated to take as long as two weeks, compared to the fatal five weeks in took to help the survivors of Winter Storm "Theodore" of 1940. The newscaster finished the evenings broadcast by saying, "The weather service has named the winter storm of 2010, "Horatio". The man said, "We have looked up the name and it means, keeper of the hours." Then he ended his broadcast saying, "Good luck to all of you on the East Coast who have only to pass your time in your bunkered down houses as Horatio gives to you hours of solitude away from the hectic world outside. God bless and goodnight to you all."

Julie laughed and said. "They stop at nothing, do they?"

"What do you mean?" Carl asked her.

"These news people, they always have to take events like these and pump them up and dramatize them. Yes, they are potentially dangerous and I'll admit that the storm will be no picnic for those experiencing it. But do they have to make this storm into something profound."

Carl said nothing. He agreed that news people worked hard at sensationalizing events for their viewing audience. But, he understood what the man meant by getting a break from the hectic world we live in and having the chance to be with their loved ones without any distractions from the outside world. The newsman had done a pretty good job making him feel almost a little envious of those in the storm. He knew if he were with Rebecca and the kids, he would be enjoying their time together, despite the stressfulness of the storm.

Julie looked at the man across the room from her. She was afraid she had said something wrong. He was being so quiet, and he was staring at a picture on the mantel. She sat there, staring at him. He was handsome. She liked his dark brown hair and tanned skin. She could see the strength in his exposed forearms, since his sweater sleeves were pushed up to his elbows. He appeared to her to have a gentle nature about him. Most men she protected were hard, businessmen types. People with lots of money and the ego to go with it. They were usually older. She assumed that it took them all their youthful years to build their vast wealth and all those years before they consequently needed protecting. She enjoyed her job. It made her feel strong, and she made good money. Julie thought how she never before worried or even cared if something she said might have upset any of the people she protected. She wasn't there to be their friend anyway. But now she hoped she hadn't upset this man across from her. She knew many things about him were different from the other men, but she wasn't yet sure in what ways. She wanted to get to know him better, if he would allow her to.

She clicked off the television and asked, "A penny for your thoughts." She wasn't sure if she was prying, but she figured it couldn't hurt to ask.

Carl looked at the girl across the room from him. He noticed that with her hair down and the professional clothing removed, she looked a little older than she had earlier. He could have sworn that she was no more than twenty-four years of age earlier that day. Now she seemed to be in her late twenties. "I was thinking about what you said" Carl told her. "I agree that they make more out these things then are necessary, But I do think they are in a way lucky to have the opportunity to take a small vacation from the rest of the world. I think that is all the newscaster meant by his remark."

Julie looked into the man's eyes and saw that the green in them from earlier had changed over to hazel. She looked into them and felt her heart grow anxious. It was pounding hard, and she was sure he could see her chest thudding from his effect on her. She tried to calm herself, but she couldn't. Something in his eyes felt like they were burning through her own and she couldn't fight the compulsion to stare even harder.

Carl felt a sudden rush of exhilaration hit him as Julie stared hard at him. He felt a reaction growing inside him. He looked at her shiny hair and longed to touch it. Carl watched her as she took her hair and brushed it back behind her ear just as Rebecca does. He instantly felt a shock to his gut as he remembered her, and he forced himself to squash his desire for Julie. Carl got up and went to stir the fire.

The alarm went off in the kitchen, and Julie went to shut it off.

Carl stood there and looked at his pictures of his family and wondered if Rebecca could feel that he was still with her. He tried to send her a mental message. "Rebecca remember me, and know how much I love you." He said to her.

Julie returned to the room with plates in her hands. They turned the television back on and ate in silence. By the time they had finished their meal, Julie had regained her composure.

"Carl, we need to discuss our situation." She told him.

Carl waited for her to continue.

"I'm not used to working with someone as young as yourself. In the past when asked what my relationship with a client was, we were easily able to say that I was their daughter. Obviously, in this case, that isn't going to work." Julie hesitated. "I can appreciate how awkward this is going to be for you, but... I feel the only logical explanation would be that we are married."

Carl thought about that, "Why do we need to pretend to be anything?" he asked.

"Carl, this is a large facility, the only people who know who you and I are, are the twenty-five people who work in Randy's section, those are all his men, we can trust them. She explained, however, the rest of the facility has people from many companies and some foreigners also. If any of them are spies, they will be looking for someone who is single."

Carl understood the logic she was presenting him with, but it didn't make it feel any less strange. He told her he understood and then he excused himself to grab a shower and go to bed.

Carl lay in bed as he heard the shower turn on. He found himself imagining what Julie looked like with warm water streaming down her body. He yelled at himself. "Get a grip and stop torturing yourself." He was in love with Rebecca, and he didn't want to consider ruining his marriage, not over simple lust. He tossed and turned for an hour and then he finally dosed off to sleep.

CHAPTER ELEVEN

Rebecca stood at the large great room window and watched as the snow and ice crept its way up the window's pane. Anne had gone off to bed an hour ago, and Pam was reading by the fireplace. Rebecca and Pam had managed to get the children off to sleep in their sleeping bags in the upstairs loft half an hour ago.

Rebecca reached for her knee and shifted all her weight to the other leg. She couldn't believe the mess she had gotten herself into. Stranded in the mountains of Virginia with a nice family and an attractive man. She thought how if she were twenty again it would have been a dream come true. But at thirty-two, she had larger issues to worry about then whether or not she had a fun time waiting out a blizzard.

Listening to Pam, describe her life earlier made it feel so unreal to her. If she didn't have those three great kids of theirs upstairs then she would have been convinced it had all been only a strange dream. She looked at her wedding rings and thought it may have been eight months without Carl, but she still felt the power of them on her hand. She remembered her and Carl picking them out. She had needed new ones because after three children she no longer was a tiny little girl as she had been when they were married. She looked at them again and decided that as long as she felt that connection to Carl she wasn't going to give up on his returning to her.

She reached down to her leg again. "I saw that, little girl." Frank said from behind her. He put his hand on her shoulder and reprimanded her for standing on her leg. "I came to say goodnight, I'm headed up to bed."

Rebecca told him goodnight, and Pam did too.

"You get off that leg of yours and let it heal." He insisted.

"I will, Sir." She smiled to Frank.

"Good, See you both in the morning." He told them and then he went off to the pink room to be with his wife.

Pam looked at Rebecca and didn't envy her for her situation. "Rebecca, are you okay, what are you thinking about over there." Pam moved her legs from across the couch and made room for the sad woman to sit down next to her. Pam patted the couch beside her and placed a throw pillow on the coffee table for her foot. "Here, take a load off that leg."

Rebecca joined her and asked, "How long have you and Daniel been together."

The blonde haired woman across from her placed the bookmark in her page and placed the book on the coffee table. She had what looked like rough hands, working hands that saddled horses and helped to muck out stalls and lay fresh hay. She was a very happy woman, and Rebecca envied her. Her life seemed to be solid and secure. She had her horses, and her daughters competed in the local circuits. Rebecca looked at a picture on David's mantle of a competition that Stacy had won.

"Daniel and I have been together since I was a freshman in high school. Well, we broke up for six months in tenth grade, but we were still in love. We were two young kids testing the water of love. We both dated someone else, but by the end of the school year, we were back together and have been ever since."

Silence fell between them.

Pam went and got them both another glass of wine. "Now we can relax and enjoy the fire while the kids sleep." She told Rebecca. She also had David's long handled popcorn cooker and was pouring in dried kernels as she spoke. "I'm sorry, I don't have any valuable advice to give you Rebecca. Pam told her, I've been fortunate not to have experienced any real losses yet in my life. David could probably help you better than me, he had a really hard time with his divorce from Suzanne." She put butter in the cooker and placed it over the fire. "I know it's not quite the same, but he knows what it is to hurt." They listened to the scraping of the kennels as Pam shook the long handle forward and backwards. "But I'd like to listen, if you'd let me." Pam looked at the dark haired woman, and wanted to hug her. The pain coming from her was so strong she could almost feel it. She didn't know her that well, so instead she asked. "What is your husband like."

Rebecca thought for a minute. "I wish I had a picture to show you, The one I had in my purse, I gave to the CID investigator." Rebecca described her husband. "He has brown hair and hazel eyes, but sometimes they are the prettiest color green. If he lets his hair grow, it is all curly like Karen's. The first thing I think of, is that Carl is a character, he always tries to make people laugh. But, he can sometimes be very pouty too. He is a great father and a good husband. I have sometimes feared that he would regret the choices he has made. He has passed up a lot of opportunities for us."

The kernels popped ferociously as Pam removed it from the fire and opened it to let out the steam. "Do you think he would make all the same choices again if given the opportunity."

Rebecca hesitated to answer that question. "Six months ago, I would have instantly told you that he would, but now I'm less sure then I was." "Now... I don't know." Rebecca felt lost. She didn't even know if she would make all the same choices again herself. Never mind, try to figure out what Carl would do. The only thing she did know was that she needed to find some solid ground before she fell. She sat there and took a sip of her wine as they ate the popcorn. "My only real plan is to figure out where home is for me and my kids." She told Pam.

Pam understood, at least she knew one thing for sure. If anything ever happened to Daniel she knew having her home was what would help her to make it on her own. It was her home and horses that grounded her and made her comfortable and safe. Pam thought that if she had her horses maybe there was something the woman next to her had too. "Rebecca, Is there anything you can think of that makes you feel grounded?"

Rebecca turned her face away from Pam. "With all the moving we did, we only needed each other, and we were home." Pam heard the light sucking in of air through Rebecca's silent sobs. "Carl was my ground, and I was his."

Daniel and David came through the door. "I came to see if you were ready for bed, her husband told Pam. We're sacking out in David's room if that is okay with you." Pam shook her head and wiped her eyes as she walked behind the couch to go with Daniel. She reached down from behind Rebecca and gave her a hug then she rushed off before her new friend could see that she was crying too.

As David came closer, she wiped her tears, so he wouldn't stare at her. He stared anyway, and asked if she were all right. He grabbed them both some blankets and then he sat in the spot where Pam had been. She asked if they were done playing chess for the night. "Mark and Kevin are finishing up their game and then they're going to crash for the night in the den." David caught the beam of a flashlight and the light whisper of

Tommy's voice. "They really hit off, didn't they." pointing to the loft. Those two are still up there reading on the couch.

"What's the story with Tommy. Rebecca wanted to know, He seems young to be working for you."

"He'll be seventeen next month. He's been working and living here for the last two years. David told her. His mom had breast cancer, unfortunately, they didn't catch it soon enough."

"What about his father?" She asked.

"He left them when he was nine or ten."

Rebecca couldn't imagine being completely alone as a fifteen-year old.

David explained. "He's in his last year of high school and I'm trying to convince him to apply for college."

"Is he really smart." Rebecca asked.

"Very, considering the amount of time he puts toward studying is close to zero." He explained to her how Tommy was a hard worker and that he really loves the animals. He has been trying to encourage him to go to school to become a Veterinarian.

She advised him not to push the issue too hard, but just to let Tommy understand that he has faith in his abilities. "But, that is something that would require a lot of ambition, Rebecca stated her opinion out loud, and it should really be his decision."

David agreed with her and said that it might not hurt him to take a year off to see where his future is going. "Working here full time and otherwise idly passing his time may be enough to convince him." He said that he wished he had gone to college while he was young. He has managed to take a few courses here and there that he felt would help him with his business.

Rebecca wasn't convinced that college was always the best thing for everyone. She told him so by saying that old adage, "Sometimes doing is better than schooling." And she told him she was better off professionally when she was nineteen than she is now. David noticed the ring on her right hand and lifted it closer to his eyes. He read BS PSYCH on the side of it. She told him it was something she needed to prove to herself, more than anything else. She explained to him that she hadn't ever finished high school and was told by a guidance counselor in junior high that she would never amount to anything other than a housewife.

"Are you serious?" David asked her.

"Completely." She told him.

"I'd like to say that that attitude was something from twenty years ago, but my academic advisor at the university pretty much said the same thing. He told me I had less than a twenty-five percent chance of graduating." She would like to think he was just quoting statistics to her, but she really doubted that he gave that speech to the young kids and men who came to see him.

David thought that the woman across from him was probably stronger than she ever gave herself credit for. She appeared to him, to be less convinced of herself and her abilities, then others around her were. The room was burning hot because of the fire. Still, he watched her as she wrapped herself up and closed herself off from the people around her, especially him. David wondered if she would ever need anyone but most of all if she would ever want him.

David got her another short glass of wine, and they talked about the storm and then he tried to steer the conversation toward her husband. But she wouldn't let him into that part of her world. She would talk about her plans after the storm had broken and the roads were clear. "I'm going to visit my mom and Carl's mom after that." Carl's mom had offered to put the kids in school up there to finish the school year, but she hadn't decided what she wanted to do yet. They discussed the farm and the calving season that was approaching. "If you can come down, you're welcome to stay with me so you can see at least one calf birthed." David said excitedly. Rebecca thought about that and told him she would like that, but she would have to let him know after she was up north, whether or not she could make it. He told her the invitation was open so all she had to do was show up at his doorstep anytime she liked. "Thank You" Rebecca replied. They heard the click of the kid's flashlight, and they both let out yawns of their own. Then David moved to the other couch, and they both fell asleep.

Carl woke in the night, stumbled out of bed and toward the bathroom. After relieving himself, he made his way to the kitchen to find something to drink. The clock on the wall said 1:00am. He felt disturbed by the dream he had just woken from. He found himself some juice and then went to the living room couch and sat down to drink it. He could recall Rebecca sitting some place dark, and there were animals all around her. He had felt warm, but uneasy upon wakening. He finished his drink and passed the strange dream off as having been induced by the wine he had had earlier. Rebecca had always teased him that he was a lightweight. He sensed his way back down the hall toward his room and noticed the light on in the bathroom. He hoped that he wasn't responsible for waking up Julie. He made his way back to bed and surprisingly fell straight back to sleep.

Carl awoke to the sound of metal clinking coming from the kitchen and figured Julie was already awake. It was still dark, and he saw that his alarm clock read 5:05am. He pulled the covers away and felt the cold air hit him hard. He reached for the khaki's he wore last night, and he pulled a tee shirt over his head. Last night the warmth of the fire was still strong in the apartment and he realized he had walked through the entire place with only his underwear on. He was glad he hadn't run into Julie in the dark.

He walked toward the kitchen and found Julie making some hot tea. "I hope I didn't wake you, I tried to be quiet." She told him.

"No, I typically only sleep around seven hours a night, on average."

She told him she was the same way and asked if he would like a cup of tea.

He told her. "Thank you." Then thought how Rebecca slept like a bear in winter. On weekends, he spent his mornings playing on his computer by himself or with Danny once he was up, Rebecca and the girls usually slept several more hours before the families day would begin.

Carl got the milk out when he heard the teapots whistle sound off.

"Would you like to take these into the living room?" Julie asked him.

Carl nodded, and they carried their cups in with them. He threw one of the paper logs on the grate and lit it.

Julie switched on the television, and they found the first morning news.

The majority of the storm was over, and the woman on the set was telling them the statistics of area averages for snowfall in each particular state. The storm had produced another four feet in some areas but up to six feet in parts of Maine. The meteorologist came on and explained the snow was expected to melt fairly quickly as he showed the viewing audience the warm air stream approaching from the Bahamas off the Atlantic Ocean. It was expected it reach the coast within the next few days. Then he explained how this could create a further problem. "If the snow melts too fast the East Coast would have to expect flash floods," the man said. Then he pointed out to them the Arctic Airflow coming down from the North. He told them, "If we are lucky then this will mix with the warm one coming this direction, if the warm one lowers in temperature as the arctic one gains in temperature, then the effects should be mild." He said that hopefully the snow would melt at a slower rate, then he explained that anyway about it, the people on the East Coast were looking at some flooding, but the rate of melting snow would determine how mild or drastic the water displacement would be. He explained, that the milder the better. That way the water would have the time necessary to work its way down the waterways to the ocean, with less flooding over riverbanks. He then forecasted the weather over the following few days for the rest of the country. He was finished, and the news switched over to the sports.

Julie noticed that Carl was uninterested in the sports, so she clicked off the television set. She finished her tea and let Carl know she was going to use the bathroom.

Carl opened the curtain to the glass door as he heard the water flowing from the shower pound against the tub. He heard the force subdue and assumed she must have stepped under it. Looking outside, he could see the light beginning to rise from behind them and come across the large mountain in the distance. Carl watched as the sun filled the sky around him and thought how unreal the weather in the east seemed to him here.

He could see something down on the ground outside, and tried to get a better look at it. He opened the door and noticed that to the side of the door stood a grill, and on the other side there was a table and chairs. These people thought of everything. Carl leaned over the banister to get a better look and saw bloody paw marks on the ground further away. He believed that the footprints were rather impressive in size from this distance.

He heard a noise inside and went back in. He didn't want Julie to find out about the cougar and go complaining to Paul. He wanted to get another look at it if he had the chance. Closing the door, he turned to see her standing there dressed already for work.

"That was quick." He told her.

"There isn't much decision involved in putting on a pant suit." Julie told him.

Carl didn't agree but said nothing. He looked at what she was wearing and supposed she was right since the only thing she had to choose was the color of the blouse she wore. Carl noticed that, today she had French braided her hair while it was still wet and had pinned it under. He excused himself to go grab a shower too and knew he needed to decide quicker today what he was going to wear. He grabbed the dark gray suit and the navy shirt with the gray tie then he headed for the bathroom.

Julie put on her shoes. She wouldn't usually dress for work three hours early. However, she needed to try and maintain more professionalism this morning, compared to yesterday. It was just easier to do, she thought, when she had a suit on.

She tried to see what Carl had been looking at outside. Peering through the window, she supposed it was the incredible sight of Mt Rainier. She returned to the kitchen and found herself some cereal and made a pot of coffee this time. As she sat at the table eating her bowl of cereal and drinking her coffee, Carl came in and slung his coat over a chair. She noticed he looked handsome in the suit and tie. He looked taller to her today, than he had yesterday and he was acting a bit more relaxed, as well. He made some toast and helped himself to some of the coffee. Then he joined her at the table.

Julie almost gagged on her food when she saw the three heaping spoonfuls of sugar Carl added to his coffee. "Matt should be here around Eight o'clock to play chess" he reminded her. She nodded to him with her mouth full and after swallowing she told him she wasn't one for chess, but she enjoyed playing backgammon. He informed her that he didn't know how to play that game. "I could teach you after breakfast if you're interested."

Carl carefully lifted the chessboard to expose the backgammon board underneath. Then Julie showed him how the layout of the board was to be set up and explained the rules of the game. "This set looks old, it's in perfect condition, but probably, turn of the century 1900." Julie told him.

"Why do you think that?" Carl asked.

"See these legs and look at the brass, but I think this is actually ivory." She held up one of her white backgammon pieces. Then she picked up one of Carl's black ones. "And I think these are onyx." She said as she stared at the chess set with its pieces covered in tiny jewels, sitting on the floor next to them.

"Wow, this thing, must be worth a small fortune." They both said at the same time.

"Do you think we should be using it?" Julie asked Carl.

"Carrie wouldn't put it here if she didn't want it to be used." He told her.

Besides he thought to himself, Rebecca didn't believe in things being looked at and not used. "What was the point in having nice things if you don't enjoy the use of them." He could hear her saying and said so to Julie. He thought Carrie would agree, and that is exactly why she put it here.

Julie beat Carl's butt without even trying. As they were putting the chessboard back into place, the doorbell rang. Julie went to answer it, and she returned with Matt at her side. "Good Morning" Matt said loudly and asked if he could get some coffee.

"Help yourself." Carl told him.

Matt returned with a bowl of cereal too. Julie asked Matt what he knew about the table. "All I know is that it was Dad's. Mom told me she had bought it at an auction house in New York as a wedding present for him." "Why do you ask?" Matt wanted to know.

"Julie just thought that it seemed very old." Carl told him.

"Knowing Mom, She probably paid a fortune for it too, just because it had Dad's initials on it." He laughed and told them, "She's more sentimental then practical, but that's one of the things people love about her." "Just wait, you'll see what I mean." He told them.

Carl and Matt played chess for a while, and then they left for work. As they walked into the building they ran into Paul, who asked Carl, if he had seen any more sightings of the cougar. "No." Carl told him. It wasn't exactly a lie, since he couldn't say he actually saw the animal. He didn't want him to have it removed, before he saw it again. "I haven't figured out what it means yet, either." Carl told him.

"I wouldn't worry about that. Like I told you already, you'll know when you need to." Paul smiled to Carl and then he spoke with Julie. Carl smiled and hoped he was right, but that didn't make him stop wondering.

They went to work. Julie and Paul met with Randy, and Carl assumed they filled him in about yesterday. Julie and Paul were gone for two hours and when she returned she was wearing a pair of jeans and hiking boots. He could see her gun strapped to her side when she removed her jacket. She was tired, and she told him she and Paul had followed the trail all the way out to a service road, but they found nothing to speak of.

Carl told her, "I noticed the trees were removed already, by the time we got here this morning."

"Paul is very efficient." Julie told him. "He must have somehow missed those trees because they were the only possible place for concealment, clear around the building." She explained to Carl. "I have a meeting with Randy in a couple of minutes. Do you think you can break away from what you're doing to join us."

He told her he could. "Give me a second to use the bathroom, if that's okay." Carl used the bathroom, and upon re-entering the hallway, he heard someone calling his name. "Carl, can you come and look at this for a minute." It was a man from their section walking toward him. He was trying to figure out if something he found were useful or not.

"Look at this. it is a note from a person named Ling Chu, sent to the General." He told Carl. It read: "My red haired son accepts the invitation to your child's party." The e-mail was from an address in New York City's Chinatown.

Carl couldn't believe their good fortune, "Harry right, keep this one quiet for a little while okay. It might be a big lead, but I need to check out something first before you announce this new information."

"Yes Sir, but this is the type of stuff you wanted me to look for, right?" the young kid asked him.

"It's exactly what I want you to look for. Your doing a great job. Keep it up." The kid beamed from ear to ear and told him he would.

Carl went to join the others already in Randy's office. He knocked on the door. Julie and Paul were in the office with Randy and he said to Carl. "What happened to you, you have too much coffee or not enough." Carl just smiled as Randy asked him what took so long in the John.

Carl explained to them what Harry had found and then he added, "What do we know about Harry." Then he added a note of caution. "If this is legitimate, Carl paused, don't you think we should wait until we have found another corroborating bit of evidence to support it."

Randy agreed with Carl, and he told them that he would look up Harry's file and check him out. He said he remembered their hiring the boy straight out of college, not long ago, so he felt fairly certain the boy was clean.

Julie told them all, her concerns about yesterday's incident. "I'm confused by the apparent lack of professionalism in the job that was done. I wonder if it isn't someone's way of telling us one of two things. Either they want to warn us that we are being watched, or they want to make actual contact with us."

Everyone thought about what she said.

Paul thought she might be right. It made no sense to him that they would smoke at all. Never mind, smoke a very strong smelling tobacco.

Randy felt that the cigar pile was possibly a message as to how long they had been watching them.

"Paul did you keep any of the cigars." Julie wanted to know. "I don't think it is necessary to test them or to research them to find out where they are from, she told them. Anyone can buy any type they wish to in our cities. But I did notice it was a very distinctive smell, and I want to smell it again in case someone tries to contact me that way. Then Julie added, "Whoever he is, he could have been waiting out there, for someone to make contact with him. But then, Why leave?" That confused her.

"Because he didn't want to be captured and locked up." Carl understood that intimately.

Randy told her he thought that she would definitely be their source of contact since the person saw her.

Paul said, "We know it is a man and judging from the size and depth of his shoeprints; I would say the guy is big. The shoe is probably a size thirteen and I would guess he weighs around 240 pounds, give or take a few."

"Right, said Julie, So I'll keep my eye open for a big guy."

"Everyone is a big guy compared to you!" Carl teased Julie.

"Maybe in body, but not in spirit." She eyed him in a playful manner.

"You're as ferocious as a big cat." Paul said to her.

"That's only because you're as gentle as a mouse." She smiled and told him,

"Yeah, yeah, and I'm a Grizzly, now get out of my office, so I can get some work done." Randy grumbled. He told them to all maintain the appearance that nothing has happened, but to keep their eyes open to any subtle change in behaviors. "If anyone caught wind of yesterday's events, then they are sure to be nervous." Randy informed them. "Send in Jason and Ed would you." He asked Paul on the way out. "Tell them I'm expecting an update on their projections." Randy figured, if anyone were listening; that they wouldn't suspect a thing. He wanted any spy under his command to be unprepared for the kill.

CHAPTER TWELVE

Rebecca could see a bright light penetrating her eyelids. She shaded her eyes with her forearm and rolled away from the light. She was groggy from sleep, and all she wanted to do was go back and be with Carl. It was no use; she wouldn't fall back asleep now that she could hear all the children thudding their heels on the hardwood floors above her. She had had that dream again. She was standing in a green forest; Her and Carl were hiking and they had stopped to look at the beautiful snow capped mountain in the distance. The dream always ended the same. She would be standing alone, as she would watch as a large cougar went running off into the forest. Rebecca thought the animal was beautiful, but it made her feel scared. She always felt sad and a little afraid when she woke up. Rebecca tried to open her eyes, but the sun was shining so brightly that it hurt. She slowly adjusted her vision and saw the boy's bedroom that surrounded her. They had been snowed in for almost a week now.

When she awoke the morning after the storm, the window in the great room had had snow half way up it. The men figured that the storm must have hit them harder than the rest of the state, probably because they were in the mountains. They decided that the snow must have been about ten feet. That first morning, Rebecca almost had a heart attack when she looked up and saw David and Daniel wearing the snowshoes and walking out toward the barns. Frank assured her they would be fine, but the animals would need food and milking. She had now spent a full week with the Henry's, and she wanted to try going with David to help feed the cattle. The snow had melted three feet in the last five days, and they thought that, by another five days, they would be at a safe height of about three to four feet of snowfall left.

They explained to the women; they could then take the snowmobiles to go check on Frank's animals and get supplies. Rebecca looked at her watch and noticed it was almost ten. She didn't like to sleep in late, in someone else's home, it felt rude to her. She got up out of Ryan's bed and dressed. She noticed her leg was much better now, but there was still a huge, nasty dried blood scab on her knee. She made her way to the upstairs bathroom to use the container of snow water to brush her teeth. She greeted the children as she went toward Jessica's vanity in the pink bathroom across the way. She looked in the mirror and decided every other day was all she could stand without washing her hair. She made plans to make the kids bathe too. Rebecca left the bathroom and turned to walk down the hallway toward the stairs. As she looked up she noticed David appear in the middle of his bedroom doorway.

He turned up his pointer finger and was crimping it in a motion for her to come to him. Rebecca saw that he was standing there partially naked and realized he had had the same idea. His hair was wet, and he smelled clean with soap. His face was thick with overgrown stubble. "I can't decide if I should grow this out or shave it off." He said as he rubbed at his chin and jawbone.

"I think a little stubble is sexy, but a full grown beard just doesn't do it for me." Rebecca told him.

He leaned in closer to her and said, "Is there something about me that does do it for you."

She was thinking the whole package worked, but she wouldn't let him know that. Rebecca could feel David's energy hit her as he put his large muscled hand to the small of her back and pulled her slightly closer. Rebecca felt a surge of lust, grip her like a vice in her abdomen and she quickly pushed him away. "Give me a break, David." She told him as she went to the stairs to make her escape.

David watched her rush for the stairs. He had felt her body quiver when he touched her. "I'll keep your advice in mind." He yelled to her. He smiled as he recognized her response as an unmistakable attraction toward him. He knew he at least had a chance.

Rebecca watched David as he entered the kitchen; he had shaven the thick growth off, and he looked handsomely clean. She could see the shadow left behind where the dark hair follicles were under his skin. She thought to herself that this clean shave of his was much sexier than the heavy growth covering his face before. He came over to her and said softly into her ear, "By this time tomorrow, he rubbed his jaw; I should be a bit sexier." Then he got himself some coffee and went to talk with Daniel.

"Would you stop torturing that girl." Daniel whispered to his friend.

"What do you mean?" David wanted to know.

Daniel left the room and David followed him wanting to know what he had meant by that remark. "David. Come on. Your setting yourself up for failure. She isn't free to love you back."

David looked at his friend and felt like decking him. "Are you telling me there is no way she could love a man like me." David asked him.

"No, David. I'm telling you, she isn't able to love you or anyone for that matter." Daniel continued. "Have you forgotten so soon, how long your pain lasted after your break up."

David said nothing.

"I just don't want to watch you hurt all over again." David's friend told him.

"Daniel, don't worry about me. This isn't the same. There isn't anything for me to lose, because I don't own it to begin with."

Daniel looked at his friend and knew he hadn't listened to a word he said, but he was going to say it anyway. "David if you go into a store and you break something, you have to buy it, right?"

David nodded, "What's your point."

"You bought it, but you never really owned it did you. You spent hours in the glass store picking the perfect one. But on your way to the register, somehow it breaks. That is a real loss, of time and money or worse if it cut you on its way to the floor." Daniel looked at the stubborn expression on David's face and decided to throw in the towel, his attempt to get through to his friend was useless. Frustrated, Daniel said. "I just want you to treat your heart more carefully then you treat your dishes." Then he went back into the kitchen with the others.

David had watched his friend talk and noticed the same pained expression on his friend's face as he had seen before, while Daniel had watched him struggle through his failed marriage. He knew his friend loved him and had suffered as much as he had during that difficult time. David stared at the fire in the den. He didn't want to put Daniel or any of his family through that kind of agony again, anymore than he wished to experience it himself.

He looked up and saw Rebecca standing there. He knew he had to give himself the chance to experience love with this woman. He smiled at her and thought, Even if I can't keep it, I want to experience the joy of it, if only for a short while.

She smiled up at him and asked if she would be able to help him with the cattle today. She insisted her leg was much better. David stared into her eyes and thought determinedly; he was willing to risk the pain. But he was equally determined that if given the invitation he would love her to his fullest while he was able.

David looked at her with his ocean blue eyes, and just stared. She knew he would tell her No, She couldn't go with him. She also knew he was only being protective because of the tree incident, but she had been in this house for five days and really wanted to go outside. She also wanted to see his animals and now she knew that his silence told her his answer. He watched her look down to the floor and then she slid her hair behind her ear as she returned her gaze back up toward him.

That gaze made him want to explode, she was so seductive, and he didn't think she was even trying to be. All she had to do, was look at him, and he'd betray all his better judgments to make her smile at him. "If I let you come you'll have to let me carry you." He stopped her, as she was about to open her mouth in protest. "I have to bring one of the guys, there is too many animals for only you and me. If you already knew how to do the grain mixtures that would be another story."

Rebecca gave in and said, "Okay." She was surprised. She had been prepared to fight for her right to simply go with him a minute earlier. She wasn't stupid enough to fight with him and make his answer change to No, after she had already gotten a Yes from him. She felt almost like a child, who had won an argument with their parent, but not the war.

David was shocked that she hadn't protested further. But he had to admit he was relieved because he wasn't up for an argument with her right now. David popped his head into the loft and found Tommy and Rachel, where they had been glued for the past five days, curled up together reading books. They only took short breathers to use the bathroom and eat. He wished he and Rebecca could have gotten along as companionably as these two had. Of course, he knew his intentions weren't as innocent as Tommy's. They both looked up at David as he leaned into the room. He noticed that Rachel's hair was in wisps falling lightly around her face, and he noticed she was a really pretty girl. After five-days together, they had gone from passing the book to each other, to having Rachel lean against Tommy as they shared it, taking turns reading. He saw Tommy's arms around her as he held the book reading aloud to her. He knew there was a sexual element to it, but it seemed harmless enough. They were both staring at him waiting for him to say something.

"What's up, David." Tommy asked.

David was surprised by their lack of embarrassment to his seeing them so intimately together. Neither of them felt the need to break their embrace.

They looked at him expectantly, "Tommy. I was hoping you could help me with the feeding."

"Can Rachel come with us." The boy asked.

She'll have to ask Rebecca." David told them. "She's coming too," he added.

"Oh, then she'll let me." Rachel said to Tommy.

They all headed down the stairs. "Are you guys almost done with those two books?" David asked them.

They told him, "Yes." with a slight regret in their voices.

"I was just wondering because I think I might have some of his other books in the den." The kids perked up and went to the den to look.

David met Rebecca in the kitchen and asked if she were ready to leave.

Everyone was confused as to where they were off to.

"I told Rebecca she could help feed the cattle since her leg was feeling better."

Daniel went to get up and grab his coat.

"That's okay, David told him, I asked Tommy to help. Take a break, Daniel, Tommy's been on his duff for days."

The kids came into the kitchen carrying three more books. "Thanks David." They said in unison. Rachel asked if she could go with them and Rebecca looked at David. He gave her a squinted expression and a little nod. Rebecca said it was fine, and Tommy ran the books upstairs as they all bundled up in their coats and then they were off.

The rest of them stood watching from the kitchen window as David carried Rebecca in his arms and Tommy had Rachel on his shoulders. "They are like two little infatuated boys, one who doesn't know any better and one who should." Daniel let out in exasperation, as he shook his head in disgust.

Frank sighed, "There's no point in your getting upset over something you can't control, Son, trust me, people have to make their own choices in life."

"I seem to remember a young man who once slept on my doorstep for three days before I took him back." Pam told her husband.

Everyone laughed as Daniel turned a shade of pink, "That's different, I was a Tommy. I didn't know any better." He demanded.

Anne told him, "No one in love acts rationally, Daniel."

Pam asked her husband, "Are you telling me your love was some stupid impulse."

"No." he told her.

"Well, then give your friends enough room to be at least as stupid as you say you were." She told Daniel.

"Come on. Let's go play a game." Frank told the men.

Kevin and Mark teased Daniel. "Man, you actually slept on her doorstep for three nights."

Frank said. "More like camped out there for 72 hours straight. Pam finally took pity on him and took him back."

The two guys laughed at their friend. "No wonder she has him on strings." Mark said to Kevin.

"All right old man; Daniel said to Frank. "This time I'm going to beat you."

Rebecca was so happy to smell the brisk fresh scent of winter air mixed with the smoke from the chimneys. She could feel the cold air burn a little as she breathed it into her lungs. She shaded her eyes from the light and tried to look up into the sky. The sun was beating down rather strong, and it felt interesting to her to feel the chill breezes mixed with the heat from the sun.

"Your cheeks are getting a bit red." He told her.

Rebecca put her arms around David's neck and turned her face inward and against his upper chest, so she wouldn't end up with a painful windburn. She caught the scent of him and couldn't help breathing in a little deeper than usual. He smelled so good she could barely resist the temptation to nuzzle her face up against his neck. She let out a deep sigh and David could feel her satisfaction at being in his arms. He only wished she would recognize that for herself. He whispered to Rebecca. She couldn't hear what he said, so she leaned in closer.

"I only wanted to feel you come closer." He admitted. "But, now I want to warn you that I'm about to yell to Tommy."

Rebecca braced herself.

"Tommy, you be careful with Rachel around those animals and in the snow."

"Where are they going?" Rebecca asked him.

"They're going to start at the other end." He told her not to worry, "Tommy will be careful. I just thought a warning might ground him a little."

They were now at the barn. He helped her onto the windowsill and opened it. David climbed in and then he reached up to help her inside. Rebecca swung her legs inside and then realized how high this window was. David had to wrap his arms around her legs and hold on tight in order for her not to drop straight down to the floor. She felt him slowly slide his arms up to her hips and then he let her body slide down against his own on its way to the floor. When her eyes met his he stopped her in midair and he concentrated as he looked into her eyes. He saw it. For just a split second, before it changed over to fear. For the first few seconds, he saw in her the same raw hunger that he felt for her.

He let her slide to the ground, and the next thing she knew he had hung up his coat and was now busy unzipping hers. He helped her to take it off and hung it next to his own coat. "Where were you just then?" David asked Rebecca.

"I don't know, I think I lost some time. My head feels hazy."

He smiled at her and took her hand and twined their fingers together as he led her out of the room.

He brought her out into the barn and showed her how they took care of the animals. She noticed that the layer of straw on the ground was compressed and deep. She could smell the slightly rank odor of stale air mixed with the smell of animals, hay and a little fresh manure. She asked about the thick straw. He explained that they let the layers build up in the winter to keep in the warmth and to reduce the strain of the concrete on the animal's legs.

They had a generator running so they could get cold water pumped from the well. David mixed together large bags of feed. She saw that most of it was corn, and there was some soybean, barley and something else that she didn't see the label for. He added some other ingredients and then told her the buckets behind her measured in different weights. There were stacks of them in the corner of the room they had come from, and he told her to get four red ones. He mixed all the grain in a cart that was pulled by a small tractor, and he started it up. She heard a loud ruckus as all the animals went running up against the wood of the stalls. They're a little excitable because their schedule is off. But they understand the tractor means dinner is coming.

He showed her what to do. She filled pails with the grain and then every once in a while David would move the tractor forward. He stopped at one of his heifers and had her come over and touch her. What kind of breed is she, Rebecca knew she wouldn't understand the difference but she wanted to know anyway. The beef cattle are all Red Angus, but our dairy cows are Holsteins. She rubbed the side of the animal's neck. And then they moved on to finish feeding the rest of them before the others got restless. David went down to the other end of the barn and had her wait where she was. The animals had been cooped up in the barn, and he didn't want to risk Rebecca being frightened by a possible aggressive bull. David gave them water and fed them. Then he and Rebecca moved on to the other building and started the routine over again there.

When they met up with Tommy and Rachel, they found them playing with the dogs in one of the dairy buildings. One of the female dogs had given birth to a litter of puppies, and Tommy was giving the mother a whole lot of praise and special food for nursing dogs. The other dogs were disinterested and were eating at the other side of the room. There were eight puppies and Rachel wanted to know if they should bring them into the house. Tommy told her they would be fine where they were. "All they need is their mommy here, he told her patting the collie's head, She'll take care of them." David asked if everything were finished up in here. Tommy nodded and looked at his watch, "Yeah, until the evening milking."

"Do me a favor, Let Daniel know we're going over to check on the horses now, okay." He said. "Oh, and Tommy be careful on your way back over to the house, the snow is still very deep."

They smiled and waved to David and Rebecca as Rachel climbed back up onto his shoulders. "Bye." They called out.

Rebecca rubbed the collie's head and asked David how far it was to get to where they were going. "It is two miles from my house to the stables and then it is a little further to get to Daniel and Pam's house beyond that.

"Can you carry me that far?" She sounded a little worried.

"Rebecca that's not that far of a distance, it isn't like I'm running a marathon while carrying you."

"Maybe I should just climb on your back, piggy back style instead."

"That won't hurt your knee?" He was concerned.

She explained that she thought it would be fine. Then she climbed up on his back, and they took off. He carried her about half way, but the thick coats were making it difficult for him to hold her up without really putting all the leverage at her knees. David found a fallen tree and he put her down on it, and they took a break.

"I'm heavier then you thought I was, aren't I?" She asked as she wondered if they should turn back.

"Rebecca, Is it okay if I take a break and just want to sit for a moment?" David asked her. "We aren't in any rush are we? Do you have a hot date, I don't know about?" He teased.

"As a matter of fact I do." She told him. David knew she was giving him a hard time.

"Oh, Yeah, who with?"

"Kevin." She smugly told him.

David didn't think she was being funny.

"Apparently word got out that I'm a woman with a sorted past."

She egged him on.

"Is this the famous past you warned me of in the hay loft." David played along.

"No, this is a different one altogether."

He looked at her and waited.

"I have a history for playing spades." She laughed as she tried to say that with a straight face.

David reached over to Rebecca unzipped her coat and pulled her onto his lap. Then he unzipped his own and pulled her closer to him, cupping his hands under her jean covered buttocks, he leaned forward as if he were about to kiss her. He looked into her dark eyes, and when his mouth was an inch from hers he said. "Very funny." In a deep, throaty voice. Then he grabbed her butt in a jolting effort to get to his feet, and they continued on their way to the stables.

Rebecca was lost in another daze for about thirty seconds and then she felt a jolt as David took a step. She reached her arms around his neck and mumbled, "What are you doing to me?"

"I'm carrying you." David told her.

"But, she whispered, that wasn't what I meant."

David knew that wasn't what she meant either. He was enjoying his affect on her. He knew if she ever decided to accept a relationship with him; that he would miss seeing her float like this. He figured this reaction in her was being induced by her intense emotional indecision. Once she chose to kiss him, he assumed her dazes would end. He enjoyed giving her those emotional highs; but the consequences were putting him in physical turmoil. He wasn't sure how much more of it he could handle. But he sure as hell was enjoying himself as he flirted with her, and disaster.

Rebecca's heart was pounding so hard she knew he could feel it. She could feel his warmth against her as she put her body against his under their opened jackets. He was burning hot. She nuzzled her face against his neck as she took in the warm deep scent of his manliness. Now she could smell that lightly grainy scent on him again. She wanted him so badly it hurt. Rebecca was so afraid that her womanly instincts were in complete automatic drive that she didn't trust herself to make rational decisions.

The heat of her was burning him. She felt so hot against him. As she rubbed her body against him, he was certain she was beyond all self-control, and he felt responsible for making that happen. He wanted to enjoy it and yet something tugged at him saying if she did this she would be even further away from him emotionally afterward. He wanted her love and affection not just her lust. He could see the stables, and he focused on that so he wouldn't get caught up in Rebecca. "Sweetheart." David said. "We're there."

Rebecca looked up at David as she felt the cold air hit her. He pulled the door open and lowered her to the floor inside. When David thumped down to the ground next to her, she couldn't help feeling self-conscious. She felt no shame for her attraction and desire to this strong, incredibly masculine man. She was only confused about how to feel about her own needs and what it would mean to both of them.

David came over to her. She looked away trying to stall as she waited for the right words to come to her. She looked up into David's eyes and saw a gentleness and comfort she hadn't expected. Rebecca realized she didn't need any words of explanation.

"Come see the horses." David said as he took her hand again and led her toward a stall. "Currently, we have twenty-seven horses on the premises." David explained that the first ten he showed to her were all boarders. Then he showed Rebecca Pam's horses. She had seven, two of them were Arabian; One was black, and the other was gray. David told her the solid black wasn't very common. There were also two American Saddlebred horses that were both dark chestnut in color. Next Rebecca was standing in front of two large horses "These are Throughbred." David told her. Rebecca reached in and stroked the muzzle of one of the Thoroughbred and then moved on down to the next stall. Inside she saw a small perky looking horse. She told the thing hello and rubbed the bridge of its muzzle. "I recognize you." Rebecca told her. David said that she was an American walking pony. "She used to belong to Stacy, but now she is Kim's." David pointed over to one of the Saddlebreds and told her the lighter one of the two was now Stacy's horse. She asked which one Cory rode. David walked further down and stopped at a stall with a medium brown horse in it. "He likes to ride "Acorn" here." He told her as he rubbed the horse. "She is Jessica's Missouri Fox Trotter and that chestnut one there is Ryan's." He explained to her that he bought them when he had first settled here. The kids were small, and they were supposed to be good horses for kids to learn on because they are gentle and eager to please.

He walked over to some other beautiful brown horses and met them with greeting rubs. "These are mine. They are Quarter Horses, they're good workers. They were traditionally used for cattle herding. Today they are more mixed breed then long ago, but they are strong and happy to work the pastures. Their pretty good with the steep terrain." Rebecca went over and touched the animals. Then she turned around at the third quarter horse's stall and saw the most beautiful black-reddish hued horse, the eyes grabbed hold of hers, and she felt like it was looking straight through her. Rebecca walked over to him and climbed up on the edge of the stable door so she could reach him better. The horse reared up and let out a loud snort at her.

David was still busy socializing with his quarter horses, when he heard the commotion as the horse got mad at Rebecca. "Rebecca get down! That one doesn't like strangers." By the time he finished that statement he was floored to hear her admonishing the animal.

"You be nice." She raised her voice to the aggressive horse. The animal looked at her and in a soft tone she spoke to it. "I was only trying to touch you, you silly thing."

David watched as the horse prick his ears in alert attention and took a step toward Rebecca.

"That's it, come here." She said even softer than the last time. She put her hand out to the animal and left it there without moving. She felt a loud and winded snort that the animal made against her hand as he got a scent and feel for Rebecca. The horse came straight up to Rebecca, and she made sure not to flinch even a little as he snorted her face and hair. Then she slowly turned her hand over and gently placed it against the horse's strong muscled neck. She left her hand solid and still against the horse until she was sure he had accepted her touch and then she made long strokes along his neck.

David stood amazed as Rebecca charmed his mustang. Then he stood there and watched as she said something even softer to the strong animal. The horse leaned into her and nuzzled his muzzle against the side of her face.

A few minutes later, Rebecca told the animal, "I have to go now, but I'll come and visit you again, okay." As she started to slowly, edge away from the large animal, he snorted another scent of her and then backed away.

When she climbed down and turned around, she found David standing there staring at her. "Wow, isn't he beautiful, David." She said to him.

"Yes he is. He's also very dangerous."

She was puzzled. "Why should he be more dangerous than any of the others?"

"Because he's a wild Mustang."

She did notice it seemed a bit edgier and skittish than the others. However, one look into his eyes was enough for her to know he was gentle.

"I got him from an adoption program out west." He told her.

He had had him for nine months and had bred him with one of his quarter horses. They expected the mare to foal soon. David gave all the horses water. She helped him to measure out and fill the horses feed bags.

When they were finished David climbed up to the hayloft and called for her to follow him. When she had reached the top of the ladder, she saw that David had opened the loft door. Once she was up there, he pointed out Daniel's house to her. They weren't very far away from the house. The stables were maybe 300 yards from the back porch. There was a thick line of trees separating the house from the barn. Rebecca could make out an older barn through the trees in the distance and noticed several gaps in the tree line. She could imagine a very worn path linking all the buildings one to another. But she also noticed that to the right of the stables there was a long strip of clearing through the trees. It ran fifty yards to the right of their house. She assumed that it was a dirt or gravel road leading out to the paved road.

"What are you thinking?" David asked her as he pulled the huge door shut again and latched it.

"I was looking at how all the buildings were arranged."

"So what do you think." He asked her. What he really wanted to know was whether or not she thought she could be happy living here with him.

"I don't know, what is there for me to think when I know nothing about farms."

David was sitting on a bale of hay, and he tapped on the empty spot next to him. She smiled at him but didn't move from where she was. "What's the matter." He asked her.

"Nothing is the matter." Rebecca told him.

"Why are all your answers vague." He said in a slightly angered voice.

She held on to the rafter by her head for strength. "I didn't realize I was being vague."

"Damn it, Rebecca there you go again. What kind of answer is that." He continued. "I wasn't asking you for a professional critique of my farm and why are you way over there, are you afraid of me or something."

Rebecca thought about what to say. She knew her answer better not be a simple "Yeah, something like that."

Her silence was killing him. He watched as she walked toward him but sat on the hay strewn floor instead, with plenty of room between them.

"David, part of me is a little afraid of you. When I'm close to you, I feel weak. And that scares me."

He looked at her as she glanced away and then she looked back at him. He saw her again, the sad girl that he had met on the first night in his parent's home. He was so happy to see her, the vulnerable girl who was open and honest. The girl who described for him her childhood and who could say that she wasn't able or comfortable telling him more. David moved to the floor to be with her. "I'm sorry I raised my voice to you, I was just wondering where the girl I met a week ago had gone." "I looked at Tommy and Rachael today, and my heart broke because I want to be that comfortable with you."

Rebecca cut in. "They're just kids, their lives are uncomplicated."

David frowned, "I know, but why can't we be able to comfort each other like we had in the barn that first night. It was completely innocent, but it felt so wonderful." He told her. "As soon as we got to my house something changed and everyday I've watched you as the space between us has become further apart."

"Carl, you don't- " Rebecca stopped herself. "I mean David, I'm so sorry." She put her hands to her head to gather her wits. "That is why, I need to keep my space from you." "I understand that you're ready to move on with your life, but I'm not." Rebecca continued. "I promised my life to a man fourteen years ago, and I'm not convinced yet that I have to accept that it is over."

"Rebecca, I'm not asking you to forget Carl or to stop loving him. I'm also not asking you to make any choices. I know you don't have enough information to decide anything. All I ask is, to know if you think you could ever have room in your heart for me too."

"I feel confused. I don't think I can answer that."

"It's not a difficult question Rebecca, all I'm asking you is; do you like me and are you attracted to me. Does my home, farm and family make you happy." "If I have the answers to those questions then I can wait for you to figure out the rest."

Rebecca looked at the dark haired, blue eyed man dressed in cowboy boots and denim jeans, clothes that she thought only he could make look so sexy and told him the truth as scary as that was for her. She took in a deep breath and steadied her voice, "I think you are a wonderful, charming and handsome man, David. Your eyes and your touch make me ache, and your smell and heat drive me crazy from your intense sexuality. You make me fall half unconscious. I couldn't image a better life then living it here with you, your family and your animals. But, she looked at her wedding rings, but.

"No, but- Please. I don't want to hear the rest. I understand." "Thank you." He stroked her cheek. "Everything you just told me is all I needed to hear, Rebecca. Knowing that, I could enjoy loving you for only one hour and be happy for a lifetime without you. Because I'll know, there could have been a lifetime with you."

David watched as tears ran down her cheeks. He reached over to her and cradled her in his arms like a child. He whispered in her ear. "Please let me love you, he felt her panic in his arms, Not sex, he said softly, I said love you."

She looked up at him and saw love in his eyes instead of passion. Rebecca reached up and put her arms around his neck as he ran his strong hands through her hair. David picked her up and laid her down in the straw. Rebecca spent the afternoon in David's embrace as they shared innocent caresses and memories of bygone years.

CHAPTER THIRTEEN

Julie tried to be extra careful as she pulled out the coffee can from the cabinet and closed the door. She awoke earlier than usual this morning and was trying her best to be quiet so she wouldn't wake Carl. She felt restless. She knew she wanted to do something other than work. She had been working for two weeks straight, and she was a little bored right now. After the cigar man incident, the excitement of this job had become limited to mentally documenting Carl's little quirks. Needless to say, the adrenaline had dropped off dramatically, she thought, at least at work anyway. She put in the coffee grounds and flipped the switch. Listening to the coffee maker percolate. She reached over to the employee itinerary for this weekend. They had listed, Friday, March 16th Dinner and Dancing. "I doubt I could convince Carl to do that." Julie told herself. She read that tomorrow they were going to have something called "Spring Anticipation." It was scheduled for the banquet hall in the main building. "That sounds intriguing, she thought to herself, what does it mean?"

She grabbed a cup of coffee and went to the glass door. Pushing aside the curtain it was too dark outside to see, but she knew there was still snow on the ground. Sitting down on the couch she noticed the monthly flyer that was left under everyone's doors. In it was a listing for movies that were showing in the theater. She recognized the names of a few of them. One was an earthquake story. One was an international spy movie. She could do without that one, she told herself. Two were comedy/romances and the last two she didn't recognize. She looked up the dates and times. She saw that they only played at 7:00pm and 9:00pm, except for the children's matinee on Saturdays. Last week she had learned of a dining hall on the other side of the facility. Julie was told that the place was only open Wednesdays through Saturdays, but it was supposed to be nice and the food good. Julie wondered if she could convince Carl to take her there and then to a movie afterward.

She heard a stirring down the hall.

"You're up early." Carl said as he entered the room.

He went to the coffeepot and got a cupful. She watched from the couch as he completed his script for coffee preparation. Pour the coffee, get milk from the refrigerator, pour a third of the cup with milk, put milk back, get the sugar bowl and add two heaped spoonfuls into the cup. Stir and sip, then add another heaped spoonful, retest, close lid and put the bowl away. She smiled, knowing he would drink down the coffee and then twenty minutes later do it all over again. She shook her head, as she wondered if Carl knew that it was a table spoon, that he was using.

Though she didn't know him well, she felt they had developed a familiar routine, which made her feel she'd known him for years.

"You up for a game." He asked her. This time he was determined he was going to beat her. Carl never realized; there was this much strategy involved in backgammon. It may not have the complicated movement that chess pieces had, but he found it very enjoyable to play. He finished his cup and went and got another. A half-hour later Julie had stomped his butt again, but at least it was a gentler stomping then the plunder he experienced more than a week ago.

"You're getting better." She told Carl. "I'm going to get ready for work."

Carl picked up the flyer Julie was looking at earlier. A schedule of movies, he looked at the titles. He went over to the glass door and looked for the cougar. He hadn't seen it again since the night he felt it staring at him. Carl wondered if it had moved on to another territory. Maybe there wasn't enough food in this area. He hadn't seen any deer since the day it killed and dragged off the small one. Carl stepped outside. He noticed that the footprints weren't visible anymore. The snow had melted quite a bit, and he thought if they were lucky maybe this would be the end of any snow for the season.

Carl stepped back inside. He looked at the pictures of his family and felt certain that if they weren't there to remind him, he would have sworn that part of his life had been only a dream. Carl looked at Rebecca and was surprised by the contrast between her and Julie. The last two weeks had felt like two months to him. Work had become so draining; that a single day could feel like a week. He thought that he could use a short escape from it. Picking up the list of movies again, he contemplated which one he and Julie, might both enjoy seeing. He recognized that somewhere along the way the words, He and Julie had become synonymous. He was beginning to find her presence a comfort, like a pair of warm fuzzy slippers that one wears to avoid the cold chill of the tile floor. He realized he had found a comfortable place somewhere inside of himself to become friends with her and was surprised it had come so easily for him under these circumstances.

Julie came into the room dressed in a light gray suit with a pale pink blouse. Carl was struck by how beautiful she looked this morning. She struggled slightly as she balanced her jacket on her arm, and put small, pink pearl earrings in her lobes. He watched as Julie turned and walked toward the kitchen. She asked him something. "Huh." He responded. All he had been aware of was the view he had of her in that tapered skirt. Carl's heart started to thud against the inside of his chest as he allowed his eyes to follow the lines all the way down. He noticed that her legs looked longer than normal because of the gray pumps that she was wearing.

Julie poured herself another cup of coffee and turned to face him.

Carl quickly lifted his gaze upward, but blushed, when he realized he had been caught. He felt like a twelve–year old caught sneaking a first peak at his father's girly magazines.

"Do you think it's too much for work." She asked Carl.

"No, it looks nice and when the jacket is on it will look very appropriate." He thought, once she covers that incredible little behind of hers.

"Are you sure?"

"Trust me, Carl told her. It's perfect." He leaned toward her ear, "Just be sure to leave the jacket on or not one single man will get any work done." He took in her rosy scent and allowed himself to stare a little too intently at her figure.

She blushed. "I wasn't sure if the silver gray and pastel pink weren't maybe too soon." Was he deaf. "Carl, I was asking if you thought that it was too soon to wear spring colors."

"I wouldn't know, he said, but I think it looks nice." Carl couldn't peel his eyes away from her legs. "Besides, I don't think that any of the guys at work would qualify as the fashion police."

She smiled and thought he was probably right. Passing him the employee itinerary. She asked, "What do you think this means."

Carl read, "Spring Anticipation." "I don't have a clue, but Matt probably will."

Julie felt pretty and cheerful in her spring outfit, not to mention a bit sexy too. She hoped that the event, whatever it was, would be something fun. "Do you know that is the first nice thing you've said to me." Julie told Carl. "Thank you." "I'll set up the board while you get ready." She told him. She couldn't resist exaggerating the swinging of her butt as she walked past Carl. She was pleased, when she caught a corner glimpse of his locked gaze on her.

Carl drank down the last of his cold coffee and went to shower knowing that today, he would take that cold too. Carl felt bad. He realized she was right. He hadn't been very nice to her. He had been civil, but not exactly nice. "I was wondering if you wanted to go to a movie tonight? Carl asked Julie when he came back dressed for work.

She saw he had put on light colors too. A light tan suit with a cream shirt and a yellow designed tie. Julie complimented him and thanked him for his choice of colors. "Yes, I'd really like to go see a movie,." She asked." Would you mind if we went to that dining hall too."

Carl's thoughts darted through his mind. "You sure you don't want to eat at home." Carl asked. This was starting to feel a little too much like a date for him. Carl looked at the disappointment in her face. "Alright, I'll go with you to the dining hall."

"If you don't like it there, we won't have to go again." Julie said excitedly.

They started their game and were caught by surprise, when the doorbell rang. "It's a little early for Matt." Carl looked and saw it was only 7:00am. He answered the door to find that it was Matt, an hour earlier than normal. "What's up?" Carl asked him.

"I was hoping to get our game in a little earlier today, because Mom just called. Randy has volunteered my services for the day to help her prepare for tomorrow's party."

"What kind of party?" Julie asked.

"It's the annual spring formal, Mom recruits people to help every year, but I'm usually, spared from the agony, off busy working." The boy told them in exasperation, "But Randy gave in to her this year."

"Carl, do you think we could help, it sounds fun." Julie asked him.

"I doubt if Randy would consider party decorating as mission essential." He teased her.

"You could never tell with Randy. If it were essential to Carrie, it might be to him too." She told him.

She was seriously contemplating this, What happened to that professional bodyguard he was assigned to, two weeks ago. "But- But Randy said I didn't have to go to any of the planned employee events, if I didn't want to." Carl winced as he finished saying that. He knew he sounded about five years old. "But damn it, I hate these things." He said out loud.

Matt told them that it doesn't matter if you don't go to the informal events, but no one misses the formal ones. "Not unless you're in surgery or having a baby." He said. "You'll have a good time. Mom never plans an outright typical and boring formal. You have to come." He told the thirty-five year old man pouting like a child.

"This means we'll have to go shopping somewhere." Carl cringed.

Julie's face lit up as she realized she had won, not on her own merit, but she won nonetheless. She was going to have a weekend of excitement instead of television.

Carl and Matt played their game of chess as Julie went to her closet to look through what she had brought with her. She always packed at least one formal dress, but she realized it was a winter black and completely inappropriate for an occasion titled "Spring Anticipation." She called Randy and asked if she would be allowed to take Carl off the compound, so they could get clothing appropriate for tomorrows party.

"Carl's agreed to go with you?" His voice was one of an incredulous tone.

"Why wouldn't he?" She asked the man.

"Julie has Carl talked to you at all about his life and family." Randy questioned the twenty-nine-year-old woman on the phone, who sounded like an excited teenager preparing to go to prom.

"No, we haven't talked about anything accept work, mainly."

Randy shook his head, "You have my permission to take him as far as the Outer Springs Mall, but don't be gone too long, okay."

"Alright, thanks." She hung up the phone and went to the small box on her dresser. Opening the lid, a tune chimed slowly as she picked out some rings that looked to her the most like a wedding set. She placed it on her left hand, feeling like a little girl preparing to convince the neighbor boy to play house. Except she was doing so with someone else's husband. She knew she should feel bad about that, but she didn't. As far as all this was from the real thing, it was still the closest she's come, and she was determined to try it on for size.

Julie returned to the living room and announced, "I've arranged for us to go to the local mall." Carl didn't look very pleased with the idea, but she wasn't going to let him spoil her time. "Matt, Do you have a car we could borrow."

"Sure, it's a blue compact parked in the main entrance. Just ask Mike to point it out to you." He handed her the keys.

They rode down with Matt in his little white cart to the main building. Carrie was with a group of women and she immediately put Matt to work on a high ladder in the great room. He was hanging a huge camouflage net with twinkle lights strung through it to look like stars. They found Mike, who agreed to take them to the car and let them out of the locked gates. "When you want to come back in, just speak to the Main building's office, through this intercom and someone will get me, so I can unlock the gate." He cringed. "It will probably take a few minute though, because Mrs. Taylor will definitely have me up on a ladder hanging something or other. I just hope I don't end up in a cast like I did at Christmas. It wasn't any fun falling when hanging bulbs on that thirty-foot high tree. She had some of the grounds crew cut it down for her out in the forest." He told Carl.

It was no laughing matter, but they couldn't help laughing anyway, once the man started laughing himself. They both told him to be careful. Then they set off for the mall.

"Where are we headed?" Carl was getting restless sitting in the passenger seat. He hated not knowing the route and how long it took to get there. He pushed the radio's buttons, but found nothing, so shut it off.

"The mall is a bit far away, you'll just have to sit back and relax." She teased and then regretted it, "I'm sorry, After everything you've been through I don't blame you for being anxious and restless."

"What do you mean?"

"Well, after being contained for six months and then being thrown here and with me."

Carl said. "You're not so bad."

"Then why have you not told me anything about yourself, I mean you've asked about me, but avoid any talk about your own life."

"I've enjoyed learning about you." He gave her a rundown of what he remembered, youngest of three children, grew up in California. Graduated from UCLA with a major in business. Never been married. Met a guy, who introduced you to this lucrative, protection business. Have traveled to forty countries. You vacation every year, for a week of skiing in the Swiss Alps, and spend another week on the shore in the Riviera. You are a beautiful woman, surrounded by rich men, who no doubt, lavish you with gifts.

"I get my share." She told him.

"It sounds as if your life couldn't be any better." Carl replied.

Julie realized. He had yet again, managed to avoid talking about himself. They needed to work on that. Except for one thing, the fact that she was alone. Julie had thought that her life was ideal. That was until she heard him describe it to her. As he did, she could list at least two downs for every one of the ups he had just equated to her life. Now, she wasn't so sure it was as good, as she had originally believed.

"We've been driving for an hour, Julie, how much further is it."

"We'll be there in a couple of minutes." She said. Julie watched Carl. He was getting more agitated, the closer they got to the mall. "Carl, are you okay?" She placed her hand on his twitching leg.

He reached for her hand and held it. "These party things aren't for me."

"Is anything else bothering you?" She gently probed for the problem.

Carl looked out the window. "She always picked out my clothing for me."

Julie filled in the name Rebecca for herself. "I can help you, I think we should get you a standard black tuxedo. What do you think?"

"That's fine with me, what ever gets us in the store and back out again quickly, is all I want." He told her. She tried to pull her hand away, Carl held on even tighter. Carl looked at Julie's face and noticed a sad strain across it. "I'm sorry, Julie. Thank You, I would really appreciate your help."

They were to the mall within another ten minutes. Then it took them less than thirty minutes to pick out a tux for Carl and have it fitted. Julie knew exactly which one to choose, and it had turned out to be a painless experience since she dealt with the salesman for him, as well. The man at the store told them to come back in an hour and his wife would be done altering it for him. They thanked him and moved on to dress shops for Julie. They planned on getting shoes last and were going into a third store, still looking for the perfect dress. As they entered the store Julie immediately found the dress she wanted. The saleswoman came over and asked if she were going to the resorts spring ball, "Every woman I know who is going has tried that dress on, but no one could pull it off. You'd need to have a fairy's figure." She said looking at the red head's body. "You just might do it." Julie went to try on the dress, and Carl sat waiting for her to come out and model it for him.

He smelt a strange odor and looked around. A large man and his wife entered the front of the store. The woman went straight for the dress Julie was trying on, but she instantly put it back, once she saw the back cut down to the waist. Julie stepped out of her dressing room and could smell that very distinctive scent of cigar smoke. "Sir- Sir." The sales woman ran over. "I'm Sorry, but you'll have to put that cigar out. This is a non-smoking building, except in designated areas."

Disgusted, the man nodded to the woman. He sat down next to Carl. Crossed his ankle over his leg, and crushed out the glowing cigar tip on the bottom of his shoe. He said, "So many rules in America. I don't know how you live here, No smoking, No drinking, No women."

Carl knew this must be the man. He sounded Russian, at least that was Carl's guess. "We have all that here."

"Yes, the man cut him off, But not, as we do." He looked at Julie. "You look as beautiful as a delicate flower." The man told her as she stood there in nude stocking feet and the spaghetti strapped gown. Her purse, with her weapon in it was on the floor in the dressing cubicle behind her, and all she could do was say, "Thank You." Then he told them. My name is Yuri Zelkovic, and this is my wife Natalia.

The woman was now standing next to Julie with a stack of dresses in her arms. She looked at her husband. "Go try them on." He told her in a loud demanding tone. She smiled from ear to ear and popped inside one of the dressing rooms. He spoke loudly. "Be sure I see each one."

She responded with a Russian slurred, American "Okay." She quickly popped out of the room with a pale green dress on.

Yuri cringed and shook his head "No" to her. She disappeared again. "This resort of yours, I've found it very difficult to get reservations for, do you think you could get us an invitation to this Ball we've heard so much about." He asked Carl. Natalia popped back out in a yellow gown. She got another "No" from her husband.

Carl agreed with Yuri. But He kept his opinion to himself. "Yes, I believe I could." He told him.

Natalia returned this time wearing a pretty morning glory blue and white gown that had a delicate lace shawl that went with it. Yuri nodded his head, "Oh, my butterfly, this one looks lovely." Natalia swirled like a young girl, so Yuri could see the whole thing and she too could see how it looked in the mirror behind her. "You did not introduce yourselves, the large man complained, as he reached out his hand to Carl."

Carl apologized, "This is my wife Julie and I'm Carl Stevens."

The large Russian man shook his hand and then took Julie's hand in his and kissed it. She felt something placed into her palm and clutched it until she could read it later. "So little flower would you help my wife get whatever else she needs to finish her outfit."

"I would love to, Julie smiled to Yuri and Natalia, so long as you two gentlemen promise to accompany us."

"Of course we will, Julie." Carl told her.

"American women." Said Yuri. "Keep their men on a two foot leash."

"Ah, But that goes both ways." Julie told him, as she latched her arm into Carl's and then gave him a small flutter of a kiss on his lips. Julie ran back into the dressing room to change. She placed the piece of paper carefully into her pocket book trying to avoid any cameras from seeing her. When she rejoined the men, she found that Yuri had decided that they were going to eat first and then finish their shopping after.

During their lunch conversation, she learned that Yuri and Natalia expected to be put in one of the hotel rooms at the resort and that they would be coming back with them from the mall. The women ran into a lingerie boutique to get undergarments for their outfits and then Carl and Yuri went into "The Black Tie" clothing store to get Carl's tuxedo. Yuri quickly picked out an outfit and the man's wife made the simple alterations while the men waited.

As the group left the mall, Julie whispered to Carl, "What are we going to do?"

"Bring them back with us." He told her. "What else can we do?"

The Russian man told them as they approached a black Mercedes Benz that this was his car and that he and Natalia would follow them.

Julie and Carl got into their aging Honda Civic and drove, leading the way. Julie quickly wanted to know what the message read. Carl read it to her. "Sandman Et al desires to help in ending the nightmare. Spring is near, and so are friends."

"What the heck is that supposed to mean?" Julie asked.

"I don't know, maybe nothing in particular, perhaps it was only meant to intrigue us." said Carl.

"Maybe." she answered. "But let's try to think it through logically anyway."

"Alright, we know that the Russians are contacting us, but the note talks about a sandman."

"So, Julie says, the Russians are telling us they are already in contact with the Arabs perhaps, What do you think?"

"That sounds good to me, I would make that assumption, Clearly the rest of the line is telling us that they know about the problem and that they possibly have knowledge that we do not."

Julie said, "I don't know about you, but I always want to end my nightmares fast, and it is usually something really bad."

"They obviously think so too if they called our problem a nightmare." Carl added.

"I think a possible Third World War counts as a nightmare, don't you."

He agreed with her there. The second line says, "Spring is near, and so are friends."

"Well, Spring is a season, but it can also mean action." Julie told

Carl.

"Okay, so that may not mean anything, but it could mean we have our D-day wrong, and it could all happen sooner than we expected."

"Friends are near." She hesitated. "That could mean that we not only have allies. but that they are close by. Already working with us or better yet, if we're lucky, even undercover working directly with General Davis."

Carl said. "That would be nice, but I hope the possibility of our Dates being off in Davis' favor isn't correct."

"Do you trust the Russians, Julie?"

"Well, my gut tells me that Yuri must understand that security has been increased, and I think that by getting themselves taken into a secured facility, they would be committing suicide if he weren't on the up and up."

"Either that or he's damn good or over-confident." Carl added.

"The question in my mind is whether any of this has a connection to you or is simply related to the project in general." She expressed her concern.

"I vote for coincidence." Carl answered.

"They are rather interesting though, don't you think?"

"Yes, Carl admitted, They are."

Carl pushed the intercom and asked for Paul. "Paul, Julie and I picked up those clients Randy asked us to meet. The ones his father-in-law provided some tobacco research for."

Paul hesitated, "Would that be Blue Skies Incorporated or Red Horizon Industries."

"I believe they are from Blue Skies Inc. Carl added. They have requested some lodging and wish to discuss their friendships and future business relationship with our Company."

"Sounds good to me. I'll be right down to let you in." Paul told him, but first he verified everything with Randy. A few minutes later, the large iron gates opened to let them through. Paul leaned into Carl's opened window. "You are supposed to take them to your place first, Randy will meet you there."

"Paul, have you been in my place, there are pictures of my family there, which won't look good, when my name is Carl Stevens and Julie is my wife." Carl was back in his element and took charge. "We'll stall by bringing them to the main hall, that way Matt can take everything down and hide it in the coffee table."

Julie led the couple into the main hall where they found everyone still preparing for the party tomorrow night. Carl was amazed at how the children's area came out. The huge net Matt hung earlier was made to form a massive mountain that the children were going to have a sleepover in. Carl and Julie went under it and instantly felt as if they were inside a cozy starlit cave. At the opening to the cave was the huge great room fireplace.

A couple of teenagers came over, and one of them asked if she could sign up their children. She explained that the kids were being assigned into small groups, and she was in charge of color-coding all the nametags. Placing all the children into manageable sizes, per each two-person high school team. "You see, each child will be placed in a group of eight kids, and their color tag will match their captains'. She whispered; Kids don't like the term babysitters."

"Wow." Julie told them. "You did a nice job with all this, but we don't have any children."

"It looks really great." Carl told them. "The kids will love it."

"Thanks. The only items left to do is finish organizing the supplies and roll out the rugs." As she said that, Paul and Mike were rolling in two large bolts of green carpeting.

"Good luck guys." They told the kids as they left to approach another couple."

"I see you're still in one piece." Julie commented to Mike.

"Give her time; the day is still young yet." Mike winced when he heard Carrie scream. "There you are Mike, I need you to help Matt string all the lights in the banquet hall." "Where did Matt run off to?" She yelled loudly.

"Here I am, Mom." Matt came strolling into the room.

"Where were you off too." She asked.

"I was only gone five minutes, can't a guy take a leak."

Carrie caught sight of the couple with Carl and Julie. "Well hello, she held out her hand, I'm Carrie Taylor."

"This is a colleague of Randy's. He owns Blue Skies Incorporated in the Tobacco Industry." Carl said.

"It is lovely to meet you both." She shook their hands as Carl introduced Yuri and Natalia to Carrie.

"My wife is very pleased to be invited to your ball tomorrow night."

"Yes, thank you very much." Natalia smiled.

Carrie listened to their deep Russian accents and didn't know if she should be proud or scared that her little corporate party jumped from hometown to international gala. "Your very welcome, It is nothing grand I'm afraid, we're all just family here."

Natalia looked with a confused expression toward her husband. They spoke in Russian for a moment and Yuri explained that she misunderstood Carrie's usage of the word family. He waved his arms around, including all the people of the grand room. "I've explain to my Natalia that you did not mean that everyone here is blood related, just related in spirit."

Carrie smiled warmly at the man and his wife. "Exactly, we'll enjoy food and dancing and play some games, like the big family we are."

Natalia asked Carrie if there were anything she could do to help. Before Carrie could answer, Julie looped her arm in Natalia's, and told her maybe they could come back down after they got them all settled into a room. As they left the main building they heard Carrie yelling, "You boys be careful not to fall off that ladder now, Mike it needs to go a little further that way. No, a little further."

Entering the Apartment, Carl noticed the picture above the fireplace in the antique style had been overlooked. Glancing at it, he figured he could pass Rebecca off as his sister, if needed. Carl and Julie carried in their things from the car and they noticed that Yuri and Natalia had too. Carl invited them in and everyone sat and relaxed as they waited for Randy. Julie made coffee and brought in some cookies on a plate. She figured their plans for dinner and a movie were now canceled, so she went to the kitchen to throw a roast in the oven. Natalia took her coffee and followed her, leaving the men to play chess.

Carl realized he felt invigorated, meeting up with Yuri and Natalia had been exciting and he felt strengthened by the excitement of it all. He went to the fireplace and lit it. Passing by the window he caught sight of something moving. Looking more carefully at the wood line, he caught sight of the cougar dragging off another small deer. Carl was distracted by the Russian voice.

"What is that you are staring at?" He was now standing next to Carl. "Ah, look at the strong hunter preying on the weak. That is symbolic of the flip flopping roles our countries have played over the decades, But look at us now, standing here as comrades. In the past, one of your people would have taken the note and run. But today you bring me to your home. I have much hope that we can solve our mutual problem together." Yuri put his arm around Carl's shoulder. "Come, let us play a game before your Randy comes to talk business."

Carl thought that Yuri's explanation of the cougar was accurate in regarding our countries, but it still didn't explain what it meant to his personal life. The phone rang, and Randy asked if everything were okay. "Are you comfortable with them or do you question their integrity?"

"No. We're good." Carl told him.

Yuri yelled from his chair at the game table, "If that be your man, You let him know we'll not be difficult guests, We'll be fine here with you."

Carl looked at Julie. He didn't know if she was laughing from shock or she genuinely found some humor in all of this. Natalia shyly told her husband maybe it wasn't such a good idea. "Nonsense, this is a big place, there is plenty of room."

Actually, Carl thought, it was rather small and getting smaller by the minute. "Yuri insists on staying here. Ah huh. Yes. That's fine." "See you in the morning." Carl hung up the phone.

"Good." Yuri expressed.

"What's good?" Carl asked him.

"Now, we get to enjoy good company and play with your beautiful set here." He held up the Fairy queen. "This piece looks much like your Julie flower." He handed Carl the piece.

"I hadn't noticed that." Carl looked carefully at the piece and then placed it on Yuri's side of the board.

Yuri set up his pieces. "It certainly is a delightful set." The man carefully inspected each piece.

Carl picked up his human pieces and set them up on his side of the board.

Yuri said, "Look, mine are a fairy tale and yours are real."

Carl picked up the human queen and noticed it looked like Rebecca, "No, look these are gnomes." He engaged the charming man.

"But in German folklore, Yuri told him, gnomes are only small humans who live in the ground under forest trees."

Carl played chess and talked with Yuri about women and food and movies. Carl looked at his watch. it read 6:30pm, "There is a movie showing at nine if you would like to take the girls to it."

"My Natalia, Carl would like to know if you would like to see a movie reel tonight." His wife beamed with excitement and clapped like a small child invited to the circus.

"I'll take that as a Yes." Carl watched the woman shake her head.

Yuri finished his move, "Check Mate." He told the young man across from him. Letting out a loud laugh, when he realized, Carl never saw the move coming.

"Ouch, that hurt." Carl had been whooped three times by this energetic middle fifties aged man.

Julie turned on the television and excused herself from their company. Quickly, she gathered her things and was thankful she had been slow to settle in. She moved it all into Carl's room and closed the door.

When she returned to the living room, she felt that she hadn't fooled the forty something year-old woman watching her take down dinner plates. Natalia helped set the dinner table and asked if they had intruded at a bad time. "No, why would you think that." Julie asked her.

"I just notice, you do not sleep in the same room together."

Julie was afraid the woman might have noticed her room with clothes spread on the bed and floor. Carl came up behind her and put his arms around her waist, "You know women, they have more clothing than they know what to do with." "Did you get your clothes cleaned up in the spare room, so I can bring in their bags." She nodded. "Thanks, sweetheart." Carl kissed her, long and strong on the mouth. Julie swayed a bit when he let go and she hoped she hadn't blown his attempt to convince Yuri and Natalia that they were truly married.

Entering the apartment felt odd, Carl sensed that someone had been inside, but he couldn't find anything that was missing. On the kitchen table was a note in Randy's handwriting that said, "Memories safe and sound, see you all at nine sharp in dining hall." Carl went to re-light the fireplace and saw the forest picture hanging above the mantle again. Carl felt relieved that the pictures of his family were safely away from prying eyes and was grateful for Randy's foresight. Carl burned the note in the fire and then went and joined the others in the kitchen.

"That was a lovely movie," Natalia thanked the young couple for taking them. The kettle whistled, and Carl poured everyone hot water. Everyone had a nighttime tea except Yuri, who preferred decaffeinated coffee with a shot of bourbon. After discussing the movie and finishing their tea, Carl informed them all that they had a breakfast date at 9:00am with Randy at the Dining Hall. Yuri and Natalia wished them good night and went off to clean up and get some sleep.

Carl sat looking at Julie as she took the braid out of her hair and ran her hands through it to release the tension its construction had created.

"Tired." He asked her.

"Hmm, Yes." She looked at Carl across the table.

"Are you ready for bed, then."

She flushed slightly as she felt the intimacy connected to those words. Julie knew if she felt like a schoolgirl, then she must look like one too. "Do you think they have seen through me." She whispered.

"I don't know." He took her hand and led her to the bathroom. "It's time for marriage 101." He whispered into her ear as he unzipped his pants.

This time she turned beat red.

Carl turned his back to her and peed into the toilet. "Married people don't have personal space, he said to her softly, Your turn." She went to the bathroom, watching Carl wash his face and then she flushed the toilet. They shared the sink while brushing their teeth. Then Julie cleaned her face too, and they went to the bedroom.

That was easy she thought to herself, but now they needed to change their clothes, and she hoped he would be discreet. No, he wasn't. Her mouth dropped as he changed into his nightclothes of sweat pants and a tee shirt.

"Well, That was really discreet of you." Julie complained.

"Discretion isn't what we need right now Julie, but yes I am being discreet, I usually sleep in my underwear."

She blushed again. She felt like a fool. She was twenty-nine-years old, and she couldn't control her hormones. Julie stripped out of her clothes and noticed that Carl had given her privacy by climbing into bed, with his back to her and had shut off his lamp. She shut off hers too and changed into sweats, a tank top and threw a sweater on top of it. She couldn't think what her problem was. After all she had been with men before, she was almost thirty for goodness sake. Men hit on her daily. Then it dawned on her. It wasn't her that was the problem. It was him. She realized, as she climbed into bed with Carl.

The movie had been a very sweet romance. Julie was surprised that Carl appeared to have enjoyed it. With his background, she thought he would have been an action film man only. Julie held Carl's hand when she noticed him crying at the point in the film where the woman refuses to marry the man, and she ends up telling him she is dying from cancer. Julie cried when the man insisted on marrying her anyway. Lying in the darkened room, Julie had her back facing Carl as she tried to sleep. "Are you still awake?" she whispered.

"Yes." Carl answered.

She flipped over. "What did you think of the movie?"

Carl flipped over to face her. They had already discussed the movie. She just couldn't sleep and wanted to talk.

She caught a glint of his green eyes in the moonlight and suddenly felt naked, despite the fact, she was wearing more clothing than any normal person wore to bed.

Carl looked at her bundled up in the thick sweater. He thought. It did nothing to make her less beautiful. "The movie was good. Julie -."

"Yes."

He whispered even lower. "I'm sorry about kissing you earlier this evening."

She smiled, "That's okay," she really hadn't minded. Softly she said, "It was quick thinking, but I was afraid I messed it up by nearly falling when you let go of me."

Carl smiled. It felt good to have such a pretty woman tell him his kiss made her swoon. "It was nice - but still, I'll try not to do it again."

She floated and then sank. Her heart was fluttering so fast that she thought she might know what it felt like to be a hummingbird. Julie found her mind moving just as rapidly. He had a way of making her brain fog whenever he came too close. He wasn't like any of the men she knew. She was losing her composure with him, and she knew she was being completely unprofessional. She felt frustrated by all this and confused. He was attractive and hardworking. What had surprised her most was that, even though he was forced to be there, he was still kind and friendly with everyone, even teasing and fun to be around. All the men at work liked him, as did the few women there. Best of all was that he wasn't arrogant like all the men she had protected. Julie lay there wishing he would kiss her again. She looked at this man next to her in the moonlight, and she saw a tenderness in his face that she hadn't seen before. She longed to feel his arms around her once more and looked away before he saw the developing tear in her eye.

Carl watched as the moonlight reflected on her face. He caught the glitter of a silver bulb streaking down her cheek. He reached across to her and gently wiped it away. He badly wanted to hold her. To kiss away, whatever it was that was making her so sad. But instead he asked, "Did I say something wrong."

"No." She insisted.

"So, why are you crying?"

Julie hesitated. She wasn't sure why herself. "Do you remember our talk this morning in the car."

"Yes." Carl wondered what any of that had to do with Julie's tears.

"Well, A short while ago I would have been thrilled with your description of my life, But now - I'm not so sure it's enough anymore."

Carl wasn't quite sure what she meant by that. "What part do you mean, being attractive, successful, intelligent." She interrupted him.

"I'm not sure, maybe the whole lifestyle, I mean being smart and pretty has landed me jobs that would otherwise have gone to a man. But the only recent relationships I've had, have been, a few nights of fleeting passion." She added to herself. There's not one person with a picture of me, held close to their heart. "I guess I'm saying that I liked your arms around me, kissing me at the kitchen sink, as I made us dinner. It's something I never expected would feel - so right." Julie reached out to Carl and placed her hand against his chest. She put her head against him and listened to his heart beating rapidly.

"Julie." Carl lifted her chin, so he could see her eyes. God, her blazon eyes and sweet scent drove him insane. It took all his might not to kiss her and instead he forced himself to speak. "I'm afraid you think I'm different from other men." The look she gave him proved him right. "But I assure you, I want you just like any other man would. That's why I think we should both just turn back around and try to sleep." He told her.

"I know you're a man, Carl, but you are different."

"How's that?"

"Because when I'd wake in the morning, you'd still be here." She reached up and placed her mouth on his own.

She swirled her tongue with his, sending Carl's emotions into a twisting tornado. Gently he pushed her away, "Julie you know I'd love to, but right now I just can't." He said, "I'm so sorry."

"No, don't apologize, I should be the one apologizing, not you." She wiped her finger gently over his mouth as if to remove the kiss and then flipped back over, "Good night" she whispered.

Carl knew he should just flip over and go to sleep too. Instead, he moved closer to her. "Can I hold you until you fall asleep?"

When he touched her, she thought she was about to burst physically, but emotionally she felt warm and calm. "Yes."

Carl fought the urge to make love to her, physically he wanted to badly, her body heat and magical scent mixed with the lightest bit of rose made him frenzied. She nuzzled her face into her pillow and twined her fingers with his. "Julie, I'm really confused right now, I've been married for a long time, to a woman that I love. I don't want to use my love and longing for her to allow myself to be with you, it's not right to do that to you or to me."

Julie leaned toward Carl. "I understand Carl, really I do." She wrapped her arm around him and nuzzled her face into his chest, letting out a sigh. It was his inability to be with her that made her care for him all the more and what made her envy Rebecca.

Carl hoped he hadn't made her feel rejected. She was beautiful and sexy. His body ached to feel hers. But he knew it was her loving acceptance of him that had calmed his passion and had emotionally lulled him to sleep.

CHAPTER FOURTEEN

Rebecca woke in the dim light sneaking its way through the pane of Ryan's bedroom window. She felt a somewhat strange sensation in the pit of her stomach. It wasn't a physical pain that she recognized. It seemed to her to be more of an uneasy feeling. Anxiety maybe, she wasn't certain. She wondered if her feeling had anything to do with her and the kids leaving tomorrow morning. It did feel rather weird that they would have to tell these wonderful people goodbye. Her watch read 6:00am, as she placed it to her wrist. The house was quieter now that Daniel and his family had gone back home two days ago. Anne and Frank had decided that they were going to stay with David a while longer, since they had a tree on their house to removed and a roof needing repairs. Rebecca test the air by pulling back the covers, she found that it wasn't too cold. However, when she put her feet to the floor, it sent a shiver up her spine. The opposite feeling of someone putting an ice cube down the back of her shirt. She reached quickly for the socks on the floor and rushed to get them on. Climbing the stairs she saw David's bedroom door was wide open, and the bed was unmade. The blankets were all heaped to one side. Walking past the bathroom, she leaned into the loft to check on her children. She noticed they were still all sleeping, rolled up in their bags. Only Rachel was on the couch in hers. She saw that she was wearing an old flannel shirt and assumed it was one of Tommy's. She worried that she had been a neglectful mother to Rachel for letting her fall in love with this older boy.

As she stood there, she tried to remember what being thirteen was like for her. A crush came back to her that she had had for one of her older brother's friends and she recalled the exhilaration she had felt when

198

she was asked by him to hang around with them. It had felt good to her and exciting, but she was okay and she knew Rachel would be okay too. Rebecca went to the bathroom and turned on the faucet. She was thrilled to find hot water. She closed the door and decided to grab a quick shower. She was amazed at how luxurious it felt to her to stand under the shower's head as it spouted warm water down her body. She would have loved to stand in it for an hour, but instead, forced herself to be quick in case others wanted to clean up too. Opening the door, she spotted David headed to his room. She waited a second and then quietly made her way to the stairs. Hoping not to get caught by him this early in the morning, when her guard was down.

"Where are you sneaking off to so bright and early." He had caught her.

"Nowhere, I was headed down to the kitchen to get some tea." Rebecca half lied. She didn't know what was the matter with her. The past week had felt so warm and comfortable between them, but now she felt - unable to face him. Like her leaving, was some kind of betrayal to him. She knew that was absurd, but it felt that way none the less. "Are you headed out, or coming back in."

"Back in, I woke up early today too."

She looked at the mess the blankets were in on his bed. Pointing to it she asked, "Did you not sleep very well?"

"No, I didn't. I worried that this was going to happen."

"What?" She asked.

"That you would put up your defenses and move on long before you actually left."

"David, I'm trying, but I don't know how to leave here gracefully."

David saw Rachel walking towards the stairs behind her mother. He smiled at the girl and then he pulled Rebecca by the hand into his room.

Rachel walked toward the kitchen and the scent of bacon. She knew Anne would be there making everyone breakfast, but she was surprised when she saw Frank there too.

"Good morning, sweet pea." Frank said.

The graceful and dainty, gray - haired woman smiled and asked if she would like tea or hot chocolate. Rachel opted for a tea and sat down at the table next to Miss Anne, as she set the timer for the muffins she had placed in the oven.

"David just pulled Mom into his room and closed the door."

Anne panicked not knowing what to say. She looked at Frank.

"Tommy says that David is in love with her." Rachel said.

"Is that bad?" Frank asked her.

"No." She paused, taking a sip of her tea. "Dad would like David and he would really like the way he takes care of her."

"Do you like David?" Frank asked.

"Oh Yes, I do very much, but that's not the problem."

"What is?" Anne managed to let escape her mouth as she twisted the towel in her hand.

"Well, I think Mom uses her heart to guide her through everything, she stirred her tea, and right now Mom's heart is too broken to guide her at all, never mind to David."

Tommy walked in through the back door. "Want to help with the milking." He asked her.

The kids closed the door behind them.

"What do you think of all that." Anne asked her husband.

"I think she's perceptive, I also think she's right." He said. "I only hope that boy of ours isn't doing something stupid."

Anne's buzzer blared. She flipped the towel over her shoulder, and she shut it off. Passing her hand along Frank's forehead she gently kissed him and then went on with her chores. She listened to Frank, discuss his plans to go pick up Rebecca's car later that day. "It's going to feel lonely around here." was all Anne said.

"Who said you have to leave gracefully."

Rebecca's breath was a little rapid as she stood there leaning against the door. David had his forearm leaning against the door beside her, and his frame surrounded her. She couldn't move any further away from him. David hadn't touched her, but for some reason she couldn't breathe. Oh my god, I'm experiencing my first panic attack, she told herself. Rebecca tried to relax and control her breathing. Just relax, draw in long, even and deep breaths and just relax, she coached herself. Her head stopped spinning, and she could now breathe without feeling as if she were inside a coffin.

"Are you okay, do you need to lie down?"

"NO, I'll be fine right here."

"Did I scared you?" He looked at her confused. "You look as white as a sheet."

She felt silly. "No, I just somehow felt overwhelmed for a minute."

David stepped back, "I'm sorry Baby, I'll get you some water."

Rebecca let her back slide down the door, landing her butt on the floor. She dropped her head down between her knees to catch her breath. Baby, she thought about David's choice of words. That was something Carl would never have called her. Babe maybe, but never, baby. Baby implied helplessness, and vulnerability. A baby is someone who couldn't take care of them self. And the definition included, she thought, someone who was less valued because of all these beliefs. Baby, that's what she spent her whole childhood being. The baby of six children, she was always considered someone's shadow or other. If she weren't following around one of her siblings, then she was her best friend, Maria's shadow instead. She had spent the last fourteen years breaking free from that inscribed role.

David returned with her glass of water. She realized it wasn't him that had overwhelmed her. Instead, it was the prospect of returning home, voided of the role she had built for herself. Without Carl's love and presence by her side, she feared the lure and easy return to her former status as family baby. "Thank you." She got to her feet and drank a few sips. David was making his bed.

"I only wanted to finish our conversation before the children had a chance to interrupt."

Rebecca sat on his made bed. "You didn't do anything to make me upset. I've felt strange since I woke up. But I can sort of thank you for helping me to understand why." David waited for her to continue. "I haven't been home in a while and now I'm returning with no home of my own. I think my family might try and convince me to move back there." "They very well might throw logic at me that could be hard to dispute. Not that any of that ever mattered before, but I always had Carl before too." "They always accepted that my life was with him. But now - it could be hard for them to understand that where they call home, isn't quite right for me." "I've always gone my own direction, but Carl was always there to back me every step of the way."

David restarted the fire in the hearth and sat there poking at it. "What is right for you? I mean - which way do you think you're going now?"

"Well, my heart is telling me to go home, it's where I know I can rest and lick my wounds for a while."

He looked into her eyes and saw the reflection of himself. He liked the way he felt when she looked at him. He felt whole and vital, everything he distantly remembered being before his heart broke in two and everything else about himself that went along with it. "Stay and be with me. Your homeless and I have a huge empty house. I would love for you and your children to make it a home. I promise you. He put his hands up in the air. No strings attached and no obligations. You can heal your wounds here until you decide what to do next."

Rebecca stared at the fire and felt the warmth. She felt safe here with David. He was strong, loving and protective. She looked at him with his large firm body and tender eyes. A man who handles overbearing animals and lugs around bales of hay as if they were pillows. Yet, whenever he touched her, it was if she were made of glass. A china doll that if bumped it would break. She supposed right now; she probably was a glass bulb. One that if, not placed high enough on the tree, one swing of the dog's tail, would send it crashing to the floor. Like high thick bows, David's arms were strong and secure. But, Rebecca understood her place. Right now, it was tucked away safely in a box, up in the farthest reaches of the closet. That way no one would get cut on the broken glass or suffer the longing for a holiday too far from near. She knew David hadn't gotten to know the real her. Right now, she was only a shadow of her real self. As comfortable as it would be for her to remain here with him, she knew it would be the cowardly thing to do.

Her silence gave him his answer. He knew it had been wrong to ask her to stay. He also knew he would have regretted it forever if he hadn't. "Would you promise me two things at least." She looked up at him. "Promise me that you'll keep in touch and please give me this day with you." He put his arms around her and longed to never, let her go. He saw in her the blue speckled egg that the spring storm had knocked to the ground, battered but not broken. He was always thrilled to see those fallen eggs, because, without the storm, he knew he would never have had the chance. But with that excitement, always came some sadness too. As much, as he wanted to warm her and protect her. He knew that he couldn't. He had to put her gently back where she belonged, and hope that when the time came, she would be at his windowsill singing the gentle song of the robin. He knew if he were truly lucky, she'd return once more to build her own nest. But for now, he was just glad to have seen her beauty and to have been allowed to hold her before sending her on her way.

They made one last trip out to the stables so Rebecca could say goodbye to Ebony. She reached into the stall, and the mustang instantly greeted her with their usual hello. She spoke quietly to him for a few minutes as she rubbed his mane. Then Rebecca pulled an apple from her pocket and held it out for the animal. She whispered goodbye and turned away from the elegantly massive creature. Ebony stomped on the ground and then banged the stall's door.

"You seem to have him under the same spell."

"He only wants another apple." She smiled as if it were her trick.

"You've never brought him an apple before, but he always acts like that when you walk away from him."

She stood leaning against the wooden wall of one of the stables. He was handsome. She thought she would never forget the way he looked today. Across the aisle from her David stood with his thumbs hooked in his blue jeans, and he wore his usual boots and white tee shirt. However, today he wore a black Stetson that framed his face making his eyes even bluer than usual. Like the salty ocean water, his eyes stung her, but without hurting. She smiled at him, "Are you going to throw a tantrum when I walk away from you?"

David shook his head back and forth. "Yes, except I'll probably wait until after you leave." He gazed at her as he leaned next to a pile of hanging leather reins. "There is one thing I'm going to do before you leave me."

"What is that." He looked more intently at her as he moved closer. He didn't need to answer that. She knew already what he intended to do.

"I've been forced to break my promise."

She looked to the ground. Her mind trying to flee away from him, but her body remained firmly in place with a will of its own.

"Please, don't look away from me, I want this memory to be perfect." She looked straight at him. She looked different, beautiful, incredibly beautiful, all he wanted to do was leave her with a memory that would guide her back to him.

She put her hand to his mouth. "No David, I don't want you to break your promise." She took her hand away and she stepped toward him, leaned in and placed her mouth on his with a power he hadn't known she possessed. He was overcome by a pounding, everywhere all at once, and he couldn't contain himself from kissing her back.

David broke free from her, "Promise me, you'll come back."

"I can't promise anything."

He leaned against her, and her body fell back against the wall. She felt the cold, ridged planks behind her and his taut form against her own. She felt conflicted. Between the overwhelming need to know him more completely as his passion burned her chest and with her need to remain as distant and cold as the surface behind her.

He kissed her again, this time with a torrential; honey drenched passion, a passion to stir every desire she possessed. A passion guaranteed to bring her back to him...someday. "Promise me." David looked into Rebecca's eyes and saw confusion in them. Through the sweet, torture of their kisses, of all the things he had wanted her to feel, confusion wasn't one of them. He wanted certainty, certainty to understand his need and wants, certainty to know he needed her to want him, to want to return to him. He watched her as he moved toward her again.

Rebecca put her hand to his mouth blocking his need from her and trying to end her own. She needed him to stop. If he didn't, she knew she wouldn't have the strength to stop herself. David took her hand in his and gently placed her fingertips in his mouth and gave her his passion through their eyes and the warm sultry feel of his mouth. Rebecca thought dying might actually be easier than resisting the magnetic pull of his will and energy. She couldn't feel that way again; that skin crawling feeling, like millions of tiny legs creeping across every inch of her body. "Not again," she told herself, not ever again." "David, please, I can't, not yet." He turned her hand and stared at the rings on her finger. "It's not that, Carl doesn't have as much to do with this, as I do. This is all about learning from my past mistakes and not wanting to do them again."

"Rebecca, you've lost me."

She let her jean bottom crash to the floor as she struggled to explain.

"You have a thing about sitting on the floor, don't you." He held on to her hands and pulled her to her feet, leading her past all the stalls and to the ladder.

Rebecca climbed the ladder taking memory of the feel of it beneath her hands, and the smell of the sweet dampened grain, as their boots tore open the slender stalks of hay. She lay in her usual spot. Where they had spent the last week telling each other their dreams and secrets, of their blazing joys and the bitter sadness of the wounds they obtained along the way. All of this intermingled with the thick air of their longing and hunger for each other's comfort. Placing his hat next to her, David joined his body against hers as he innocently enjoyed their last afternoon sheltered from the snow outside. It was here that they slowly melted the winter within them. It was in this haven that he had managed to connect with her, and it was where he had become whole again in her arms.

"What were you trying to tell me down there?"

"I was young once and I remember making love for the wrong reasons."

"Are you saying that making love to me would be wrong."

She saw the pain in his eyes as he turned his gaze away from her, and she reach for his jawbone. She felt the light stubble on his face, as she guided his gaze back toward her. "I'm saying that if either of us were to feel badly afterward, then yes, it would be wrong for us to make love. At this point, I don't know if it would feel right when the heat of it was over."

"So, your saying your love for Carl would make our love making feel cheap." He looked into her eyes and saw pain, pain which his own insecurity had caused, "I'm sorry."

"I told you. It has nothing to do with him." She looked away from his eyes. "I am trying to tell you that I would feel bad, if I realized too late that I'm, not in love with you." She hated this conversation, She wanted to run away. She covered her face. "Once I used sex unknowingly, to find out if I were in love with Carl or someone else and the truth of it hurt so bad, It took me years to get past that pain that I had caused to me and everyone else." She waited for him to say something, but he didn't. He did guide her hand away from her face and swept her hair bangs away from her eyes. "I don't know how I feel about anything at the moment. But I do know that when I make love with you. If and when, we make love, then you will know that I love you. But I'm not willing to risk that pain by finding out the hard way."

"Rebecca, I know what you're saying and I agree with you. When Suzanne left me, I did something like what you are saying. I had a one-night stand with an old high school friend of mine. That is, I knew it was a one-night stand, but I guess she hadn't and I still feel badly about that. We hadn't talked at all, not like you and I. We had just plunged right into it, and it ended up a mistake. I just want you to know that I never intended to make love to you, not today anyway. Besides I'm not even prepared."

"What do you mean."

Washing his hand down his face, he looked straight at her. "I haven't been with anyone for two years, he told her softly, I don't have any protection." He felt silly at his age talking about this. He watched as the corners of her mouth curled upward, and he instantly turned a shade of crimson.

"David you haven't been with anyone for two years and I've been with only one man for the past fourteen years." "I doubt we need to worry about safe sex."

He looked at her with those eyes and placed his large hand across her abdomen, "Your still very young." He watched as the smile dropped from her face and he wondered what he had said to upset her. "What did I say."

She smiled; she had forgotten about that. It wasn't something she thought about very often. Her ability to have babies was removed five years earlier and she hadn't regretted that choice ever, until perhaps now. "I can't have children anymore." There she said it and maybe that would change how he felt, but she couldn't help that.

"Were you sick." He put his hand back down on her as if to heal her.

"No, David, I just decided that three kids were enough, and I got tired of taking pills and worrying every month. She looked away from him. Danny's birth wasn't the easiest thing to go through." He was so large that I had a doctor on one side of me and a nurse on the other, each pushing to expel the mound inside her body out. "They broke his collar bone to get him out."

He turned her face toward his and kissed her as the tears rolled down her cheeks. "I'm sorry it was so difficult." He wasn't sure why she was so upset about something that happened so long ago, unless... "Do you regret having that done."

"No." she wiped her tears off.

"Then why are you crying?"

"Do you?"

"Rebecca, I have two kids already and you have three." She just stared at him. "I do have to admit it would be nice to know what our kids would look like if we had any, But that curiosity isn't enough to make me wish you still could." "I never really thought I would want any more kids either, to be honest." "Look at me, you silly thing, do you know how crazy this is." David wiped away her last tear. "You can't decide if you love me, and you refuse to make love to me, yet your crying because you can't give me children." "You are insane, do you know that."

"Yes, I told you I was too confused to understand my own feelings, but I promise as soon as I know I'll fill you in okay."

He hugged her, "I'm going to hold you to that promise, but I'm not going to wait for long. In some parts of the world women are allowed one year to wear mourning clothes and at the end of that year they are married off to a new husband." "They don't let the living go on as if they were dead. I did that for two years, and you brought me back to the living. I think they're pretty smart. So, If you don't come back to me by June, then I'm coming after you. To make sure, you're not too busy dying to live."

"You promise."

"You know my track record with promises, but I'm usually good for my word."

She sat up, picked up his hat and pushing back her hair from her face, she placed the black Stetson on her head. "How about I hold onto this for you as a down payment to your promise."

She looked silly. It was too big, and she wore it too far back. "My favorite hat, you want me to give up my favorite hat, I don't think so." "Do you have any idea how long it took to get it fitting perfectly." David swung his leg over her and straddled her hips. At the same time, Rebecca fell backward against the pile of hay behind her.

"No, she teased him, I never seriously intended for you to do that." She picked up the hat that had popped off her head when she hit the hay. Then she placed it on his head. "You are obviously, very attached to this hat, besides it looks much better on you." David adjusted it and then he leaned down and hovered his body above hers, by propping himself up on his forearms. The feel of him covering her was exciting and comfortable at the same time. She wanted him to kiss her, but she remembered his promise. "Please kiss me."

Did she say that? He'd waited so long to hear those words that he wasn't sure if he imagined it. Her eyes, he noticed had a special allure to them he hadn't quite fully seen in her before. "Say that again." He paid careful attention to her eyes this time. "David, I want you to Kiss Me - Please." He saw it, the fire in her that made him want to tear their clothing off and soak in her femininity, basking in her silky feel, as if he were immersed in a warm tub of water.

He was staring at her, but he was really staring straight past her. She realized he was lost in his own thoughts. It hit her. The brick landed squarely against her head. She knew that it had been the wrong thing to say. She had forgotten all reason and had instead plunged straight for the abyss despite herself. She couldn't believe she had done that to him, she had confused him, it was so unfair of her to do and she wished she could take her words back.

David looked into her face and saw the moment had passed. Where was he, he was sure a week ago, he would never have hesitated for a moment to fulfill that same request. Rebecca struggled to set herself loose from under him.

"Where are you trying to run off to."

She stopped squirming beneath him. "I. I suddenly felt very uncomfortable, I'm sorry." She squirmed once more.

"Rebecca, he smiled at her and placed his hands down on hers to stop her attempt from leaving him, "Wait. You don't just say that to a man and then try and run away a second later."

"I'm sorry, I shouldn't have. It was wrong of me to say."

He felt the tense, stiffness of her body beneath him and was afraid to let her go.

Rebecca felt the warmth radiating from his hands, and it calmed her. She felt his hand move down her arm and over to her waist, and she closed her eyes to enjoy his touch. She opened them again to find him staring at her.

When he touched her smooth waist and slowly moved upward, he watched as the fire in her eyes had turned to fear. She closed her eyes, and he knew he had lost the moment. That pure moment when she had wanted him. The moment that had taken him by surprise, and had his body floating from the delight of her honest desire for him. He had taken a minute too long to respond to her, and now he knew he had to wait for that moment to be given to him again. He needed that clearness, the unobstructed vision of her seeing him directly with no thoughts or distractions of anything or anyone else between them. He would wait for her. For that pure, honest feeling before he would ever touch her creamy flesh again.

She felt his weight come off her. She opened her eyes and saw him lying next to her. Looking at her so warmly, gently. "I'm sorry."

"No, Please don't apologize." He found a piece of long grass in the hay and played with the feathery tip of it. He ran the soft spines of the caterpillar end down the side of her throat and let it play against the flesh exposed by the V in her sweater. He felt his body surge as he watched the rosy hue build across her chest.

He placed his hat on the bale of hay beside him and lay his head down against his upper arm and she heard a light sigh come from him as she watched his chest rise and then gradually fall. "I'm really good at destroying people aren't I."

"No, don't say that, because it's not true." "You haven't destroyed me at all, and what you said wasn't wrong either, it was the most sincere thing I think you've said to me." He threw the piece of grass back into the hay. Using the side of his thumb, he ran his hand down the length of her throat and watched her arousal flush her chest. He drank it all in and solidified this memory to hold him over until the day he saw her again. "Thank you -For wanting me." He said. Running his fingertips gently across the side of her throat, he felt a light tingle and tiny goose bumps rush across her skin. "I think I've grown up some too, because I know that I'm more than willing to wait for our perfect moment to come again." He reached down and kissed her with a gentle, but growing passion. Gently he parted her lips and softly ebbed his tongue with hers sending them both crashing and spent until yet again he returned to her. David let himself feel the intense flame that they both shared. He carefully extinguished enough of the oxygen feeding it, to allow them to both feel an easing of the burn within them. Reluctantly, he slowly, purposely withdrew his mouth from hers, knowing that this was the only point where that possibility would still exist. To continue, if even for a second longer, he knew he would have lost all sense and control. Two things he was determined he would not do with her, not here and not now.

"Ah, Hmm." Daniel cleared his throat.

They heard Pam's voice. "Our little love birds visiting again." Daniel nodded to her. "Hey guys, how are you?" She yelled up.

"Hi, Pam, we're good, thanks for asking." David called back.

"Jeez man, I'm really sorry, but can I get a couple of those." Daniel stood at the end of the ladder and pointed to the bales of hay.

"No problem, we were just getting ready to come down anyway." David got to his feet and pulled Rebecca up by the hand.

Daniel really doubted that judging by the look of the embrace he found them in.

Rebecca looked at her watch. It was later then she had thought. "Do you need to get over to the barns." She looked at David.

"No, Kevin and Mark said they would look after things today."

"Jerry is probably done with the car. I should go get it."

"Dad told me that he and Tommy were picking it up around noon."

"He shouldn't have done that, I could have gotten it."

"You know Dad by now."

She smiled. Both his parents were very nice.

He threw a large square bale down to Daniel and then another. "Thanks." His friend yelled up to him. David turned back to find her adjusting her clothes and trying to fix her hair. "You don't need to do that, he grabbed hold of her waist, You look beautiful." David pulled a small strip of straw from her hair. "I'm going to go help Daniel for a quick minute, okay." He kissed her and went down the ladder.

Rebecca stood at Ebony's stall door and reached inside to stroke the animals long, black mane and the length of his thick neck. "I'm amazed at how he has taken to you." Rebecca heard coming from her side as she turned and saw Pam walking her way. She smiled at her. but also kept to her emotional tending of Ebony. She was unsure if Pam were referring to the horse or to David, but she assumed she meant the horse. "He's gentle, he's just a little sad."

Pam knew she was referring to the horse, but she could just have easily been speaking about David. "Rebecca, I like you and your kids are great too, but I have to tell you, I'm worried about David."

"I know." Rebecca looked at the woman struggling to explain.

"I mean, I'm worried about you too, but." She didn't know what she wanted to say. It was hard sitting back and watching, having no power to ensure that everyone ended up un-scathed from the fall.

"Thank you." She looked at the woman next to her with her blonde hair pulled back, and French braided, wearing jeans that were worn above the knee from where horses legs rested as she tended to and mended their hooves. "You know I don't want to hurt him. That's the last thing I want to do."

Pam hugged her, "I know, she said gently, Try not to give him false hopes, okay." "Good luck to you." She started to leave and get back to her horses.

"Pam, why do you assume that I'm going to hurt him?"

"I don't, I don't know you Rebecca, but I do know him."

"What does that mean."

"David is a romantic, Rebecca. If he isn't flying, then he has to be bleeding. There's nowhere in the middle for him."

Rebecca sat on the couch reading the last chapter of her book. The fire in the hearth was burning strong, and she fully enjoyed herself as she sank into David's couch and looked around his room. Probably the most masculine room she had ever been in and probably ever would. She soaked in the feel of the wood all around her and breathed in the scent of the fire. She counted the guns and crossbows hanging high on the wall behind them. Watching as the glow of the fireplace bounced off all the walls and reflected in the great room windows. Looking at all the animals, she let her eyes absorb the colors of the tan deer and caribou, the gray spotted owl and the brown of the moose and jackrabbit. The red fox with its white tipped tail and the golden bobcat with its whiskers and fur, which looked like a beard. The bass with their mouths wide open as if in shock. She wondered why he had such an assortment and what it meant to him. Rebecca watched as David sat on the brownish black grizzly with Danny playing a board game. A sarcastic little "sorry" came out of Danny's mouth as David moved his piece backwards.

"That's alright. I'll get you back."

Rebecca saw the wide grin on Danny's face as he slammed David again. David rolled the dice and made good on his promise. Danny took it in stride as he moved his piece back four places.

"Are you looking forward to visiting your Grandma's."

"Uh... yeah"

"What does that mean."

"Well... it will be nice to see them."

Rebecca pretended to be absorbed in her book, when she glimpsed Danny looking at her.

"But what?" David asked.

Danny lowered his voice a little. "But, I'm afraid Mom's going to go back to being sad again."

"She doesn't look too sad."

"No, not here, but in Tennessee we could talk to her, and she wouldn't hear a word."

"I like her better here. With you - she's more like when Dad was around."

"How's that?"

"She smiles and laughs, and hugs me more." The two of them were quiet as David took his turn. "And you know what." Danny threw the dice as he looked around the room.

"What?" He slid the tiny piece for him.

"Dad doesn't hunt, But I think you'd be friends with each other, and Dad likes it when Mom's happy."

Rebecca couldn't control herself. She hid behind the book so Danny wouldn't see her face. She was grateful when the girls and Anne called him to come and get a warm cookie that had just come out of the oven. She put the book down, and David saw the stream of water running down her cheeks. He came over to her, and she made room for him, he chose to climb behind her and he placed his arms around her and picked up her book.

"You okay."

She looked up at him, "I guess I didn't need to worry so much about his understanding."

He kissed the tear running down the bridge of her nose, tasting a hint of its saltiness on his lips. "Kids are free with their love."

"But, Rebecca wiped her face; teenagers aren't quite as accepting."

Karen came in carrying a tray of the cookies they made with Anne and two glasses of milk. "Hey giggles." She beamed when he called her that.

"Thanks sweetie, did you have fun playing with Stacy and Kim today?"

"Yeah."

"Did you let them know that we're leaving tomorrow?"

"Yeah, I did, they have to go back to school tomorrow too."

"Rachel said to let you know that she went out to the barns with Tommy."

"Okay." She hugged her daughter. "Goodnight."

A few minutes later they could hear the whisper of Frank reading the kids a story up in the loft. "School, tomorrow's Saturday."

"Yeah, The School Board, decided to add Saturdays, instead of two weeks at the end." David read the page that Rebecca was on. "Wow, this is some good stuff." He looked at the cover to make sure this was the same story Rebecca had bought in the corner store. "There wouldn't be any reading aloud of this in front of the kids."

"Oh, come on, it's not that bad."

"No, Not bad at all."

She took the book and put it back on the coffee table. "David, why do you have all these animals."

"It's a hobby, one that I grew up doing with my Dad and friends."

"Did you hunt everything in this room."

"Well, hunt no, not exactly, but kill, Yes." "I eat everything I hunt. But sometimes things need to be put down for one reason or another." "Like that fox that kept getting at my mother's chickens a few years back." The bobcat was something similar. A friend of his was having a problem with his sheep."

"But what about the rabbit and the owl?" She turned her head to look up at him, and could hear the thumping of his heart in his chest.

"Now, rabbits are good eating, but the owl was an animal I found with a severely broken wing that couldn't be fixed, the vet tried but he had to put it down."

"Do they bother you?" David wondered.

"No, not really."

"But the grizzly did, didn't it?" he asked.

"Yeah, It did, but not as much now. I mean - I think what I do is colder."

"What are you talking about Rebecca."

"Going to a grocery store and picking and choosing what I want to buy. I'm not completely naïve where the food comes from, but I haven't had to face the reality of it before either. Before seeing and feeding the cows here with you."

"Does that mean I've made you into a vegetarian?" He tickled her as he asked that.

She laughed, "No not at all, but it seems your hunting is more honest somehow."

"That's sort of nice of you to say, but not everyone has the stomach for hunting and cattle is my livelihood. I want people to go to markets and buy the milk and steak."

She shook her head in agreement, "And believe me I will, I don't have the stomach to be a vegetarian, all the power to those who can, but grains make me ill."

"Are you getting tired yet?" He looked at her and hoped she said no, he wasn't ready to let go of her yet and was dreading when he would be forced to. He looked at his watch. He felt silly when he caught himself counting the hours before she left.

"Do you feel guilty for not working today?"

"Not at all, sometimes Kevin or Mark will take a whole day off just to go fishing." She knew they were both stalling, not wanting to turn in for the night. "You have a long drive tomorrow."

"I can take No-doze and suck down colas and candy bars."

"That's real healthy." He got up and threw pillows to the floor hitting the grizzly's head and followed that with a blanket. He led her to the floor and they carefully folded themselves to the others shape and lay there silently together. Rebecca thinking how stupid she was for needing to leave, and wondering if she would regret that decision, dosed off to sleep.

David carried her to the bedroom, on the way he saw Rachel come back inside and was headed for the stairs. "Rachel, Wait a second." David entered Ryan's room, and Rachel pulled back the covers for him as he placed her mother in the bed and drew the covers back over her. They went to the kitchen and David poured them both a glass of juice and handed her one of them.

"How are you doing?"

"I'm okay." She said looking into her glass.

"Do you miss your Dad."

The tears welled up suddenly in her eyes. "It's so hard."

She avoided looking at him. "What is?"

Her voice wobbled, "Watching her with you, it's like she's forgotten all about Dad."

He heard her suck in a deep breath as a shudder racked her body from the sobs. "Believe me; she hasn't forgotten your Dad."

She looked up at him. "She's just trying to figure out how to go on." He explained.

"I know." She wiped her running nose.

"Well, I just wanted to let you know how much I like your mother, and you kids. And if, in the future, your mom were to decide that I could maybe fill a small section of the hole in your lives - I would be honored for that chance, with all of you." He hugged the girl.

"Thanks David, I like you too."

Rebecca was suddenly rushing down a river in a large yellow raft with white rapids ahead of her and then just as suddenly she was safe and stable on the ground once more. She was walking in the forest again with Carl, and they were laughing about something. He pointed out the cougar to her and he kissed her and held her for a moment, she felt safe. She felt strong and content. Then suddenly she was looking into the cougar's large green eyes and felt that same strength and contentment that she had with Carl's arms around her. She stood there alone as she watched him bound away into the forest, strong and confident without looking back. The last thing she saw was the golden tail of the cougar as it disappeared into the evergreens. She woke and found that she was in Ryan's bed, the last she had remembered was being in front of the fire. She couldn't believe he had carried her, and she had sleep through it. She hadn't done that since she was six years old, when she remembered her father carrying her up the stairs to her bed. He was sleeping there peacefully beside her. He hadn't even removed the belt he wore with the large buckle. She needed to use the bathroom but lay gently back down so she wouldn't wake him. The dream had left her sad, but she felt the strength and confidence of Carl and the cougar both by her side. She knew she had the power now that she needed to forge straight into the forest like the cougar had and continue on with her life. Looking at David, she wasn't sure where he or anyone fit into the picture of her life. But she did know that she was grateful to have met him. She knew she would keep her promise to him. She would let him know what it was she wanted; when she knew herself. Right now, she was just happy to have woken well rested and strong enough to take on the rest of her life.

There wasn't yet, any sunlight trying to force its way through the blind on the window. She rolled over and tried to fall back asleep. She felt his arm slide across her and she reached for him and twined her fingers with his.

"See. I did manage to sleep with you."

"You did that the first night we met."

"Yeah well, I'm just a hard man to resist."

He had no idea how true those words were. She wished she knew the right words to say to him, but she didn't. She didn't want to respond with something trivial, yet no words were coming to her, except "Thank you."

"For what."

She turned back to face him. "I don't want to leave here without your knowing how much my time with you has meant to me."

"No. Wait, Rebecca. We're not saying goodbyes remember. We

agreed. You are going to go off for awhile and figure things out for yourself, but for good or bad we are going to see each other again. So no, goodbyes. Let's just leave it at I'll see you in June."

"Okay." She responded. David turned away from her and started to put his boots on.

Rebecca threw back the covers and let the cold air hit her, the house felt like a warm day in July when the fires were going, but by morning it was always a reality shock to the cold march weather outdoors.

"Where are you going." David asked.

"I'm going with you." Rebecca answered.

"No, it's still early. You should get some more sleep before your drive."

"Why are you going, if it's still early."

He looked at her. "I want to get it done, so I can get back and see you and the kids off."

"Well, I want to help you."

He looked at her there shivering and stubborn, "Alright." He answered.

She grabbed a thick sweater from the chair in the corner and threw it on over her tee shirt and found her black work boots in the kitchen. David had already started a fire in the wood stove, and he had put a teapot on to boil. She heard the toilet flush and listened as his boots pound against the planks of the wooden hallway floor.

"Are you sure you want to go, it is really cold out there this early in the morning." He sort of liked that she wanted to go, but he was hoping to have this quiet time working alone to gather his thoughts and prepare himself for her leaving.

"Do you not want me to go?"

He was quiet as he poured out the water into their mugs, "Tea?"

"Who's putting up defenses now." She walked away and closed the bathroom door behind her.

Rebecca returned to the kitchen and found a note left for her with her fixed tea. "Sorry Rebecca, I don't mean to hurt you, I just need a little time alone, David." She took a sip of her tea and found it exactly how she liked it. She took a few more sips and then grabbed the silver flashlight off the counter and her jacket from the wall, and she headed out into the darkness towards the stables. It felt strangely dark and a bit chillier then she thought it would be, but the path was well memorized from her and David's walks there during the past week.

She listened to the sound of an owl in the distance. The moon was still shining bright enough to guide her through the trees and down the snowy path which reflected its glow. As she neared the stable door, Rebecca thought she smelt a smoky scent, but not the smell of Daniel and Pam's chimney. As she reached to pull open the heavy door, she turned back and caught the small orange glow of a cigarette about twenty feet away. Rebecca felt her heart surge, and she quickly decided to take her chances inside the barn, she knew she couldn't out run whoever it was, not all the way to the couple's house. Seeing the glow coming closer, she opened the door enough to get inside and closed it behind her. She searched around the wall trying to find the light switch, but couldn't, and she couldn't manage to find a lock either. She then fumbled with the flashlight and dropped it. Dropping to her knees, she felt frantically; all across the cold concrete slab, beneath her to find it. She heard the rattle of the door wheels on the sliders begin to squeak from movement. Finally, she felt the cool metal cylinder, gripping it, she ran for the other end of the stables. As the door slid open, the bay aisle filled with the last of the moonlight. Reaching the dark at the other end, she turned as she heard the heavy footsteps and saw the bobbing of the glowing tip approach. A streak of neon orange fell to the floor, and she watched it bounce and send glowing sparks flying. It then disappeared, as she heard a gritty sandpaper scraping sound against the concrete, when the hard sole of his shoe twisted to extinguish the butt.

"Where are you, lady?"

She heard her heart echoing in her head. He sounded foreign, European maybe, she wasn't sure. She felt for the latch and slowly opened Ebony's stall door, only a few inches at a time. Reaching in, she put her hand up for him to smell her and then she crawled into the stall. Closing the door behind her, it creaked.

"I only want to talk to you."

He was getting closer. She thought he might be German. She wasn't stupid. Strangers do not wander onto private property at five in the morning and want to "only talk" about anything.

"What secrets are you hiding."

She heard him open a stall door and then another.

"I'm not leaving here, until you tell me what you know."

He was to Ebony's stall. She stood and placed herself against the wall on one side of Ebony, and the man was at the door on the other.

"There you are."

She turned the flashlight on the man. He was about a foot away from the door and was tall, maybe six feet two inches and he had brown hair and a mustache with dark eyes to match his disposition. He sheltered his eyes and reached for the door. Ebony reared up and slammed the door with his two front hooves giving the man his full force and a loud snort as an added warning.

"Just tell me the truth, Rebecca, and I'll go away and leave you alone."

"I don't know what you're talking about."

"Carl, where is he?"

"Why don't you ask the government because I know nothing, it seems a spouse isn't in the need to know category." She kept the flashlight in his eyes.

"Don't you think that it is strange for a man to be buried in Arlington, but his family knows nothing about it?"

"No. I'm never surprised by what the government does. Did it occur to you that maybe they wanted me to think he is still alive? Better watch out, the hunter may be the one being hunted." She knew she was lucky he couldn't see her face or she would have given her brave front away. She saw anger rise in his face.

"You think you are so smart."

His nostrils flared and his eyes narrowed, she knew not why he was after her, or what he thought she could possibly know.

"You won't be so smug after I adjust that attitude of yours."

The man with the black eyes threatened her, and she realized his heart was just as black. Rebecca placed her shaking hand onto Ebony's side. She felt a surge of fear filled adrenaline course through her body as the man opened the door. She saw rage in his eyes and knew none of this had to do with Carl or anything else for that matter. This man was just an opportunistic prowler, and she had happened upon his path.

He stepped toward Rebecca and the mustang flailed up and crashed down upon the chest of the intruder, knocking him to the ground, then while he was still down he stomped on the man again. The man pulled himself away from the horse, across the aisle he struggled to rise to his feet. Ebony placed himself between the man and Rebecca, nudging her slowly backward to the corner of the stall as he gave a verbal warning to the man.

"You won't always have that beast to protect you."

The man slid the rear door open next to Ebony's stall, and the dim beginnings of daylight streamed inside as he exited the building. She heard what was now to her, his very distinctive voice. "You! What are you doing here? You're joking, you have a thing for this bitch too?"

"Ka-Blamb!"

Rebecca heard a blast of gunfire outside the door, and then it closed shut. She felt the echo of the shot and its ringing in her ears as the force reverberated against the stable's walls. She tried to move toward the door of the stall to find out what happened, but Ebony refused to let her out. She hugged the animal. "Thank you, Ebony." "Shh, thank you." She stroked the side of the animals neck trying to calm both of them down. A few minutes later she heard a shuffling on the ground outside. About five minutes after that the stable's door opened at the far end letting in the first light of early morning.

"Who the hell is in here?"

It was Daniel's voice, "Daniel? It's me, Rebecca. I'm - I'm down here with Ebony." She saw the figure of Daniel approach with a shotgun in his hands. She knew it wasn't him who had made that shot ring out. It was not the sound of a shotgun that she had heard. It was definitely a handgun of some kind.

"What was that noise we heard, the horse was upset and then we thought we heard a weapon." Daniel asked her and called to his wife. "Pam, it's okay, you can come in."

"Rebecca, you okay." Pam came in with her hair down and a pajama top on with jeans and a coat.

She didn't know how to explain any of it, because she didn't understand it herself.

"Are you hurt?" Daniel saw a little bit of blood on the stable floor.

"No, I'm okay."

Pam looked at Ebony and found only a little blood on one of his hooves. "He's okay, it's not his." She told them.

"What happened Rebecca." Daniel asked her.

"I don't know. I mean - I'm not sure."

"Let's get her inside." Pam told Daniel.

They brought her into the house and called over to David's. "Hello, Anne is David there, Rebecca is here and something happened but she's not completely coherent." "Right, We'll bring her over." Pam hung up the phone.

"I need to check on Ebony first, he was really upset." Rebecca insisted.

Daniel went out with Rebecca as she checked on the mustang.

"Daniel, I'm fine, why don't you just let me walk back to David's."

"Because David would kill me if I let you do that, besides something happened here and I intend to get to the bottom of it."

"Pam needs to get the kids off for school, and you don't need any more hassles than I have already caused."

"The kids can miss one more day, it won't bother them any."

"Alright, but let me brush Ebony for a bit to calm him down, okay."

"That's fine, I need to tend to all the others anyway."

Rebecca felt bad for deceiving Daniel, she wanted to see what was on the other side of that door, and she wasn't sure what she would find. When he had walked all the way to the other end and had entered a stall, she slowly opened the door and peeked out. She thought she could still smell the faint scent of the carbon from the discharged weapon.

There was Nothing. Her fear of finding a dead body lying there was dispelled. She opened it further, enough for her to slip outside and then closed it behind her. Stepping out back, she noticed a pooled spot of blood on the ground. She looked all around and noticed a small area in the snow where there had been a small scuffle. She saw tracks leading away from the stable, only one set, and she noticed they were deep. She followed them, every once in a while along the path she would see a tiny spot of blood in the snow. The track led her around the house and out to the paved road on the other side of some woods. Whoever it was they had carried the man and were long gone by now. She followed the path back to the barn and covered the bloody snow along the way. When she reached the stable door, she noticed a paper note jabbed into it with a small pocketknife. It had been too small and too high up for her to notice before. Rebecca pulled it down. "Don't ever worry about this man bothering you again." She didn't recognize the handwriting. The pocketknife had a worn emblem on it. It was hard to make out, she thought it was vaguely familiar, but she couldn't say she recognized it any better than the handwriting. It didn't help that it was more than half worn off. She put it in her pocket with the note and debated about whether she should tell any of this to David.

She knew that she didn't want Daniel or Pam knowing what happened. She didn't want them to know a stranger had invaded their home. Or that, he had probably been killed by another stranger. Even worse, Rebecca thought, was that she was the reason it all happened. Why tell them and make everyone upset when she was sure that it was either over or would follow her, when she left later today. She covered up the blood stained spot of snow and went back in, to actually, check on Ebony this time.

Rebecca brushed the reddish black coat of the large animal that had protected her. She knew the stables had been her best chance of evading that jackal. She shuddered visualizing that vile man, who like a mangy, rabid dog had wished to sink his canine teeth into her. She wondered who spared her from that loathsome creature's stalking her again. Rebecca couldn't fathom any of this, and she simply couldn't imagine someone killing another for her sake. She felt no guilt over the destruction of that man. She wasn't responsible for what had happened to him. As she saw it, it was the depth of his own character that had sealed his fate, not her. Whoever her silent knight was, she couldn't help wondering if his act of protection were performed out of callousness or great fortitude. The note made her think it was the latter. She preferred not to think that there might be other cold blooded snakes lurking in the corners somewhere waiting to strike out at her. Instead, she rather believe that there was a stallion out there, watching her, ready and waiting to trample any other slithering, hissing vermin which dared to sneer it's fangs at her. She read the note once more and slid it back into her pocket, satisfied that whoever he was, he was a friend.

"Rebecca, are you sure your alright." Daniel was standing there with Ebony's food and was ready to clean his stall.

"Yes, I'm fine. Really, It was no big deal." She gave him a firm expression to assure him. "Someone sneaked up on me and Ebony protected me, and he left."

"It sounded like more than that."

"Well, I don't know what else happened."

"Who was it."

"I don't know who he was, but Ebony here slammed him pretty good though."

"Did the man touch you."

"No, he never had the chance."

"Good, Good job Ebony, he pat the horse, you're a good boy, aren't you."

"Why were you even out here." The dirty blonde haired man looked at her with his confused gray eyes.

"It's my own fault really, I was acting like a child. David and I had a minor argument. He went off to the barns to be alone, and I decided to come see Ebony."

"Do you mind if I ask what your fight was about."

"It was stupid, yesterday he accused me of being distant and then this morning he did the same thing to me, so I called him on it. But I didn't give him a chance to respond right away, I expected he'd wait, while I used the bathroom, but he didn't."

"He probably wouldn't have confronted your accusation anyway. He likes to think things through, before he says his peace. When he's really upset about something he goes hunting, gets his thoughts straight and then he comes back, and talks about it. If I know David, he probably wanted to get his emotions in check before you left this morning."

"Well. That just goes to show, how well I don't know him, because it seemed to me he always had no problem confronting me, all strong and confident."

"He is those things. He just needs time to sort out his feelings, so that he can express them eloquently." Daniel filled the mustangs water trough. "I haven't seen him this happy in a long time." Looking up at Rebecca, "You've made him happy, I can't tell you how wonderful it has been to see him whole and spirited again, Thank you."

Rebecca saw the expression of pain in his face. She knew Daniel, like Pam, was worried about their friend. "Daniel, I really care for David and I'd really appreciate it if we could keep what happened here to ourselves."

"You floor me Rebecca, who are you?"

"What do you mean?"

"I mean, look at this horse, if he reacted the way I believe he did, then something serious happened here in this stable this morning. But all you're worried about is how everyone else is going to react to what you're not telling us. The only thing I can't figure out is if you are acting this way to be brave or deceptive."

"I don't want everyone to get all upset, when there is no reason to. The problem is over and it's not going to happen again."

"What problem is over and how do you know it's not going to happen again?" She turned to see David standing there heavy of breath and very upset. "What the hell is going on here, he demanded to know, and why the hell are you even here, anyway." David was now yelling. He was so happy, to see her standing there and all in one piece. The message he received was confusing and disturbing all at the same time. It was all he could do to get here without hitting a tree.

***He could see through the binoculars that she had kept her cool. "Good girl." She had gone back over his tracks and had destroyed them and covered all the blood. She still had it. He thought. That instinct to think things through and get the job done. He was glad he had gotten there early today in preparation for her trip. If that son of a bitch had hurt her, he would have ensured the man had died much slower and in a much more gruesomely manner. He knew the barbaric pig. His gut had told him, way back then, That he should have destroyed him. When he had met him in Kosovo. He hated to think of the cruelties that must have been inflicted by that sick boar as he rutted his way through the world during the past five years.

He was glad she was safe. It killed him though, to watch her with this man. He had wanted her, but he had respected her marriage and had never tried to pressure her. Even though, he had craved for her help in quieting his loneliness. He had sensed her attraction to him. He also thought it was partly her response to his for her. She was a strong woman; no matter how flirtatious he had been with her, and no matter how many times he had invaded her personal space, she had never backed down or was less professional. Now he had killed a man for her, and he wanted more than anything for her to know it had been him who had protected her.

"David, come on buddy you need to calm down." Daniel was sure his friend was going to push Rebecca away by doing this. He knew she wasn't the type to be thankful for a man treating her like a child. Daniel stepped between David and Rebecca, "Think about how you're acting."
"She's fine, look at her."

He stepped back and let his heart stop pounding. Looking at her, she did look like she was fine, but then, what was all this about. He was angry with himself not her. He tried to calm himself, to slow the blood coursing within him. He had been stupid to run off this morning, instead of just facing her and his feelings. If he could go back, he would never have gotten out of that bed this morning. He would have held her until he was forced to let go. If only, he looked past Daniel and into her eyes, she looked away for a moment and he knew she was hiding a secret. He was able to tell now when she was holding something back. He had spent too much time watching her every tiny nuance, not to notice. He saw in her the truth. Something had happened. She was too honest to have the skill to hide her emotions. He saw it, the brave front she was attempting to project, trying to appear carefree so he wouldn't be the wiser. He recognized it in her face. He had seen it before on the deck of a ship in the Persian Gulf. That allowing of yourself, to feel the fullness of your fear, and pushing on despite it. That was all bravery was. He knew, because he had felt it before himself, he also knew anything less wasn't courage, it was mere ignorance.

He looked at his friend, "Thanks Daniel."
"It's not me you need to thank, it's that horse of yours."

David looked over to Rebecca and saw that her regular pale coloring was coming back. Her dark features emphasized her frail complexion. He liked how she looked like a porcelain doll, But now he knew that that look was deceiving, she wasn't quite as fragile as she appeared to be.

"Whoever it was, Ebony gave him a good pounding according to

Rebecca." Daniel saw that his friend had calmed down now. He walked over to Rebecca and gave her a light hug. "Have a safe trip Rebecca."

"Thanks Daniel, tell Pam there is nothing to worry about." They smiled at each other and waved as he left the stable.

David walked up to her and fought wanting to hold her, he was unsure if she wanted that at this moment. Looking at David she couldn't figure out what he was thinking. She had seen rage like his before. It wasn't something that frightened her. She knew he wouldn't have hurt her. It was only rage induced by helplessness.

"I'm sorry, I shouldn't have run off to the stables."

"No, you should have been with me. It's my fault."

"It's no one's fault, besides, I'm fine."

"Are you going to tell me what happened?"

"I don't know, I haven't decided that yet."

"I know that, can I hold you now."

"Please." They both said at the same time.

She may be confused about everything else in her life right now, but one thing was certain. She felt safe in his arms and knew she would miss that.

❋❋❋

He hit speed dial and held the gadget up to his ear, "Yeah it's me. No. I have a package left at the prescribed coordinates. No, it couldn't be helped. Yeah I'm fine. No. Damn it - This is my case. No. NO! He doesn't need to know anything. She's fine. Yeah, zero nine hundred hours, destination Charlie Tango. Yeah, there could be possible delays. ETA is eighteen hundred hours. No, teams are no longer necessary. Roger Sir. Yes. Over, Out." He put the phone back in his pocket and picked the binoculars back up. There she was with him again. He understood this guy's attraction to her. She had a way of looking at you. Where the shine in her eyes made you feel like you were the center of the universe. He wanted her to know. To know that he had done well, he had been assigned CID, but then his application had been picked up quickly for CIA. He knew she would have been so proud of him. Her smile made his heart ache, he knew it did that to everyone, but he felt it no less knowing that. When he caught wind of this assignment sitting on his boss's desk, he insisted the assignment be his. He was given a hard time about taking it. It wasn't a high priority to the man, but it was to him. He'd sit out in the dark in this damn freezing, wet snow forever, to see her smile and look at him with that glow in her eye one more time.

      Looking in the rearview mirror, Rebecca adjusted the black Stetson and watched David look at her and the children as she pulled the car down the gravel driveway. The children were waving madly at the three of them standing in the driveway, waving back. Rebecca rolled down her window and reached her hand out to wave also. Taking one last look in the mirror, she saw David turn and walk toward the barns. Then she closed the cold air away again. She clutched the piece of paper in her hand and shoved it in the pocket of her jeans. She turned and followed the road out to the main highway the way Frank had told her to go. Seeing the sign for the interstate she put her blinker on for the I-81 turn.

      Rebecca listened to the silence in the car and knew that each of them had fallen in love with these people in one way or another. She charged the car up the mountain ahead of them and through the cut through the mountains which left cliff faces of exposed rock. She absorbed the scenery around her, noticing the rock had thick layers of ice covering it. In some places, it was so thick that the ice glowed with a sky blue hue. One spot looked just like David's eyes and she smiled when she realized that ice had a way of burning you from its intense cold, the way his eyes had burnt her. There was nothing cold about David, though. He was one of the most inviting and comforting people she had ever met. As Rebecca rounded the corner of the mountain, there before her was a valley and another mountain ridge in the distance. In it, she noticed a small town, one like David's and farms cut into the snow-covered mountains beyond. She saw that many trees had been lost, but that was good she thought, it made room for new growth.

      The people here would have a lot of work ahead of them, but they would be left with the warmth of fires for many years to come. With it would be the refreshed and rejuvenated forest giving them a whole pallet of bright new colors to behold from their porches. She rolled down the window only a little, enough to smell the clean winter air and hope to catch the scent of a fallen pine. She listened as the roar of the water rushed down the side of the rock walls on both sides of the highway. The sun was beating down with a summer's force and she thought about how beautiful these mountains would be in a week or two. When it would be covered in the lush green growth of thick pastures and the sight of wild daffodils and crocuses would be mixed into the hillsides of scattered grazing cattle. Soon the fences would be covered again with sweet honeysuckle. Then would be the period when daisy's, golden rod and Queen Anne's lace would dominate. Once the drowning sun of summer hit these hillsides, only the hearty purple thistle would have survived its sweltering heat.

Rebecca felt blessed. She had been given the opportunity to see into a world she otherwise would never have glimpsed, and it was all she thought it would be. Yeah, life was difficult for everyone, but that doesn't mean that they don't still have a slice of heaven on earth. She knew she was predisposed to seeing the world through rose colored glasses as one of her professors always complained about, but she knew that using clear or worse black ones didn't always make things any better. Change, change was what he was always concerned with, maybe things did need to change... sometimes. She couldn't help thinking that some things were good as they were and she thought these mountains were probably one of them. Maybe that was naive thinking on her part. She didn't care, right now the optimism of her rosy vision was comforting, and she wasn't willing to give it away.

Rebecca read the sign for Arlington and knew she would end up there eventually. Right now though, like her view of those mountains in her rearview mirror, her spirit couldn't afford to give up hope, not yet. Driving past the sign that would lead her to the national cemetery. Rebecca looked at her wedding rings and willed herself to continue believing that its soil held no significance to her life. It was a lie. He was only trying to rattle her, but somehow her rings seemed to her to have lost some of its luster.

Rebecca avoided traversing the big cities and instead continued up I-81 forging her way into eastern Pennsylvania. Where she would then take a sharp turn east, toward home and to where she knew she would really find out who she was, what she wanted and if she were strong enough to command her own life. She looked at the children in the back seat sleeping and then over to her daughter reading in the seat next to her. She wondered if she should talk to her about Tommy. Deciding against it, she flicked on the radio and settled herself for the long drive ahead.

CHAPTER FIFTEEN

Carl woke in the darkness to the familiar sensation of Rebecca by his side. Sliding his body toward hers, he caught the slight scent of roses. Carefully he turned back away from the woman pretending to be his wife and reached out for the wristwatch that he had placed on his bed's side table. His arm felt strangely disconnected from the rest of his body, as if it belonged to someone else. Pushing the button on the watch, the neon glow appeared to wobble. The ripples kept time to the soft ticking of the timepiece, and Carl watched as each second, another ripple made its way across the crystal. It reminded him of the effect a rock makes to the surface of a pond. The way it had when he went pond skimming as a small child. He remembered carefully picking out the perfect stones, ones as flat as this watch's face.

Through the waves, he strained to make out the time, 4:30am. Reaching his feet to the floor he couldn't feel the rug beneath them. Stepping across the room, he moved toward the bathroom. Each step felt void of the weight of his own body. Surreal, Carl realized, that was what he was feeling. It was a bizarre, interesting feeling being disconnected from his body and the environment around him. A walking dream, he thought, as he reached his seemingly, wobbly arm out to the door handle.

Stepping inside the bathroom, the cold surface of the tile floor jarred him half way back to reality. He closed the door behind him and flicked on the light switch. That was all that it took. The unforgiving wattage of the light bulb filled the small room and shocked his over dilated eyes. Jerking his hand up in defense, Carl sheltered his eyes and slowly allowed them to adjust before he removed it. Though he felt back to normal, the image in the mirror betrayed him. Inspecting his reflection,

Carl noticed that the green in his eyes were normal, and so was his olive complexion. The dark brown hair was the same too. He couldn't place what it was, but he felt strange somehow. He felt an odd sensation and recognized that he felt like a fraud. It wasn't him; he realized. As much as it was the world he was forced to function in.

Carl took in a deep breath and regained his composure. Taking in another equally deep breath, Carl gave himself his wife's speech. He knew she would be telling him that he could do this. As much as he hated hobnobbing and dressing up. He knew her counsel would be correct; he would make it through this day, and manage to convince everyone along the way that Julie was his wife. No one said that they had to be an old married couple, if Julie acted like a newlywed, then that is what he would pass them off as being. He knew that he needed more rest to face the stress of this day, so he headed back to bed and climbed gently in with the rose scented girl who would pretend to be his wife.

Julie woke to the stream of light entering the bedroom window and was amazed that she had slept so long. 7:00am. She couldn't remember the last time she had slept past five in the morning. It never mattered what time she went to bed something always triggered her to wake at 5:00am. She looked at Carl lying next to her. Julie thought about how she usually slept in the center of the bed, not used to sharing it. She hoped she hadn't hogged the bed during the night. She went to the bathroom to clean up and decided she better grab a shower now, before everyone else was up.

Carl heard water pouring down like rain, he roused himself further and noticed it was the shower in the bathroom. He assumed it was Julie since she wasn't in the bed anymore. He knocked on the door, then cracked it and yelled her name.

"Yes." She answered.

"I'm coming in, okay."

"Ah. alright." She listened as the stream filled the toilet.

"I'll go and make some coffee." He told her.

"Okay." She heard the door close behind him.

She went to the bedroom and tried to figure out what she should wear this morning. Catching her reflection in the dresser mirror, she stopped to see how she looked. She felt really well rested, and Julie thought that it showed in the mirror. This morning there was no need to cover up any dark rings under her eyes and her skin looked a bit more colorful also. She worked at French braiding her hair and decided to leave a couple of wisps out to frame her face. From the closet, she grabbed a black pantsuit and a pretty coral silk blouse that she thought emphasized her eyes well. Then she strapped her gun to the side of her ribcage and put the jacket on over it. Grabbing her shoes, she went to join Carl in the kitchen.

Instead, she found Natalia sitting there with a cup of coffee, and there was a small plate of muffins on the kitchen table that she must have baked, because there weren't any in the apartment yesterday. "I hope you don't mind I made these?"

"Not at all." She took one as the woman pushed the plate toward her. They were still warm, blueberry, but it needed butter. Julie poured herself some coffee and then asked where the men were.

"They are outside on the balcony." "I made Yuri go outside to smoke that nasty thing he's addicted to."

Julie thought they smelled pretty good, but the second hand smoke probably wasn't good for anyone.

"You look very pretty. Is that how I should dress for breakfast this morning."

"Thank you. I haven't been to the place we're going to, but I heard it was nice there." She told the woman sitting across from her. She couldn't help noticing her dark brown hair with a little gray mixed into it. Julie looked at her eyes, and saw that they looked as if they had been through a lot in their lifetime. She was very pretty. She looked like she was wiser than they were maybe supposed to believe her to be. "What is it like in your country?"

"Before the fall of communism, it was just a very difficult life. But now with the developing of democracy, it is scary and very chaotic, before we understood to be careful of the government. Now half the time, we don't know whom we need to watch out for. We don't know if the boy next door is in the mafia. It is men like Yuri, ex-KGB that are trying to bring some order to the chaos there. They also have the same struggles from before, trying to stay in the loop globally. Unfortunately, there are some who wish to take advantage of our countries current state of disorganization. That is why we are here, for your people's help."

Julie understood what she was telling her. Their country couldn't face a major war, at best it would send them back into communist rule and at worst it would destroy their nation completely.

Carl stood with Yuri outside on the balcony. They watched as mount Rainer sat, strutting its stuff in the distance, awing them both. "It is very beautiful here. This place has a way of making you forget there are real problems out there, like the one we are facing now."

Yuri agreed, "Yes, it is very pretty here. You wish to keep some perspective, the large man told him, Then you just imagine what that mountain would look like after a nuclear explosion."

Carl cringed. That thought did it; he couldn't see it at all anymore, he imagined the mountain all dark and the trees standing charred black with death. This man next to him had lived the cold war. Carl was fortunate enough to have that end when he was in his teens. He could still remember seeing the films teachers said the communist children were seeing in their schools. Films that were full of exaggerations about the bad things in the United States; crime, drugs, poverty etc. He assumed both sides must have exaggerated.

Yuri stoked on his cigar one last time and then they went inside.

Carl excused himself to shower and then he put on a suit like Julie had. They needed to meet Randy at nine in the dining hall. He was told the name fooled you. It was actually an upscale restaurant, and he knew that they would be expected to have on a tie and coat.

As they entered, everyone couldn't avoid looking up. The chandelier caught all of their attention, dangling there in mid air, it was huge, making the room appear smaller than it actually was. The room was half filled with people already. He knew the place was popular, but he hadn't expected a crowd at nine in the morning.

Carl was further surprised when he saw Carrie there with Randy. He thought for sure that she would be finishing up last arrangements for this evening's affair. She was as elaborate as always, wearing a bright yellow suit and white blouse. Six rows of pearls were wrapped around her neck and with it earrings to match, shaped like huge flowers in her lobes. Her blonde hair was down to her shoulders with the ends scooped under as always. She was really quite intimidating, sitting there straight backed, a woman of strength and fortune. But she was also as warm and inviting as always. He really liked her, and he wondered if that were obvious to everyone, not that that mattered. Everyone liked her. It was her gift. Either that or bred into her. Carl didn't know which.

The couple stood as the four of them approached the table in the middle of the room. There would have been no other suitable place in the room for them to be seated, the Taylor's were center of the room type of people. He and Rebecca; were much more comfortable in a corner somewhere, where they could be alone and not feel stared at by others. He introduced his new friends to the Taylor's and then they all took their seats. He noticed that Yuri and Natalia were both center people too, but he hadn't expected anything otherwise, considering the line of business they were in.

However, he was surprised to see that Julie felt slightly uncomfortable, she was busy looking around and playing with her napkin in her lap. "Are you okay?" He whispered into her ear.

"Yes, I feel uncomfortable, my back is to the door."

He understood. It was the training in her.

Randy caught their eyes and asked the waiter for a different table.

She smiled to him and then he let them pick their places first by stalling Yuri and Natalia with conversation. She chose the seat that allowed her to see both the front door and the service door to the rear. She was much more at ease now, and it was very noticeable to Carl, and he presumed it was to Randy too.

The rest of breakfast went well. They had talked about nothing except this evening's event and a few other insignificant things. Carrie told them that the reason for the children's sleepover in the Great room lobby was because the major attraction tonight was a dance contest. A dance until you drop - that started at ten this evening and went until there was only one couple left standing. "The prize is a Hawaiian cruise, she said excited, so the participation should be good." The women's group she was in charge of had voted on the contest and the prize. Not to mention, a few other surprises tonight, such as the entertainment and the theme of the dance. Her father even decided he was going to come to this one. Carrie explained leaving out the details. "I won't spoil the surprise." Carrie sipped her coffee and became tight lipped.

Randy told them they would have a few other unexpected guests tonight also. Carrie looked at her husband with a look that told the rest of them that she hadn't been informed of this new information. "I didn't want you to get nervous." He looked at his wife. "We'll have some very important guests tonight. However, I'm not allowed to say who, for security reasons." He winked at his company. Everyone made their own guesses, but no one said anything. Carl didn't think that there would be very many people in our country who could make Carrie nervous. Randy patted his wife's hand. "Don't worry, Your parties are wonderful."

"That wonderful?"

"Yes honey, really. Don't even think about making any changes."

She took a deep breath, "Okay."

They finished their meal and then they all went over to Carl and Julie's to have a cup of coffee. Carrie was pleased to see that the chess table was finally getting put to use after all these years. "Matt told me that you are teaching him how to play chess, Carl."

"Yes, he's getting pretty good too. Of course, I have yet to beat

Yuri."

"Would you like to try me Randy." The gray haired, round and incredibly tall Russian man enticed the Major with a spark of competition in his eye.

"Why not." Randy took off his jacket and took one of the seats.

"Julie. Randy told me that you dragged Carl off to the mall yesterday."

"Yes." The young girl said excitedly. "Would you like to see my dress?" The women went into the bedroom, and Julie showed them the flowing rose pink dress with the silver lace that covered the bodice, and the silver lace shawl and shoes to match.

Carrie looked at the back of the dress and saw that it came down past the small of her back, "Wow, how daring, you'll look beautiful."

"Thank you. Natalia bought a dress yesterday too."

She showed the woman her dress, and they all thought it was very pretty and perfect for the woman's dark features. Natalia thanked them both. She loved the dress and had been thrilled shopping for it. Being able to look through racks of dresses was something these women probably took for granted. She ran her hand across the blue silk gown and knew that she didn't. Having breakfast in the fancy restaurant, the movie last night and this dress were all privileges she would remember for the rest of her life.

Carrie looked at her watch and at the pretty, yet plain woman who was in her age group and thought of a great idea, at least she hoped it would be. "I have an appointment that I have to go to, she reached up and touched her hair, would you both like to come and get fixed up for tonight with me." Julie's mouth dropped. She knew all the salons in the immediate vicinity would have been booked a month in advance. Carrie took that as a "yes" and she pulled out her cell phone and called her very sheik hairdresser and made sure he could fit them all in. "He says he can fit us all in at noon." She smiled at them. "And don't even think of bringing your purses ladies because this girl's day out is on me."

Julie looked at Carrie. "What about Carl?"

"That man of yours will be fine with Randy, newlyweds." She smiled over to Natalia.

Natalia thought that could explain a lot.

Carrie ran down the hall to explain things to Randy.

Julie told the other women that she would use the restroom and then be right with them. She ran through the bathroom and through to the bedroom beyond. She removed her gun and holster and instead put a smaller gun in her handbag and went to join the others in the living room.

"You know I can stay here with you men." Julie mentioned in an almost pleading tone.

Randy insisted she go with the other women.

Carl met her in the kitchen. "I'll be fine."

"Promise you won't go anywhere while I'm gone."

"I promise. We'll stay right here." Carl looked at her in his perfectly comfortable and confident manner, "Go on Julie, they're waiting."

Julie hesitated. She kissed him quickly on the lips, goodbye and felt uncertain if leaving wasn't a mistake. When she heard the helicopter, she knew that it was. "Are we going all the way to Seattle?"

"Well, of course we are, some of the best hairdressers are there."

"Carrie." Julie started to complain, and stopped.

Paul escorted them out to the helicopter. "Don't worry. You have to look your best tonight. A lot of important people will be there. It could open a lot of doors for you." He told her, before she joined the others inside the aircraft. She knew that was true. Normally she would have been very enthusiastic about that prospect, but lately her drive was missing.

The pilot asked if they were headed to 'The Day Spa.'

"Yes. Jackson, will be expecting us at noon."

He nodded in understanding and lifted the metal bird and charged forward.

"Ms. Taylor you look wonderful." The young man exclaimed from behind the marble counter.

"Carrie, sweetheart."

"Of course."

"Do you want the full package today."

"Oh, bless your heart, but we couldn't, not enough time today, but thank you." She knew they usually expected clients in by 10:00am for full packages.

"Would you like me to lighten this up for you, to be more spring like." He was playing with her hair, and they hadn't even fully entered the salon yet. Julie thought they obviously have had a long time business relationship. "Well." He looked at her friends. "I know exactly what would be perfect for each of you. Ms. Taylor you may not have the time for the whole package, but rest assured you'll leave here looking like a million dollars."

"I always do, Honey."

He introduced them all to his helpers today and led them into the back where he could wave his magic wand.

Yuri stomped Randy's butt too, and now Carl didn't feel quite as bad. "Is anyone hungry." Carl watched as both men shook their heads that they were. Carl looked at his watch and told them that he could throw some steaks on the grill. The men reset the chessboard and started again. Carl thawed a few steaks and searched the cabinets for some spices or sauce. Going out to the grill, he started it and sat on one of the chairs as he waited for it to warm up. He threw the steaks on and went to the kitchen to microwave some potatoes. Returning to the balcony, he saw the movement of something tan on the ground below. He stood very still and wondered if the smell of the steaks cooking had brought it out of the woods. Looking through the slats of the balcony, he could see the size of the animal below. It was huge. Its paws were roughly the size of his hands with his fingers spread open. The creature looked up at him, and acted as if Carl were just another object it its environment. It was beautiful. He knew it must have had a full belly because Carl felt no fear of being its next snack.

The cougar looked up at him again and stared into his eyes. They were light green, and they looked like they were three times the size of his own. He felt safe with the animal there below him, like it had taken Julie's place protecting him while she was away. The animal just sat there looking out at the woods the way Julie had the first day he had met her. Carl checked the steaks and then placed them on his plate and went back inside. As he closed the glass door behind him, Carl saw the cougar bounding into the woods and watched as it disappeared into the forests green foliage.

The knob rattled, and the door burst open. "I love that color, it is so pretty." Carrie had both of the women with her feeling like they were the most beautiful in the world. Julie felt like Cinderella after the fairy godmother had waved her wand, and now she was on the way to meet the prince. Carl stood in the kitchen washing the dishes from lunch. "Did you girls eat something, Carl yelled, I can throw on some steaks for you."

Julie came in and swirled around. "Thank you, but Carrie took us out to lunch." Her auburn hair had been given strawberry-blond highlights. They had done her nails in rose pink polish to match her gown and her makeup looked flawless.

"Wow, you look wonderful."

The salon had put her hair up to reveal her slender neck and the wisps were curled. Carl thought that she looked straight out of a portrait in the Metropolitan Museum. Once she was in her outfit, he knew he would be the envy of the other men. Carl could tell that she felt pretty, and she should because she was beautiful.

"Would you ladies like some hot tea." Carl placed a filled pot on the stove.

"Yes, a cup of tea would be nice, it certainly isn't spring out there yet." Carrie wrapped her arms around her and rubbed at them.

Randy was involved in the game he and Yuri were playing, and Carl thought that Randy wasn't one to accept defeat kindly. Yuri made the killing move and Randy was forced to accept his loss. He turned the piece sideways on the board, "Good game Yuri, I'm glad we're on the same side in other venues."

The older man laughed, "You put up a good fight Randy. Thank you, it was a good game."

"Should I make a fire, or do you think the scent would soak into our clothing."

"How very considerate of you to worry about that, Carl. A fire would be lovely." Everyone agreed with Carrie.

Julie asked the men if they wanted some tea with them, but instead Randy and Yuri both had coffee with a shot of brandy. Carl had his usual extra sweet coffee and then Carrie and Randy left to get ready for this evening.

The others all agreed to meet them down at the banquet hall an hour early so they could help Carrie with last minute arrangements. "That gives us three hours. Yuri commented. "I think I'll take a short nap to get me through the night." Natalia smiled and told him she didn't wish to mess up her hair. She would just relax out here. He twirled his wife as she stood to give him a goodnight kiss and he told her to rest so they could win that trip to Hawaii.

Julie didn't doubt that they were probably wonderful dancers. She never learned any official dances except a standard waltz. "Carl, do you dance?"

"Ah. No, not really."

"Good, That puts us in the same boat."

"Well, you must learn to dance a little. It would be rude not to at least start the dance contest," Natalia told them, "The first few dances at the very least."

They knew that Natalia was right. She turned on the radio, "Not the right music, but it will do." She taught them both the basics to a few dances, the fox trot, the tango, a waltz and a polka. Then she commanded them to continue practicing while she went to freshen up in the ladies room and get ready to go.

With the coffee table moved out of the way, soft music on the stereo and a crackling fire in the hearth, the young students did as they were told. Gently Carl held Julie. Carefully stepping one way then the other, his hand pressed warmly against the small of her back. Leaning into her ear he said quietly, "I think we're getting the hang of this." Carl felt a small shudder work its way through her. He didn't think she could possibly be cold, not with the fire going next to them. He looked into her eyes and caught a subtle feeling that she was sad. "Is something wrong."

"No."

"Are you sure."

"Yeah."

He wasn't convinced, but he wasn't going to push the issue either.

"I got something yesterday. When I went into the tux store with Yuri, I saw a vest that matched your dress, so I bought it."

"Let's see it." She smiled. "That was so sweet of you." She knew how difficult going shopping was for him yesterday. She urged him to try it on.

"No, you'll have to wait to see the whole package at once."

"Well then, let's get ready because I can't wait to see your outfit."

In the bedroom, Julie watched Carl enter the bathroom and then heard the shower turn on. When he came back out she saw the steam flow out the door and smelt the fresh scent of after-shave. Julie breathed in a deep breath of the drifting scent. It smelt heavenly to her. The warm manly scent tickled her nose as she took in another abundance of air to capture the scent of him from across the room.

She was standing in front of the mirror, and he could see her reflection in it. Very beautiful, slim and pale with the sensual dress that clung to her hips ever so slightly as it draped its way to the floor. The back, which was facing him, was bare all the way to her butt. He watched as she adjusted the necklace she was trying on. With her long pale arms raised to her neck, the length of her back was emphasized to reveal her slender waist and the small of her back. If it were even an inch lower, he knew the world would see the creamy beginnings of her delicate shapely bottom. Imagining her white silky form sent a shiver up his body and an equally jolting response elsewhere. Carl put on the vest and buttoned it. He was right. It matched her gown perfectly.

Turning to face him, "What do you think, this diamond heart or these pearls."

"With the silver lace I would say the diamonds definitely."

"I thought so too." She took the pale pink pearls out of her ears and replaced them with diamonds to match the necklace.

"The necklace is very pretty, a little large maybe for your delicate features though."

"Yes, well the man who gave it to me was feeling especially generous when he bought it for me."

"Hmm... that doesn't surprise me."

"I had saved his life and the bullet proof vest I was wearing at the time, was pierced at my heart."

"Are you serious."

"Absolutely."

"Should you be dressed like that then."

"Well, he had a more definite and certain enemy."

"Who was it."

"Let's just say that he had a wife who wasn't happy with the share of his fortune that she would have received if she asked for a divorce."

"She tried to kill him and you."

"No worse, she hired a hit man."

"Oh my god, what kind of people do you work for."

She smiled at him, "People like you, it's why I make the money that I do, remember."

He felt bad. "I didn't bring this on myself."

"Believe it or not. He didn't ask for his wife to be a shark either."

"Well, it is very pretty." Carl touched her slightly to lift the heart and noticed the beginnings of a rosy flush grow across her chest.

"Thank you." She gazed straight into his eyes only a few inches away. "The cold feel of it reminds me to stay sharp." She thought the subject was dampening their mood. "I love your vest, it was very thoughtful of you to notice it matches my dress." She looked at the two of them in the mirror. "We look like we belong together, I like that." Carl smiled at her and brought her shawl up to her shoulders. Then they joined the Russian couple in the living room.

They entered the lobby filled busily with teenagers wearing white t-shirts that each said captain, with their name under it. They were setting up the last of the supplies needed for the sleepover. Carrie had ordered two caterers, both of which were running around preparing last minute details. One was a fancy caterer from Seattle and his staff of about fifty people, and the other was a local woman who had been tasked with coming up with the children's menu.

She had done a wonderful job according to Carrie. The whole menu consisted of finger foods. Carrie knew the kids would love not having to use silverware, but she had been appalled and told the woman that that would be incredibly time consuming for her and her small staff. The woman agreed to let a couple of teenage volunteers help her. Carrie had been careful to pick very serious young adults and told them that this could end up being a good summer job if they worked hard. This local woman was a great cook. Carrie had hired her to cater smaller diners they had at the facility, and she also did meals for the buffet dinners they had monthly.

They saw the two young girls that Carrie picked out heading over to a corner of the great room. That corner sometimes had a bartender handing out drinks, but for tonight the bar had been converted into a small kitchen by the maintenance staff. It was covered with a clown tent and was accented with a ton of twinkle lights. Each person of the catering staff was wearing a different clown jumpsuit and they had on their chef hats. A couple of them even wore paint and one man wore a red nose. Everyone in the lobby was enjoying watching them prepare their children's meal. Many people who knew the woman and her staff were busy complimenting them. She told the parents that the last thing they had planned for the kids was an ice cream sundae jamboree. Every child would get to go through the rainbow tent following the line of tables as each makes their own sundae. They had a whole Ice Cream Shoppe full of toppings. The teenagers were busy crushing packages of candy bars and placing them in bowls. The parents left wearily, hoping their own evening would be as fun as their children's promised to be.

Julie was amazed at the amount of children lining up to be assigned to their captains. Then each child was given a piece of tape and marker to label their sleeping bags. The adults watched as the stack of bags against the wall began its assent. Carrie came into the great room and clapped her hands loudly to get everyone's attention. "Welcome everyone, please get your children to their proper captains first, but then you'll need to join the others in the ball room, I'm afraid it is less exciting there at the moment. She took a deep breath, I'm sorry about that, but the caterers need their room. Thank you." She greeted individuals as she made her way through the busy lobby to check on all the staff. "Julie aren't you beautiful." She greeted them all.

Inside the banquet hall, were two women seated at a table. The first let them know from a chart behind her where they were seated. The other checked off their names, and each couple was handed large sticker numbers for the contest. Carl and Julie were seated at a large round table with four other couples from the project. Julie pointed out to Carl that Yuri and Natalia were seated at a table with Carrie's parents, so far they were the only two couples seated at that table.

The stage to the front of the room was tri-tiered and draped in pleated satin cloth. The stage was well lit and was set up for a big band. To the side of the stage, was a quartette setting up. They listened as the cello, two violins and the viola were tuned, and the players warmed up. Harold was telling them all that the quartette was dinner entertainment. "But for after dinner, Carrie managed to get Davie Artrello and Missy Travis." Sheila hit her husband, "You weren't supposed to tell anyone." They were all surprised. Davie Artrello had been herald as the new Sinatra and Missy Travis was a famous singer of blues and pop. "Davie and Missy agreed to perform for the dance contest with short breaks of course, Sheila pointed to the fifty style jukebox in the far corner, During the breaks we're going to use the jukebox to keep the contest going." Helen said excitedly. "Can you believe the prize, a two week cruise leaving from Seattle and going to Hawaii." Sheila added. "And it's not only to Oahu, the cruise starts in Kauai and then goes to Oahu, Maui and then the Big Island."

"Wow, it should be a good contest." Julie commented.

On everyone's plate was a rolled up and ribbon tied small cream paper, Carl thought it was probably the menu. It was stuck out of a tiny brass wire basket filled with mints and around the baskets were assorted candies each decorated with tiny flowers of hard frosting. The floral bow from the basket flared up and then a litany of tiny colored ribbon strands extended from the large puffy one. It was a very pretty presentation, and Carl knew Rebecca would have loved to see the table with the high rose topiaries and the accent candles all around them.

Tiny fairy lights hung from the ceiling surrounded in green sheer cloth. It create a soft glow and add to the garden park theme. The low pile gray rugs that were around the room had been hand-painted to look like stone patios. Carrie and the women placed park benches everywhere, especially around the dance floor in the center. Strands of lush green ivy were woven with flower garlands made of roses. Each climbed the park lampposts that glowed in the softest light he had ever seen. The scent from the roses was surprisingly strong. Carl looked around the room and felt as if it were a park filled with flowers of pink, white, crimson, yellow and even purple. All of it mixed with so much green that it was difficult to believe that it was March outside. The glow and warmth of the candles made it feel as if it were a warm June evening. The slow, gentle twinkle of some of the fairy lights even gave him the impression of fireflies.

People were piling in now, and it was interesting hearing the low rumble of voices in the room. The quartette began playing, and the people began to speak more naturally. Carl listened as the low rumble transformed into a loud thunder of talk and laughter. He liked how the music was loud enough to enjoy; but soft enough so you could easily speak with others at your table. Julie whispered into his ear. "I think they want us to be a little distant from everyone tonight. We need to try and blend in, and just enjoy ourselves." "Let Randy or anyone else come to you if they want to talk to you." Carl nodded to Julie. She was beautiful. He couldn't smell her rose perfume over the roses in the room, but he knew she smelt like them tonight too. She reached for his hand, and he could feel the rings on her finger.

"Are you doing okay?"

"Yeah, I'm doing very well, actually. These couples are familiar and the noise is comforting."

"Good." She smiled at him.

"Did I tell you how beautiful you look tonight." He thought that she definitely looked like the fairy queen from the chess set. All she was missing were the wings.

"Thank you." She felt really pretty. Hearing Carl say so, made her feel more beautiful still.

The place was almost filled now. Gowns and black tuxedos were everywhere. Many men wore accents to their wives gowns, and Carl noticed that Randy wore a yellow vest to match his wife's yellow flowing gown. He noticed she had simply switched from the yellow suit to the elegant gown. She still wore all the pearls and the sight of her was stunning. Matt was at a table across the way with Harry from the project, and he saw that they had young ladies with them.

"What are you thinking about Carl." Harold noticed the man across from him was off somewhere else.

"Matt Taylor over there, I didn't think he had a girlfriend." Carl saw Matt's arm around a pretty brown haired girl around his own age.

"That is our daughter Emily." Sheila explained that she was home visiting for spring break, "She goes to Brown."

"Apparently, she and Matt hit it off instantly, yesterday." Harold told everyone.

Helen lifted her brows, "Not a bad catch." Helen and Sheila looked at each other and nodded in agreement.

Helen's husband said. "Someone who can go to Brown University doesn't need to catch anyone."

Harold agreed with Ed and told his wife not to encourage this for their daughter.

"Harold, She can have both, a career and a marriage, besides Matt is a nice boy. She could do much worse."

"Okay, I agree with you, but she is finishing school, I haven't shelled out that much money to have her quit half way through."

"What is her major?" Julie asked.

"Biology."

"She must be very smart."

"Yes, she is. She wasn't popular in high school. Not like the Taylor's boys, that's probably why Matt didn't recognize her yesterday."

The whole table turned to look at the kids.

"They look nice together, don't they?" Debra, Jason's shy wife, said softly.

"Do you know that they went out last night, and it was eleven o'clock when they pulled into the drive, but Emily didn't come in until 4:00 am." Sheila said.

"You didn't tell me that."

"Harold, please. You would have embarrassed her."

"Your damn right I would have."

Helen laughed at him. "Harold your daughter is twenty years old, are you going to run off a guy courting a girl who is two years past the legal age."

"Hell Yes!"All the men at the table yelled.

"All they did was talk."

"How do you know that." He questioned his wife.

"Because, I believe my daughter, and because I recognized the look on her face. Come on Harold, you saw her this morning, she's in love."

Ed said, "Are you sure it's not lust."

"No." Harold told them. "Sheila's right, my little girl is in love - and he better not hurt her."

All the men at the table looked at Harold, and recognized the day, the day when your child is not really your small child anymore. They didn't envy Harold. He had reached a milestone in his life, one that was happy and sad. His daughter was in love, but she was also ready to leave home, the home Dad had made for her, and that meant that Harold was old.

Carl realized that Matt had found the girl, the one where he had told him that he would just know she was the one, and he was proud of him for not running scared. He saw her, and he went for it. He took that scary risk of getting hurt. His reward for his bravery was that pretty girl on his arm, and he saw that Matt looked very happy, like he was the prince of this ball. Carl looked across at Emily and wanted to be able to see his girls fall in love and tell his own son that one day the girl of his dreams will be standing there and it is up to him to risk his heart for her love.

Carl's thoughts were broken by the commotion. Outside, overhead was a large helicopter. It's sound managed to penetrate the building. Even with the music and the loud chatter, the thudding of the birds blades were deafening. Everyone was excited because they knew that there was an important guest arriving. Somehow since yesterday, it had leaked out that big people were coming, but no one knew who it could be. Now the moment of truth had arrived, and they were about to have their suspicions put to rest.

The place became very quiet as a precession of people entered the hall. First came many men in dark suits and Carl noticed they wore ear pieces. Julie leaned toward him, "Secret Service." That was what he had thought. Then entered a girl with a pixie hair cut, wearing a lime green gown. "I know her. She guards Senator Guthrie, here she is now." The fifty year old woman walked in with her husband on her arm. She looked lovely, was wearing a peach gown and was very pretty with slightly gray hair at the temples. The announcer spoke into the microphone. "We are pleased to be joined this evening by Senator and Mr. Guthrie from our great state of Washington. Everyone applauded. Next through the door was an older man with white hair, and he was dressed in a dress blue military uniform with ribbons covering his chest. On his arm was his wife in a pretty sequin and gray gown, her hair was pulled up and was blond though Carl thought that maybe it was naturally the same color as her husband's. The announcer: "General and Mrs. Harding of the United States Army, 82nd Airborne Division." Then came through the door, Randy and Carrie. She looked nice, calm considering her guests tonight. "Our lovely hosts tonight, Major and Mrs. Taylor." Everyone cheered loudly for their own couple that they all loved.

Then no one else came through the door, and so everyone went back to their talking and laughing, until the American Anthem started and everyone rose from their chairs. They all stood a little perplexed as the quartette finished the anthem. The announcer: "Ladies and gentlemen please remain standing." The quartette made the first few cords of a march, "Ladies and Gentlemen, The President and First Lady of the United States of America, James and Mary Cartwright."

They looked younger in person then on television. She was a brunette, and she wore a lavender gown with white gloves reaching up to her elbows. She had her hair pulled up and held with jeweled combs made of amethyst and diamonds. He wore a tuxedo. It was plain, but had a black silk pleated cummerbund. His youth made the outfit look dashing without the need for any additional ornament. He was dark haired and had commanding, yet gentle eyes and a smile that made everyone think he was intelligent and charming, which he was since he graduated from Harvard Law School. He had been Attorney General under Chamber's presidency then he ran a term as governor of California and now he was the second youngest president ever. Carl knew they had two small children, he wondered where they were until the little girl came running in to her mother's lap. The little girl was probably six years old, and she was wearing jeans and a sweater. It looked angora, but she still looked like a regular American child. The nanny came to get her, and their son came with her. Carl guessed he was about Karen's age, 10 years old. He was covered from head to toe in preppy designer clothing. The brother convinced his younger sister that she should go with him. Carl overheard him tell her on the way out. "If you stay with mom you'll have to eat lobster and steak."

"Yuck."

"Well, come with me and you can have wienies in a blanket and nachos. I was also told that later we get to have sundaes, and I even saw a lady dressed like a clown say she might make fried dough if everyone is well behaved and neat, so she has enough time to make the batter."

"Fried dough, we only get that at the beach."

Carl laughed. He was really good with his sister. Carl watched as the parents followed their children to the door with their eyes, and the boy waved that everything was okay. They both waved back and then they engaged the people sitting next to them with conversation.

Julie saw the look in Carl's eyes as he watched the Cartwright's children. She knew he missed his own, and she didn't blame him one bit, she wasn't even a mother and she found the Cartwright children charming, as she was sure his own were.

Carl wondered if they planned on informing the president of their situation. He didn't know if they had enough information yet. Yuri's presence was a definite plus. It helped that a KGB agent was here asking to help. That was proof enough that something was up. Now all they had to do is figure out what the general's plan was. With the president and a senator on their side, they could probably end this easily. Perhaps only a little evidence would be enough to force a mandatory early retirement on General Davis. "Ed did you know that the president was going to be here tonight?"

"Yeah, I knew."

"Can it all be finished tonight?"

"That I don't know, he looked at Carl and then at his partner Jason. Carl, You're not involved with this tonight. Randy's orders."

"Carl." Jason smiled at him. "Man, we couldn't have gotten this far without you."

He knew that was true. They had spent six months and hadn't gotten anywhere. In the last two and a half weeks they not only found lots of information, but they also made contact with Yuri. He knew he wasn't responsible for all of it, but even making contact with the Russians was a byproduct of his coming here. He couldn't help feeling left out of the loop. He was disappointed, and the others saw it on his face.

"You don't understand, the rest of the guests haven't gotten here yet."

The announcer broke their conversation: "Ladies and gentlemen our hostess asks that everyone take a moment of your time to fill in the entry forms at each of your place settings, Thank you."

Carl untied his ribbon and read the inside. It wasn't a small menu as he thought. It was a small tear off form at the top and a description of all the door prizes to be given out at the end of the evening. Cute idea, he thought, that way, even if you did not have the energy to win the dance contest and the grand prize, you still have a chance at winning something. People loved to win things and Carl thought that Carrie and the women were smart, it ensured that most people stayed until the end of the party.

He read the list of prizes. 20 pair of tickets to the movie theater, 15 coupons of dinner for two to the dining hall, 10 hundred dollar gift certificates to the Outer Springs Mall, 5 romantic getaways for two; consisting of a two night stay at Bear Lake, compliments to include champagne and gourmet dining by Mrs. Treaburn.

Everyone at the table was busy discussing the prizes. They all dropped their forms into the box that one of the catering staff was carrying from table to table. Julie threw her form into the box and thought about what the men had told them. She was baffled that she and Carl hadn't been told about anything that was going down tonight. She figured it probably never had a chance to come up since they haven't been away from Yuri and Natalia for a moment since their arrival. She was really glad that she made arrangements with Paul last week. She remembered the first rule of her job, always have a contingency plan and make sure as few people knew about it as possible. For this mission, the only people to know, was herself and Paul. She chose Paul because she trusted him and because this was his world, these endless forests. She knew he would have the perfect place, somewhere that only his people would know even existed at all. She was right, and this past week he took her there and they left crates of supplies and spare clothing. Now she was really glad they hadn't put it off until the following week.

Everyone heard another aircraft flying overhead. They all sat there expectantly. The announcer interrupted the quartette again: "Ladies and gentlemen our final guests of the evening have arrived. General and Mrs. Davis of The United States Army, 25th Infantry Division. Everyone applauded. They were older looking than the Harding's, but Carl knew they were the same age. This man had salt and pepper hair, but his face was more weathered than Harding's. Carl figured that was probably due to his being an Infantry Officer for twenty years. His wife was pretty. She was auburn haired like Julie and she wore a gold colored dress that matched the stripe down her husband's leg of his dress blues. It looked lovely on her because of her dark Hawaiian tan, and she wore bold gold jewelry to match. The announcer: "Our entertainment for this evening, Please give a round of applause for the graciousness of their company this evening, Missy Travis and Davie Artrello." She was tall and had long blonde hair to her waist. Her dress was all glitter and made of black sequin, to look like a lace design. It made her look naked underneath. Huge diamond and onyx earrings hung from her lobes. On her arm was Davie looking so young and handsome with a winsome smile that matched his voice, he was wearing a standard tuxedo and his youth made him look straight out of GQ. Behind them came in four men that looked as if they were their bodyguards.

"Oh damn." Carl heard Julie say under her breath.

"Everything okay."

"Yeah, I just know one of them."

"Which one."

"The leech that looks as though he is on steroids."

"Okay."

"He's the guy who got me started in the business."

"Really."

"He looks different now, he wasn't a wrestler looking thug before. Hard to believe by looking at him that he has a degree from Cal Tech."

"That sounds unfair of you."

"Believe me you wouldn't say that, if you met him."

"Well, then you'll have to introduce me to him, later. So I can hate him too."

"Sure." She answered, but she knew she wouldn't need to, he would manage all on his own to make Carl hate him. What she wanted to know was what he was doing here. She recalled being told, by a mutual friend of theirs, that Richard was now out of the protection business. It had lost its appeal for him. She was told he moved onto a more lucrative career field, only she hadn't been told what that was. Now she was more than curious.

CHAPTER SIXTEEN

Rebecca sat in the recliner of her mother's living room sipping at a steaming hot cup of bedtime tea. She was grateful that her mother had the foresight to ask her sisters to wait until tomorrow to come visit. She felt amazingly tired. She hadn't realized earlier how drained she really was. The last couple of weeks had been stressful, and that was only a small stress compared to the last seven months. Her realtor down in Tennessee had called to tell her mother that they had received an offer on the house. Her mother told her that the realtor wasn't sure if she would be able to sell without a current power of attorney from Carl. She would talk to the real estate agencies attorney and let her know. She hadn't thought about that, she thought it was up to date, if she had to she would just rent it out instead. Anyway, right now she wanted to avoid thinking about everything all together. She needed to sleep. That was for sure. She only knew that she needed to sleep.

Rebecca's mom sat over on the couch and avoided talking about Carl. She talked about the weather, and she talked about current events. She was the master of small talk and sometimes that could be a comfort, and at other times it was the most annoying thing she knew. There were times when she wanted to scream. "The weather is irrelevant, Mom, how are you, are you happy or sad." Sometimes she wanted more from her than she was capable of giving and she knew that and instead she smiled and continued to talk with her about the weather. She knew it wasn't exactly her mother's fault that they had nothing to talk about; she was the one who chose to have a life separate from the rest of her family. That distance left holes in her relationships with her mom and her siblings.

She had been mostly content to be a couple with Carl, off

245

somewhere gallivanting to new places, setting up a temporary home and then tearing it down again to go off to someplace new. But that was all changed now. It was now time for her to chose a place to settle permanently. She knew one thing for sure. It wouldn't be here in Connecticut. As soon as she crossed the border of New York State and entered Connecticut she was certain. Entering Danbury was scary and crazy. Life here was a mad rush, and she wasn't a fast paced type of person. She liked the open spaces of farms and the open space of the ocean. She knew that she would choose to live where one of these two serene environments were plentiful. Not in a place where the rush of cars and the jammed packed feel of buildings were the norm. She liked driving from one town and not seeing anything except farmland for miles on end before she found the next town. But here you drove straight from one town to the next without ever knowing you had except for a sign on the side of the road. Unlike the south, these northern towns usually didn't even welcome you to their town. Most of the time there was a cold sign that simply stated you had reached the town line. She noticed people here didn't look at each other and forget talking to anyone you didn't already know. It was rude here to look at some one and even ruder to greet them at all. Down in the south it was the opposite. You would be rude if you didn't look people in the eye and say good morning or whatever greeting was appropriate at the time. It amazed her that this country could be so different from one region to another. She wanted her kids to grow up in the south, where most people were happy, where striving to succeed in life wasn't a dire need. Competition with the Jones's' was an excepted norm in the north. Who was she kidding. It wasn't excepted, it was expected. Having any less drive coined you a failure. The irony to Rebecca was that to avoid failure many of these people here, and she admitted elsewhere, simply strive for things they know they can succeed at, instead of trying to do things whose outcomes were uncertain. She hated coming home. Here she had to play by their rules and that made her feel like a failure.

Rebecca didn't live by these rules. She didn't find value in the same things that a New England upbringing instilled in the people who lived here. Rebecca really missed Carl. He understood her like no one else did. He was the only man she knew that felt and believed in the same things she always had.

She drank her tea and looked at her mother over there across the room from her. She was aging. She looked so much older every time that she saw her. She knew she was older too. She was now, herself, the age she remembered seeing her mother and aunts being when she was small. At 33, she had gray throughout her own hair, but kept it dyed most of the time. Rebecca saw her aunts in herself, when she looked at her hands and when she looked in the mirror. She looked at Karen sleeping at the other end of the couch where her mother had sat brushing her hair. She wanted more than anything for her children to grow up to be happy. To be people who took joy from their failures, as well as, from their successes. She knew she would teach them that the attempt is more than the outcome. She would teach them that you only grow from trying and learning new things. She would be proud of her children. Adults that she will have raised to enjoy life. She wanted so badly for Carl to be with her and to see them too. Happy with whatever it is they decide they want from life, and hoping that that changes almost daily, choosing never to become too complacent. These were the things she wanted for her children.

Rebecca looked at her mother. She wished they had had a better relationship. She'd had learned how easy it was to lose the people she loved. She didn't even remember if she had made sure he knew how much she loved him. They had made love, but she wasn't sure if he felt loved. He had just silently left when he had been called in on alert in the middle of the night.

The army did that all the time. Used the phone roster and called everyone in and timed them to see how long it took the unit to get assembled. Practice in case the real thing ever did happen. Rebecca knew how the real thing happened, and it wasn't any rapid movement of troops. It was slow and planned out. It had taken a couple of months before Carl's Medi-Vac Unit had been deployed. Toying with everyone's emotions, they were sure one minute and then unsure the next as to whether or not they would be deployed.

She knew that she and Carl weren't the type to display generic emotions. They didn't kiss each other goodbye every time one of them went somewhere. They were more secure in their relationship than that. They knew they loved each other. She never questioned his love for her, and she just hoped he didn't question hers for him.

She remembered the night her father had passed away. She was here staying with her parents. Carl was away at a military school and they hadn't set up a home yet and were in limbo. She remembered the way her father had kissed her mother, before he went to bed that night. It was something she would never forget.

God, she hated being in Connecticut. She hated the memories that flooded her when she was here, some good and some not so great. Rebecca thought that here she would always feel like a small child, someone who had never grown up. The only thing she ever regretted was not having friendships with her siblings. But she knew it went both ways, if they had really wanted to be friends with her they could have come to visit. Not anyone had ever done that. They had busy lives, but so what, everyone did, didn't they.

She had only just gotten here, and she already knew that it would be a short visit. Just long enough to visit with everyone. Then she would move on to her mother-in-law's house. Rebecca felt sorry for herself. She recognized the feeling, sad and pitiful. She felt sad over her loss of Carl, the only person she ever really needed. Happy to be anywhere in the world as long she was with him. She basked in her own pity and knew she needed sleep. Rebecca gulped down the last of her tea. "Good night Mom, I'll see you in the morning." Worse than her own pity, she felt her mother's as she watched her youngest daughter, probably now a widow like herself, walk down the hall toward the back bedroom. Rebecca saw her daughter sound asleep in the bed and she carefully pulled back the covers and climbed in next to her.

⚜⚜⚜⚜⚜

Carl sat there and slowly sipped at his glass of wine. He wasn't one to drink much. It always made him sleepy. He ate the last piece of his steak and pushed his plate slightly forward. He didn't really like lobster, so he gave his to the others and was now watching as they performed what looked like delicate surgery upon the bright red creatures. They were all really enjoying themselves. Picking at it with forks and dipping the meat into the small bowls of melted butter.

Carl looked around the room and thought it was like a dream, too pretty to feel real. Carrie had done a nice job. He looked over at her. She looked very comfortable sitting there with the president on one side of her and a General on the other. Randy's day had come, and his father in law was here at the same table to witness every moment of it. Carl was happy for him. He only hoped the evening worked out the way everyone hoped.

Maybe if he were lucky he would be going home soon. That thought made him happy, and he took a large sip of the wine in front of him in celebration of that idea. He listened as the quartet played a song he recognized, but couldn't quite place. He excused himself from the table and told Julie he was going to use the restroom.

She couldn't very well follow him in there, so she let him go. Noting to herself to get Paul's assistance in helping to keep an eye out for Carl while he maintained security of the building. "Don't get lost. The dance will start soon."

"I'll be right back." Carl said.

Carl went to the lobby. The kids were all hyperactive with chatter and movement. He saw feet where heads should be and knew they were all flying on the sugar of the ice cream sundaes. He saw two secret service men guarding the children and wondered if they were happier being out here or were wishing they were on duty inside the banquet hall. He bet they all pulled straws to see who could stay out here with the kids. One of the men was about to put a large fried dough covered in white confection to his mouth, and he knew that they definitely fought over who would protect the children. At least he would have.

Mrs. Treaburn was handing out fried dough to all the kids and looked like she was pleased with how the evening had gone. He had learned that the man in the red nose was her husband. He was helping out with tonight, but he was actually the local sheriff. How cute, he hadn't noticed it earlier, but now Carl saw that he was wearing his star on the clown jumpsuit. He handed the president's daughter her fried dough with a little bow added.

Carl found the restroom down a hall and then made his way back to the dance hall. He found that the waiters were done collecting all the dinner plates. They were busy refilling glasses with the last of the sparkling wine. Carl saw a cart come rolling out through the kitchen door. He had forgotten about dessert. This was starting to turn into a very long evening, he thought to himself as he forced a smile when he reached the table. He wasn't even hungry for dessert, but he took a slice of the fancy chocolate cake and was grateful for the coffee they served with it.

He sat listening to the women talk about the best shops in the area to get certain items. "Sara does the best hair, but if you want your nails done professionally, then no one is better than Cindy over at Nailed Shut." The best place to do your grocery shopping was at the supermarket down on Wilson Road, but if you want the freshest fruit and vegetables, then Saturday mornings, you should go to the Turner's stand located on the corner of Pine and Maple.

"Isn't that where the Ice Cream Dairy is located."

"Yes, their brothers, Ray Turner owns the Dairy Creamery and his brother Jed has a corner of the parking lot for his stand."

"So, Carl asked, is the ice cream really good too."

The ladies were surprised he was listening. "It's the best around."

Carl wasn't interested in talking about sports. Which was what the men were discussing, the upcoming opening season of baseball. They were busy talking about players stats and coaches strategies. Not something Carl knew anything about.

The announcer interrupted. Finally, Carl thought, He was thankful that the dance contest was about to begin, the sooner they got this started the sooner he could leave and go back to the apartment. Julie took one of their numbers and placed it against the center of her chest. Carl followed suit and placed his on the left lapel of his tuxedo jacket. The announcer explained the rules for the contest to everyone. They were rather simple; you must remain dancing while the music is going and you may change dance partners from dance to dance. But no one was allowed to leave the dance floor except during intermissions. Anyone who broke these simple rules had their number removed by one of the four judges and they were retired from the competition.

Davie and Missy began the contest with a duet and everyone only half danced and half watched the performance. The next song was one of Davies latest hits. Holding Julie, Carl could feel the smooth silky feel of her skin and now when he leaned close to her he could catch the unique scent of rose mixed with the heavenly scent of her body. The song ended, and everyone switched partners.

Carrie switched with Julie. "Are you having a nice evening."

"Yes." Carl lied.

"It's alright to admit it's not your cup of tea."

"Well, Maybe I am a bit uncomfortable."

"Bored, you mean."

Carl blushed, caught a little by surprise that she pegged him so well.

"I have become so used to doing these by now that I get most of my enjoyment from planning them and actually putting them together."

"You did a beautiful job."

"Thank you. I didn't do it alone. It did come out nice though." She looked around, "Didn't it?"

The song ended, and they switched again.

Across the way, Carl could see Julie dancing with the large ex-boyfriend of hers. He watched as the man placed his hands on her, much too low as far as he was concerned. Carl watched them carefully as he tried to move the woman he was dancing with closer to Julie and that thug. Now Carl was getting pissed, he saw Julie pull the man's hands up to her waist twice now. Carl watched as the man put his hands even further down on her butt, this time reaching inside the back of her dress to do so.

"Excuse me." Carl said to the woman he was with as he heard the song winding down. Carl swiftly moved across the room before the song ended fully,

"Get your hands off my wife."

"Excuse me."

"I said, get your hands off my wife."

"This guy really gets into his part. Julie, where did you find this one."

Julie looked really angry. "Richard, I told you three times I wasn't here on business." She held up her hand to the animal standing in front of her and prayed he didn't recognize the rings on her hand.

"I'm married. This is my husband Carl, Carl Stevens."

"What a winner, Julie, Did he take your name?"

"We just happened to have the same name, thank you very much."

"Do you really expect me to believe you married one of these science nerds."

Carl put his arm around Julie, "Why don't you give it up and go harass someone else."

"Yes, Richard, I expect you to believe it, because I am married. If you ever listened to me when I spoke to you, instead of hitting on me, then this whole scene could have been avoided, Good bye, Richard."

The large brute walked away, but she wasn't sure if he believed her.

Carl took Julie in his arms. "Are you all right, I could see him groping you from all the way across the room."

He held her close, so close she could feel his entire body against hers. She liked it. She liked how he made her feel safe and she loved his defense of her, even if it were a show, "Thank you."

"He made me so mad, what makes him think he has a right to touch you like that."

"He just thinks because I was his once; that I'm forever his to touch as he likes."

"He's a jerk."

"I know, I told you that you would hate him."

Carl looked down at her and looked into her eyes. She looked upset still. "Are you sure you are okay."

"Yes."

"Why do you look scared then."

"Because, he isn't in protection anymore, I'm afraid he is here looking for you."

"You think he was hired by someone." Carl asked.

"I'd bet that he was hired by General Davis. Julie answered, "I'm afraid that he doesn't think that we are really married."

Carl leaned down toward her and pulled her body even closer to his own and there on the dance floor he kissed her for everyone to see. Julie was in heaven. She melted into Carl and absorbed his affection. She felt his hard shoulders with her hands and gripped them tight when she felt his mouth close onto her own. The moist, soft feel of his kiss almost made her stumble.

Carl felt her grab onto him even tighter as he kissed her a second time. She felt wonderful, and he was reluctant to draw himself away from her. They finished dancing to the blues song that Missy Travis was singing. "Are you ready to leave now." Carl asked Julie.

Julie looked at Carl and then she looked around the room. He seemed to see only her. Everyone around them, although they were mere feet away, felt far away from them. Julie thought she couldn't be happier, until she noticed Richard across the way and felt fear build inside of her. "Yes Carl, I'm ready to leave. Can we go now?" She was dragging him toward the table to get their things.

"Where are you two going." Harold wanted to know.

"We're going home."

"Already - have fun."

Julie grabbed her shawl and Carl, and she headed for the door. On their way out of the banquet hall, she saw Paul go into the bathroom.

"Julie, slow down, I'm going to use the bathroom before we leave, do you need to."

"No, I'll wait for you over there." She leaned against the wall as she watched the children sort through the sleeping bags against the opposite lobby wall. Richard came out of the banquet hall as if he were looking for something. She hid behind a couple of teenagers and hoped that the dim light of the lobby's fireplace would help shade her from his view. The only other light came from the twinkling lights under the children's tent that intermittently blinked here or there. Julie kept her eyes locked onto Richard as he slithered his way through the children and past the fluttering light of the huge stately fire in the lobby's hearth.

Julie watched the overbearing man walk through the lobby and wondered why she had ever dated him. She couldn't remember what she had seen in him five years earlier. She watched as he made his way toward the bathroom. Julie held her breath. She hoped that he wouldn't run into Carl on his way out to meet her. Paul came out of the bathroom with Carl, and they ran into Richard on their way. She could see heated words being yelled, but couldn't hear them over the rumble coming from the mass of children preparing themselves for bed. Julie tried to get over to the men, she weaved her way through the crowd as quickly as she could, but she was too late. She heard the blast. Hiking up her dress, Julie reached down to her thigh to find her gun. Pulling it out, she aimed over the crowd that was now on the floor and fired when she had him in her sight. Blamb, the sound even jolted her. She ran to get to Carl and found that Paul was on top of him. The red head struggled to pull her heavy friend off of Carl.

He was unconscious. She saw blood everywhere and felt every inch of Carl's chest. She realized that he was fine and had only been grazed by the bullet. However, Paul had the thing lodged in his chest and the blood was dark red and oozing out everywhere. She felt unsure what to do. Julie slapped Carl and got him to his feet. She checked Paul. "Get him out of here." She heard a light whisper tell her. He was hurt badly. Paul had taken the bullet in the chest only inches from his heart, and she knew it was probably meant for Carl. He was dazed by everything that had happened and was only now coming to his senses. He had hit the floor hard when Paul pushed him out of the way. She saw Richard lying there, a bullet to his head and knew she hadn't had a choice. She regretted having been right about why he was here. But now she needed to worry only about Carl and get them both out of there.

The secret service had been slow to reach them. Julie and Carl were lucky that they had been caught up in securing the president, his family and the senator. It had allowed them enough time to get out of the building unnoticed. Julie had Carl running now. They rushed to the helicopter pad. "Pete, Do you remember the coordinates that Paul gave to you."

"Yes"

"Quickly!"

They were off the ground within seconds, and flying through the darkness into the depths of the wilderness. "Remember, Pete. No one is to know where you dropped us, not even the secret service. Go and see Randy as soon as you get back, he will take care of everything." "Also, only tell Randy that we're safe."

"Yes, Ma'am."

"Carl, Are you okay."

"Yes."

"Good, because we have to rappel from this aircraft."

"We have to do what!"

"We have to rappel."

"Like this." He pointed to her gown.

"Yes, we have no choice. You do know how, don't you?"

"Yes, of course I do."

The helicopter stopped forcing its way forward and instead began to hover in place. Julie reached behind the seat and pulled out a duffel bag. She unzipped it and took out ropes and some metal clips. She secured a large metal clip to the floor of the helicopter. Tying on their seats, Carl looked out the opened door of the helicopter and couldn't see anything in the darkness outside. The thick of the night appeared impenetrable. It was by the light of the moonless sky that Carl was thanking heaven to be alive. Carl looked above the blades the best he could and saw that there were no stars either. Julie clipped the metal to the ropes and she threw the heap out the door and then followed it a second later. Carl clipped his seat to the ropes and felt the slack tighten for a minute. He knew that Julie was below him holding the ropes, ready to jolt them to the ground if he were about to fall. He could see her in his mind standing there with her silver heels dug into the dirt as she steadied herself for his decent. She awed him. She was the most amazing woman that he knew and probably ever would. One minute earlier he had seen her preparing to jump out of the helicopter. All bare legged, with the rope seat tied to her, bunching up her gown, and exposing her slim sleek legs. Carl watched as her high heels pushed her off and away from the aircraft.

Carl waved to the man in the pilot's seat and dropped himself into the unknown below him. Down to the waiting arms of the most astonishing woman in the world. When he hit the ground, the dark of the night was still as black as it had been from the inside of the helicopter. Carl knew if he waited a few minutes his eyes would adjust to the darkness and he would be able to walk with fairly clear vision. The sound of the helicopter became distant. He realized that, in place of the thwacking of blades, he could now hear the rumbling rush of water in a fast moving river. Carl felt in the darkness for Julie. Reaching his arms outward he felt her and pulled her closer to him, "Are you okay?"

"Yeah, are you."

"I'm fine, did you land alright with those heels on."

"Yeah, I just twisted one of my ankles a little."

"How bad?"

"I'll be alright, at least until we get where we're going."

"Where are we going?"

"Paul brought me to a place that we could use in case we needed it. But the problem is that we have to get to his cousin's house first, so he can bring us there."

"You mean you don't know the way."

"I mean, no one outside the tribe knows the way there. It is a sacred place to them, and its secrecy is guarded from outsiders."

"Do you know how to get to his cousin's."

"Yes, it is about two miles upstream, of course it would be easier if it were daylight and I had proper shoes, but what the heck I always like a challenge."

"I'm beginning to fully comprehend that truth." Carl could see her pretty well now. He reached through the shade of night toward her face and gently gripped it with his hand. Guiding his fingers across the side of her cool cheek, Carl lifted her chin upward as he leaned toward her and softly placed his lips to hers.

"What was that for."

"Thank you."

"For what."

"For saving my life."

"Oh that, don't mention it."

"Are you sure you're okay."

"Yeah I'm sure, let's not talk about anything now okay, we need all our energy to get to the cabin."

"Okay."

Carl reached down to feel her ankle, "ouch." It was too dark for her to anticipate his touch and hide her pain. He knew that was good because otherwise she would have insisted she were fine. He reached for her waist, "Ready?"

"Yeah." She knew when not to fight. "I'm ready."

He lifted her and she wrapped herself around his waist and was happy for the warmth of his body against her exposed legs. Julie felt warm and safe like a child held by their parent. She wondered who were doing the protecting, her or him. Perhaps they both needed a little protecting. She gladly snuggled her face into his neck and settled herself for the long walk ahead. Breathing in Carl's reassuring scent, Julie let out a sigh and tried her best not to think about the two bloody bodies she left lying lifeless on the floor of the lobby.

Carl now knew what it felt like to be protected like a president. It was a good and bad feeling. Good because Paul put his own life second for a man he barely knew. Bad because Paul could die for protecting him, a stranger. How do you Thank someone for that, he felt guilty and prayed that the man would be okay. Then there was Julie. She had killed someone to protect him, someone who she once must have loved. He didn't even know what that pain must be doing to her. He held the woman who saved him and knew he would always be indebted to her for his life.

CHAPTER SEVENTEEN

Rebecca was standing next to a stream. She felt happy. It was beautiful where she was. The canopy above her sheltered her from the falling of snow. She could imagine the trees from high above her covered in heavy snow on the topside, but from where she was standing it was warm and safe. She watched as the tiny flakes of glistening white fell, ever so slightly, through the huge evergreen canopy. She was surprised that the stream had frozen ice along the surface of the banks, yet she felt no cold at all. It was amazingly dark in this forest of hers. She could see well for about twenty feet around her, but beyond that it was almost pitch black. Rebecca couldn't explain what she was feeling, it was a strange contentment, a sense of being with others even when she could see no one else around her. She was certain that she wasn't alone. Maybe what she felt was love, but whatever it was, Yes love, she could feel it surround her, protecting her from the cold and the loneliness she had been feeling inside her. Rebecca heard something and looked around her to figure out where it was coming from. Through the hazy light around her, she could make out the image of something trying to emerge from the shadows beyond her vision. A few minutes later she found herself standing inside a cluster of deer. They had approached as if she weren't even there. A family of them had stopped to drink from the ice cold babbling water. Then it occurred to her that she wasn't really there at all. This magical world was only a dream.

"Oh, No, please she told herself, not yet." But it was too late, the realization that she was in a dream had made it fade, and she was now in complete darkness. Rebecca slowly felt herself awakening and found she was in a dark room. She brushed the form of someone beside her and remembered that she was next to her daughter. Reaching out to her, she brushed her hair back and noticed that her touch had made Rachel start to stir. It made her wonder when it was that children stopped feeling completely safe. She knew that Danny still felt it. She could touch his head, brush back his hair, and kiss his forehead without his waking up. She remembered how Rachel would always smile when she gently stroked her forehead. She had missed noticing when it was that Rachel had stopped feeling safe. She wondered if it had happened during this time when her Father left them or if it had occurred earlier.

Rebecca slowly lifted her body from the bed trying not to disturb Rachel's sleep. She looked around the room and saw all her mother's familiar things. Dressers filled with pictures and knick-knacks. Teddy bears and other stuffed animals lined the top of her shelving. Many of them she had sent to her mother over the years while she had been away. She never knew any practical things her Mom would have needed. She lived so far away from her that she sent her very unpractical things. That was when she managed to remember special dates here or there. Rebecca wasn't very good about those types of things. She had been known to buy someone a birthday card and not send it to them until the next year or even two years later, if ever at all.

She closed the bedroom door behind her and went into the next door on the right. Closing it, she flipped on the light switch and was blinded by the harshness of the electric light. She grabbed the wash cloth and turned the faucet to lukewarm. Placing it under the stream of water, she felt a welling in her eyes and forced them back. Rebecca looked in the mirror and saw the silver gray at the roots of her hair. She felt old, and thought how she was too old to be starting over. She knew that was stupid. She would yell at anyone else who told her such nonsense. Old was just an easy word to use. She knew she felt overwhelmed, weak at the prospect of facing her family and all the questions which were bound to be asked of her tomorrow. She would probably be flooded with the emotion of pity pouring from everyone.

At least it would be Sunday. That meant that everyone would be off at church tomorrow morning, so she wouldn't have to find answers for the bombardment until that afternoon. Rebecca was thankful for small miracles. Mornings weren't her best time of day. She had always been a night owl, like her father. That was what her mother had always told her, anyway. Even as a small baby she was supposedly up at all hours with her father, as he sat at his drafting board. She thought that she could remember being that small too.

She made her way down the hallway. Halfway down she noticed

that the television was turned on, and she heard the sound of someone trying to sell something. "Hi, Mom." She was sitting there not really watching the television, only half listening to it for comfort. By the light of the television screen, Rebecca could see her mom lift her cup of coffee to her mouth and take a sip from it. Then she saw the movement of her mom's hand toward her face again, and caught the bright glow of her cigarette as she drew from it. Her stomach jumped into her chest, and she knew it was the cigarette that gave her the start. She forced the adrenaline to slow in her blood by remembering the feel of David's arms around her that morning. She forgot when it was while growing up that she stopped hugging her mother, and forced herself to give her a hug. The only way she was really ever able to hug her was when her Mom was sitting at the table. She gave her mother a quick hug from behind and then rubbed her shoulders a minute. "You look a bit tense." Her Mom was all bones. She thought that she was a bit anorexic. She would easily blow away if any good gust of wind hit her.

"You can't sleep?" Her mom asked.

Rebecca always thought that her mother's habit of inhaling coffee and cigarettes was what made her have this ritual in the middle of the night. But now she knew it wasn't just the stimulants that she was partaking of in the wee hours of the morning, it was the solitude that she enjoyed. Something her home never had except at three in the morning. Rebecca suddenly felt guilty for leaving the bedroom and disturbing her mother's moment of quiet. "A dream woke me. I'm sorry for disturbing you."

"Don't be silly, sit and have a cup of tea with me."

Rebecca filled a cup with water and put it in the microwave. Then she searched the cupboards to find the tea bags.

"They're in the canister on the counter."

Another downfall of seeing her mother only every couple years was that she never knew where anything was kept. The house always looked different to her too, every time she came home. Everything was always, only vaguely familiar.

"The kids look good. Are they doing okay?"

"Yeah, they're hanging in there pretty well." "I think they're spirits are pretty high, considering everything."

"They seem so, they can't seem to stop talking about the Henry's and David. Did you weather the storm well with them down there?"

"Yes, everything went fine, the kids loved it there. Who wouldn't with the unique experience of it all, it was really very exciting."

"So, what is the story with David."

"Not much of a story to talk about really. He's just been through a difficult divorce, and he used to be in the military, the Navy - but now he runs his family's cattle ranch." She didn't think her mother was buying what she told her. The woman sat there drinking her coffee and drawing at her cigarette. Rebecca avoided her eyes.

"What has happened, Rebecca?"

"What do you mean?"

"I mean, everything. What is going on, there has to be a lot you're not telling me." "Look at you and the kids, you can't hide that something has happened." She looked at her daughter and hoped she wasn't pushing too hard. She usually stayed out of her business. However, now things were different, there wasn't Carl around taking care of her any longer. She was worried about her little girl.

Where should she start? She wondered. The better question she knew was how much she could tell her mother without her getting her upset. She knew she wouldn't tell her about this morning. She wasn't sure if she could ever tell anyone about this morning. The problem is, she had uncertain knowledge about Carl, and if she told anyone about it, then they would want to know how she got that information. She wished she had just stayed in bed and avoided this conversation. It was all too complicated. "I don't know where to begin." She knew she couldn't put off her mom or anyone else in her family the way she had David. Her family was different. They didn't respect that you didn't want to talk about something. She was the same way usually. But she knew they would get upset if they knew the truth, and she didn't want to get them upset. Or else they would give her a hard time about moving on. She thought to herself, "Grow up Rebecca, just spill it, be an adult and maybe they'll treat you like one." She wasn't sure if that were true or not, but it sounded good to her. She watched as her mother lit up another cigarette. "Mom, are you okay." She watched her mom's hand shake a little as she placed the long white stick in the ashtray holder and went to fill her cup with more coffee.

"Rebecca, You never hesitate to say what you are thinking or worry about what people think. This means things are worse than I thought."

"No Mom, I'm okay, really. It's just that things are really complicated and I don't have half the answers myself. But I promise you we're doing okay."

She opened the refrigerator and poured some milk into her mug. The glow of the box shut off as she closed the door. Rebecca listened as her mother's slippers scuffed the floor on her way back towards her chair. Her Mom sat there silently pouring sweetener from the small pink packet into her coffee. Rebecca knew she was waiting for her to say something. "Where do you want me to start?"

"Anywhere you like. But while the kids are asleep, starting with Carl might be best." The gray haired woman looked sympathetically at her daughter and then lowered the volume of the television set.

"There isn't much to tell you there." Rebecca filled her mom in with the details she knew, which were very little. Then her mother asked her about her trip to Virginia and Rebecca told her what she knew about the Henry's and everything there too, with a few exceptions, meaning details about David. Rebecca drank down the last sip of her cold tea and told her mom she was headed back to bed. Exchanging goodnights, she made her way back down the darkened hallway and to the bed with her sleeping daughter in it.

"Are you going to tell Grandma about David asking you to stay with him." The light voice floated to Rebecca in the dark.

"How do you know that he asked us to stay with him?"

"Come on Mom. Everyone could see he fell in love with you, besides Tommy told me and David too sort of."

"Do you wish I had said yes?"

"I don't know."

"Well, I wasn't sure if it were the right thing either. That's why I said no, for now. Who knows maybe if things.-" She didn't know what she wanted to say exactly. She wasn't willing to give up yet, and she sensed that Rachel knew that. "I'm not ready yet."

"I know, Mom." The young girl hugged her and then she turned over and went back to sleep.

She thought about how Carl wouldn't recognize their daughter if he saw her now. She had changed so much in the past eight months. She figured tragedies must tend to do that to people. Rebecca remembered the forest and cold stream from her dream earlier. The way that she felt safe in the center of the herd. It was with that thought that she eventually dozed back off to sleep.

❦ ❦ ❦

Julie tried to take some of her weight off of Carl's arms. In the darkness, she felt for his shoulders then she wrapped both arms high up around his neck. Oops, she slipped and banged the back of his head.

"Damn."

"I'm sorry, I was just trying to help ease my weight from your arms to your shoulders."

"That's okay, You're not very heavy." She couldn't weight much more than a hundred pounds. and Carl thought that she had to be losing all her body heat with only that slip of a dress on. He was right. She shivered against him, and he tried his best to wrap his coat around her bare back, it almost closed, but not quite. "Are you cold, would you like my coat?"

"I'm good, your warmth is keeping me warm. Thank you, but could we stop for a second."

"Sure, what's up."

"I want to take these heels off, they must be digging into your back."

"Just a little."

"You should have told me sooner."

Carl put her down and noticed the river beside them was moving to a softer sound now. He reached to touch the bank and found it was solid ice for a foot inward and then the water only felt like ice.

"How far do you think we've gone?" She stood there before him, shaking and bare foot.

"Ready?" He lifted her back to his chest, and she melted back into him once more. He did have to admit he preferred her cold feet against his back rather than the cold pointy heels that had been jabbing him every ten feet or so before. "I think that we've walked about a mile, but in the darkness and this cold it is difficult to be sure."

"In the daylight this walk seemed rather short, I'd say that it took, maybe a half an hour." Not that she had any concept of time right now. She realized now that it seemed to have completely stopped for her when she heard the first gun shot in the lobby. Only now was everything beginning to feel somewhat real to her again. Perhaps because she was starting to get some feeling back into her limbs. Carl's body was very warm, and she knew he was the reason she wasn't at this very moment, frostbitten from head to toe.

"Are you warm enough?"

"Yes, believe it or not I'm quite cozy."

He believed her because her feet stopped feeling like ice ten minutes ago and now her warmth was also keeping him comfortable too. In fact, he was having difficulty concentrating. Had been, since the day she introduced herself to him standing two feet away and again every time she stood within three feet of him since. She was so feminine it hurt. Carl groaned slightly when he felt her breath against his throat. It had been so long since he was this close to a woman. He thought it was her warm, sweet scent that was helping to keep his damn blood coursing so swiftly through his veins, despite the friggin-ass cold. But he couldn't deny that carrying a half-naked woman through the woods was reason enough to be plenty warm.

"Carl, do you smell something."

All he could smell was her deliciously sweet scent, but he told her "No."

"There it is again, did you catch it."

"Yes." She smelt heavenly.

"Is it smoke?" Julie asked.

"Yeah, I did get that, I think it is wood smoke."

"We must be getting close then." Julie felt the back of Carl's head and felt the lump that had formed there. "Is it causing a headache or any other problems."

"No, I was knocked out for a minute, but I feel fine."

Julie smelt the scent of the wood fire getting stronger. She was both happy and apprehensive. She longed to get there and sit by the fire, but she didn't want to have to tell Paul's cousin, Luke, what had happened. Julie thought of all the blood pouring from her friend's chest and fought back tears from trickling out of the corners of her eyes. She buried her face into Carl's neck, and instead let out a deep sigh to accompany her shudder.

Carl recognized the feel of stress relieving itself, the reality of the evenings events was probably coming full force into Julie's mind. If that shudder he felt come from her was any indication of how she was feeling, then he knew that she was fighting her emotions from flooding her. He held her a bit tighter in an effort to comfort her and felt her respond by clinging back. Carl tried to think of something to say to make her feel better. but he knew, there were no such words in situations like this. Not when they had just killed their ex-lover and watched as their friend lay bleeding on a cold tile floor. The image was enough to upset even him, and he was a stranger to one and only an acquaintance to the other. No, there were no words of comfort, but he could hold her as long as she needed him to.

Carl breathed in deeply the reassuring scent of the girl in his arms. When he looked down at her, he caught the glimmer of the huge heart around her neck and instantly understood the true value of that gift. What he had seen earlier, merely as a retirement fund in her old age. Appeared to him now, as the precious jewel that represented an even more precious commodity, a man's life. A life which Julie had saved and which Carl now understood all too well, himself. He understood how it felt to owe his life to another. Carl knew this debt would be something he hated had he owed it to anyone other than Julie. Carl looked at her and caught the silver glitter of a tear rolling down her cheek. He knew he could stand this. He could stand owing his life to this fragile redhead.

Then he thought about the sweet, jolly man who had jumped in front of him. The man with the kind voice and the twinkle in his eye as if he knows something no one else in the world knows. Carl prayed that he would survive the bullet wound so he could thank him. He wasn't sure how, but he knew that he wanted the chance to try.

They heard the sound of a dog in the darkness beyond their range of vision.

"What is it, boy?"

"Is someone out there?" A heavy voice called to them.

"Yes." Julie called out. "It's me, Julie Stevens."

He turned a flashlight on and beamed them in the face. "Everything okay, did something happen?"

"We're okay. But, Yes, something did happen." Julie said. "This is Carl, the man that Paul and I are protecting."

"Well, get in the house first and then you can fill me in on what's happened." He led them into a small entryway where boots stood dripping and coats were left hanging to dry. It was also a shelter to the rest of the house from wind, cold and what other element nature was hell bent on hurling at his cabin. Past the tiny entryway was a cozy large room, he had hand-made blankets hung over all the windows to keep the warmth in and the cold out. Julie remembered them now. They had been pulled open, to let in what little daylight there was in this forest, when she had been here before. The quilts were now covering the windows completely, and that was why they never saw any light coming from the cabin on their walk here. Luke pulled out a pot and filled it with water. They saw a woman lean over the loft's railing to poke her head out and see who was visiting at such a late hour. She was quick to lean back into the loft, and they listened as Luke spoke to her. "It's alright Love, you can come down, these are friends of Paul's. They could make out a figure pulling on some clothing and the girl appeared wearing some sweat pants and what looked like one of Luke's flannel shirts. It came down almost to her knees. She was very young and very pretty, with dark brown hair that came down to her butt. She was probably a good ten years younger than Paul's cousin. After putting the pot on the fire, he reached his hand out toward Carl, "I'm Luke, Paul's cousin." He was larger and darker than Paul, and he wore his hair traditionally, braided down his back.

"Nice to meet you. Sorry to be invading your home so late at night." Carl said.

Love placed a blanket around Julie's shoulders and guided her over to the fire to get warm.

"Well, I guess something pretty bad must have happened for you to be hiking to my house in those get ups." Julie turned to look at him, "Why isn't Paul with you this time?" Luke could see tears running down her face.

"He got shot. I tried to see how badly the wound was, but he told me to get Carl out of there. I don't know what condition he is in, but I do know it was bad - in the chest somewhere."

Carl looked at the man standing before them. He appeared distressed by the news, but was careful not to show much concern. Carl thought it was his way of trying to maintain control of this situation and hold onto hope for his cousin.

"Are you both okay?"

"Julie has twisted her ankle." Luke went to Julie and reached out to her ankle to inspect it.

"It is a bit swollen, it was probably good that you carried her. I'll see what I can do for it. How about you, did you get hurt?"

"I'm fine, Just a small bump on the head, that's all. Paul was keeping me safe by pushing me out of the path of fire. So, so it was he who, unfortunately took the bullet. I'm sorry."

"Don't be sorry. Paul was doing his job. But even if he weren't, he still would have taken that bullet. That's just the kind of man he is. Don't let it consume you that he got hurt, it's not the first time he has been shot." Luke took the boiling pot of water off the fire. He carried it into to the tiny kitchen.

Carl noticed a lit oil lamp on the table's center and was surprised to see a refrigerator in the corner. From a tin that Luke pulled out of the cabinet, he filled a strainer full of dried herbs of some sort. "This is a family tea. It has been passed down for ages, I hope you like it. It is good for the body, it has plants in it that are excellent for helping the body to rest and heal itself." He finished steeping it and then poured the pot's contents into five mugs that he had placed on the counter. Opening the refrigerator, Luke pulled out a bottle of milk and offered some to the others. "It is rather sweet already, you most likely won't need any sugar."

Julie thought that Luke didn't know Carl or he wouldn't have assumed such a thing. She was surprised, when Carl sat drinking it, as it was, without adding anymore sweetener.

Then Luke pulled out another tin and into the fifth mug he put some of the black substance into the hot tea and replaced the tin.

"Your cabin is beautiful." Carl commented to Luke as he sat staring at the stone fireplace. He liked how the fireplace had a brick oven to the side of it. "Do you use the brick oven?" He looked around the small kitchen and noticed there was no stove.

"Yes, I do all my cooking on the fire and in the brick oven. I have a small generator for the refrigerator and the hot water tank, but otherwise I use oil for light and wood for heat." Love disappeared and returned with some clothing for them to change into. She handed Carl a pair of sweat pants, a tee shirt, sweatshirt and a pair of tube socks. Then she gave Julie a similar outfit, wished them "goodnight" and disappeared once more into the loft from which she had come earlier.

"The bathroom is through there." Luke told them. Julie went to change first, when Carl came out he found that Luke was soaking a towel with the mixture of tea and black stuff and was placing it on her ankle. "There, hopefully that will make the swelling go down. Try and get some rest and in the morning I'll lead you out."

"Good night." They all said in unison.

Carl looked at the room lighted by the orange glow from the fire. Under different circumstances, he would have thought this place very romantic. Right now he only wanted some sleep. Surveying the room the options were a couch, a chair and an area rug not far from the fire. Love must have brought them a sleeping bag at some point, because now he saw one rolled up and placed to one side of the couch and next to it were two pillows and a thick blanket.

In a whisper, he told Julie. "You can have the couch and I'll take the bag and the floor."

She whispered back "Okay." Julie hobbled over to the couch once she saw that Carl's back was turned to her.

When he rolled out the bag against the floor, he caught sight of her strained movement from the corner of his eye. "I saw that, is your ankle really bad?"

"It hurts a little more than before, now that the numbness from the cold has worn off."

"Is Luke's medicine helping at all."

"I don't know, but he did tell me that it would get worse before it gets better. So we'll see what happens, I guess." Julie settled herself on the couch to get some sleep, but the images from earlier keep intruding her mind. She turned her body one way on the couch and then she shifted again.

"You can't sleep?" She heard Carl's voice call to her through the darkness. The fire had died down, and now it was a large pile of bright red embers.

"No."

"Me either."

"I can't get all the blood out of my mind."

"I'm sorry, it must be very difficult for you."

"What?"

"Killing your ex-boyfriend."

"Isn't that every girl's fantasy."

"Julie, I'm not buying that nonchalant attitude of yours."

"What do you want me to do, break down and cry."

"Yes, if it will help."

"Well, it won't Carl, and for the record he is my ex-husband."

"What! You didn't tell me you were married."

"Yeah, well, I don't really count it as a marriage. It lasted all of one week."

"Why?"

"Why what, why did I marry him or why did it last only one week."

"Yes."

"I was just young and stupid. We went to Barbados on vacation right after my first assignment was done. On a whim, we got married, but by the time the vacation was over, I realized how dumb marrying Richard had been."

"Why was that?"

"He went down to the bar while I finished packing to go home and when I came down to find him to go to the airport. Well, let's say I found him alright, All over a girl in the bars bathroom."

"What a piece of work, I'm sorry Julie."

"Thanks, but it was my own fault. I should have known he was a piece of shit. I mean, everyone told me so, I just didn't want to see it." "Now, I really know he had no scruples. In the protection business sometimes it can be very questionable who your protecting and why. Do you know what I mean?" She paused. "I don't always know if the person I'm protecting, is the good guy in the situation. I like to think that my guy is the good guy. But Richard was so obviously working for the bad guy." "Hell, he was the bad guy." She paused again. "Shit Carl, I don't know, maybe I've only been trying to fool myself. But I've always felt there was a difference between killing for money and killing to protect." She paused. "Your awfully quiet over there, did you fall asleep."

"No, I'm listening. I don't know what to say, except that I believe there is a difference. You saved my life Julie. But I guess the most important thing is how all this leaves you feeling, whether or not you're comfortable living with the nature of your job." Carl hoped what he said to her was the right thing. Damn, she got awfully quiet herself. All he knew was that he didn't want her upset because she saved him. "Julie, you still awake?"

"Yes."

"What are you thinking, did I say something to upset you."

"No." He could hear a wobble in her voice and knew she was fighting back tears.

"Are you okay?" Through the dark of the room, Carl could hear her sobbing lightly.

She sucked in a deep breath. "I can't tell, usually I can feel the difference, I'm normally okay with this. I killed a bad guy, but why be upset, he was the bad guy after all. But this time I can't tell if - am I the bad guy?"

Carl got up and stumbled his way to the couch. "Don't be silly, Julie, of course you're not the bad guy." He wrapped his arms around the small girl and pulled her into his lap. She leaned into Carl and wrapped herself around him. She shuddered in his arms, and he tightened his grip around her. Slowly Carl could feel her shudders subsiding as her tears rolled down the side of his throat. "But Julie, I could see why you are feeling terrible. You had to kill someone who you once cared for, and you can't pretend that it hasn't upset you. If you didn't feel really bad. Well, then maybe, you would be a bad guy, but sweetheart there is no way you are bad in any way." He lifted her face up to see her eyes. "I'm sorry that you had to kill someone, but I am so grateful to you, to be alive."

"Thank you. Thank you for talking to me and for holding me."

The death of the fire, allowed Carl once more to smell the sweetness of his companion. That hint of rose that captivated his senses and made his heart leap to get closer to her. Carl slowly let her perfume guide him to her throat, where the scent was the strongest. The delicate fragrance mixed with her honey scented hair was driving him crazy. He slowly felt her hands lift under his shirt and feel the length of his chest, sending his mind soaring to the tree top, of the owl that he heard hooting outside. Gently he could feel her soft lips glide across his jaw searching in the darkness for his mouth. He could feel the tenseness of his own body melt away as the heat of hers intensified. Carl gave into the intoxication. Bringing his mouth to hers, he allowed her need to possess him. Carl felt the length of her legs and the desire of the woman against him. He could feel the smooth silky feel of her flesh against his and had suddenly realized that he had taken off her shirt in the haze of their shared heat.

"Oh shit, I am so sorry."

"Why?"

"I didn't mean to take off your clothing, and I went too far. I'm sorry."

"Carl, don't apologize, I helped."

"Yes, I know, but you were upset."

"Carl, We were both upset, and we both need the comfort of each other's company, there is no shame in that."

"I know, but."

"I know, you're in love with someone else. It's okay, really, I don't have any expectation beyond the moment."

"You may not, but it doesn't feel right, at least not here or now."

She had completely forgotten where they were. She knew he was right, and so she felt a little foolish. "Maybe your right, I did get a little caught up in the moment. It felt like we were still back at the facility for a moment." She was too embarrassed to admit she had had this conversation with him in her mind already. She had been ready and waiting for the reaction to her that he had just had. She knew she was upset. and she tried not to show it. Thank goodness for the darkness. But damn it, they were grown adults. She was a grown adult, damn it. She could protect her own heart from getting hurt. She didn't need him to protect it for her. She wanted to be with him, and she knew there was no future with him. She couldn't help but to feel sad, why was it that the good ones never wanted her. What was it with her luck with men. "Yeah, Yeah." She told herself. She knew that it was her own fault. She should know better than to let herself want someone who is married. "No." she corrected herself. "It's not that he's married." There are plenty of married men that would have jumped her in a heartbeat. It was the fact that he is a good man. It was this that she knew was the real factor that attracted her to him. It was the essential element that had been missing in her life, not a lack of men, just a complete lack of good ones.

He wasn't sure what the heck he thought he was doing. Maybe that's the problem he wasn't thinking at all. The only thing he could say for sure right now was that he was tired. It had been a long day. A day spent looking at an incredibly beautiful woman. And damn, she did look so beautiful in that pink gown. Of all things, he couldn't get the thought of her in the helicopter out of his mind. She looked so sexy with that lacy silk dress pulled up to her waist exposing her sleek long legs. It didn't help that all evening he had sat imagining what her silky body would look and feel like. He knew it was the image of the silver gun strapped to the inside of her thigh that had sent him over the edge.

The entire walk here had been excruciating for him, trying to block the images of her from his mind. Especially with her against him as she was. But even still, how stupid could he be. "You idiot." He wanted to slap some sense into himself. He knew it was moments like these that people did things that they lived to regret later. Of all things, the last thing he wanted was for her to regret making love to him.

She was too fragile right now to make any choices. He was sure of that. Making love to a crying woman is almost always a huge mistake. He knew that if he ever did decide to be with Julie, then he would be damned to make sure that he would feel okay about it afterward, or else he knew he would never be able to look at her or himself in the mirror again. He never was very good at playing the field, not even when he was single. Besides, she had been hurt too many times, and he wanted to be careful with her. Not to mention his own heart was a bit fragile itself right now.

He wondered if Rebecca had decided to move on with her life. Carl tried to stop himself from thinking about her. That world of theirs seemed a lifetime away from him, and he knew it would do him no good to think about her and their marriage right now.

He brushed back Julie's hair from her face. What now, he wondered, do they stay in these woods for a month, a year, for how long. Carl felt the energy drain from his body. He hated this insane assignment he was on. It hadn't been his choice to do this, and he resented it all. But the worst thing was not knowing if he would have a home to return to when it was all over, that is if he even survives this at all. He knew, now it would be impossible to find out anything about Rebecca and the kids. He looked down at the red haired girl in his arms and felt guilty for thinking about his family while he was holding her. A woman who had saved him from being killed and who without, there would be no possibility of ever returning to them. "What do we do now?"

"Try and forget that I made a fool of myself and get some sleep."

"Don't say that, you didn't make a fool of yourself, but I agree we need to get some sleep."

"Yeah right, come on. How many times do you need to tell me your not interested."

"Julie, I wouldn't say I'm not interested. Things are just very complicated and now is a bad time to discuss this. God! You must know that I'm attracted to you."

"I know, your right and I'm sorry, this is a bad time. We really do need to get some sleep. To answer your question, I guess all we can do is go to our safe place and wait for contact from Randy."

"But I thought you said that he doesn't know where we are."

"He doesn't need to, all we have to do is read the paper and he'll contact us through it."

"Really, I would never have thought of that."

"It's pretty standard, The trick is your code, but sometimes just putting it straight for everyone to see is the perfect way to hide it."

"I don't understand."

"Don't worry you will. Now let's get some sleep because we have a long walk tomorrow."

Carl gently rose from where he was with Julie on the couch and returned to his bag on the floor. It was now comfortable on the floor since the fire had died down to embers. "Julie, I do think that you are a beautiful woman, and under different circumstances I wouldn't have hesitated for a minute. Good night." He waited to hear her respond, but there was nothing said and so Carl blinked once and was instantly rendered oblivious to the room around him.

Julie listened to the gentle words given to her by a man which she knew was honest. He had never told her anything that he hadn't honestly believed and so she knew he wasn't just trying to make her feel better. She trusted him as much with her own life, as he had trusted her with his. She equally trusted him with her heart. It was the word circumstances, however, that had her thinking. She knew that could imply many things, but there was no need for her to know what that meant right now. She knew she would find out what he had meant eventually.

CHAPTER EIGHTEEN

Rebecca was startled awake when she heard a thud and rattle sound come from across the house. She opened her eyes to find that the light from the window was beaming straight at her. She reached for the pillow on the bed next to her and slammed it into her face to block out the pain caused by the light. Although she found the brightness of the sun disturbing to her unprepared eyes, she did notice that the heat of it on her body felt very comforting. She felt so warm, and the sun was so bright that if she hadn't known better, she would have thought she were in her own bed back in Tennessee, where Carl would be brewing coffee and making breakfast. When she opened her eyes the nightmare would have been over and the only thing for her to do, would be to join him in the kitchen and drink her coffee and tell him the whole thing as she sat there watching him cook. He would have burnt the bacon. He always burnt the bacon. This house was too quiet to be her own in Tennessee. She wondered if it hadn't been Tennessee that had been the dream.

Rebecca listened for more sounds inside the house and realized that she must be alone. Her Mom must have managed to convince the kids to go with her to church this morning because she didn't hear a single sound coming from the living room. And that was unheard of in her mother's house. There was never a quiet moment, either the phone was ringing or the television was going or else the house was full of relatives. Even when no one was here this house had had noise in it. She recalled how when her parents went out they would always leave the radio on to keep her father's dog company. But that was a long time ago and now that he had passed on, and the dog had also, Rebecca assumed that her mother had stopped that ritual.

She slowly lifted the pillow from her face and squinted to see the time on the alarm clock beside her, 8:45. Her Mom must have run behind schedule this morning because church was at nine o'clock. She hoped that it wasn't the children that had made her late and she thought that it probably was Danny who had held them up. She wondered if the kids had been given a choice in whether or not they wanted to go with her mother this morning. She could see the girl's being interested in going, curious about what it is like. She knew that Danny wouldn't have wanted to go, but then of course he wouldn't have had a choice if the girls had decided to.

Rebecca covered her eyes once more and wondered who it was that had opened the shade to let in the light, Rachel or her mother. It didn't matter. She knew she needed to get up and shower before her family got together for Sunday dinner. If her memory served, then she knew everyone would be here at the latest by 1:00pm. If everyone came that would mean a very full house, overwhelmingly full. She felt weak at the prospect of having to face them all. Worse was that she hadn't even decided yet what she was willing to tell everyone. She knew they couldn't keep quiet about anything, and she wasn't willing to jeopardize Carl's chances of returning, if he had any. At best her sister would have everyone at church praying for Carl's safe return and at worse her mother would be calling her state representative demanding to be told some explanation for her son-in-law's disappearance. She knew the most important thing she could do was to stress to her family the importance of keeping this to themselves. She also knew she needed to believe that Carl was still alive, at least until someone contacted her once more anyway. After all, they did tell her that the investigation was still open. However thin that thread of hope was, it was still something.

Rebecca felt there was no sense in delaying getting out of bed any longer. As much as she wanted to stay where she was and not get out for days, she knew the possibility didn't exist. Besides, she was starting to feel a tight pressure in her abdomen, the tea she had late last night was taking its toll on her bladder. Quickly she reached across the floor to retrieve one of Carl's old Army sweat jackets and swiftly zipped it up and headed to the bathroom.

When she made her way down the hall to the kitchen, she stopped to look at all the old photographs hanging in her mother's hallway. She remembered many of them. When they were taken and why, First holy communions, confirmations, weddings and graduations. Then there were anniversaries, family picnics and a whole litany of school photos. Rebecca saw one of herself and cringed. She never understood why her mother insisted on keeping that photo of her. It was taken in elementary school, and she hated it because she looked like a beaver in it. She should take it out and burn it, but she knew her mother would kill her if she did. There was a picture of her Dad, in it he had his arms around her mother, it was a Christmas shot. They looked pretty happy together. He was probably in his mid- fifties then, before he got ill. His hair was jet white, and she had been told he supposedly had a full head of gray hair since he was 27 years old. Rebecca had always thought that was a slight exaggeration, except now she believed it, because she has been dying the gray out of her own hair for the past eight years.

In the kitchen, she poured a cup of coffee from the machine sitting on the counter, and took a seat at the breakfast bar that separated the kitchen from the living room. Instantly, she recognized her mother's handwriting on the slip of paper placed on the counter. It was addressed to her and only told her what she already had known. That she took the kids to church and that they would be back sometime around 11:00. Dinner would be at 1:00. Rebecca sipped at her warm coffee and switched on the television set. To her surprise, last night had been rather eventful to the country and she caught how the reporter was making the most out of this breaking news. She flipped the channel only to find that almost every channel was covering the event that took place in Seattle late last evening. Rebecca was impressed because the number of cable channels had become massive over the last few years, yet what ever had happened managed to consume every network. She figured it was worth finding out, so Rebecca left it on. But first she switched the channel to the network that she felt had a newscaster who always presented the news with the least bias. Wow, now she was interested, even he was a bit upset, she could hear the marked elevation in his voice.

"In case you have just joined us, It has been brought to the attention of our West Coast office early this morning that there has been an attempt on the president's life. We learned that the President and Mrs. Cartwright were attending a charity ball last night at the exclusive Peak View Resort, where apparently there was an attempt made on his life. The elite Washington Resort is well known for its high profile clientele. It is also known that joining the president at last night's function was Senator Guthrie of Washington, they were accompanied by her husband and at least two, high ranking military officials. We have yet to learn of the exact status of President Cartwright at this time. However, it has been reported that a secret service agent has been seriously injured. The name of the agent is currently being withheld until family has been properly notified. We can tell you that the gunman has been reported as dead, but his identity has been withheld pending a full investigation. We have been informed that The White House will be giving an official statement about the status of the president sometime in the next hour. We will notify you, our viewing audience of any news breaking information pertaining to these events as soon as we receive any. But while our reporter Maria Sarsky stands by at the White House pressroom, lets join anchorwoman Sandra Connelly, with retired FBI agent Gerald Jones." "Thank you John, Agent Jones can you tell our news listeners what is likely to be taking place right now in the investigation at the scene of this terrible incident?" "Yes Sandra, Routinely the FBI agents on the scene."

Rebecca shut off the television. The news wasn't likely to change anytime soon. and she wasn't in any hurry to sit there and wait for what would probably be hours before any word on the president was actually reported. Strange though, they almost always knew instantly whether or not the president was actually hit by a bullet. Maybe they were just being more cautious for once, before they panicked everyone in the country. Anyway, she had more important things to do and worry about right now. She had to decide what to do with the rest of her life. Rebecca let out a deep sigh. She was well aware that knowing what she didn't want wasn't the same as knowledge of what she did. And right now she was in really short supply of the things she did want.

Sitting in the stillness of her mother's house, she felt she could do with a quiet drive by herself. It was one the things that she had really enjoyed doing while she was young, and living here with her parents. She especially liked driving out to the Rhode Island beaches and spending time walking on the shore. She made a mental note to herself, to take a trip out there for a walk before she moved on to Vermont to visit Carl's Mom.

Today was a good day, warm and sunny for a winter morning, perfect for taking a short drive through the old back roads that she used to enjoy as a teenager. The ones with the twisting and winding roadways that could barely hold two cars and that ran through woods. Land that had been divided centuries ago by stone fences and that in the summer were lined with wild flowers. She hoped she could still find her way through that old system of roads without getting lost. Encouraged by the idea of seeing the back roads, Rebecca quickly placed the coffee cup in the dishwasher and ran to get ready to leave.

Cleaned with freshly dried hair, Rebecca slipped into the black jeans that Anne had given her, and over her tee shirt she threw on David's old sweater. It was even colder here than she had expected it would be. It made Rebecca appreciate the thick cream knit sweater that was large enough to cover her hips. She pulled on her black work boots and reached for her coat, the long black wool one that David had complained to her would cause her death. She didn't care; it looked nice, and this sweater of his had sleeves, which were long enough to fold up over the outside of her wool coat. Digging through her purse, she found her car keys and placed them inside her coat pocket. Then before leaving she was careful to use the mirror to place David's hat properly on her head. The way he had shown her how to wear it. Careful not to set it too high up on her forehead, but instead a little lower over her eyes. Looking around the house, she felt as though she were forgetting something. Without figuring out what it was, Rebecca, with purse and car keys in hand, closed the door behind her. In the car, she buckled her seat belt and when she looked into the rearview mirror to back the car out of the driveway. Rebecca glimpsed the emptiness of the seat behind her and realized it was her family she was missing. She thought how, if her world were normal it would be Carl sitting here in the driver's seat right now. As they drove down the windy roads, when he spotted a hump in the road ahead he would speed up to get the dropping effect of a roller coaster. The kids always cheered and asked him to do it again and again. He had always made things exciting, even something as simple as a drive through the woods.

Rebecca swallowed hard, as she gently guided the car out of the drive and onto the road. Then she turned the car toward the business district before heading out of town. When she felt another uncontrolled emotion grip her, she reached over and cranked up the radio as loudly as she could and began singing just as loud. Turning down the radio, Rebecca pulled into the drive-thru of the Donut House and ordered a French vanilla cappuccino and dozen-donut holes. Then she pulled back onto the main road and headed out toward the Old Mill Town Road.

In town all the snow piles had been colored black with dirt and exhaust. Out here, Rebecca could see that the integrity of the white snow had remained intact. It was amazing, how high the snow along the Old Mill Town Road still remained. Rebecca realized that Connecticut had to have been hit much harder than they had been hit by the storm in Virginia. She looked closer to the wood line as she rounded a corner and saw that the forest had few fallen trees and realized that they must have been spared from all the ice that the southern states were hit so hard with. She was sure it would melt fast and wished she had thought to bring a camera. Rounding another corner, Rebecca was surprised to see the entrance to the old historic grain mill open. Turning the car into the entrance, she slowed the car down to a crawl and was careful not to slip off the narrow, barely plowed road. She continued on inching her way into the small dirt parking lot. She parked the car and found that the only other vehicle was that of a forestry ranger. She hadn't even known that Connecticut had forestry rangers. Well, she supposed, it wouldn't be unheard of, for there to be a couple, maybe. But she certainly doubted that this state needed more than that. She couldn't recall ever having seen one before today.

Rebecca grabbed the bag of donuts and took a bite out of a chocolate glazed one, while she contemplated what a forestry ranger would be doing here on a Sunday morning. Other than a few deer, squirrels, chipmunks and the like she couldn't imagine what would be of such high importance to drag someone out here. Of course, unless someone had broken into or damaged the old mill, teenagers probably. When she was in High School, she would come out here and make out with boyfriends and she was sure others had too, both then and now. Wouldn't that be stupid, she thought, to vandalize the mill, all that would do is ensure that this little park became closed to the public. Swallowing the last of her fourth tiny donut with the contents from the bottom of her coffee cup, Rebecca decided to venture out of the car and hike up the path to the old stone structure.

It was further and steeper than she remembered. It was also just as beautiful. The two hundred year old field stone building stood there as it had forever, graceful and elegant by the side of the river. Looking in the window Rebecca was always impressed with the way it had been constructed. The large grinding gears, which took most of the space inside the building with the large water wheel attached to it for power. She walked around the building to the other side so she could get a better look at the water wheel.

Rounding the corner Rebecca froze when she saw a trail of blood and debated on whether to head straight back to the car or to go and investigate. Looking closer at the ground. she could see that whatever it was, it most definitely was not human. That was a comfort and so she decided to risk following it for a short distance, telling herself, if it weren't briefly up ahead then she would turn back. Other than the first spot of blood, the trail she followed was very sparse of blood, following the drips she wondered why the animal had carried it off so far from where it had caught it. Maybe her driving up had forced it into the woods.

Rebecca was about to give up and turn around when she thought she could see something on the ground up ahead. Approaching it, she covered her nose with her hand when a breeze carried the strong scent of blood at her face. When she saw the size of the deer torn apart, she reconsidered the wisdom in her decision to follow the trail. Instantly she headed back to the car fearing the culprit had been a bear. When she could see the stone building once more, Rebecca stopped long enough to place her hand inside one of the paw marks on the ground before her. Yeah, definitely a bear. That would be a first for these parts. She wondered where it came from. It was probably long gone. She consoled herself. It had to be just traveling through. She would bet that it had moved on hours ago at the very least.

Reaching the parking lot she found that another car was now parked across the way. Rebecca looked around, but saw no one, she knew there hadn't been anyone at the building as she passed it. They must be hiking. She thought. Then hoped they didn't have a run in with the bear, if it had decided to stay. Rebecca felt a stillness come over the air around her and felt the hairs on the back of her neck tingle and rise. Looking around at the forest, she felt an odd sensation of someone watching her. Taking off her hat for a minute, she listened to the woods surrounding her and scanned it once more, this time looking more carefully for disguised shapes at the bases of trees. Satisfied that she was going insane, Rebecca continued to her car.

"Stop where you are and whatever you do, stand very still!"

Preparing to go around the hood of the car, over to the driver's door, Rebecca suddenly did as she was told. Across the parking lot from her, a man emerged from the hiking trail. Dressed in green and pointing a gun, she did as he told her. It was as she stood waiting for his next instruction that she noticed the head of a large animal rising above the side of her car. The animal leapt onto the hood and looked Rebecca directly in the eyes. She was dumbstruck, not from fear, but from the deja vu she was experiencing, face to face with this awesome animal. It was so close to her that she could feel the strength of its powerful presence envelop her. As it starred her in the eye she felt that it meant her no harm, its large green eyes were gentle to her own. The huge animal bounded down from her car, and it brushed the side of her body with his own, the way a house cat would, except that his force would have knocked her over if she hadn't been braced against the vehicle. Watching as the long tail passed her eyes she heard a loud popping sound. It was the roof of her car unbuckling from the release of the large animals weight. Turning to watch the animal leave, Rebecca was hypnotized by its beauty. Boom, She jumped and stood there shocked by the sight of the animal scattering and then dropping to the ground. The single shot of the riffle had taken the animal down almost instantly.

"Don't worry, He's only tranquilized."

Rebecca leaned over the cougar and touched his nose. He was

completely unresponsive, which she could tell from his glassed over eyes that he would be. The animal had only a swallow breath. "Are you sure you didn't give him too much?"

"Yes, he'll be fine. I would think you would be screaming at me for not shooting him earlier?"

"He wouldn't have hurt me, but why hadn't you."

"By the time I made my way back here to take a break, I saw that he was about to pounce. All I could do was warn you and hope he didn't decide to use you as a play toy to sharpen his claws." "You see he's a pretty big boy, the man patted the animals side, he's likely twice your weight maybe more and if I missed him and hit you instead, You'd be dead."

"Thanks for waiting. Like I told you, he wouldn't have hurt me."

"You mean to say that you weren't scared of him."

"No, I was afraid it was going to be a bear."

"Bears usually attack only when they feel threatened, Cougars if hungry enough might go for prey of your size."

Rebecca placed the black hat back onto her head. "So, what's going to happen to him?"

"Some Zoologists from the Bronx Zoo are headed up to take some tests and chart his movement. I was told some colleagues of theirs have been doing a study out west and they lost track of this guy a few months ago." He lifted the head of the animal and showed her the device stapled to the backside of his ear. "Then they'll transport him back out West, too dangerous to leave him here."

"Well, thanks for the warning."

"Would you like to have dinner with me tonight or some other time?"

"Guess they don't let you out of these woods very often, do they?"

"No, they don't, but why do say that?"

"Thanks, But if I weren't wearing these gloves you'd see that I'm married."

"Oh, sorry." "You know anyone would be scared to come that close to this animal. I would, So why weren't you?"

"That's a long story and I'm sorry, but I really need to get going or I'll be late for something." Rebecca went to the car and unlocked the door.

"Rebecca, you don't remember me, do you?"

"I'm sorry, Rebecca looked at the man closer, No I don't?"

"We went to school together, High School, I'm Todd Greenfield. Ninth grade Biology and Gym."

"Wow, Yes, of course I remember you, how have you been?"

"Oh, pretty good and you?"

"Me too, Pretty Good." Rebecca smiled at the man standing before her, amazed to see a face from so long ago. Then she lifted her glove sleeve and looked to the time on her watch, 12:30. "I'm sorry, but I was telling the truth when I said that I needed to get going."

"Sorry, of course. Rebecca, Now that you know that I'm not just some crazy guy in the woods. Are you still married?"

"Yes, actually." She pulled off her glove to expose her rings." I really am married."

Todd gave her a warm smile. "It was nice seeing you again."

"You too." She took one last look at the cougar. "Take care of that big guy."

"Someday you'll have to tell me that story of yours."

"Maybe someday." She got in the car and waved to Todd as he went to the forestry truck and opened the back to expose a huge cage.

Rolling down the window Rebecca yelled out to him, "Do you need help getting him in."

"Are you sure. I wouldn't want to make you late."

"Yeah, I'm sure. The story alone will be enough to pardon my lateness."

"Thanks, if you don't mind. I'd really appreciate it."

Behind the wheel once more, Rebecca took the turn towards home and pondered silently if there had been more to that cougar than there seemed. Blinded by something beaming off her side mirror. She looked in the rearview mirror and caught the reflection of something in the forest behind her. Glimpsing the streak of a rabbit in front of her, she hit the brakes to slow the car. When she looked back up, whatever it was, it was gone.

CHAPTER NINETEEN

Carl woke to find the cabin empty except for himself and Julie. He didn't have to look in the loft to know no one was there. The evidence was in the room around him. Dirty dishes in the kitchen sink, the lingering smell of breakfast was hanging in the air and most obvious of all, the note left for them on the table by Luke. The scratching on the piece of paper informed them that he had left breakfast plates in the brick oven and that he would return shortly.

Carl was shocked, his watch said 10:00am and he was completely perplexed as to how he managed to sleep through Luke or Mary cooking on the fireplace next to him. Checking on Julie's ankle, Carl found that it looked perfectly normal. But, what was more unusual to him was that she was completely unresponsive to his touch. Julie was always a light sleeper, and she had never slept later than he had. Feeling her cheek, she felt normal and her breathing was even. So he stretched and went to use the bathroom.

When Carl came back, he went to the oven to get his plate of food and returning to the table with it, he spied his teacup from last night. Freezing cold, Carl decided to place it in the brick oven in an attempt to warm it back up. When he went to retrieve it, he heard the door to the cabin open and then felt the floor rattle as it slammed-shut.

"Don't drink that." Luke had returned, and with him he had brought some boots and jackets.

"Sorry!"

"I said don't drink that. I'm sorry. I should have thought to dump that out." He pointed to the fireplace, "Grab that kettle and I'll make us some coffee."

Carl did as he was told and brought the kettle over to Luke.

Luke emptied Carl's cup into the sink and rinsed it out. "I should have told you last night that there was a natural sedative mixed into the tea. But I was afraid that in your and the girl's agitated state that either or both of you may have refused it and then have gotten no rest before our hike today."

"Did you go into town this morning?"

"No, only over to my brother's place so that he could care for Love while I'm gone."

"Is she ill?"

"No, she's carrying, but we've lost one before and so she needs to stay bed rested as the doctor's advised her."

"Congratulations!"

"Too soon for that, But the doctor says after the first trimester, it should have taken hold. Do you have any?"

"Yes, I have three children."

"Wonderful, so heaven has blessed you then."

"Yes. Yes it has." Carl watched as Luke rolled up his sleeves and knead dough on the white floured surface of his kitchen table.

"You can put that back on the fire." He motioned to the kettle that was sitting on the table's corner. Carl hung it back onto the wrought iron hook and then placed the mitt back on the mantle. "I think your friend will be knocked out for probably another hour." Luke informed Carl as he formed the dough into a long loaf, then took out another bowl and started to knead its contents. "We'll throw these in the oven and wait for her to wake up, no point in rushing her, she'd be too groggy to walk all the way there anyhow." He made another loaf, "Then you can take these with you."

"Thank you and thank you also for breakfast."

"Sit and finish it before it gets cold." Carl sat back down, amazed at how hungry he was especially after all that food he ate at the banquet hall last night. Last night, Lord that felt like ages ago. "Have you heard any news about Paul?"

"The Radio isn't giving out many details. But no matter, I don't suspect that it is the actual story anyhow."

"Why, what have you heard?"

"They're saying that an attempt has been made on the president's life. Their also saying that Paul was an agent injured while protecting him. Not quite the truth, huh?"

"No, not quite."

Luke placed the loaves in the brick oven and then went to gather a few things from his cupboards. Placing the canned goods and a bag of rice inside a backpack. Luke said, "You're going to thank me for this later, I've had the food that comes in those brown bags."

Carl laughed. He knew exactly what he was referring to, MRE's. They are called meals ready to eat, and Carl had had more than his share of them. "If you're really hungry, they're not that bad."

"No man should ever become that hungry."

He knew Luke was right and was grateful for the supplies he was gathering for them. Carl knew too well the effect of too many MRE's in a person's digestive system, constipation from hell. Luke also placed a jug of wine and a small tin of his family's tea inside another bag.

"You be very careful with this. He pulled the tin back out, You only need a small pinch to a cup of water." Luke made sure he understood him, waving his hand at him in lecture.

"I understand. Thanks."

"Be sure you only use it when one of you is sick or hurt, it's not good to use as a sleep aid, regular use would make it less effective."

"Okay, I hear you. Thanks, Luke."

"Don't mention it."

Carl finished his breakfast and rinsed his plate in the sink. Then he watched Julie lying on the couch sleeping so soundly. She looked calm, somehow that picture of her didn't fit well. He had thought of Julie as always restless, and since she was usually up before the sun was, he thought that her sleep was probably never this peaceful. Carl watched as Julie turned in her sleep and knocked the cover loose. He checked her leg once again and then placed the blanket back over her. "That stuff you put on her ankle last night seems to have really done the trick."

"Yes, it looks much better, for now."

"What do you mean?"

"By tonight, she'll probably need another dose of the tea and then a day or two off her ankle completely." Julie turned once more. "Looks like she's about ready to wake up, why don't you go ahead and try those boots on for size." Luke motioned to the small pile of boots and coats that he had brought in with him. Carl reached for the brown boots and tried one on and then the other. They were a little too big but better than too small he thought.

"Do they fit alright?"

"Yes, Thank you."

"Not too small, are they?"

"No, not too small."

"Good."

Julie stretched, and found Carl walking back and forth in some boots he was apparently testing out. "Morning."

"Good Morning." Both men returned.

"Goodness, what time is it," she looked at her wrist and found no watch. She had forgotten that she was dressed up last night and had left her watch at the apartment. Carl looked at his and told her it was 11:00am. "I thought we needed to get an early start."

"You needed your rest more, besides I had some errands to take care of first."

Julie looked down at her ankle and was surprised to see it was perfectly normal. Pulling the covers off of her, she stood and walked over to the bathroom door.

"How does it feel?" Carl asked her.

"Okay, like I twisted it a couple days ago."

Luke thought that was because the tea hadn't fully worn off yet. It would hurt like hell in a couple of hours, but he kept his thoughts to himself. Carl had retrieved Julie's plate from the brick oven and had been careful not to close the door hard, to avoid making the bread fall.

"I'm sorry everyone is waiting on me." She looked across the table at the men staring at her.

"We're not waiting on you at all." Carl answered. "Luke put bread in the oven and so we're waiting for it to finish baking." Carl got the coffee and gave her some and then filled his and Luke's cups for a second time.

"That must be what smells so good, it was making my stomach rumble in my sleep."

They filled Julie in on the little news that was being broadcast. It wasn't a surprise to her. "We need to sit tight a couple of days and Randy will contact us after all the media hype has calmed down." Julie finished her food and thanked Luke. Then she tried on her boots and was glad that they were a little tight rather than loose, this way her ankle was well supported, and she wouldn't have to worry about a second twist.

Luke took out the breads to let them cool, and everyone prepared to leave. Carl trying on a coat and a backpack. Julie putting on her jacket and waiting for instructions from their guide.

The dog barked outside. "Shh, Hawk." They heard a voice yell. "Bang, bang!" A fist pounded against the front door. Luke put his pointer finger up against his lips and motioned for them to enter the bathroom. "Coming!" Luke yelled. Carl and Julie squeezed into the small bathroom and held their breath and positions as quietly as they could. Listening they could hear faint voices.

"Sheriff, What brings you by?"

"Could I come in?"

"I was just headed out."

"Please. It will only be a minute."

"Sure, come on in."

"Luke, I've come by to let you know some bad news. Last night at the Resort Paul got shot. He was flown to a hospital in Seattle. I didn't want you to find out from the radio, so I hope you don't mind I came out here."

"Of course not, thank you, sheriff."

"I know I'm on official business, but you can still call me Bill."

"Yes. Of course, What happened last night?"

"Do you mind?" Bill motioned to the kitchen chair. "I can't rightly say. Paul got shot in the chest by some man. And at about the same moment, a girl in a pink dress shot the man. Mr. Taylor and the FBI have asked me to keep what I saw to myself. SO, you didn't hear that from me. You know; folks around here have always thought there was something funny about that resort." Bill picked up a cup on the table and put it back down. "Mr. Taylor assures me that what I saw was not what it looked like. Whatever that's supposed to mean. People were shot, how can that not look like, what it is, A Crime!" The man shook his head in disgust. "When weird things go on up there and its strangers, that's one thing. It shouldn't be, but it is. But now it's Paul, one of us." Bill picked up another cup and placed it in the center of the table.

"So, have you heard any news about Paul's condition."

"No, only that he is in intensive care." "Where's Love, Luke?"

"She's sleeping, doctor's orders."

"Luke, I don't know what's going on here, but I'd bet you have two people hiding in your bathroom. You always were a terrible liar."

"I don't know what you mean?"

"Give it up, Luke and call your friends out. I know there are two other people here with you because both of these cups are still warm, and I watched you drink out of that one. But also, I already saw Love at your brother's place before I came here." Bill laughed. "Even as a kid you always worried about the next question and not the one you were currently answering."

Julie and Carl came out of the bathroom. "We would have climbed out through the bathroom window, but it was too small."

"I knew that too." The gray haired man with the star on his chest grinned. "So, should I be shaking your hand and saying 'How do' or should I be slapping hand cuffs on those little wrists of yours?" Bill stared at Julie.

"Preferably, shaking my hand." Julie extended hers out to the man. "Julie Stevens, and this is Carl." They removed their coats and took a seat. "There isn't much I can tell you." Julie started.

Luke held up his hand. "I'll explain. You know that Paul was once Secret Service and that afterward he went into civilian protection."

"Yes."

"That's what she does and she was working with Paul."

"The man you saw her kill last night, was a gun for hire and Paul got shot protecting someone else."

"Him?"

"Yes." Carl said sadly.

"That's pretty dangerous business you've got yourself involved in. Wouldn't you rather be off somewhere making babies or something?"

Julie got angry. "That is a very sexist thing to say, I'll have you know that I'm good at what I do."

"Calm yourself down, little lady. I believe you. Don't take me wrong now, But women like you, tend to be interested in shopping, charity luncheons and PTA's."

"What kind of women are you referring to?"

"Women of education and wealth." The sheriff stated the obvious, then changed the subject back to last night.

Julie barely heard the things the men finished discussing. But she did vaguely realize that the sheriff had left and that the men were ready to leave. Julie had been struck by what the man had said to her.

"Julie, Are you ready?"

"Yes." She grabbed her coat and rushed out the door, hearing Luke slam and lock it behind her.

Following the river, they hiked a distance and then needed to cross over it at a junction where it split into two rivers. Looking back, Julie noticed that it didn't actually split. It only appeared to do so, because the water was forced to divide around a small island. With Luke ahead of her and Carl right behind, Julie watched the landscape they were passing through, the huge cedars smelt incredible, and the thick moss underfoot was like a thick padding to her feet. It was cold, and in some areas there was snow on the ground, but most of the time it was dry, but had a frozen quality to it. Every once in a while, a deer or two would pop their heads up and look at them. Then go running off in the distance to avoid contact with the humans, as they made their way through the animal's homes.

Occasionally, Luke would stop and look at tracks made in the snow, but he never said anything. Julie noticed that Luke had picked up speed and she altered her own and stuck close the Luke's heels ahead of her. Looking back, she saw that Carl had followed suit and so she kept rhythm with their guide ahead of her and allowed herself to think once

more about the words of the sheriff. "A Woman of Education and Wealth."
She repeated to herself. Julie found herself for the first time re-evaluating
not what she wanted in life, but who she was. Weeks earlier, she would
have not only called him a sexist pig, but also a man of poor judgment.
After all, she was no woman of education and wealth. She was a girl
raised on a farm in Northern California. Yes, she was a girl who had a
degree from UCLA in business, but she got it on full scholarship. She was
a girl who had earned lots of money, particularly because she didn't look
the part. She was the poor girl who because of wit, luck and willingness to
play a dangerous game was brought into circles of status and wealth. Julie
looked down at her manicured hands with the large rings on her fingers.
Yes, she thought, she was once the uneducated poor girl raised on a
vegetable farm, with soil stains on her hands and dirt under her nails. But,
she wondered, Is that who she was now?

CHAPTER TWENTY

Rebecca took the last curve of the Old Mill Town Road headed toward home. The cougar had been very heavy. She was glad that she had stayed to help, even though she doubted that he really needed any. It gave her the chance to touch the cougar, an experience she doubted she would get again. The animal had been pure muscle, and the weight of him proved it. Looking at the clock in the dashboard, she hoped she was right, and her story would be enough to forgive her being late for dinner. At least it gave them something else to ask about instead of Carl. That gave her some relief, even if it would be short lived.

Pulling up to her mother's little bungalow, Rebecca saw that the driveway was full and pulled her car to the curb with the other three cars already there. The small yellow bungalow would be jammed packed with family, people she no longer sees very often. It is always a little uncomfortable at first, making adjustments to how people's appearances have changed, but shortly after her nervousness had calmed, everyone's personalities would come though as she remembered them and then it would feel like her family once more. Looking at the large front porch, to one side she could see her mother's wicker furniture draped over in large plastic covers and to the other side she could see the old wooden swing that had been painted a million times. If it were warm enough, she would be tempted to sit out here until someone realized that her car was outside, at which time she could pretend that she had just arrived. She knew that even if it were warm out, she wouldn't actually do such a thing, even though she might desire to. Perhaps she could steal another minute to collect her thoughts. Too late, no such luck for her, the door had opened.

"Hurry up and get your butt in here." Her brother, Donald yelled.
"Hey Donny, how are you?"

"Where have you been, we've been waiting for you." Her mother stepped out in a sweater and her Sunday clothing. "I was just about to call the police and have them start looking for you."

"Mom you know I would have needed to be missing for at least Twenty-four hours first."

"You know she doesn't care, she'd call anyway." Her and her brother shared looks. "Yeah, I know." They both chuckled.

"Come on. We're starved." Her sister, Angela, ran out to hug her. "How are you doing kiddo?" Kiddo was more symbolic than it seemed. Angela did think of her as one of her kids, since she had changed Rebecca's diapers when she was a baby.

"I'm hanging in there, how are you?"

Once she stepped through the door the air was drenched in madness. Everyone wanted to know, first of all, where she had run off to and why she was late to dinner. The room was full of questions and comments and hugs and kisses all around. Rebecca answered the easy ones and avoided anything that required more than a paragraph to answer. All while searching to find each of her children, and greet all of her nieces and nephews at the same time. Danny, she saw had set up permanent residence on her brother, Robert's lap. Karen was thrilled to be getting all of her older cousin's attention, playing with her hair and talking about little girl things. Rachel, she couldn't find.

"Hey Mom, where is Rachel? Did something happen, is she hiding out in the bedroom?"

"Yeah, she's in the bedroom, but not hiding out, she's talking to some boyfriend." Robbie answered.

"It's Tommy." Danny fluttered his eyelashes and tilted his head in a teasing gesture from his place on Uncle Robbie's lap.

"Well, go tell her that we have to eat now."

"Okay, but where were you Mom. We've been waiting an awfully long time for you."

"Let's get dinner started and then I'll tell everyone at once."

Danny went running down the hall to the bedroom and returned after cracking the door open and yelling loud enough for the whole house to hear. "Get off the phone, Butthead, it's time to eat."

The small two-bedroom house was wall to wall with people. Everyone had filtered through the tiny kitchen, where dinner had been laid out by her mother and sisters buffet style. Then it was each man to his own to find somewhere to sit. The dining room table was full of men, containing her brothers, brother in-laws and nephews. Danny had been given a high footstool to sit on, right next to Robbie, of course.

By the time Rachel joined the others to eat, everyone was too busy putting food in their mouths to keep up the full force of their previous conversations. It gave Rebecca's head a small break from the noise, and now she was better able to focus on the quieter conversations going on around her.

"Hey beautiful, Come and give your Aunt Emily a hug before you get a plate."

Rachel went to hug her Aunt, and while passing her mother she said, "Mom, I told Tommy we had to go eat, but that you'd call David later." She spoke in less than a whisper.

"Thanks sweetie." Rebecca would have asked, if it had been David who had called or Tommy, but she didn't want to fuel questions for the others. Rebecca was in no rush to eat, she positioned herself out of the path of traffic, between the couch and the breakfast bar and picked up a piece of turkey from a platter.

Rebecca studied the faces of her family and listened to them talk while getting familiar with the montage before her. Her Mom had reversed her house so that the living room and dining room were switched. Her reasoning for this was that she liked to be able to watch the television while she prepared meals. Rebecca thought that this made sense since most of her time was spent in those two rooms. In the open space between the two rooms, where a wall would have been, had there been one, laid a table cloth on the floor and all the nieces were gathered around it with their plates.

"Rebecca, why don't you take off your hat and stay a while." Her sister, Vicky, yelled from across the room. "It's not something I'd have expected you to wear."

Her husband yelled over. "It's a nice hat, Rebecca."

"Thanks Larry, Why do you think it doesn't suit me, Vicky. I mean - I did live in Tennessee for six years."

"I didn't say it didn't suit you exactly, but I guess it's a little more earthy than I think of you as being."

"Becca, I like it. It's a little big maybe." Emily was her sister closest in age, and at one time, they had been really good friends.

"Thanks Em." Not that it really mattered to her what they thought of a hat that wasn't even hers, really. She turned around to the wall mirror behind her. Rebecca looked at herself in the hat and imagined the blue eyes that it belonged to. She wondered why he would have called her; a day is hardly any time to have thought about his offer. She hung his hat on the wall hook and went to the kitchen to grab a plate of food. In the living room, she could hear her sisters bickering at each other.

"That's great, Vic, I think maybe you've upset her."

"Well, excuse me. You know I didn't mean to."

"Give her a break, really with all she's been through."

"Angela, It was a comment about a hat, give me a break, will you please."

"I'm absolutely fine Guys, really. Why don't we just forget it, okay." Rebecca heaped some food onto her plate and covered it in gravy, swiping a roll on her way to the living room. She thought it might be friendlier to sit with the girls on the floor. Rather than choose any group to sit with, Rebecca instead stood centrally located with her back against the front door.

"Becca, you abandoning us, just because Vicky doesn't like your hat?"

"Don't be silly. I'm just comfortable here." She let her back slide down the door, and when her butt hit the floor she allowed her legs to fold under.

"Rebecca, you'll get sick sitting there."

"I'm fine, Mom." There was a draft blowing straight at her butt, but it was still better over here, alone. She knew her family was just stalling through dinner, at least the best they could. What they were really interested in knowing is all the juicy details of her screwed up life. She was waiting for the one question that would steam roll it all.

"The hat isn't Mom's." Rebecca heard Danny tell her brother Robbie.

"It isn't?" He looked at Rebecca with a smile as he listened to her son betray her.

"No, it's David's. She's just holding onto it for him." The boy said casually, without ever knowing he had exposed a secret she was trying to keep from the others.

"Yeah, until June." Karen added.

The room got quiet, quicker than the men had run for the food earlier.

"Well, aren't you a couple of little traitors." Rebecca looked to her son and then to her daughter.

They looked confused.

"Rebecca!" Her mother shouted.

"Chill out Mom, I'm only teasing and they know that."

They could tell their Mom wasn't really mad, but she wasn't completely happy either. "You didn't say it was a secret Mom."

"I know sweetie, I didn't say it's a secret because it isn't." Rebecca said. "Well, I guess you guys can tell them the rest if you like." At least she didn't have to tell the details herself. "Go on. It's okay, tell everyone the story."

Danny looked at Karen and Karen looked at her brother, then they broke out. "David's in love with Mom." Danny said first, followed right behind by Karen. "He asked us to live with him."

Rebecca's mouth dropped along with everyone else's in the room. She covered her face as best she could with her hands and wished she were still wearing the black Stetson to hide behind. "I didn't mean that, I meant who he is and where he lives, that kind of information."

"NO, No guys, you did good, laughed Robbie, you cut right to the chase, and that's what we all wanted to know." He tickled Danny, "Good job, Kid."

The room was again cluttered with intense noise.

"Spill it, Becca."

"Out with it, Kiddo."

"Come on, start talking."

"And we want to know the whole story."

"Come on."

"Come on." They all hounded her.

Rebecca looked to Rachel. "Sorry Mom, You set yourself up for that one."

She knew her daughter was right too. It was her-own fault for trying to avoid simply telling them everything from the start. She told them all the details that she knew about David. Including his offer and the deal they had made with one another.

The phone rang and everyone scattered to throw away plates and clean up the dinner mess. "Aunt Rebecca, the phone is for you." Her nephew told her, "Before you answer it, can Casey and I take the kids to a movie this afternoon?"

"Sure, if they would like to go. That would be nice, thanks." She wasn't fooled. She knew her sister had asked him to take the kids out. That way everyone could find out what was going on with Carl, without the kids being here to make them uncomfortable.

"Hello."

"Hello, Miss Garner, Is that your maiden name or married name, Ma'am?"

"Excuse me, Who is this?"

"Excuse me. My name is Gina Russell. I work for Channel 13 news. I was informed that you were approached by a wild cougar this morning and wondered if you would like to comment on your harrowing experience?"

"It was less than harrowing and no thank you, I wouldn't care to comment." Rebecca hung up the phone.

"Who was that Rebecca?" Her mom placed a covered dish in the refrigerator.

"No one important, just some reporter from channel 13, she wanted me to comment about this morning." Rebecca rinsed a platter and placed it in the dishwasher.

"Oh yeah, Becca, You never told us where you were." Emily ripped off a piece of plastic wrap, covered the bowl and handed it to their mother.

"You're kidding, a reporter, What happened to you this morning?"

Rebecca thought. Nothing; compared with yesterday morning. But she kept that to herself. "I only planned on taking a short drive and then getting back here before everyone arrived."

The front door slammed shut. "What happened to the hood of your car, Aunt Rebecca?" Her nephew came in from putting the trash out to the curb for her mother.

"Rebecca, were you in an accident?" Vicky asked her sharply.

"No, I went for a drive out on the Old Mill Town Road and when I got to the Mill entrance it was open, so I went in to sit and drink my coffee."

"I know that place, all the kids from school go out there." Angela glared toward her son. "Oh, But not me, Mom."

"Yeah right, give it up Craig, like you and Shelly have never been out to the Old Mill." Casey gave her cousin a hard time.

He pushed her, "Thanks Casey!"

"HEY! What's going on over there." His Dad yelled.

"Nothing, we're listening to Aunt Rebecca's story about why she was late."

Rebecca left the small kitchen and entered the living room so everyone who wanted to hear her story could. "So, as I was saying, I decided to take a ride out the Old Mill Town Road and I stopped at the park because it was open. Drank my coffee and then walked up to the stone mill. But when I rounded the side of the building, I could see blood on the ground, I looked closely at the snow tracks, and since I was sure they weren't human I decided to follow them."

"That's not very smart of you, Rebecca." A low, but firm voice said.

Other than Hello; that was the first thing she had heard him say to her, and it was a scolding. Gary was her sister Em's husband, and he was always quiet, but not because he had nothing to say. Rebecca took her scolding, "Yeah, I know Gary, but what did I know, I thought that it was probably a fox that had gotten a rabbit or at the very worst maybe a wild dog that had gotten it hours ago." Gary sat there staring at her with a smirk on his face. She couldn't fool him; he knew she was lying. "All right, So I knew it wasn't any fox, But curiosity would have gotten the better of anyone here." "Except maybe you Gary, she teased. You would have gone home to get your rifle first."

"Not me."

"Or me." Said some of the women.

That didn't surprise her, other than Emily. Most of them wouldn't care to go camping, never mind hike through woods searching for wild animals.

"How big did you say that track was?" Her brother Donny asked." "So, what was it?"

"I didn't say, and hold on because the interesting thing isn't what it was as much as how I found out." She explained everything. They all sat there staring at her in disbelief. "It was incredible, the way it stared straight at me with its huge green eyes."

"A cougar, are you insane Rebecca."

"It wouldn't have hurt me."

"You're just lucky it had a full stomach."

Her family had freaked out exactly as she thought they would. Everyone was busy talking about her story as they all scattered to watch games on the television or finish cleaning. Rebecca went to the kitchen to help the others finish the dishes and make fresh coffee. With her hands in a sink full of soapy bubbles, Rebecca stood washing the silverware for dessert.

"What was that you said?" Her lanky brother asked as he passed her.

Looking up from the sink, Rebecca saw Robbie carrying four beers.

"I said, Carl would have thought it was pretty great."

"I doubt that." Everyone in the kitchen responded.

What did they know, they barely even knew Carl. She finished what she was doing and dried her hands.

"Hey Robbie, Do you remember Todd Greenfield?"

"Yeah, he went to school with you."

"Did you know he was a Forest Ranger?"

"Yeah, I think I did hear that. Oh my God, was he the ranger today."

"Yeah." She said.

"You know he had the biggest crush on you."

"No, he didn't." Rebecca half laughed.

"Yeah, he did Rebecca."

"I didn't know that." She said surprised.

"Well, that's because you only had eyes for Jason Harper." Her brother did a mimic of Danny. She knew why Danny liked him so much. He was still a child himself.

"Stop that."

"Don't deny it, Rebecca. You were so lost in Jason Harper."

"No, I remember well enough myself, I don't need to be reminded."

"So, you saw Todd today, Did you know his wife passed away a few years ago? Damn, I'm surprised he didn't ask you out."

"As a matter of fact, he did." Rebecca walked away from her brother.

"SO!" He yelled across the room.

"So what, I told him I'm married."

"Why did you do that?" Vicky wanted to know.

"Gee Sis, maybe because it's the truth."

"Rebecca, You really -"

"Let it go Vic!" Larry yelled to her.

She sat down at the dining room table, where her brother-in-law was already sitting reading the Sunday paper. "Come on Gary. You can't tell me that you don't think that was a great experience. Come on." She coaxed him. "Admit it. You would have liked to have been there."

He sat quiet for a minute. "Maybe, but I agree that you're nuts."

Karen came over to hug her goodbye. "You guys off to the movies."

"Yup. Mom, wasn't it scary?"

"Actually, No, it wasn't. The way it looked at me was gentle. I knew it didn't intend to hurt me." "But anyway, the ranger was there to save me if he needed to."

Gary looked at her as she boldly lied to her daughter. They knew the truth, but the kids didn't need any more stress than they already had. The others came and said goodbye too.

"So Gary, when is the family conference scheduled for?"

"I have no idea what you're talking about."

"Come on."

"I have nothing to do with anything, so don't ask me."

She sat there for a minute. "So when, over coffee and dessert?"

"That would be my guess."

Rebecca picked up the classifieds. "And the subject: moving on with my life or moving back here."

"That sounds right."

She flipped her page. "Thanks."

"No problem."

Folding the paper, she placed it back on the table. Rebecca certainly wasn't surprised. She couldn't decide if she felt honored that her family loved her enough to care so much or angry that they still treated her as though she couldn't make decisions for herself. Maybe she felt a little of both. But she did know that the best way to have a conversation with her family about Carl was to initiate it herself. That way, It was her who had brought up the subject and therefore she who had the power. This way she could assert that they were not in charge of her life, and that was the way she was going to keep it. Rebecca knew that time was of the essence, or else they would run her over like road kill.

Rebecca heard the coffeepot perk its last, long sound. The clatter of plates and coffee mugs had started which indicated to her that it was now or never for her to say something first. Rebecca joined her mother and sisters over near the counter and asked her brothers which dessert they wanted. Handing Donny his plate, Rebecca made her move. "I wanted to thank you all for today, I mean, I really appreciate that everyone has respected me and the position that I'm in and hasn't probed me for details that I can't give, Thanks." Rebecca could have heard a pin drop as she handed Larry his dessert plate. If Rebecca could have, she would have patted herself on the back for a job well done. She cut another slice of cake and waited for someone to speak. She knew her thanking them wouldn't stop them from having their planned family discussion of her life, but she hoped that she had at least set some boundaries.

It was her brother-in-law Larry who broke the silence. "Funny that you mention that because there was something that I wanted to discuss with you."

"What's that, Larry?"

"It's about Carl!" Her sister chimed in.

"Vicky, please!"

"What, she's my sister."

"Yes, and without so many words she has asked you to butt out of her business. So please let me handle this one." Larry reached into his pocket and pulled out a piece of paper. Handing it to Rebecca, he said, "I think this may be what you've been wanting to know."

Everyone in the room wanted to know what it was. Larry lifted his hands to the others to silence them. Rebecca carefully looked the document over. "How did you get this?"

"A friend of mine, who is now in the FBI acquired it for me."

"You shouldn't have done that, I hope you don't get into any trouble."

"Don't worry about that."

"Thank you!"

"You're welcome."

Larry was a State Trooper, and she stood staring at the certificate as he explained to the others how he had run Carl's social security number through the database at work and only came up with deceased. So he contacted an old buddy who had gone Federal.

"Larry, can I keep this?"

"I don't see why not."

Rebecca knew that what they saw in this certificate of death and what she saw were two different things. To them it was a confirmation that Carl was dead and that she could now accept it and go on with her life. To Rebecca it was the bit of information that she was prepared to go to Arlington Cemetery herself to know for sure. Whether or not her husband's body was in that grave.

But now she didn't need to go all the way there to know the truth. It was right here on this page before her. Typed on it was the word "Marker" on the lower left corner in the box titled burial or cremation. Rebecca folded the paper and placed it in her pocket.

"Are you okay, Kiddo." Angela looked at her confused.

"Yeah, I'm fine." Rebecca sliced another piece of cake and placed it onto the next plate on the stack. Then she poured herself a cup of coffee and went to the refrigerator to get her creamer. She listened only faintly to the voices in the room around her.

"There's a house down the street from us that is for sale."

"Oh, We know of a great little place not far from us too."

"The school system is better out that way too."

"Our school system is very good."

"And Rebecca you can still go on with your schooling just as you planned, the University down the road has a great psychology program."

Rebecca leaned against the stove and sipped her coffee. She listened to them all as they planned her life for her. Making suggestions and offering advice on schools and neighborhoods. Not one asking if she even wished to live there, just assuming that she wouldn't want to be anywhere else. She didn't blame them for assuming she would want to come home, a few years ago she would probably have done nothing else. She was different now. She had grown up some and maybe by living away from everyone for so long; she no longer needed to be surrounded by family to feel safe. She smiled at them and knew she wouldn't argue with them, not about why she should do this over that. Everyone would have their valid arguments. She knew she would too. It wasn't worth the fighting. She was grown and would make her choices on her own, not that she didn't love them for caring, she did. This was about her, and about her and Carl. It was about fourteen years of loving and growing. About years of learning, learning what it was she wanted from life and what made her happy. Rebecca placed her cup in the kitchen sink, grabbed her coat and hat, waved to her brother-in-law sitting at the dining room table and closed the door behind her. As it latched shut, she heard the others asking where it was she were going. She didn't stop or turn around long enough to answer them. But she did hear Gary say loudly, "OUT!"

CHAPTER TWENTY-ONE

Carl looked ahead and saw that Luke had stopped once more. Instinct told him - correction; training had told him to hang back when he was marching in a line formation. Either way it was a hard thing, to break old habits. Carl forced himself to keep up with the others and to suppress his ingrained reaction to hang back and to take cover. You're not a soldier anymore, he told himself. By all rights, he should be home with his family, enjoying time alone with his wife in bed or playing in the living room with his children. He should be worrying about nothing except whether his wife would make them a real home cooked meal or if she would want to call out for a pizza. And face it, who actually worried about such things. You worry about paying the bills, concern yourself about whether your wife will feel up to fooling around, and stress about having to return to work the next morning, hopefully on time. Other than these, life posed few problems - other than the concern factor.

That was for every other Joe in this country of ours, except Him. The irony of this situation was the fact that here he was; no longer a soldier mind you. Happening to be walking through a forest and for the first time in his career, which he couldn't help reminding himself was over. Yet, walking through these woods he was acutely aware that there was a real possibility of an enemy out there, somewhere, waiting to pop him off. Carl wished he had his rifle, So he could use it on the person who put him in this situation, and to get this whole damn thing over with, once and for all. Not on Colonel Dobson of course, General Davis. Yes, General Davis. After all; he had believed his life was worthless.

Carl felt himself getting angry, and then angrier still when he thought how close the man had come to killing him. But then his heart broke, when he thought of how Paul looked lying there with a bullet in his chest. Carl let the image sink in and realized he would much rather beat General Davis at his own game then just simply shoot him. Hurt him, where it hurts most, politically.

Carl looked into Julie's eyes as she turned back to check on him. They looked to him to be preoccupied. She was deep in thought about something and Carl hoped she hadn't paid any mind to that old time sheriff. He was just a 1950's poodle skirt and leather loafers thinking grandfather, who didn't possess a thread of modern views. She shouldn't have allowed it to get her so upset, and he would tell her so when they had a free moment to talk.

Carl looked at his watch 3:00pm, judging by the pace they were keeping and the amount of time they've been walking, he figured they must have traveled about nine miles. He noticed that they had been steadily going uphill for the last hour, but now it was starting to become steeper still. The trees had changed to pines, and he saw that the trunks were not as thick as they had been earlier. Carl's knowledge of the outdoors was limited to the places he had been while in the military, but he was fairly sure that they were climbing up a mountain. If that were the case, it seemed to him silly that it wouldn't be obvious, but he thought that it must be a very large, and gradual mountain that they were climbing.

Another hour later, Carl found that they were walking through a foot of snow, and they were still steadily climbing upward. By now it had become apparent to him that they were, in fact, climbing up the side of a mountain. They had stopped only once to rest for a few minutes and drink water. At the same time, Julie had been given some of the wine Luke had brought along in hopes that it would ease her pain. Then they had taken up their line formation once again and trudged onward. Not that Carl would have normally complained, which he didn't, but he was feeling rather winded from having done zero running during the last. He had to stop and count... a couple days short of nine months. When he was in his cell, he had had the availability to work out only his upper body and mid-section, now Carl regretted that, and wished he had complained. More accurately, it was his lungs that were complaining now. He wouldn't mind a swig or two of that wine himself.

Another half-hour had gone by when Luke stopped once more. Not far ahead from them, they could see a rock face. Carl lifted his head skyward. It went almost straight up for about two hundred feet. Beyond it was a massive mountain covered with snow and in the distance Carl could see many other mountain tops on the horizon. Carl looked at the cliff and wondered how in the world they were meant to climb it. They had no climbing gear and Julie had a bum leg. Carl was sure they needed a short break, so he sat down on a boulder and stared out at the view.

"Hey my friend, you look a little down-hearted, don't you like the view?"

"It's beautiful, but where are we going?"

"We're there."

"Where?" Just as he feared, Luke pointed up toward the cliff.

"You see those tree scattered ledges on the side of this hill.

Hill was an understatement if you asked him. "Yes."

"Count up three ledges, do you see that slightly larger clump of trees."

"Yup."

"That's it."

Carl knew that he must have missed something in this equation. "I mean no disrespect, but how is a clump of trees helpful?" Luke's face broke out in a wide grin, and Carl could see he was purposely being vague to give him a hard time.

"It's not the trees that are important. It's what those trees are hiding. A secret cave, one that my ancestors have used for centuries. A sacred place to us, it was used for religious purposes, some say it was a special place because it's location brought them closer to the heavens. Later it became a hiding place for our people and a safe haven for warriors to plan battles, during the wars with white men. After that it was used secretly to continue our religious and cultural traditions once white men said we no longer could."

Carl sat quietly for a minute and soaked in the history of the place that they were being brought to. He wondered how the ancestors would feel about a white man being brought to their sacred place. He thought of Paul, how easily he befriended others, always happy to see old faces and greet new ones. And Luke, how he opened his home to them, strangers in the dark of night. The open heartedness of these men warmed his own. He stopped thinking of how circumstances were all against him and began seeing how blessed he was. These men had looked out for him, a complete stranger. Even at the risk to themselves and their loved ones.

"I'm honored that you would bring me here, Thank you."

Luke looked up at the rock cliff. "You are a warrior in need of a safe haven, aren't you?"

Warrior? He supposed he could be called that. "I guess I am."

"No need to thank me then, we're following tradition."

Carl knew there was more significance to Luke's tribe allowing them to use the cave then he was letting on, but Carl let it go. "How do we get there?"

"It's not as difficult as you might think." Luke stood and waved for them to follow him. Around one hundred and fifty yards to the right of the rock cliff was a path through trees, not actually hidden, but not obvious either. It was a steep climb, but nothing compared to climbing the face of the rock. The path weaved a bit here and there, which made the climb that much easier then straight up. Along the way Luke began picking up pieces of timber, so Julie and Carl followed suit. By the time they had reached the ledge, each of them had a full load of firewood. Carl was happily surprised that the ledge itself was not as narrow as it had appeared from below. It was probably a good five feet wide, but at times it may have been as narrow as three feet. Carl estimated the distant from the start of the ledge to the opening of the cave to be the length of a football field, give or take a ten yard line or two. Then again, given his experience with a football field, he very well may have misjudged this estimate, though he strongly doubted it.

At the opening, Carl dumped his load of firewood and took off his backpack to get out the flashlight that Luke had handed him when they left this morning. Turning it on he saw nothing except darkness past the beams reach. So he looked into Luke's backpack to find his flashlight. The bag, he had taken from Luke so that he could help guide Julie, hobbling as she now was, over the narrow expanses of ledge. With both flashlights now directed into the cave, Carl tried again to see inside, but again was met with only darkness beyond the combined beams cast. He thought it must be a very deep cave. Wondering where the others could be or what could be holding them up, Carl turned to look back for his companions. Only instead of finding his friends there, he met large green eyes in place of theirs. Carl quickly shut off the beams to the flashlights, so he wouldn't startle the animal by inadvertently shining him in the eye. Carl was pretty sure that it wasn't his cougar. This one had gray fur up the bridge of its nose and along his ears. But then he hadn't been this close to the cougar at the apartment. It sat there and stared at him, intently looking at his face, not moving a muscle except to twitch his whiskers every once in a while. When he had had enough, he casually walked away down the ledge and rounded a corner out of Carl's sight.

Carl looked back the other direction and finally saw Luke and Julie getting close to the cave entrance. He found that they had abandoned their loads of firewood, and instead, Luke was now carrying Julie on his back. The closer they came to him, He realized that Julie wasn't conscious. "What happened?" Carl helped to lift her off of his new friend's back. Julie's head had a good deal of blood trickling down the side of her face.

"I'm not sure - she was walking ahead of me and she either twisted her leg and fell or she fainted from exhaustion. By the time, I got to her she had hit her head pretty hard on a large rock."

They set her down in the opening of the cave and checked her body over for breaks. When they straightened her legs out it was obvious that she had somehow broken her ankle. Her foot faced sideways when it should have been straight.

"OUCH!"

"My God, that has to hurt!"

The men stared at her leg and were thankful that she was unconscious, even if it did complicate her condition more. Both men looked at the other. "What should we do?" They both said at the same time.

Carl knew she needed a hospital, but that wasn't likely to happen anytime soon.

"Should we risk turning it and putting a splint on it?"

"I don't see how we have any other choice, Carl answered, but I think we should get her out of the cold first."

Luke grabbed the backpacks and Carl lifted her. Carrying her in his arms, he followed Luke down the long entrance of the cave and finally came to a large room at the end. Luke found a lantern and lit it. The room shone, as light from the lantern, bounced off its walls. Carl instantly felt that he had stepped back in time. Around him were walls covered in depictions of native history, Luke and Paul's ancestor's history to be precise. Scenes of hunting groups, battles and animals were the predominant themes of the ancient artwork surrounding him. To one side of the room, were boxes of supplies. They had been placed to one side of a large wooden box. It was heavy and thick, but most striking about it was the carvings of native life on the sides of it. Carl felt movement in his hands, looking down to Julie he could see that she was returning to them.

"Ouch, she reached up to her head, What happened to me? I feel like a truck has hit me."

Carl set her on the ground.

"You must have fallen?" Luke explained that she was walking, and the next thing he knew she was on the ground with blood coming from her head, so he carried her to the cave.

"We thought that we should get you inside out of the cold before we fixed your ankle."

Julie looked forward to her feet. "Oh Shit!" It was in a lot of pain, but damn, "How the hell did I manage this?"

Carl looked through the supply boxes and only found a bottle of drug store pain relievers. He doubted it would help too much. "Here, take some of these." He handed her two pills. Luke took out the bottle of wine and handed it to her.

"I guess liver damage is the least of my worries right now." She threw the pills to the back of her throat and washed it down with a few large gulps of the wine. Luke reached for the bottle to put it away. "Thanks, but I think I'll keep it."

"Alright, but not too much with that knock to your head."

The men busied themselves with searching through the supplies to find a way to splint her ankle. They found a blanket and shirt that they could use. Julie guzzled down Luke's wine. She looked at her sideways facing foot and drank more.

"I think you've had plenty." Luke took the wine jug from her hand and resealed it.

Carl ripped the shirt into strips. "Are you ready?"

"Yeah." Julie thought Carl had been talking to her, but realized he had been speaking to Luke, when she felt his hands come down on her shoulders to brace her.

Carl felt the inside of her boot first and found no blood. "That's good anyway."

"What?" She asked.

"It's not open." Then he placed a knee on her good leg and gently turned her ankle back into place.

A yelp came from Julie as she tried to stifle the amount of agony she would allow the others to see her in.

Carl placed the folded blanket around her ankle and tied the strips around it to keep it in place. "There that's the best we can do for now." He said. "I'll finish getting the fire wood before it gets too dark to see out there."

Carl first brought the load back from the cave entrance so Luke could get a fire started and then he went back down the ledge path to find the wood left by the others. Finding it, he brought it to the entrance and then went back to try and find some large logs. When he returned he found that the firewood at the entrance had been removed. He carried his find; four, good sized dry logs back to the others. When he got there Carl was surprised to find that on the ground were many large animal furs and in the center was a fire. Julie was now lying on the furs with a sleeping bag beneath her. Luke was busy rigging together a tripod that he was making to hang a pot over the fire. "Wow, this is pretty nice." It was nicer then the drippy tents and canvas cots they used in the Army. "Is there anything I can do?"

"Not for the moment, sit and relax."

That sounded like a good idea to him, only as long as there was nothing else to do. The walk there had been so long and tiring that he feared he wouldn't have the strength to get back up once he sat down. He noticed that Luke had removed his boots and Julie had only her hurt one on. She had dosed off, but their voices had stirred her. He took off his boots and sat down next to the fire. The comfort of the furs and sleeping bag made him realize that everything else could wait until morning. The fire had taken the dampness out of the room and in his new warmth, he noticed he didn't need a coat to feel comfortable and so removed his. He sat watching as Julie drifted in and out of sleep. Carl knew that all they really needed was food in their bellies and some well-deserved rest.

CHAPTER TWENTY-TWO

Rebecca drove into town and looked at the old familiar buildings lining the main street. Most things were exactly as she remembered them. But on the right, she noticed a small storefront that was new to her. She parked the car and studied it for a moment. It had an old styled sign, hand painted, which read Patti's Tavern. The building's front had an old arched door with a small sign stating the business hours tucked into one of the little square windows. The arch of the wooden door had the greeting "Welcome Friends" and to the right of it was a posted menu. Rebecca tried to look through one of the bay windows to the tavern, but from where she was, it was difficult to see anything. She surveyed the clientele by looking at the vehicles parked in front of it. It seemed to her to be a pretty average crowd, so she risked entering it alone. Inside, Rebecca was greeted by a friendly, pleasant speaking woman standing behind the bar. She called out a welcome to her and asked if she were there for dinner or just ale and conversation. Rebecca glanced across the room and noticed most sitting with stew bowls and breadbaskets, but some were in the corner watching the game and sipping beers. The woman answered for her. "I'll just let you sit here with me for a bit, and if you chose to you can always switch to a table if you like." She smiled warmly at her as she placed a menu on the bar far away from the bitter coldness that blew in with the constantly opening door. She waved and yelled "Evening" frequently adding names behind it as she poured drafts. A man yelled back, "Evening Patti", indicating that she was the owner of the place. Something Rebecca had already thought was the case, since her voice was thick with an Irish accent. Rebecca relaxed a bit and took off her coat and was about to hang it over her chair. "What's your name now?"

305

She couldn't help smiling at the charming woman before her, "Rebecca."

"Rebecca, That's a lovely name. Rebecca, Could I offer you some coffee or a glass of wine. I don't think you're really an ale sort, but how about a nice glass of white wine."

The woman had pegged her well. "Thank you, I suppose one wouldn't hurt."

She poured her a tall glass of wine and then said she could hang her coat and hat on the peg at the end of the bar if she liked. Before moving on to other customers she let her know that they specialized in stews, but would be happy to make her just about anything she liked.

"Thank you."

Through the back door Rebecca saw an exact version of the woman before her, only younger. There was a man and another young girl who were busy pouring ladles of stew from huge pots. Rebecca also glimpsed huge sheets of biscuits coming out of the ovens. Reading the long list of stews on the menu she tried to decide on which one to try.

"Patti always hands new people the menu, but regulars know to choose one of the stews listed on the black board over there." A man's voice said to her as she sat with the menu open before her. Looking up she found Todd standing beside her. "I see you've found the best thing to come to this town since time began." Todd told Rebecca loud enough for Patti to overhear.

"Thank you, Darling." Patti said to Todd with a wide grin. "Always nice to know we're appreciated."

"Patti, I'm surprised the mayor himself hasn't given you and your husband a commendation."

"There he is over there honey, you can suggest it to him yourself."

She winked at him and poured him a draft placing it before the seat next to Rebecca. Todd motioned to the chair. "Do you mind?"

"A nice young man such as yourself, I shouldn't see why she would." Patti commented.

Rebecca smiled at her and then told Todd. "No, Please."

Having completed her mission, Patti ran off to wait on others.

"Nice lady, don't you think?"

"Yes, she seems very nice."

"Did you decide on a stew yet?"

"I was thinking maybe the Beef."

"The corned beef is very popular, but I have to say that the regular, is one of my favorites, he patted his belly, it hits the spot very nicely."

She laughed. "It must after being out in the cold all day."

"So, where is your Husband, Todd looked around the place, I'd like to meet him."

Rebecca sat silently for a moment. "He isn't here."

"Oh, well, maybe another time then."

"Maybe."

He sipped at his beer. "So, did our story this morning excuse your lateness?"

"Well, let's just say that the story didn't help too much."

"Come again?"

"It was a great story, but the thrill of it was lost on my family."

"Well, I can't say as I blame them, after all you could have been killed."

"Not you too, I told you earlier that it wouldn't have hurt me."

"Yeah, Rebecca, I remember you saying that, but how do you know?"

How could she explain to a stranger that the cougar; as crazy as it seems, is her husband and it would never hurt her. For all she knew, maybe it was there to protect her. She could have sworn that someone was watching her. "Maybe you can't accept this answer, but in all honesty. I can't explain how I knew it. I just did."

"Rebecca, I can accept that."

Patti came and took their orders and Rebecca noticed the tavern was getting packed tight with people. "Pretty popular place, Huh?"

"Yes, it has been since day one, everyone has tried to get her to move to a larger location, but Patti insists that it's the tight quarters that make everyone friendly and feel like a large family."

Rebecca watched as people went to the back of the bar and found chairs stacked in the corner. Carrying the chairs with them, she noticed how others made room at the tables for them to join in. Rebecca thought that the open camaraderie was something that Patti must have initiated, and she agreed that it did feel as if the place was one large family.

Rebecca ate her stew and sipped her wine as she felt the tightness of the room and its people brush by behind her. In a roar of cheers, Rebecca heard everyone yelling to Todd. Turning around, she could see the television had been turned up slightly, and Todd was on it. The reporter who had called her for a comment was on with him, and they were discussing the cougar from this morning. Everyone was laughing and cheering for their friend. Every once in a while, someone would walk by and slap him on the back and ask him something about the cougar. The next thing she knew, Rebecca was staring at the television, which was displaying an old driver's license of Rebecca's and she could hear the wretched reporter quoting her non-remark. "According to Rebecca Reynolds her experience was less then horrific." The television blared out at everyone.

"Did you really quote that?" Todd laughed.

"Sort of, I said no comment. And look at that horrible photo she dug up, I look like a criminal!"

"Not quite that bad, but it is better to, just make a short comment, they're going to get their story with or without your help."

"Thanks for the advice." Rebecca threw down enough money to cover her bill and went to use the bathroom before she left.

As she came out of the ladies room Patti thanked her and told her to be sure to come back again, then she wished her a good night. Rebecca felt a chill and reached for her coat as she scanned the slightly dark and hazy room around her. She saw that Todd had moved from the bar to over where the men were watching the game. He waved for her to come over to where he was. "You headed out?"

"Yes, I need to get home." She smiled at her old acquaintance.

"I hope you're not mad at me for telling the reporter about you, most people like to have a few minutes of fame, Sorry."

"That's okay. Todd, this morning were you watching me before the cougar thing happened?"

"Watching you. No, like I told you I only knew you were there when I came down the hiking trail and saw the cougar preparing to pounce."

"It's okay, I wouldn't be upset if you were."

"No Rebecca, I wasn't watching you, but do you think someone was?"

"Well, I'm not sure."

"Let me walk you to your car. Alright, Just to be safe."

"Thanks." Rebecca put on her coat and hat and went to pull out her gloves when a chill shook her body. She could feel a piece of paper in her coat pocket. One that she was sure wasn't there before. She left it where it was and gently pulled out her gloves as Todd held the Pub's door open for her. "Thank you."

"You never did tell me that long story of yours or others I suspect."

The last thing she needed to do was to involve any others in her troubles. "Maybe another time when I have more time, Bye Todd, Thanks for walking me out."

"So long Rebecca, don't mention it, and you be sure to take care."

"I will, you too." She said as he closed her door for her and waved.

Rebecca pulled away as he went back inside the pub. Her mind was flying all at once, and was making her unable to think straight. The slip of paper was foremost on her mind, but then there was also her picture and address plastered all over the television to consider too. Her heart pounded as she made her way back to her mother's house. She pulled into the drive and noticed that most of the cars had left. Robbie's truck was still there, and Em and Gary had waited too. The house would be a lot calmer now. She debated on whether to read the note here in the car or in the house. She decided on here. Taking a deep breath, she pulled out the note and turned on the overhead lantern. It was a small square note like the kind left for her yesterday morning, but this time there were no knife marks stabbed into it. It only read, "Time to leave, your friend." As she went to turn off the light, the door to the house opened and Emily and Gary stepped out.

"There you are, we were about to give up on waiting for you."

Closing her car door, they all went back inside.

"No one meant to upset you, Rebecca." Emily said as she closed the door.

Robbie was playing video games with Danny and the girls were having their dessert.

"I know, Em."

"So, what is the problem?"

"I want to make my own decisions, and I have a lot of things to think about right now." Of which they knew nothing and she knew it was best to keep it that way.

"Do you mean, David?" Her mother handed her a package. "It arrived a couple of hours ago, mailed overnight delivery."

Rebecca held the box and read the address carefully, even going to her purse to pull out the slip of paper he had handed her himself yesterday with his address hand written on it. They matched; both the address and his handwriting with the one on the package. Rebecca debated on whether or not she should go outside to open it, just in case. Then hopefully, she would be the only one to get hurt if it wasn't what it appeared to be. For god's sake, she told herself, why would anyone want to blow her or her family up. Rebecca carefully opened the package to find a rose-papered package with a note attached. "I found this in town a few days ago and wanted to give it to you yesterday morning. Anyway, you understand. May it be a lovely memory for you to keep, I know I will. Love David." Inside was a crystal globe thick with white snow and glitter. The scene was of a farm with a red barn, horses and pastures.

"Well, isn't that pretty, Becca."

"Look Mom, It looks just like David's farm."

"Yes, it does, wasn't that sweet of him."

"Mom, did you know that you were on the 6:00 news?"

"Yeah honey, I saw it." Rebecca clutched the note in her pocket. "Hey kids, when I was out, I talked to your Grammie on the phone, and she told me that all the kids were starting back to school tomorrow. She really thought that it would be best for you guys to start then too."

"Oh Mom, I was supposed to see Tina tomorrow, and we were going to go skating too."

"Rebecca, you just got here!"

"I know Mom, but the kids really shouldn't miss school."

"Why don't you guys go get your things together."

"Rebecca, what's up, why are you leaving. They can start school with the kids here on Wednesday."

"Emily, I never said that I was staying, everyone just assumed that I was." Rebecca rushed to get her things that were in the living room gathered, her gift from David and the wrappings she shoved back into the box. As the kids brought their bags out to the living room, she handed Rachel the keys from her pocket as she went to get her things from the bedroom. With bags in hand, she placed them in the car and hugged her mother. "Bye Mom, I'll call and let you know we're there safely."

Rebecca saw Robbie and Gary share looks. Gary yelled for the women to get in out of the cold and he leaned toward Rebecca and palmed a piece of paper into her hand. Rebecca recognized the paper right away. "You dropped that. Do need to use one of our handguns?"

"NO. No, Thank you, Gary. Strangely, I think that's what this friend is for."

"Take care, Rebecca." Gary gave her a hug.

"Be careful, Sis." Robbie hugged her and then leaned into the car. "I'll work on that game and next time I'll beat you."

"Yeah right, Uncle Robbie."

"See You."

"Bye." Everyone in the car returned.

***She had left quickly. That made him feel good, he knew he had gained her trust or else she may have ignored his message altogether. In which case, his job would have become much more difficult by midnight. He pulled out his cell phone and hit the speed dial. "Yeah, it's me again,

we're moving, destination Victor Tango, ETA 23:00 hours." "Yeah."
"Contact was unavoidable." "Yes, Sir, I'm aware of the situation." "Yes, Sir."
"Reason will be broadcast at 23:00 your time." "Exactly, Sir." "Trust me, Sir,
everything is running smoothly on this end." "Yes, that was my fear too,
Sir, the botched job could lead to hastiness." "I understand." "Yes, Sir."
"Roger- Over. Out." He understood the man's nervousness, but he needed
to remember why he had hired him in the first place, he wouldn't let
anything happen to Rebecca. She had a good head on her shoulders, was
sharply aware of her surroundings and he knew with her insight and his
protecting her, she would be fine.

Here she was, once again running and for the second time in only
two days. She stared at the white lines in the dark and wondered how she
would explain to the kids why Grammie would be so surprised to see them
on her doorstep unexpectedly. She would be happy, but certainly
surprised by their arrival a week earlier than planned.

Rebecca reached into her pocket and felt the hard form of the
pocketknife. She wasn't sure what her next move was going to be, but she
knew she needed to trust the man giving her the notes. How could she not
trust someone who had killed a man for her sake. She wasn't naïve. She
realized there could have been a reason other than her safety, that caused
him to kill. But she trusted her own instincts and they were telling her this
guy was on her side. Besides, nothing has really changed, she told herself,
only sped up. She was going to move on anyway only now she was doing
it sooner and without a plan figured out ahead of time. No matter, she
worked well on the whim.

"How long does it take to get to Grammie's, Mom?"

"About four hours."

"Do you think she'll be awake when we get there?"

"Are the others sleeping?"

"Yeah."

"I don't know if she'll be up, but she will be happy we came."

"I didn't think that she'd be expecting us. Is everything okay, you
only drive without the radio on when you're really upset and need to
think."

"Sometimes I forget how observant you are, Rebecca reached over
and held Rachel's hand. Yeah honey, I think everything is okay, but the
news casting wasn't the best thing to happen and instinct told me to move
on."

"So, what's the plan now."

"Well, I'm only deciding what to do as I speak to you now, But... what do you think about staying with Grammie for awhile?"

"We'd rather stay with you."

"I'd rather keep you with me, but I think that there is a couple of problems with that. I haven't decided where we should live yet, and if I keep you out of school too long, then all of you will be kept back a year." Least of all, was the fact that she was being followed by someone, and would rather leave them out of harm's way. But she mentioned none of this to her daughter.

"Well, I would rather not be kept back a grade."

"So, is it a plan then."

"Yes."

Rebecca pulled into the drive and looked down to the dash, 10:30. The porch light was on, and a dim flickering glow came from the living room. "It looks like Grammie's awake." The curtain moved in the window and let light escape. "Wake up guys, we're here."

The kids stirred, and Rachel woke her brother by giving him a good shove.

"Dang, Danny. Your breath smells like a horse's butt. You better not kiss Grammie or you'll knock her out."

"Look who's talking, Butthead."

"Okay guys. That's enough. Karen wake up sweetie, we're there."

The door slowly swung open, "Who's out there?"

"Hi mom, it's us."

"Hi, Grammie!" Danny ran towards his grandmother and locked her in a hug.

"Rebecca! Kids! What a surprise, hurry up and come on in out of the cold."

As soon as Rebecca stepped up onto the porch the hot air and comforting smell of burning wood came flying at her face. The wood stove was burning full force and felt like heaven compared to the sharp, cold Vermont air outside. In a matter of minutes, the children had rosy cheeks from the heat and were pulling off their sweaters. Rebecca did the same and was thrilled when her mother-in-law offered her a cup of tea. Throwing a kettle on top of the wood stove, she asked the children if they would like hot cocoa and was immediately met with "Yes, please." in unison, and Danny asked if she had marshmallows too. "Of course I do, I bought them especially for you, kids, because I knew you were coming."

"Grammie, When does school start back?"

Karen asked as if wanting to catch her mother in a lie. Rebecca held her breath.

"School starts back tomorrow, but I'm afraid the schedule has been expanded to Saturdays because of the storm. Otherwise it would have been a full three weeks added to the calendar."

"Virginia is doing that too, Grammie, Rachel said, And Connecticut."

"But they don't start back until Wednesday." Karen added.

"Why three weeks, Mom?"

"Because we had been hit hard earlier this winter with snow and had a week added already before the storm had hit." "It had been a nice break to get days off, but no one wants to lose their summer break. The teachers and children both would be tearing up the walls by thanksgiving if we didn't get a summer vacation."

Carl's Mom had worked in the school system for nearly twenty years. She was a slightly eccentric woman, older, but you would never find gray in her hair. She wore flamboyant colors and laughed easily. It was her bright and cheery nature that made the children she worked with like her so much. Always smiling and quick to be helpful, but slow to make judgments of others. Rebecca liked her. She was probably not the perfect mother to Carl, because face it, there were no perfect mothers. Everyone has their stories, and her mother-in-law's was Carl's father. But, Mom was a survivor and if raising four children alone isn't story enough, Well then, she was a woman of many stories. At any rate, Carl had survived his childhood well enough to be her knight in shining armor, and that could not be devoid of his mother's doing. Rebecca knew her kids were in good hands, and if that meant that they lived on Alfalfa sprouts and tofu, then she knew they would be returned to her with few scars for their hard time. Carl's mom loved their children and Rebecca knew fully-well that they would be spoiled, beyond spoiled, by Grammie for the duration of their stay with her.

Rebecca also knew that as a mother herself, right now she was unable to provide her children with the stability and protection that they needed, but their Grammie could. Rebecca sipped at her tea and let a deep breath of relief escape her. Sure that her mother-in-law would keep her children safe. Rebecca went to the car and brought in all the children's belongings and placed her personal bag on the floor next to the couch. She made her groggy, children drag their things upstairs to the bedrooms Grammie had laid out for them. Then instructed them to get cleaned up and ready for sleep.

"Grammie will come and kiss me goodnight, right?" Danny asked his mother.

"She wouldn't miss tucking you in Danny. I'll let her know that you're ready for bed." Rebecca hugged him and kissed his forehead. "Good night."

Both girls hugged her as they made their way from the bathroom to their beds. "Good night, Mom." "Good night Girls, I love you."

Down stairs, Rebecca found Mom watching the end of the news. She also found a stack of blankets and a pillow on the couch. She doubted that she would need so many blankets with the wood stove going. Rebecca picked up the pillow, hugging it as she sat down next to the stack of blankets and stared at the television set. She asked her what had happened with the president. "He's fine, his guard didn't make it, though. The shooter was some environmental activist that was upset about Cartwright's veto of the pollution bill that went to congress last week."

"What a waste!"

"Yeah. The world is full of crazy people. It is a shame that man had to die for nothing, or worse something stupid like that."

"Hum." She agreed. The kids were hoping you would kiss them good night."

"Well, of course." She watched as Mom stood and made her way to the stairs dressed in her red and black poke-a-dot bathrobe and large black fuzzy slippers. Rebecca wondered if she knew that she looked like an oversized Ladybug or if it were just an extension of her having taught Biology for almost twenty years that had manifested itself in her clothing. Her kids loved her quirks, and she had to admit she did too. It was only that, Rebecca couldn't help wondering if her choice of clothing were conscious or unconscious. Curious, but she'd never ask.

"I told the children that the school had a problem with the heating system and so school had been delayed a day."

"Was that really on the news?"

"Yes." She told her daughter-in-law, "But why don't you tell me about the cougar in Connecticut and maybe why I've had the privilege of your showing up on my doorstep unannounced."

"I'm sorry, it was really rude of me."

"Rebecca, I'm not mad, only concerned."

Rebecca told her about everything that had happened in Connecticut with the cougar and her family. She showed her the death certificate and told her what she thought. "Look here Mom. Under Burial, Cremation or Removal; wouldn't it make sense to type anything other than "Marker," that is if there is a body.

The woman held the paper and shuddered, "Rebecca, Are you sure you're not just seeing what you want to see. Carl was my son, and the last thing I want is to give up hope, but honey you have to accept the reality of all this. Look it says here "drowning", could it be that there is only a marker, but because they couldn't recover his body."

"Mom. No. How can you think that he's dead!"

"I don't want to, but the evidence is right in front of us."

"Then why hasn't the military come and told me the truth."

"I don't know, Rebecca."

Only, she knew about the man in Daniel's stable. And what about the note man, he wasn't a figment of her imagination. She wasn't convinced yet that Carl was gone.

Carl's mom had opened a bottle of wine and brought over two glasses, "Here, I think we could use this."

"Thank you."

"Rebecca. Put aside for a minute, what has happened to Carl and answer me one question. What would he have wanted you to do?" She lifted her hand; "Wait. Put some thought into it and then answer."

Rebecca set aside the man who had been killed and the man following her and all the unanswered questions that had been consuming her. She thought about Carl and about the life they had planned together. The answer that came to her was simple, "He would have wanted me to be happy, it was the only thing he ever wanted."

Rebecca was back in her kitchen in Tennessee. Staring out the window as the movers had packed her house.

"Man Dave, she's out there, she needs to pull it together."

"Shh, give the lady a break will you."

"All right, You deal with her then."

"Ma'am, Ma'am... we're going to take a lunch break, we'll be back in an hour."

Rebecca gulped down some of the wine Mom had given her.

"I think he'd want me to pull it together, he wouldn't recognize me, running scared and out of it as I've been."

"Give yourself a little more credit than that Rebecca, but I agree, he would want you to be happy and he would want the kids to be happy too." "I think leaving them with me for a while and taking some time to yourself would be a good idea."

"Thanks Mom, I think your right."

The first thing Rebecca planned on doing; was to stop running. She would decide things for herself, not out of confusion, or fear, or lack of confidence in her own decisions. Instead of letting the world run her, she was going to take charge again herself. Rebecca ran out to the car and grabbed the road atlas. The first thing she needed to do was to decide where she was going to go first, not by whim, but by deliberate planning. If she ended up unhappy there, then she would plan a new route.

"What are you doing, Rebecca?"

"I'm taking back my life."

Mom poured them both another glass of wine and toasted Rebecca's declaration. Then they both poured over the atlas discussing good places for her to start her search for home.

CHAPTER TWENTY-THREE

Carl stared out at the world around him and smiled. Taking in a deep breath, he realized he felt exhilarated. He was sure that the cool fresh air and the amazing view around him were responsible for this feeling within him. He had by now adjusted to the altitude. No longer experiencing the dizziness, and shallow breath of a few days earlier.

In the distance, Carl could see a large bird soaring through the sky. "Wow." That was incredible he said aloud. The bird had dive bombed toward something on the ground. Then had swooped upward as quickly as it had fallen downward. He could only assume that it had caught a rabbit or rodent of some kind.

Carl reluctantly forced himself to return to the cave. He hated to leave Julie for very long, and he had already been gone for almost an hour. Reaching the ledge, he picked up the fresh pile of firewood that he had gathered before climbing to the top of the mountain, and carried it to Julie who had lain in and out of consciousness since their arrival to this secret hole in the side of a cliff.

Carl was worried about her health, but had to admit he enjoyed feeling needed again, even if she were hardly aware of his caring for her. He worried that maybe she had had too much of the wine and feared it more likely that he hadn't measured out the sedative tea correctly. She had fallen off to sleep that first night and since had barely woken long enough for him to get sips of water and a spoon or two of food in her before she was out once again.

Carl found a large pot and went outside to pack it with snow. Five days without a shower were more than enough for him. Returning with it, he placed the pot on the tripod that Luke had made and added some

317

more wood to the fire. Then he settled himself to a game of solitaire. He had found the deck of cards among the supplies and had been entertaining himself with them ever since Luke had left. Not that he was completely bored. Carl was surprised to find that he welcomed the time alone. The past month had been crazy, and he was glad for the time to stop and think. He couldn't help but wonder about his own life. Whether his old one still existed or if this new one were what he was left with. Nine months was a long time to be gone. Particularly if she thought he were dead.

Carl had been with Julie for over three weeks now, but it had seemed to him more like three months. He figured, almost being killed had a way of intensifying every minute that you remained breathing. Like Julie for instance, Carl sat staring at her, lying there as if she were a character from some children's fairy tale, she was so beautiful. Her beauty had increased the minute he watched her jump from that helicopter. He had known she was incredibly sexy and strong. But now, now he was awed by her strength. That and the courage she must have sustained in order to bear the pain of climbing up this mountain. Both humbled him.

Carl watched steam start to form, and rise out of the pot of water. Reaching a finger into it, he quickly pulled away his hand and removed the pot from the fire. Dipping a cloth into the water, Carl leaned over Julie and gently wiped her face clean and then washed her neck and arms too before undressing to wash himself.

Julie felt the warmth of something and then the cool it left behind. Slowly her eyes came into focus, and she could see the bright flames of the fire before her. She could make out the shadow of someone reflected around her. The dancing of the flames and the shadows made her feel dizzy. Closing her eyes again, Julie tried to gain her composure and attempt to sit up. She tried to swallow, but her throat felt slightly stuck and in one quick motion she re-opened her eyes and pushed herself into a sitting position. Once her eyes were above the fire, everything around her seemed to stop its dancing. Before her, was a man, broad shouldered and standing with his back to her. She noticed he was nude, and she slowly let her eyes cast downward to the shape of his behind. Watching him bend down she heard the sound of splashing water. And then Carl swung around with the pot in hand reaching toward the fire.

"Damn Julie, I thought you were out cold." He put the pot down and grabbed a towel.

He attempted to cover himself. But she thought, fortunately for her; it wasn't before the fire had the chance to illuminate the gift of a body God had given him. "I was, but I guess I got lucky." She thought she saw a bashful look come across his face as he tied the towel around his waist. "How long have I been out?"

Five days." He couldn't meet her eyes, at least, not standing there nude. He knew he wouldn't be able to control his reaction to her.

"Carl, what's with the shyness all of a sudden, You weren't too shy, to pee in front of me, remember."

Yeah, he remembered. That seemed a long time ago. Besides things were different then, she was different. They were on a mission for God's sake. "Yeah, I know, But everything isn't the same now." She didn't seem like a giggly little kid to him anymore.

Carl warmed the water back up and then rinsed again, but this time she gave him a little privacy. Then he dressed and went out to get more snow, so Julie could clean up too. He placed the bucket of snow on the tripod and went back to his cards.

Julie was confused, what had happened while she was asleep? She didn't see how things were any different than they had been before. "Were you lonely all by yourself for five days."

"Well, I wasn't exactly alone, You were still here, and I had to keep us warm and fed." Carl looked at Julie. "Do you want to get clean and change clothing?" He placed his finger in the water though he knew it wouldn't be hot enough yet. "This will be ready in ten minutes." When she nodded yes, he went to the supplies and gathered some clean clothes. Carl then carried her over to where he had arranged a makeshift bathroom. Behind stacked boxes was a large stump for sitting and a towel and washcloth. In a small bowl were soap, tooth brushes and paste. He set her down on the stump and helped her to remove her sweat pants from over her boot. Then he brought her the pot of hot water and left her to go make some dinner.

"Carl, she yelled slightly, I hate to tell you this, but I have to pee something fierce."

"In the corner, Julie."

"You want me to pee in the corner!"

"It's not very civilized, but in the corner is a lidded container, I've been using it and then taking it out to dispose of in the woods later."

"Oh." Julie saw the medium sized container and the roll of paper. "That'll work."

She finished cleaning up and then came back out, and found that Carl had made them canned-chili and rice for dinner. She was so hungry; he could have cooked her a rat, and she would have eaten it. "I guess I didn't think this place out very well, did I." There was no bathroom, or decent water source, and there was only one way in or out, which would be tricky in the dark.

"Well you were thinking safe and remote, to reduce the chance of anyone finding us. It definitely is those things." Carl smiled at her with her wet hair dripping down her shirt. She was hopping on her one good foot, trying to get back to her place on the rugs. He grabbed hold of her and easily swung her up into his arms. Then carried her back to the spot where she had lain comatose for all those days, while he sat wrestling with all the thoughts cramming his head. He only hoped she wouldn't fall back asleep and leave him again.

"The food smells wonderful." She leaned forward to try and catch a glimpse of their dinner. She took the coffee cup that Carl handed her. "Carl, Thank you for taking care of me." She tried to look into his eyes as she spoke to him, but he wouldn't take his eyes away from the fire and the food he was preparing.

"It was my pleasure." He told the truth, taking care of her had made him feel actually normal for the first time since he had kissed Rebecca and the kid's goodbye.

"Are you glad to be among the living again?" Before she could answer he asked, "How's the ankle?"

"Well, it feels a lot better actually. I won't be wearing heels for a few months, but it's not in any pain."

"That's good." He stirred the rice. Too bad about the heels though. Carl thought about the pretty silver ones she wore less than a week ago. And the pink dress cut down to her ass. "Want to play rummy?"

"Okay." She picked up the card he threw down.

"Dinner was good. Thanks." Julie looked at Carl. She knew something was different, but she couldn't figure out what it was. He seemed distracted, edgy maybe. "Carl, is everything okay?"

"Yeah." He looked into her eyes, the color of sunset and lied. Then he dealt out seven cards each, and flipped over the top one from the stack. In truth, he wasn't sure how he was, he wasn't sure of anything.

They sat playing cards in silence, except for the sounds of glee that came from Julie every time she won. Carl was glad to hear the sound of her voice, even if it were being used to gloat at his expense.

"So, What did you do while I was sleeping, besides keep us warm and fed?"

"Not much. I played a lot of solitaire."

She knew that, the cards looked very worn in. "What did Luke say before he left?"

"Just that he'd try and get back out as soon as he could. Hopefully with some news."

"He gave no ball park guess as to how long it would be before he'd return?"

"No Julie, why? Are you bored with me already?"

"Carl! What's your problem? I'm only trying to figure things out. Damn!"

"There's nothing wrong. I'm fine!" Just frustrated, his mind, his body and his spirit. But most of all he ached for his life and his home. Ached for his wife and children. Ached to feel the warmth of another and starved for the emotional satisfaction that came with that. No, there was no one thing wrong with him, everything was wrong.

If she could have gotten up and walked out, she would have. But this damn leg of hers kept her a hostage to Carl's bad mood. She sat there, angry and proud. She'd said or did nothing wrong and didn't deserve this treatment. It wasn't her fault that she had become a burden to him. This Damn leg. She punched it. She hated feeling helpless and of all people she hated Carl seeing her this way. Pitiful and childlike, incapable of even peeing on her own. And damn it, she wasn't going to cry - she wasn't.

Carl looked up from his cards to find Julie twisting her head, forcing her face away from his direction. It was the unmistakable sign of a proud woman refusing to let him see her cry. He knew it all too well. What a prick he had been. Carl felt bad. He shouldn't have taken his frustrations out on Julie. "I'm sorry Julie, I didn't mean to get snappy and mean." She sat there looking away from him refusing to speak. That was okay. He deserved that. The opposite of what he had wanted. But poetic justice he supposed. He had sat there watching her voiceless for the last five days, and now she refused to talk to him. It was his own fault, still he couldn't help wanting to hear her soft voice. Even a good chewing would have been welcomed.

Julie laid down facing away from him. Carl hoped she wouldn't fall back off to sleep and refuse to wake up. Carl played one last game of solitaire and put the deck away. Laying down himself, he tried to find the right words. Sorry wasn't good enough, and he didn't know what else to say. "Julie, Are you still awake?" No answer. "Do you need some help using the bathroom before we fall asleep?"

"I'm sorry that I'm a pain in your butt."

"What are you talking about?"

"Me, my leg, I'm a burden to you."

"Are you serious, Julie!"

"Well, why else would you be so angry with me?"

"I'm not."

"Yes Carl, You are upset about something."

He wasn't sure how to answer her. She was right. He was upset. Not with her but because of caring for her. She had been a reminder. "Caring for you has been a comfort, a sad comfort. It's been a reminder of everything that I have lost. Things that I may never get back."

Julie turned back toward the fire and Carl. "I understand Carl, at least, I think I do." She knew that he had had, what she has been wanting; a spouse, a family, a home. What did she know of these things, nothing, except that she wanted them to. Not an empty apartment in Los Angles that she spends three days a month in. And not any more lonely nights spent with makeshift lovers between jobs. What had she been doing this for? Why? Five-years spent protecting wealthy Businessmen. Feeling strong and confident. But had it been worth the loneliness? Julie wasn't sure anymore. Then there was the sheriff and what he had said to her.

Carl looked into Julie's eyes, only Julie wasn't there. She was lost, deep in thought, as she had been on their walk up this mountain. He wanted to know what she was thinking so intensely about. Why her expression was so sad. So confused.

"What are you thinking about?"

Julie startled to the sound of Carl's voice. "I'm sorry, I guess I was off somewhere else."

"It looked that way. Where were you?"

"Wondering how I have gotten myself where I am now, about to be Thirty, with no clear direction in my life."

"You've lost me, Julie."

"That's the point. Look at me, Carl, my relationship with you is the strongest one that I have. We have a business relationship, not exactly something that could be categorized as lose-able. You have a life and people to lose. I have nothing worth losing. Jewelry, a bank account and a worthless apartment that I don't even use, are all I have. I understand how my life went in this direction. I followed love into it. It's why I continued in it, for so long, that I am only now beginning to understand."

Carl sat waiting for her to continue, but she said nothing. "And?"

"I have you to thank really, and Sheriff Treaburn."

"You're not taking anything that old-coot told you seriously, are you?"

"Well, Yeah, I am."

"Julie, you have to be kidding, the man thinks women still belong in the kitchen slaving over a stove."

"He didn't seem to have a problem slaving in the kitchen himself and doesn't seem to mind that his wife is making a pretty good living at it." Julie snapped back.

"Yeah, so long as she's making it doing a woman's job." Carl couldn't believe that she had been suckered into believing the man's load of crap.

"Carl, I think that you have misunderstood me. I know as well as anyone that PTA meetings and charity events aren't exactly my style. But there was something that Sheriff Treaburn said that made me start to think. He called me a woman of education and wealth."

"Yeah okay, but also one to be reckoned with."

"I'm being serious, Carl."

"So am I Julie, You are those things, but your many more as well, your strength in body and character supercedes that of most people. And your sweet nature and heart match it."

"Do you really see me that way?"

"I don't see you that way, You are. The other night at the party you were in your element, I was awkwardly out of place, but not you. You were cool and comfortable."

"I wasn't always. I used to hide behind my work. Telling myself to relax and blend in. Hoping no one would notice how out of place I felt. But somewhere along the way I stopped feeling that way. I'm not sure when, but it probably had something to do with the objects given to me that had helped me to blend in easier."

"You mean things like that." Carl pointed to the huge heart diamond around her neck.

"Yes, this, clothing, the confidence I gained from my job and the attention that men gave me. In the role of my work, I felt included, but I never forgot that I was a farm girl. I could fit into their world, but I wasn't part of it. At least that was how I felt."

"How do you feel now?"

"Stupid, I got so caught up in my job and the people I protect that I didn't see past it and them. I think now that in some circles, it was only me who saw myself as an outsider. I wonder if I hadn't held that view, then maybe." She hated to admit failure. "Maybe, I would have made other choices."

Carl lay there propped up on his elbow listening to Julie. Watching as her hair danced its mahogany color in the firelight, highlighting her new strawberry streaks. He enjoyed her voice, the way in which it gave him comfort. He longed to touch her, to feel the warmth of her body, and the feel of it cradled against his own, as he listened to her, explain her life. The choices she had made and why, the regrets, the mistakes and the misunderstandings. As she wiggled her body closer to the fire, Carl caught a look of restrained agony in her mouth, as she moved her damaged leg to join the rest of her body.

"Here." He handed her the jug of wine. He wasn't going to risk the tea again.

"Thank you." Julie drank down a large gulp and handed it back.

Carl took a swig and refocused on Julie's voice and the words that she was speaking.

CHAPTER TWENTY-FOUR

Rebecca rolled down the window so she could feel the cold winter air against her face. It was perfect, crisp and full of the scent of salt. Only a slightly fishy scent blew in off the marshes along the shoreline. There was no snow to be seen here along the shores of Rhode Island. Rebecca steered her way down the road ahead and did her best not to get distracted by the sound of the ocean and the caw of the seagulls lurking above. She needed to find a hotel. Not that there was a lack of them, only a lack of open ones in the middle of winter. Rebecca decided to take her chances and headed down a residential side road. After taking a few turns, a right or maybe two, and then a left a mile further down. She finally came upon a bed and breakfast. The sign in front of it wasn't advertising either way, whether they were vacant or occupied.

She pulled the car over to the side and hopped out. However, before she could reach the front door to the house, it had already been burst open by an old man and he was calling out to someone behind him. When she reached the steps, she was being greeted by a couple in they're sixties.

"Can we help you?"

"Hi, I saw the sign and wondered if you had any available rooms."

"Well, I can't say if we do or not."

"Oh - Okay, Well, would you know of any other places around maybe." Rebecca smiled at the frail looking couple.

"I doubt that there is this time of year. We don't get many visitors, at least not without a reservation."

Rebecca turned a little red in the face. "I'm sorry, I didn't even think to stop and call ahead. I usually stay in the bigger hotels, but they

325

all seem to be closed up."

"Well, Miss?"

"Oh, I'm sorry, Rebecca, Rebecca Reynolds." She held out her hand.

"Miss Reynolds, the lady smiled, I guess we could give you a room if you could give us a half hour or so to air it out and change sheets and such."

"Thank you. That would be excellent Mrs?"

"Whittle dear, but call me Ena and my husband is Harry."

"Please, call me Rebecca. I hate to ask, but how do I get back here?"

Harry shook his head and then explained how she was to get back to the main road and also gave her the phone number just in case she got lost. She asked if the beaches were open, so she could go and take a walk. They told her they weren't officially open, but that she would have no problem getting onto them. Then they recommended that she should plan to eat at their house, unless, she planned to eat only snack cakes from the local gas station. Dinner would be at six. She thanked them again and then hopped into her car and followed Harry's directions back to the throughway. She stopped at the gas station and bought a soda and a candy bar to tide her over until dinner. She also picked up the free real estate magazines near the counter.

Pulling into the gravel parking lot to one of the local small beaches Rebecca noticed that hers was the only car there. This didn't surprise her since it was so cold outside, and it was after-all a workday. She grabbed a blanket from the back seat and placed her keys in her pocket as she made her way toward the beach. Surprised to find the lifeguard's chair standing, Rebecca climbed to the top of it and wrapped herself in the blanket. She stared out at the gray water for what seemed like hours and listened to the pounding of the waves against the shore. She watched as an occasional barge or boat passed by in the distance and was grateful for the absence of any others on the shore. She was sure that she was competing well with the clamour of the ocean before her. Angry for the curve which life had given her, sad about the absence of her only friend in the world, but also fearful for her future. She let it all come out, the pain she had been feeling for the last eight months and suppressing for her children's sake. Hell, in all truth, for her own sake. She was afraid that if she had let it start, it would never stop. But what scared her more was she was unsure if she were crying for Carl or herself. Then she decided that it was irrelevant. Pain was pain no matter what the source. That she could sort out later.

Through the garbled view, from tears in her eyes, she saw a streak of brown go flying past at a racing pace. Following it, she heard a loud whistle. Wiping her eyes, Rebecca made out the figure of a dog running down the beach and turned to see a man stepping off the boardwalk in the direction of the Retriever. Upon the second whistle call, the dog sharply turned around and streaked back as quickly as it had run off.

Rebecca tried in vain, to get the tears out of her eyes. The next thing she knew the brown blur was standing at the bottom of the lifeguard's chair, and was barking insistently up at her. "Bruno, Quiet Bruno!" Her eyes cleared, and she saw the man walking toward her. "Sorry, he gets over excited when I bring him here." He pulled the dog by the collar, knocking him down from his attempt to climb the chair. Then he ran off chasing a wave in protest. "I've never seen you here before, are you a local?"

"Excuse me." Rebecca gathered her wits. "No." She glanced at her watch, I'm staying at the Whittle's bed and breakfast. Actually, I should be getting back there now. Their expecting me."

"Are you okay?"

"I'm fine, thank you." She wanted him to go play with his dog, so she could get down off the chair and head back to her car.

"Are you staying with Ena and Harry long."

At least he knew their names. She trusted he was probably a local himself and not some stranger following her around the country. "I haven't decided yet."

"Well, maybe I'll see you around here again, I'm Doug and you've met Bruno, he waved. Have a good night."

"Rebecca. You have a good evening too." She waved and then went to her car.

Back at the Whittle's she was greeted by Harry and told that dinner was almost ready. He asked how her afternoon had been. Then Ena came into the room and gasped, asking if she were all right. "Shh, Ena that's none of your business." Rebecca hadn't looked into the car mirror, but she assumed she must have looked bad. "Did you not protect your face from the wind, it looks wind burnt badly, I should think."

"I'm fine. Ma'am."

"Go cool your face dear, with a wet cloth from the bathroom."

Rebecca did as she was told and heard Ena call to her as she reached the landing that they had another visitor, so she should lock the adjoining bathroom door.

"Yours is the second door on the right, dear."

Rebecca carried her bag up with her and was sure she heard Harry tell his wife that she had been crying and was not wind burnt. Though in reality, she was probably both, swollen from crying and a little burnt. The door next to her own had a do not disturb sign hanging from the handle. Which she thought was strange at this time of the day.

She opened her door to find a pretty room with a large brass bed and down comforters covered in large pink print flowers. The dresser had a vase with pink sweetheart roses and baby's breath that looked like Queen Anne's lace. The bathroom door was closed, so she knocked softly enough not to disturb someone in the other room, but loud enough for them to answer if they were on the other side of it. No response, so she tried the handle. Inside, the room was bright and cheery with yellow flowered wallpaper and towels. Washing her face with a cold cloth was refreshing to her sore face. She soaked it, long enough to feel normal again and then hung the cloth on the towel bar on her door. Then she went to have dinner with the Whittle's.

Rebecca had been pleasantly surprised when dinner turned out to be ordinary. She feared it would be, quiche or some gourmet dish, she expected to be given in a bed and breakfast establishment. She hadn't wanted to have the need to sneak snack cakes into her room, but she would have if she needed to. So you can imagine how at ease it made her feel when she was served a pork chop, green beans, mashed potatoes and gravy, and a dinner roll.

At dinner, she learned that the man in the room next to her was working on his dissertation, and so he didn't wish to be disturbed. Rebecca retrieved the real estate magazines from her car then retired to her room to call her kids and turn in for the night. Passing the door next to hers, she found a tray of dirty dishes on the floor outside. Picking up the tray, she brought it down the stairs for Ena. Entering the hall to the kitchen she could hear the Whittle's speaking.

"Such a charming and handsome man, it would be a shame if she doesn't get to meet him."

"Ena, I think she's married."

"Is she!"

Rebecca called to give them warning, "Mrs. Whittle I found this in the hall." She yelled slightly as she entered the kitchen.

"Ena, Dear. How sweet of you, I could have gotten that."

"It's no problem, I wanted to come down and thank you for the flowers in my room anyway."

Ena smiled at her, but Harry beamed too. "You're very welcome, and be sure to help yourself to the kitchen, if you find yourself hungry at any hour."

"Thank you, goodnight."

"Good night." Both returned.

Rebecca called the kids and her mother-in-law to let them know where she was and gave them the address and phone number. Telling them about the Whittle's and how Mr. Whittle must have driven quite a long way to find the fresh flowers that they had put in her room for her. She hung up with her children telling them that she loved them and that she would call again in a couple days. "Be good for Grammie, Bye."

After using the bathroom, she changed into sweat pants and a tank top for the night, but left a pair of socks on. Climbing into the large downy bed, Rebecca pulled the fluffy covers all around her as she sat reading the book of houses for sale. The windows rattled, and she could feel the wind working its way through the panes of the window somehow. Tink, tink, tinkle. Wow, she thought, it's raining ice against the house outside. The end of March was still, something of a bear up here in the north. Thinking of earlier that day, she glanced through the house ads some more and then shut off the light.

❀❀❀
❀❀❀

***In the bathroom, he washed and prepared for sleep himself. Putting his ear to the door, he heard nothing. Her towel was damp, and the washcloth still saturated with water and her scent as he smelled it and then carefully placed it back where it hung. Pulling out a knife from his pocket he gently jimmied the door unlocked. Studying the room he realized the storm had now blown over because the moon shone in through the window and highlighted her lying there in the bed. She was beautiful even while sleeping. He decided to sit in the corner chair for a while. Her breathing in her sleep was soft, but he could hear the beginnings of a cold lurking in it. He had wanted to strangle her earlier for sitting in the freezing wind as long as she had, what was she trying to do, kill herself by getting pneumonia. This job was killing him. As close as he was to her now, he understood why he was ordered to keep his distance. He wanted to touch her, to feel her soft skin and the feel of her mouth against his own. A luxury he had never allowed himself. She turned and was talking in her sleep. He wanted to know what she was saying, but didn't need to get closer to know it was a nightmare that she was experiencing. It was agony to watch her and be unable to comfort, to wrap

329

her in his arms and tell her; "It's alright, I'm there now, I'll protect you." He stayed until she stopped whimpering in her sleep and then he let himself out. Closing the barrier between them once again.

Thankful that the sun had come in and woken her, Rebecca turned to find it was 9:00 am on the table clock. Feeling more like a guest in someone's home then a paying customer, Rebecca wanted to be up and dressed, way before noon. She showered and dressed without much fuss and entered the kitchen to find that the Whittle's were making breakfast, and they had company with them. A gentleman in his mid-forties, Rebecca wondered if he were the elusive gentleman in the room next to hers.

"Rebecca, this is our son-in-law Phillip."

"Nice to meet you." They shook hands. No, not the strangely quiet man next door.

"Look what he brought us for dinner." Ena held open a brown paper bag with four dark brown lobsters in it.

"Oh, Wow." She was sure she hadn't sound very convincing.

"Not your cup of tea, dear, I'll make you a steak instead." She looked at Harry, "All the more for us then." She told him as she licked her lips and thanked Phillip as she handed him a plate filled with eggs, bacon and fried potatoes.

Rebecca sat and ate her breakfast with the Whittle's at their kitchen table. She listened to the couple and their son-in-law talk about fishing and about Donna and the kids. She amazingly enjoyed herself, sitting there almost like a fly on the wall, as they talked and she sat eating and drinking her tea. Before he left, Phillip asked if she had ever been on a fishing boat and if she cared to come out with him tomorrow morning. "Not much sun bathing to be done around here this time of year." Phillip added.

Rebecca thought about how strong the waves were yesterday at the beach. "Is the water a bit strong this time of year. I'd hate to get sick on you."

"That's not a problem. Mom, has motion pills you can take beforehand."

Ena told her, "Go, you'll enjoy it."

"Well okay, if you think I'll be fine, then I'd love to go, Thank you."

"Alright, I will pick you up at 6:00am tomorrow." He said as he went out the back door.

"That was really nice of him." Rebecca commented to Ena and Harry.

"He takes lots of people out, who come to stay with us."

"Should I offer to pay him." She was genuinely unsure.

"If he were taking out a family, then I'd say yes." Harry told her. "But you won't get in his way and he's likely to put you to work."

"Sounds fun, I'm glad he offered. I want you to know that I've noticed you haven't asked all sorts of questions."

Ena waved her hand in the air. "We've learned over the years that if people want to talk about themselves, they'll do it without any prodding from us."

"Thank you." Rebecca rose from her seat, and cleaned off her plate, putting it in the sink with the others.

She went back to the beach again today. This time bringing the atlas with her. She sat wrapped in her blanket up in the high chair as she thumbed through the maps. She liked it here, but it was very expensive judging by the house ads she looked through the night before, and it just didn't call out home to her. Mostly, it was way too cold to her liking. Plus summers would be too short here. She loved the heat and brightness of summer and she knew she wanted to live where that was fairly long. She immediately flipped to the atlas of Florida. After catching a quick glance at it, she knew it wasn't for them either. Swamps and alligators didn't appeal to her. That left her the eastern shoreline states from Delaware to Georgia. She closed her eyes and let her finger drop down to the map. Landing on Norfolk Virginia. No, she thought, too much history with David and besides, I just moved from one military town, I'm not going to another. She closed her eyes to try again.

"Hi, how are you today?"

Rebecca jolted out of her own skin and looked down to find Doug standing there in front of her. His dog was down the beach chasing something. Judging by the dogs pouncing movements, she thought that something might be a crab. "I think Bruno is about to get a pinching."

"He's learned well enough by now not to get too close."

"Is that a French accent that you have?"

"Yes, I grew up in Montreal before moving here twenty years ago." He smiled. "Is there enough room for another up there?"

He seemed harmless. "Sorry, of course." She slid herself to one side of the chair as he climbed up.

"What is that you're looking at?"

She held up the road atlas for him to see.

"You planning a road trip."

"Actually, I'm deciding where to live."

"Really, That's a strange way to do such a thing, don't you think?"

"I don't know, I think it is as good a way as any."

"People usually have a reason for where they move to."

"Why did you move here?" She asked.

"Well, this was where my wife's family lived. She passed away three years ago from cancer."

"I'm sorry." He only looked about forty, she thought, she must have died young.

"Why don't you move here?"

"I think it's a bit too cold for me." She wrapped the blanket closer around her.

"Only eight months of the year." Doug assured her.

They both laughed.

He closed his eyes and dropped a finger down on the map in her lap.

"Savannah, Georgia." She read aloud. "I don't know, maybe it's not the way to choose." They both laughed again.

"Why isn't there someone here with you, pointing their fingers on your map." Doug pointed to her wedding rings.

What to say. At least the government and Larry supplied her with some answers when people asked. "My husband has passed away too, in an accident."

"I'm sorry, Automobile?"

"Drowning."

"It took me awhile to stop wearing my ring too."

They took Bruno down the beach for a walk, and talked some more about places to live, and ways to go about choosing. None of their ideas seemed to work for Rebecca. She decided; she would wait a few more days to see how she felt about it then.

***

*** "Hi. Yeah, Everything is fine. Oh, you enjoyed the telecast did you. Yes, she followed the note I sent right away. She's doing good. We only couldn't shake, Frennier. I'm not sure what he's up to, but I've heard everything and he appears harmless. So far anyway. He's doing his job like all of us, Sir. Yeah, really? Any news yet - no. Well, I'll keep you informed on this side, Sir. Roger, I hear you. New orders - Roger. No reasoning with our enemy. Mission: Eliminate any and all serious threats. Yes, Sir, I'm sorry too, Sir. Send General H. my condolences, Sir. Thanks for the warning. Roger, Sir. I understand. Time and destination unknown. I'll be ready, Sir. Over, Out."

He watched as Rebecca got into her car and waved good bye to Frennier. Then he pulled a knife from his pocket and caught the man before he got into his own vehicle. The man went stiff behind the blade to his throat. "What do you want with the girl, Frennier?"

"What's this, I mean no trouble."

"You better not mean her trouble, because you know I'll come find you and finish this." He heard the distant sound of a car coming up the gravel road and put away the blade.

The man yelled to the dog to be quiet, and they exchanged a look and a few last words. "I thought my job was done here, but by the looks of it, I might have been wrong."

"No, you're not wrong."

"Then what gives."

"She's just a personal friend I'm watching out for."

"Maybe more than a friend, huh." Frennier laughed.

"No." He responded coldly, clutching the folded blade in his pocket.

Frennier got in his car and gave a smile and a wave. "So long." He said out the window.

Rebecca woke early the next morning. She slammed her arm down against the small box and looked to see the red blurry glare of 5:00am. She thought her eyes were unable to focus, until she realized it wasn't her eyes at all. A perfectly clear 5:02 shone on her travel alarm clock. It was completely pitch black outside as well as in. Rebecca was surprised there wasn't a street lamp lit anywhere along the road. She switched on the light next to the clock, nothing. Unsteady, she tried to force her body to rise and shower. Cringing when she realized she would be forced to forgo on a shower this morning.

She was about to reach for the bathroom handle, when the sound of the toilet flushing made her jump back. It was the first sign of life she had heard from the gentleman next door. Curious, she put her ear to the door to see if she could catch a hint of his voice, but only heard silence. She heard the slow sound of water running and rapid tooth brushing and then a few minutes later she heard his door slam shut.

Entering the bathroom, she realized she had been too late, without power she wasn't going to be able to flush the toilet or run the water in the sink. The elusive gentleman had beaten her to it.

In her room, she threw on blue jeans and David's sweater. From the dresser, she reached for her jewelry and purse and ran down the steps so she wouldn't be late meeting Phillip. On the kitchen table, she found the motion pills that Ena had left for her to take. She took two and retrieved a small glass of orange juice to wash it down. Her watch said 5:45am. She looked around the kitchen and realized she couldn't do much there either, without power she couldn't make tea or toast. She did, however, find herself a bottle of water and ran back upstairs to brush her teeth and wash her face. At 5:55am Rebecca rushed back to the kitchen and waited for Phillip.

She heard the front door close and was surprised that he came in that way, when yesterday he had used the back door. Rebecca went to the front hall to meet him, but instead found no one at all. Returning to the kitchen, she found Phillip entering the back door.

"All ready to go?" He flashed her a comfortable smile.

She smiled in return, "Well, I'm a mess - but yes, I'm all ready."

"Don't worry." Phillip, rubbed his own head to show her his morning had been just as rough. "The fish won't mind."

The Harbor was a forty-minute ride north, and they had stopped for donuts and coffee along the way. Phillip was a man who liked to talk, which made Rebecca feel at ease; since she wasn't one who liked to do a lot of talking herself. He filled her in on sites along the way, and she enjoyed the worn comfort and rattle of the old pick-up truck as they charged down the freeway. She sat listening to Phillip explain the history of the towns they passed through, pointing out which ones his parents and his in-laws were originally from. Telling her that Harry had been an elementary principle and that his dad had long retired from fishing himself.

Rebecca was awed by the view when Phillip turned into the harbor parking lot. The gray sky was beautifully lined with an assortment of masts bobbing up and down in the water. Phillip pointed out to her where the pier was and handed her a couple dollars, directing her to get them some more coffee from the café. Then Phillip explained that he would load up the boat with the equipment from the truck and meet her back here.

Rebecca walked in the direction of the café and noticed that the pier was lined with other buildings too. She purchased the coffee and thought she recognized the man walking toward the bathrooms, but quickly decided that she must be mistaken. Then instead of heading straight for the truck she walked in the other direction for a few minutes. Hoping a few minutes wouldn't bother Phillip any. Curiosity had gotten the better of her. She needed to know what the other buildings contained. She found that some sold imported goods and that others were service businesses to sailors and fishermen. She didn't have time to walk the whole length, but could tell that at the end of the pier was a seafood restaurant and bar. Next to it she saw a small storefront with a picture window. She could barely make out the sign above it that read Gallery. Rebecca looked at her watch and then looked back down the pier from which she came. If she finished walking to the end, she knew it would take at least fifteen minutes to get back to the truck. So instead she headed back, right then and there, but made a mental note to go back later to see the rest.

"There you are." Phillip closed the truck door and was carrying a wound up pile of cords with large hooks on the ends. "Was the café packed this morning?"

"No, not too bad." She felt guilty. "I sort of got side tracked, sorry."

"Donna loves to look at all the shops down here too."

"They are very interesting."

"You didn't make it all the way down to the end, did you?"

"No, my conscious pulled me back before I got that far."

"When we get back, you'll have to finish your walk, the shops at the other end, are better than interesting. Donna would say beautiful. I'd say expensive, but I have to admit the stuff is pretty."

They had been one of the last boats to pull out of the dock that morning, and they were one of the last to pull back in that evening. Rebecca watched all the boats making their way back into the harbor as Phillip was about to reach the entrance himself. She was amazed at the size of some of the boats with what looked to her like crews of six or seven men, but most were medium sized with crews of two or three. When she asked Phillip if he had a crew, he told her that he had one full time employee, who had the week off, because his wife just had a child. He also hired teenagers for the summer and some weekends. As Phillip docked the Donna Maria, named for his wife and daughter. She felt the full effect of the harbor with all the fishing and sailboats lining the docks. It was wonderful. Everywhere full of movement and energy. Men yelling to crewmates as they prepared to bring in their catches to the market. Before she could ask what they were to do next, Phillip told her to go ahead and finish checking out the pier shops as he finished cleaning up and then they'd bring in their catch for the day. She stripped off her rubber boots and coat. Phillip hosed them down, before she hung them up to dry. Then she rushed off down the dock toward the pier waving to him as she went.

She felt like one of her children rushing over to the pet shop to stare at the puppies in their cages, only she wasn't sure what she was to find. Passing the café she noticed that it was now packed with men of all ages, men that were well built from the hard work of ocean fishing. She passed by a shop where some men were busy buying repair parts for boats or rope for netting among other things she didn't recognize. Further down the pier she noticed that the shops had changed, now they began to look upscale in décor, glass doors with bright brass handles and electric lanterns hanging on either side of the doors. One storefront window contained collectibles of porcelain, silver and glass. Rebecca looked at one of the vases and saw the tag read $2000. The next window shop contained dishes and the next wool rugs. She then came across a fine jewelry shop, but didn't bother to stop and look. She was never one for jewelry really, what a waste of money she thought, but the brass mantel clock was pretty.

She was finally there, the large picture window that she read this morning. It was an art gallery and in the window stood paintings on easels. One of which caught her attention more than any of the others. It was vibrant, blues and greens with white capped waves. There was no sun in it anywhere, yet she felt it was a clear, bright summer day. It made her almost feel the warmth of the shore on a ninety-degree day. The sand seemed so real to her that it nearly glittered. What truly spoke to her was the family of dolphins in the ocean. They were jumping and dancing in the cool water, and they seemed so happy, yet one was somehow slightly separate from the others and the color of the water around it was slightly duller. It talked to her of togetherness and cheer, yet there was an element out of place somehow.

"Don't you just love that painting, there is an air of mystery to it."

Rebecca turned to find a woman in her forties standing there next to her, she never even realized someone was there until she had spoken to her.

"It's a Cavanaugh, would you like to see a couple of others that he painted."

Rebecca smiled at the woman, and then she looked once more at the painting in the window. The tag to the corner of it said $1000. "I wasn't actually shopping today, just looking through the windows. I smell of fish." She said shyly.

"I don't mind and most of my customers don't show up until after having dinner next door."

Rebecca followed the woman inside and toward the back of the shop. On the left-hand wall, she had three more paintings by Cavanaugh. One was of a child playing on the shore chasing a seagull. One of a fishing boat pulling into a harbor at sunset and the last was of a sailboat gliding past a long rock jetty as the waves hit against it. But these didn't have a way of hitting her heart quiet the same way that the dolphins had. It was special. She wasn't sure how or why, but she knew that it was.

"They are very beautiful, aren't they?" She stood staring at them with the art dealer.

"I don't think everyone sees how very beautiful they actually are. The artist was in his eighties when he created most of his paintings, except the one in the front window. It was his final piece before he passed away. It's my favorite."

Rebecca looked at the woman. "It does seem to be laughing and crying at the same time, at least that's what I feel, when I look at it."

"You sense that too." The woman smiled at her.

Rebecca glanced back at the pictures on the wall, and then she glanced at her watch. "Thank you for showing me the paintings. I really must get going, thanks again."

"He was a wonderful artist, he was an extreme recluse though. You know he lived the whole of his life on the shore of North Carolina." The woman handed Rebecca one of her business cards, before she let her out of the store. "Just in case you decide you're interested."

"Thank you." Rebecca placed it in her pocket as she left.

Stopping outside the window once more, before she went back to meet Phillip, Rebecca studied the painting again. She couldn't shake the feeling that it was a place where she could be sad and yet had to be happy at the same time. It was just the place of serene comfort she was looking for. Was she interested? Rebecca glanced at the price tag again and almost choked. $10,000 was a little out of her price range. But, at least, now she knew she wouldn't be agonizing over a decision that she thought was a $1000 purchase.

At dinner, Rebecca told the Whittle's about the wonderful day she had had, and by dinners end she told them she would be leaving tomorrow. She went to her room and called her children and mother-in-law and told them her new plans. Then she pulled out the atlas and planned her route to North Carolina.

CHAPTER TWENTY-FIVE

Carl heard a ringing in his head and felt warmth against his body and in his hand. The pounding hit him hard when he tried to use his brain to remember last night. It had been nice listening to her talk, and sitting companionably together sipping wine, but that was where his memory ended. Carl lifted the covers. Under it, he found himself bare with only briefs to cover his lower half, Julie he noticed was only wearing the same. But what was worse was what Carl didn't find, the condition that he had been presented with every morning for the last nine months.

Carl reached for a shirt and pulled it on over his head. It was cold. He quickly pulled on the rest of his clothing and noticed the empty gallon jug beside the burnt out fire. Grabbing it, he swore at himself for being a damn fool and walked toward the cave opening. Instead of going up, Carl chose to go down, following the path all the way to the bottom of the cliff. He looked back up at the ledge of trees that hid his companion. Then turned to head in the direction of the sun. Walking through a clearing to the east of the mountain, Carl followed it through and past a line of trees to the river that Luke had told him was there beyond. The same river that he had seen from the mountaintop. The one that Carl knew they would be forced to follow out if no one came to get them. He reached the jug into the brisk current and filled it a third of the way full, swished it around, emptied it, then refilled it to the top this time with the ice cold water. Carl spied a boulder perfect for sitting on further down river.

He sat down feeling the deep cold beneath his butt. His hand felt the hovering of warmth on the surface of the rock from the sun almost half way into the sky. Jerking his hand away, Carl tried to avoid the penetrating cold that his butt was experiencing and shoved both fists into his coat pockets to warm them. Staring at the swift flow of water before him, he tried again to remember what had happened last night. Other than talking for a couple of hours and drinking the wine, Carl rubbed his head as he struggled against the haze and throbbing of his brain, Nothing. He could remember absolutely nothing, and it was driving him crazy. When one took the step of committing adultery, Carl thought to himself, most would probably think it nice to at least remember that they had done it. But he had to admit he didn't feel an ounce of guilt, bad yes, but guilt, not even a little. What does that mean? He was so confused. Maybe he could deny that anything had happened. Then fear hit him. What if she remembered. He sucked in a deep breath - Was he any good?

Carl wanted to punch himself in the nose. He deserved it. He knew Julie was going to be sad to know that he never intended to be with her and worse he couldn't remember any of it. Carl became agitated, What was it she had told him that night in Luke's cabin? He was the kind of guy who would be there in the morning. "Shit, God damn it." He yelled out loud not caring what bird or squirrel he might offend. He sure as hell was not like any of her other lover's. He'd make sure of that. He wouldn't break her heart and most of all he wouldn't make her regret what they had done. Carl hurried to gather firewood and the jug of water to take back to Julie. Hoping with all his might, she would be laying there still asleep when he returned.

He would make it up to Julie for leaving her side. Even though he knew she hadn't been literal in her meaning about his being there the next morning. The least he could do; was not go running off before she even woke up. He wondered how much, she had had to drink last night because it was certainly not like her to sleep so late in the day.

Carl scanned the forest for wildflowers, but found none, it was early yet he supposed. He did, however, find a couple of bushes with pussy willows blooming on them. He pulled out a folded knife from his pocket and cut down a handful of branches covered with the puffy, white protrusions, telling himself they would have to do. Replacing the blade, he piled his gift for Julie on top of the woodpile and continued on his way to the cliff trail. When Carl reached the base of the trail he thought, he heard something. Then he heard the scraping, thumping, thwack again. Rocks were somehow falling down the side of the cliff. Carl glanced up and noticed the large figure about to enter the cave entrance. It was Luke. There was no mistaking the giant man with the long dark braid down his back. Happy to see his large friend and excited at the prospect of news, Carl quickly carried his load up the long weaving path to the top, stopping only once he reached the ledge.

Carl heard a scream and then heard the blasting shot of gunfire. He had dropped his load and was now running to reach the entrance. Carl saw a blur of colors cross his eyes, brown, green, gray, red, and then pitch-black. His eyes were unable to focus from the sunlight to the darkness of the cave. In the distance, he saw a couple of beams of light, shoot one way and then another. He pulled out his knife and slowly, silently unfolded it, locking it into place with a muffled click.

He could hear men's voices now, as he slowly felt his way down the side of the cave wall, giving his eyes time to adjust. "What are you, a bunch of dogs?" A voice barked loudly indicating that he was the top dog. His men, which sounded to Carl like three, all murmured responses. "Get Sanchez off of her, and the rest of you had better just zip back up your pants because our orders were to secure them unharmed and that includes the girl."

"Unharmed means breathing." One man remarked.

"Unharmed means not a scratch, and if you question my authority again Wolf, You'll wish you were Sanchez."

"Yes Sir." The man answered with only enough sarcasm for it to slide under the act of insubordination.

Carl's eyes had adjusted, and he could see two men leaning over the dead body, a third man was ransacking the supplies. "What a waste, and for fucking, Christ sake, Snake, take her gun away before you lift him off of her."

Julie was struggling to get loose from the carcass on top of her, but with no success. The man was large and the dead weight of him must have been cutting off her supply of oxygen. Carl could now verify that there were three men and the leading Alpha Male. Five, if you counted the dead guy. The men struggled to lift him.

"Man, Toad should have lived up to his name."

"What do you mean, he was as horny as they come."

"Light Man, Small and Light, the guy never stopped eating."

"Yeah, Pussy." The younger one laughed.

"Knock it off!" The Alpha yelled.

"So, where is he?" He asked Julie.

Carl knew his chances were slim against four men. Five, if Luke were with them. He knew he would be lucky if he were able to kill one of them with his knife. Normally his best bet would have been to go for the leader. But under present circumstances, He was the only thing controlling this pack of ravaging coyotes. Carl thought it best to go for the worst of the other three, Wolf.

Whatever happened after that, three of them against him and

Julie were better odds then four. Three against three would be better yet, but Luke was sporting a pretty good poker face and Carl couldn't be sure whom it was meant to benefit.

Carl waited for the right moment to make his move. He knew it would need to be swift with the element of surprise on his side. Julie was now up off the floor, and being interrogated by the leader of this pack. The rest of the men were busy packing supplies in their rucksacks. Luke caught sight of Carl and motioned for him to leave, with a subtle jerk of his head toward the door. Carl refused, shaking his head No in response. Luke then stood arms crossed and motioned with a finger to his shoulder. Carl knew he was trying to warn him that they were Special Forces. Carl already knew that. It was their mistake that made him unafraid and willing to risk getting killed. The Alpha dog already said that they weren't to be hurt. Why the General had changed his mind about that, Carl was curious to know, but it was seeing Julie sitting there with her body half exposed that had him wanting to kill someone.

"Here." The man threw her a flannel shirt hitting her in the chest and followed it after with a pair of sweat pants from the floor. "Cover up and stop tempting my men to disobey me." "Now tell me where the Sergeant has gone off to."

"I don't know." Julie snapped back, yelling loud enough for everyone to hear.

"She's lying, do you want me to persuade her into telling the truth, Sir."

"Shut up Roach and finish what you're doing." "Wolf, why don't you go outside and take a look around."

It had sounded like a casual request, but the other soldier moved quickly to follow the orders given him. As the man came closer, Carl sucked his body closer to the wall and into a dark nook. He held his breath as wolf came closer and he forced himself to wait just a second longer. Carl's heart raced. He hoped it wouldn't give him away. He reached out and took Wolf's shoulder from behind and quickly, before he lost his nerve; Carl slid the sharp blade across the man's throat. It was as wolf's body began to sink to the ground that Carl noticed the large body running down the cave entrance. Carl was knocked to the ground. He could feel the weight of at least two men on top of him. To his surprise, he heard a gunshot. Time suspended as Carl waited to feel a bullet enter him, but nothing hurt, other than the knees in his back. Looking to the light outside, Carl saw Luke still sprinting for the opening and heard one more shot ring out. Then the last thing Carl saw was Luke's body falling over the side of the cliff before everything went black from one crunching blow.

CHAPTER TWENTY-SIX

Rebecca turned on her blinker when she saw an exit sign indicating scenic route 17. It was already one o'clock in the afternoon, and she was eager to start her search for the perfect house. She was surprised, for the last day of March it seemed pretty warm to her. Rebecca rolled down the window. Breathing in the cool fresh air, she allowed her arm to bask in the sunlight. At the stop sign, she halted the car. Her heart sank when she saw the choice of directions she could take. Left read Camp Lejeune Marine Corps Base and Jacksonville. Right read Wilmington. Rebecca turned right.

At the first gas station she came to, Rebecca stopped, filled the tank and bought a local map. Searching the map, she planned a route and set off southward bound. The first few roads she took felt imposing. The houses spoke for themselves. Huge, contemporary, vertical siding with large sheets of glass for windows. They dominated everything around them. Rebecca couldn't see the massive Atlantic past the houses. A few of them were for sale, but she couldn't imagine, never mind care, how much they must cost. She quickly crossed one road off the map after another.

Her afternoon had been a waste, and she really didn't know what she had expected. She was fooling herself if she thought that the home of her dreams would just magically appear. It was going to require a lot of hard work, and she knew her first stop would be an ad rack for real estate catalogs. That, and a decent hotel which hopefully had a good takeout menu. She was tired, and all she wanted to do was shower and order something in.

Rebecca turned back onto the main road and followed it hoping to find a hotel. Finally she found a sign for one pointing right, but she also noticed a road sign leading left, back toward the shore. It read Cavanaugh Drive. Rebecca quickly swerved into the left lane and stopped at the red light ahead of her. She jumped when the driver behind her, laid down hard on their Beemer's horn. "Sorry." Rebecca yelled out her window as she waved to the woman behind her. The light turned, and she pointed her car shoreward bound once more to see if the sign had merely been a coincidence or if the painter's house were really located on the road named after him. Following it, Rebecca was disappointed once more when all she found were more of the same houses. She came to the end of the paved road and started to turn around when she caught the hint of an orange sign hidden in the dead over growth of sea grass.

Stepping out of her car, Rebecca pushed aside the dead weeds and read the sign. House for Sale, with the arrow pointing toward a dirt and gravel road ahead. Ripley Road. She followed it for a short way to where the road made a sharp bend. Around the corner was a small community. A neat row of beach houses dotted the dirt road, five lining the shore and five placed up on the hill behind these. They were beautiful, not too large taking up all the available land or too high reaching into the sky and blocking the view. The house for sale was located all the way to the end, on the shore. The lot that it rested on looked larger to her then the others. She couldn't help but notice the house was beaten up pretty bad.

Rebecca parked the car on the edge of the road and got out. A warm breeze hit her and pulled her forward a step. Catching her balance, Rebecca stepped onto the overgrown back lawn and assessed the house. The house itself was perfect. A small gray shingled cape cod styled house, with back stairs that were too dangerous to climb. She rounded the side of the house, perched on its nine twelve-foot beams, she found another set of stairs toward the front that were beaten, but still sound. Rebecca could see that they led up to a small porch balcony and the front door. There was also a large wooden sign in front of the house. She stopped to read it, Private Property; trespassers will be prosecuted.

Rebecca stepped onto one stair to test it, then decided to take her chances. She heard creaks and felt it quaking as she climbed, but she assured herself that they were safe enough. Cupping her eyes, she peered in through the front picture window, to find some rubbish laying on the floor, and an old rug thick with dust and dirt. There were a couple pieces of furniture left behind by the owners, but they seemed at home sitting there, even by their lonesome. It was the object that awed her next that told her this was the place she was looking for. To Rebecca's delight there was a stone fireplace in the living room with an old wooden mantle jutting out above it. Which she immediately could imagine had held a large model ship. Turning out to sea, the view struck her heart, and the wind smelt of salt. But it was the sound of the waves hitting shore that called out to her, Home.

Glancing inside again, Rebecca assessed the house. With chunks of plaster lying on the floor, she knew the walls and ceiling would need to be replaced, and she was certain it needed a new roof and possibly siding, but if most everything else were solid, she was sure she could fix it. On her way out of Ripley Road, Rebecca wrote down the phone number. "Yes, Hello, could you give me the address to this number." "Thank you." She hung up and found it on her map. Not in the city as she thought, but close in fact.

Rebecca slowed the car as the number approached and pulled over when she found an empty meter stall. Plopping coins in and turning the crank, she read two hour limit. Searching the brick storefronts. Rebecca glanced down at her paper to reconfirm the address when the brass plate before her read: Jeffery McCandless Attorney at Law.

Inside the solid, dark door was a bright waiting room with a receptionist typing behind the desk.

"Do you have an appointment?" The woman looked at her as if she were certain she hadn't.

"No, I'm sorry I don't have one, I found the number to this address on a 'For Sale' sign."

The woman said nothing, but picked up the phone and then replacing it, asked her to take a seat. "Mr. McCandless will be with you in one moment."

The door to an inner office opened and out stepped a tall, thin man in his late fifties. Dressed for business, she was sure he had replaced his jacket only seconds before opening the door.

He extended his hand, "Hello, I'm Jeffery McCandless."

She shook it. "Rebecca Reynolds."

"Please come in." He closed the door behind them.

"Please." He pointed to a chair. "Would you like a cup of coffee?"

"No, thank you." She responded, as she sat in the chair across from him.

"So, how can I help you?"

"I'm interested in a property that had your number listed on it."

"What property is that?"

"Ripley Road."

"Yes, I do represent the owner of that property." He turned to face a cabinet. Flipping through he pulled out a client's file. Facing her once more, he began to describe the property. "The house was originally built in 1901. It was bought by the current owner's father in 1935, was updated a couple of times since then. There are three bedrooms, two upstairs with one down. There is the main living area with fireplace and a small kitchen/dining area. The first floor has one full bath. Of course, the owner is selling it as is."

"But." He explained. "The lot is a very nice size." "An entire acre, almost unheard-of in ocean front property today." He showed her the survey. "But the right side of the property does border a public beach." He asked if she were still interested in the property and if so was she prepared to make an offer. Rebecca told him she was and that she would like to offer one hundred and seventy-five thousand.

The man in front of her closed the file. "Ms. Reynolds, The property is worth more than that." He said flatly.

"Mrs." Rebecca looked at the man eyeing her like she were insane and mustered the courage to say in one quick breath. "I know the house needs some work, so I can only afford what I've offered." Then while he was still dazed she added. "Does the house have any severe water damage that you know of?"

He couldn't believe they were actually having this conversation. Any person in their right mind would have the house demolished and put a new one up in its place. "Mrs. Reynolds, the house will need to be gutted and the roof and siding will need to be replaced."

Rebecca smiled having guessed correctly what needed to be done. "I understand, that is why I can only afford the one hundred and seventy-five thousand."

"All right Ma'am, I'll relay your offer, but I wouldn't hold my breath if I were you."

Rebecca thanked the man and lifted her purse in a motion to leave his office.

"Oh No, Please wait." He told her as he flipped through a large Rolodex on his desk. "I can call him now and save us both the time for responses."

He couldn't believe he was about to call his client with this joke of an offer. But he was obligated to bring forth all offers and in the past three years there had only been one. Which his client had rejected even though he had told him it was a perfectly reasonable offer of Eight hundred thousand dollars flat. He located the number and began to dial.

Rebecca heard the computerized sounds coming from the receiver. "Wait!" Rebecca said, "Before you make the offer could you tell me if the contents of the house are included in the sale?" She knew she was pushing her luck, but the rug and the desk were perfect.

"I'll ask." He told her. Mr. McCandless finished dialing the number, and Rebecca couldn't help but hold her breath.

"Hello George. This is Jeffrey, How are you?" "Yes, things are well." "No, this call isn't in regard to upcoming tax filing." "Believe it or not I have a woman here, her name is Rebecca Reynolds and she wishes to make an offer on your Father's place." "Yes, this is a pleasant surprise, but wait she has a couple of questions before she actually makes the offer. She would like to know the condition of the inside, and she would also like to know if the contents are included in the sale." "Yes, that's correct, she intends to fix it up and live in the original house." "What, But, But don't you want to hear her offer first."

Rebecca was disappointed. The least he could do was to hear her offer.

"Alright then, I'll draw up the paperwork right away." He hung up the phone. "Congratulations, Mrs. Reynolds. You've bought an incredible piece of property."

Rebecca was speechless. She just bought the house that she and Carl always dreamed of living in. She found it, and now she only hoped that if he were alive; that he would find it too.

She was so excited she had trouble sitting in her seat. She had so much to do. She needed to call her brother and have him come tell her everything she needed to have done, and she needed to get a small pickup truck for hauling supplies. "Mr. McCandless, do you know if the plumbing and electrical is sound enough to have it turned on?"

"I would recommend that you have a licensed electrician and plumber look at it first. Mr. Cavanaugh lived there right up until he passed away at the age of ninety. However; that was six years ago, and the place has taken quite a battering since."

"Cavanaugh, it was Cavanaugh's house?" Rebecca was surprised. That run down house was where he created that magical painting.

"Yes, he was a writer and then he dabbled in painting in his later years, do you know of him?"

"Yes, I've seen a few of his paintings, they're beautiful."

"Yes, it was a shame he stopped writing though." He said sadly, but then went straight back to business.

They discussed the legal details, and he told her that she should come by tomorrow to sign the paperwork and to finish up any odds or ends.

Climbing into her car, Rebecca checked the time on the dashboard and found it was close to dinnertime. But since the sun was still high on the horizon, she easily convinced herself to drive back to the house for another look before heading to a hotel for the night. Gravel crunching under tires, Rebecca slowly drove past the homes that were her new neighbors. Most looked to be closed up, no cars, trashcans, or other signs of life were visible. A couple had lights on, and two blew billows of smoke out their chimneys. Rebecca came to the old Cavanaugh house and what was to become her own home. She hesitated a moment, staring first at the house and then further down the dirt road. Deciding that the sun would linger quite a while longer, she drove the car down the dirt road to find where it led. After a half mile of crunching and turns, it brought her out to a paved road. Turning left she followed it until she came to the opening of the public beach that Mr. McCandless had spoken about in his office. Taking the turn she found the four-lane, main road leading to the beach. It was first cluttered with small houses lining every inch of street. Then she found they turned into storefronts the closer she got to the boardwalk.

Now deserted, she imagined it filled with people dressed in bathing suits and shorts. Many of them wearing bad hats. Everyone wearing sunglasses, either covering their eyes, placed on top of their heads, or dangling from straps around their necks. She imagined people toting umbrellas and beach chairs. Babies waddling behind, with parents calling to them, urging them forward.

She saw closed up tourist shops, selling beach supplies and jewelry. Ice cream shops and fudge shops. Photo shops and clothing shops. Ones that sold clothes only wearable during their one week of vacationing, because wearing them anywhere other than at the boardwalk would put anyone in serious fashion violation.

Rebecca came to the Pizzeria and saw that it was open for business, so she parked the car and went in. There was a bell that 'clanged' when she entered, and she noticed a television on in the corner, hanging high near the ceiling. Soon after entering she was greeted by a round man with a happy face, dark features and hair with a hint of silver scattered throughout. "Can I get you something?"

Rebecca glanced at the menu board and found slices unavailable out of season, so she ordered a small cheese pizza and a large soda to go. He handed her the drink, then disappeared around the corner. Rebecca heard talking going on in the back, and she took a seat to wait for her pizza. She thought about walking up onto the boardwalk to get a look around, but it was late in the day and a bit chilly even though tomorrow would be the first day of April.

The man looked around the corner at her and then yelled over to her. "You visiting or are you new to the area? It's a little early yet for visitors."

"I'm buying the old Cavanaugh place down the road."

A woman tossing pizza dough in the air leaned her head out from behind the wall. "You bought that house."

Rebecca smiled, a proud smile, "I sign the papers tomorrow."

"The place is supposed to be haunted." Both of them told her at once.

Rebecca laughed, "In what way, do you mean haunted?"

The woman, as round as the man and with features and hair as dark as his own, had a glint in her eye that told Rebecca that this was a story she took great enjoyment in telling to others. "People who have been out to look at it, say that it chills them to their bones to be on the property, and some say that old man Cavanaugh's ghost is still there, refusing to leave and scaring everyone away that goes there."

"Well, I was just out there, and I felt perfectly warm and happy."

"Okay, but don't say we didn't warn you." The woman commented as the man handed her the pizza.

Rebecca handed them the money and extended her hand. "By the way, my name is Rebecca Reynolds, nice to meet you."

They told her they were Tony and Maria Margatelli and wished her good luck.

"Oh, I'm sure I'll see you again soon, since I'm a pizza addict." They waved as she carried her things and pushed the door open with her back. It clanged as it closed shut behind her.

Rebecca placed her food in the car and went next door to the drugstore to buy a notebook and pen so she could start making lists of things to do. At the very top of her list, she knew would be Call the Kids! On her way to the register, a rack of cards caught her eye and reminded her of David. Scenes of winter saying "wish you were here" tugged at her heart and made her feel a bit guilty for not having talked to him since she left. She hadn't even put a card in the mail thanking him for the water globe. And last night when she stayed in the hotel in Charlottesville, she forced herself not to call and let him know she was there. She worried he would have come to see her, and the last thing she needed was to be distracted, the way David distracted her. It was far too easy for her to stay safely in his arms. For now, she knew it would be comfortable with him, but what worried her was the unknown of tomorrow. It could be six months or a year from now, but eventually tomorrow would come. What if she woke up in tomorrow, and found it was a mistake. But oh, how she missed David - his strength, his comfort, his tenderness. She had to admit she missed him badly.

Rebecca picked out a card, one with children playing on the shore, a crab dangling from the little boy's swim trunks. "Having a crabby time, how are you?" It reminded her of Danny and the girls, and she thought David might appreciate that too.

She drove back to the house and pulled out the throw from the back seat, so she could sit on her beach and eat dinner. Rebecca finished her second slice of pizza and closed the box to start writing her list. It was then that she felt a warm breeze surround her and thought that maybe she wasn't alone after all. "Mr. Cavanaugh, I love your house, and your son agreed to sell it to my family and me." She spoke to the man, who had lived the whole of his life in this house, while she stared out at the ocean before her. "I can't wait to get inside; so I can shake out the rug to see better what the colors are. I'll bet you kept an old wooden ship on the mantle, because that is what I plan on searching antique shops to find."

All of a sudden she heard a splash out in the water. Rebecca yelled, "Look!" Swinging her head to find only an empty beach around her. She wanted to show Carl and the kids the family of dolphins playing outside of their new home. Except they weren't there for her to call to. Instead, she said, "Did you see that Mr. Cavanaugh." She sat and watched as they leapt and danced, until finally they were gone. Then she picked up her things and looked inside the house one last time before heading to the hotel.

❈❈❈

Carl woke to a throbbing pain at the back of his head. but was surprised, by the warm comfort around him. Focusing his eyes was difficult. Carl tried again, but was only able to see a blur in front of him.

"Oh, thank god." He heard Julie say and then felt her hand touch his forehead. "Are you okay? I wasn't sure if you were ever going to wake up."

"How long have I been out?"

"Four days." Julie said as she touched his hair and realized that he didn't look up at her. "Are you alright?"

"I can't see anything except a blur." He felt around him. "Where are we? Are you alright? Did they hurt you?"

"No, Yes. You can't see anything? They hit you so hard that I wasn't sure if you would make it, I wasn't sure if you were in a coma." She answered frantically.

He grabbed Julie's hands as she reached up to his eyes. "Julie slow down, I'm okay. Everything is just blurry."

Julie sat next to Carl on the bed. "No Carl they didn't hurt me. I'm okay. She got up and moved to the small window. A window that was too small to break out of and on the tips of her toes looked outside to describe it to Carl. "We are in a cabin somewhere, still in a forest, all I can see is snow and trees. They covered my eyes on the way here. It didn't feel like it took very long. We walked for a while and then we rode on ATV's for about a half hour maybe."

"Did you see Luke? Was he shot dead?" He asked. "I only remember hearing a shot and seeing him fall."

"I don't know, they said nothing about him and they covered my eyes before leaving the cave."

"When they walked you out did you go east, north, south, which way? Was the sun in your eyes or at your back?"

"I don't know Carl, I was carried. I just don't know. The sun was neither, in my face or at my back. If I were to guess, I'd say we went north.

"Can you remember anything else?"

"Well, I do remember hearing the river and then not hearing it at all anymore."

"So, then maybe, we traveled more north-west."

"Yes, maybe."

"Have you seen anyone?"

"Only Sir." No other name, Just Sir." He brought food once in a while and then yesterday he did a lot of shouting at the other men and then he came in and left those." Julie pointed to five brown packages of meals ready to eat on the floor. "I ate one."

"What did he leave?" Carl shook his head, "No voices since?"

"MRE's. No, nothing since, she said, and since there was no peep coming from you either, I thought it best to sit and wait a while, besides there is no way out, I've looked. The walls are solid log. The window is way too small and the ceiling too high."

Carl felt the wall behind him and agreed. "You should try to escape if you can."

"I won't leave you." Julie answered him harsh and quick.

"Julie, Be reasonable, you're not in a position of protecting me any longer." He said in a curt tone, "Promise me that you'll try to escape if you can."

Julie was glad he couldn't see her. Her ego was crushed, and worst of all, was she knew he was right. She stared at her leg. "I promise Carl, if my leg will let me. I'll try." She answered. "Do you need to use the bathroom?" Julie asked.

"Yes please." He stood, and she took hold of his arm to lead him.

Julie yelled through the door. "You let me know when you're ready to come back out, and in the meantime I'll make us one of these fabulously delicious meals."

Carl just about choked on her words, but then as hungry as he was right now; it would probably taste as good to him as thanksgiving dinner

CHAPTER TWENTY-SEVEN

Rebecca loved the feel of her new heap. It was a mostly red, twelve-year old pick-up truck. That was better off for the wear as far as she was concerned. The man who had it for sale in his front yard had told her its engine had been rebuilt three years earlier. It probably needed new tires, but otherwise it was in good shape for its age. What he hadn't told her was that it needed new shocks, but to Rebecca, the squeak and bump of her new material hauler added to its appeal. She loved the noise it produced, and when all things were considered, the thing had serious ump even with a full load. It was cheap to boot.

Pulling into her dirt drive, Rebecca unloaded the truck and checked her watch for the time. Nine thirty and she still had a whole half an hour to spare. Jingle, jingle; jingle; jingle, she hated the girly sound of the new cell phone she had acquired, but the sales man had told her it was the most affordable one. Now she knew why. Its annoyance was making her wish she had gone with the next affordable one. Jingle; Jingle. "Hello." "Yes, that's correct, 100 Ripley Road, ah huh, the old Cavanaugh place." "Bye." She pushed the button and threw it back onto the cab's seat.

A couple of minutes later she heard the crunching of gravel coming from up the road. A man parked beside her and hopped out. "Hi, Mrs. Reynolds, I'm Oscar Thomas, We talked yesterday on the phone."

The introduction was actually unnecessary since his name was plastered to the side of his truck, right over "Licensed Electrician, Serving Wilmington for over 30 Years." "Yes, Thank you for coming out so quickly."

"Sorry, I'm so early, my morning appointment was quicker than expected. I hope it's not a problem my coming out an hour early, but being

I was out this way already."

"No, not at all." Rebecca could hear a loud rumble in the distance. "But, I'll need you to move your truck." She quickly hopped into her own and parked on the street, with Oscar pulling in behind her.

Within sight was a huge dump truck and after a couple of words and the passing of a check, Rebecca was promptly served with a thunderous rumble and the haze of a three ton load of gravel heaped onto the driveway and skillfully dumped along its length. With a final wave of a hand, the man and his dump truck rumbled steadily back up the way they had come.

The sound of another vehicle came charging down the road. This time, it was a long tractor-trailer hauling a huge trash container. They quickly moved their trucks back into the end of the drive, so that the man could maneuver the dumpster into the back yard. He positioned it fairly close to the house and after signing some forms and paying the man, he too drove off, headed back toward Cavanaugh Drive.

"Sorry, about all that." Rebecca smiled and waved for Mr. Thomas to follow her.

"No problem, it looks as though you're all ready to get started." "Who's your contractor?"

"My brother has taken the job. He'll be here tomorrow." She said. "Careful for that stair."

Upstairs in the kitchen Rebecca pulled out a file full of documents she had obtained from the town hall. Containing all the information she could get on the Cavanaugh house. She showed everything to him. Unfortunately, it wasn't much.

"Mrs. Reynolds, after your call yesterday, when I realized that it was old Mr. Cavanaugh's house that you had bought, I looked upstairs in some old file cabinets of mine and found these. He held billing statements of work he and his brother had done for Mr. Cavanaugh over the years.

Their names had been in Jeffery McCandless' file, part of which now belonged to her. "Did your brother say if he could make it out today."

At the completion of her question, they both heard a clomping sound come from the front stairs. In came a man identical to the one standing in front of her, except in his hand he carried a pipe wrench. The three of them walked through the house checking it for possible problems.

Thanking the men, Rebecca told them she would call when they were ready for the bathroom installation upstairs. For now, the one she had downstairs and the kitchen were fine.

Walking the Thomas' out, she noticed the high pitched jingle coming from her cab. Picking up the phone, she waved goodbye to the men getting into their trucks.

"Hello."

"Hey little girl, How's it going?"

"Hey Robbie, It's going great. I just got the okay on the plumbing and electrical and with any luck it'll be all hooked up by five tonight. Between my own judgment and theirs, we think the roof has been the major problem. But you're the expert, I'll let you decide when you get here tomorrow."

"Today."

"What, you said tomorrow at the earliest."

"Yeah, well I worked late the last two nights, so that I could finish up early. I was just too excited to get down there and see your new place."

"Wonderful, Where are you now?"

"I'm on 95, almost to Richmond."

"Great, Do you have anything that you need me to get started on before you get here."

"Just a sleeping bag and a beer, some hot food couldn't hurt either."

"You got it, see you soon, and Robbie - thanks for doing this for me."

"No problem. See you soon, Sis."

By the time her brother arrived, Rebecca had not only managed to get the water and electric turned on, but she had also picked up some essentials; A coffee pot, toaster, some kitchen utensils and pans, cleaning supplies and some groceries. Had ordered hot pasta from Anthony and Maria to be picked up at five thirty and was in the process of putting together a couple of beds she found for cheap. From an antique and thrift shop that the Margatelli's told her about, located not too far down the road. She was surprised to find a pair of white wrought iron beds for the girls room and was thrilled when she found a beautifully carved master bed for her own room. It amazed her the things people would throw away over a few nicks and scrapes. A little sanding and stain and it would look like new. A few bed linens and towels and otherwise they would have to make due until her household goods shipment could be delivered once the house was underway.

"Rebecca." "Rebecca!" "Hey, where are you. This is the greeting I get after coming all this way."

"Hi Robbie." Rebecca came out from her back bedroom and gave her brother a hug Hello. "What do you think?"

"It's Awesome Rebecca, what a view." He said. "Really beautiful, well it will be with some work." He looked around. "Yeah, it's definitely the roof that's taken the worst of it. We might as well gut most of these walls and ceilings. It's not worth keeping this plaster and that way we can put in better insulation."

"What's the plan." Asked Rebecca.

"To pee and eat." He answered. "But tomorrow first thing, to put up sheeting on the roof until it's a bit warmer, and in the mean time we'll get started inside." Robbie asked. "What's your vision for this place Rebecca?"

Rebecca excitedly went over to the desk she started sorting through yesterday. She handed Robbie two old black and white photographs, one of the house that had written on the back '1937' and the other a photo of a family in front of the house dated '1943'. "I want to restore it back to its original look, but with a few added conveniences. Tomorrow, I'll call Mr. McCandless and see if he wouldn't mind digging up a few more pictures for me."

"That sounds good, It might require a little salvaging, but I think we can manage."

"Let me show you around the house first. I don't think we'll need too much." She walked Robbie into the bathroom. "Look, their all original pieces."

"Rebecca these are in really good shape just a refinishing is all they'll need."

To Rebecca the arrival of her brother set everything into motion. She was an excited child, ready to start pulling things apart, so they could put it all back together again, solid, safe and secure. She smiled at her brother and at the house around her. And for the first time, in a very long time, she truly felt that her future lay in her own two hands. She grabbed her brother's arm with a grateful tug. She said, "Come on, I'll show you the rest and then let's go eat."

❀ ❀ ❀

Carl stood in front of the window, the images before him unable to be made clear. Brightness and white and streams of rainbow colors danced in his eyes. It made them hurt. Carl closed his eyes and rubbed them, letting the darkness soothe and refresh them. After a few minutes rest, he opened them again. Carl's heart leapt to his throat, and he jumped back away from the window. The rough image of a man's face was right up against his own, eye to eye. Carl stumbled, catching himself from falling completely.

"Did you see that?" Julie asked, "One of them was just there."

"Yes, I saw the outline of a face and saw eyes." He answered. "It surprised me."

"It would have surprised me too, the way he popped up like that."

"Well, I guess their back." Carl was afraid of what was in store for them.

"Yes, I guess so." Julie wasn't sure if she should feel anxious or relieved. They had finished their last meals yesterday, and hunger was starting to set in, but hunger could be a minor discomfort compared to the pain these men could inflict. "At least your vision may be coming back."

"Yes." Carl agreed, "Thank God for that."

The door flung open, "I'm glad to see that you're up and about, I was afraid my men had been over zealous in their retaliation upon you. But just to be sure, there will be a doctor out shortly to take a look at you and while he's at it, he may as well take a look at you too." He motioned to Julie. "We can't deliver the General's golden boy damaged, now can we." One of his men carried in some plates of food. "Thank you, Snake, I suggest you eat and rest because as soon as the doctor leaves we'll be moving out."

"Oh and you. You may want to thank your boyfriend here. He smirked at Julie. Your name wasn't on the General's list. But fortunately for you, I like to save my wild cards until I'm sure I don't need them any longer. Maybe we'll find out if you're a gambling girl Miss Stevens." He slammed the door shut as he left.

"Don't let him rattle you, he's just trying to keep our spirits broken." But even as he said this to her, Carl was surprised to think he almost missed his old cell.

CHAPTER TWENTY-EIGHT

Rebecca stared at the white piece of paper tacked to the board. "Laborers needed: good pay, flexible hours, Call Rebecca." At the bottom of the page, only one of the phone number strips had been pulled off. She wondered if she should take out an ad in the local newspaper.

"Hi Rebecca, how are things going over your way today?"

"Hey Tony, I'm good. We could use a couple more hands though." She pointed to her flyer.

"Peter Jacobson's son took that one yesterday, said he was going to call you and try and convince his friend Ryan to call too." Tony disappeared behind the wall with an order slip and reappeared with foil wrapped loaves. "Larry is a good kid and now that all the after school boys have been laid off at the plant, he could use the work. He's hoping on a basketball scholarship for next fall, Tony shook his head, but not counting on it."

"Well, I could sure use the help."

Tony handed her two Styrofoam containers. "I'll let him know that my best customer is waiting on his call."

"Thank you, Tony and thank you too, Mrs. Margatelli." A hand waved around the corner. "Maria, sweetheart, see you tomorrow."

"Bye." The door clanged behind her.

At the end of her driveway Rebecca reached into the mailbox and pulled the letters out, throwing them on the seat beside her. One letter stood out from the others. It was not the plain white look of a bill, but cushioned between two of those, was a rose print envelope postmarked Virginia. Rebecca reached for it and gently pulled it open.

Dear Rebecca,

Thank you for the postcard. You're very welcome for the globe. The funny thing is that the winter has been bitterly cold since the snow melted or perhaps it is because you left with it. I miss your feisty nature and gentle touch. There is still time left to visit for the calving season. My home is always open to you, should you desire it. Please do not be a stranger. And don't forget our promise. I won't.

I hope this finds you well.

Love, David.

Rebecca placed the mail on the counter, poured a soda for herself and a beer for her brother then announced "Dinner" in a loud yell.

A loud crash came from the living room and along with it a cloud of dust. With goggles on, a mask over his mouth and a hand waving through the chalky air, Robbie emerged covered in white plaster. "Food?" "Ahh, Rebecca I like Mrs. Margatelli's cooking, but we have to find a Chinese takeout place or something for a little spice of variety." All this sauce is going to make me start pooping red."

"I promise, tomorrow, I'll find something new." Rebecca stared at the card on the top of the mail pile.

"What's this?" Robbie picked it up and gave it a quick glance over. "So, what's the deal with you and Mr. Cow farmer."

Rebecca glared at Robbie, giving him an evil eye as good as their mother's.

"Okay, David. Now unfreeze me from a pillar of salt. So." He waited for her to answer his question. "Well, if you decide to take him up on his offer, I'll take this place off your hands."

Thanks, but I'm keeping it. She thought, even if it turned out to be only a summer home.

"Hey little girl." Robbie waved his fork. "Where are you, Becca?"

Robbie stared at her, covered in white except for the circle around his mouth, where his mask was, but was now shoveling ravioli into it. "Thanks for the offer, but I think I'll keep it."

"So, You didn't tell me what's going on with you and this guy?"

"That's the problem, I don't know how to answer that, The guy is great. I'm just not ready to make that kind of decision."

Robbie could see the strain in his sister's face. "Well, then don't worry about it Rebecca, when the time comes you'll know."

"What if I don't?"

"Then you'll do what all of us do. Make the best decision you can and live with the outcome."

Rebecca hoped it wouldn't come to that. She had to believe that her heart would know the truth. That it would know her desire, the true rhythm of her will, and that when the time came she hoped her heart would be that much stronger for its knowing. Rebecca put faith in that she still had time. June was a long time away. For now; she didn't have to know her heart, didn't have to know her mind and didn't have to know her emotions. She just had to be open to them, willing to listen and willing to feel. Right now, she felt satisfied. She dawned on her gear, pulled up a crowbar, cranked up the music loud and tore down the walls.

Rebecca placed her crowbar in a hole that looked to be hidden by a picture. The outline of which had been solidly etched by time, long ago. The plaster came down easy. Crumbling to the floor with simple tugs. Rebecca neared the bottom of her row and felt the crowbar hit against something inside the wall. Giving it a yank, books yellowed by age poured out of the wall. She fumbled through the rumble to gather them up, shaking them off carefully. They were untitled, merely dated with a year on each one. She opened one to read, "George is sad, yet I too am too mournful to change this. Perhaps it is best to send him to Eleanor." Rebecca gasped and quickly closed the book. It felt wrong to read something hidden and so clearly personal. She piled up the books counting ten in all and went to place them on the kitchen counter. Grabbing a juice from the fridge, Robbie came in to get another beer. "Here you go." Rebecca passed one to him.

Rebecca opened the top cover, one more time and read. "Nine is too young an age to be surrounded by such misery, but my sister Eleanor is full of light and happiness. She would make a good mother."

"What is that?"

"I found them in a wall."

"Are you kidding, didn't you say the owner was a famous writer?"

"No, Robbie, I couldn't. You told me yourself that this house is worth more than I paid."

"A lot more."

"Besides, this is not fiction, this is personal. Read this first page." She handed him the book.

"How can you be sure it's not fiction?"

"Well, I guess I can't, but it reads like a journal to me."

"Could be, where did you say you found them?"

Rebecca showed him the wall and at the same time they both noticed another hole further down the wall with the same trademark stain around it. Robbie grabbed a crowbar and yanked the wall down. Behind it another fifteen books were revealed, all dated in consecutive years from the first ten.

In her hands, Rebecca knew she held a man's life. A life that she had no right in holding, never mind in reading. In that moment, she knew in her heart what to do.

Rebecca plopped her coins into the meter and walked directly into the bright office that held the familiar stern face of Jeffery McCandless's secretary.

"Good morning, Mrs. Reynolds, do you have an appointment this morning."

The woman knew full well that she hadn't, but Rebecca refused to allow the woman frazzle her. "No, Miss Stouter, I haven't an appointment, but I would appreciate just a moment of Mr. McCandless's time, if he is in."

"Have a seat and let me see." The woman said as she picked up the phone.

The door popped open and out jumped Jeffery McCandless rolling his sleeve up instead of down, this time expressing a casual liking toward her instead of his straight business face. "How are you this morning, come in, come in, have a seat, would you like coffee."

"No, thank you." Rebecca placed her bag on the floor beside her chair.

He poured himself a coffee, placing way too much sugar in it, reminding her of Carl.

"Are you alright?" He touched her arm.

"Yes. I'm fine."

"I was asking how the house is coming?"

"Good, It's coming along well."

"Good, did you receive the note and pictures that I sent? George is so excited by your decision to restore it."

"No, not yet, thank you for sending them, I'm sure they'll arrive anytime."

"Well, if they don't, let me know and I'll send more."

"Thank you."

"Is that why you stopped by today?"

"No. Actually, I wanted to bring you these." Rebecca reached down and pulled out a few of the Journals.

"What is this?"

"I found them in the living room wall."

Jeffery lifted a cover and Rebecca could see the shocked look on his face, as shocked as Rebecca was to find them. "Do you have any idea what you have here." He looked at her from across his desk, business face back on.

"Yes, I believe I do, there are more." She lifted the bag up and placed the rest of the journals on the desk.

His poker face dropped, "Rebecca, technically these belong to you. You understand what I'm telling you, do you not."

"Yes, I do." She smiled at him, both staring, both knowing full well that there were millions of dollars sitting on the desk before them. "They belong to Mr. Cavanaugh."

"I don't know what to say, I'm speechless, George will be very grateful Rebecca, Thank you."

"Thank him for me, for the pictures and the house." She got up to leave. "Come on out and see how it's coming sometime, when the weather is nicer we can have a lemonade."

"Ice tea, Rebecca, down here we drink iced tea. Maybe I will, Goodbye and thanks again."

"Goodbye Mr. McCandless."

"Jeffery, my dear, call me Jeffery." He showed her to the door with a wave so long.

Rebecca smiled and waved back. Then crossed the street to hop back into her heap that would carry her back to her rebuilding. Rebuilding of her home. Rebuilding of her life. Rebuilding of her.

❈❈❈

Carl could hear garbled voices, and if he pressed his ear to the door hard enough, he could actually hear the words coming from the irritated man in the other room. The ringing in his ears was gone, and he even had, clear vision for fractions of seconds at a time. Like a camera shutter flashing in his eyes, it was difficult to make out, but it was better than complete blackness. For short spans of time, he would let the images flash against his retina's trying to piece together the events happening around him. Ear to the door and eyes to the window across the room. It was torture knowing the window was right there. A sheet of glass nailed shut. It only required a little force and he could be out. But like them, he knew the crash would have them all in there long before he managed to get both legs out. Running would be a nightmare.

So all he could do was listen for clues and wait. He wondered if Julie were doing the same. Carl saw an image in the forest outside. A movement. Big and brown. Again, it moved behind another tree. More of them, green, moving and hiding. The voice from the other room became louder.

"I told you I wanted him unhurt."

"The girl was hurt already. They took out two of my men, Sir. It was all I could do to keep them alive.

"I didn't expect it to be easy. Why do you think I sent you? You should have gotten rid of the girl and what happened to the Indian?"

"He was shot and fell from the cliff."

"And the body?"

"Gone, Sir."

"In other words, you don't know if he's still alive and now the girl has seen all your faces. Get rid of her."

"Frankly, Sir, you hired me for my experience and judgment. My call was to keep the girl. If you want him to talk, you'll need her."

"Frankly, Captain, if I want him to talk, all I have to do is snap my fingers and the wife is mine."

"Actually, Sir, that would be a mistake. Unless you want a world of shit to come your way, and I mean a world. Chinese, French, German, Russian, Japanese."

"Enough, But what I needed him for, he can't rightly do without vision, now can he."

"I wouldn't know about that, Sir."

"No shit you wouldn't, because you were ordered to bring him here unharmed. End of orders. You weren't asked to think. That's my job."

"But, Sir."

"It's all irrelevant now. Are you a good soldier? Are you willing to die for your country, and our commander-in-chief? I am."

"Of course I am, but what has that to do with."

BLAMB. Carl jumped away from the door. He saw a flash of tan and eyes in the window and then it disappeared. Ear pressed again, "It was a simple yes or no answer."

"Why." Carl heard a garbled voice say, barely audible, through what he realized was the sound of choking up blood.

"There is no better way to ignite unity, then through the aftermath of atrocity. The stages have been set. The only thing left to do, is to smother the smoke."

"Clean the rest of this mess up, Snake."

"Yes, Sir."

Carl heard a door slam and a helicopter take off and fade away. Then, he heard gunfire and yelling, coming from the other side of the cabin. Carl broke the window. Picking up a large shard of the glass, he took up position behind the door, waiting for Snake to come after him next. When the door flung open, Carl shoved hard to fling it back in

Snake's face. Shutter after shutter flicked before him. The image of the door, flashing, becoming distorted by the growing pain. When the door reopened, the brown figure stood still. Carl swung and stabbed the glass toward the image before him. It didn't move. The eyes came into focus, a shutter of a cougar, a shutter of a man. The flash of a cougar. The flash of a man. Carl couldn't stand it. Was he seeing a man or a cougar or was it the hallucination of a dying man. Had he been shot and was now bleeding out? He hadn't felt anything. Whatever it was, it stood there staring at him with large eyes, the largest he'd ever seen.

"Oh my god." Came a voice from behind the figure. "Carl, what have they done to you."

"Randy?" Carl called out, dropping the shard from his bleeding hand.

Carl heard a loud tear and saw the tan figure come forward and wrap his hand tight to stop the bleeding. "You're alright now, we've come to get you." He heard Luke say, as he pressed his hand tight against Carl's to clot the bleeding.

"Careful." Came a voice from across the room. "He can't see."

"Julie, Are you okay." Carl saw a flicker of red; then her face came clearer into view for just a split second, before she hugged him.

She put her hand over his eyes. "The doctor said to keep them bandaged, Carl." She wanted to yell at him. Why! Why, would you do something this stupid? But she already knew why. She wanted to turn back time. To go back and protect him as she had been hired to do. But time couldn't be reversed, and she couldn't change the fact that she had failed him. She wanted to kiss him, and hold him, and tell him that it was all over. But to look at him, was all anyone needed, to know that it was anything but over.

CHAPTER TWENTY-NINE

Rebecca heard a loud banging and turned down the radio to decipher where it was coming from. "Hello" came calling from across the house. Rebecca followed the call, to find an older gentleman standing in the doorway. He appeared to be in his sixties, was distinguished looking, with slightly thinning gray hair, a man who was not plump, yet not thin either. He was; Rebecca thought. Robust and somber looking, with horn-rimmed glasses and wearing casual but obviously upscale clothing. Rebecca was confident that Wal-Mart fell nowhere in his vocabulary, except when reading the stock market page of The Wall Street Journal. He looked clean and crisp, and Rebecca cringed to think of the mess he was stepping into.

"Hello, can I help you?" She asked, uncertain if she could.

"Miss Reynolds." He stated with assurance as he extended his hand to her. "I'm George Cavanaugh."

"OH, Hello Mr. Cavanaugh." Rebecca wiped her hand across her clothes and then met his.

"I wanted to Thank you personally for what you did for me, Thank You."

"No problem." Rebecca smiled.

"NO, seriously." He said to her in a firm tone looking at her intently. "Thank You."

"You're Welcome." She answered.

He handed her an envelope.

Rebecca peeked inside to find many photos.

"I'm afraid they're all black and white but I can describe to you the vividness as best my memory serves."

"Thank You, would you like to come in and have a cup of ice tea or hot tea even."

"Yes, I'd like that."

She led him to the kitchen, grabbed a towel and quickly wiped the seat and table clean before he could sit. "Iced or hot?"

"Iced would be nice, Thank you."

Rebecca took out a Tea-stained white plastic cup and placed inside it, some ice and poured tea from an equally stained plastic pitcher in the refrigerator. She wanted to crawl under a cabinet when she handed it to him. "Sorry, Plastic cups, are all I have right now."

"This is fine." He took the cup.

Rebecca refilled her own and joined him at the table. They pulled out the pictures and discussed how the house looked when he was a child. Then she showed him around and explained what they had planned for the interior of the house. She showed him the place where the journals had been hidden all these years.

"Hidden behind old photos of my grandparents and my mother." George told her, not surprised by his father's choice in hiding places. "They were the only people that he truly loved." He said in a low reflective voice. Then he turned to Rebecca and said, "I thought those holes in the wall were put there by vandals, this place was broken into a time or two, a few years back." He glanced around the room. The roll-top desk and the rolled up rug were both placed to the side of the room. He wandered over toward the desk as he looked at the view out the front window. "I forgot how beautiful the view was from here, and I see that you kept the things left behind."

Rebecca felt guilty. Like she had taken something that didn't belong to her. "You can take them if you like."

"Why, I thought you wanted them?" He questioned her.

"Well I did, but if you would rather keep them. She held her breath slightly, They just - they feel like they belong here and I do love them." She admitted shyly.

The man smiled at her and reached for her shoulder.

Rebecca looked up from the counter to see him smiling at her.

"They do belong here, I hadn't the heart to remove them from the house."

She smiled back, thankful that he didn't want them, she knew the house would feel empty without them in it.

"I'm glad that you bought the house." He said to her, as he reached for his coat. "My father would be happy you're here."

"Thank you, Mr. Cavanaugh."

"George. Please call me George."

"I'll try."

"Thank you Rebecca, for the journals and for the kindness you've shown this old man before you." He patted her hand.

"Please stop by to visit and see the progress my brother and I make on the house and thank you for letting me borrow the photographs."

"You're welcome, maybe I will stop by sometime."

"Good, I hope that you will, goodbye." Rebecca waved as he started down the rambled stairs. "Careful on those stairs, so long." He waved back and in a few moments he was gone, driving steadily down Ripley Road, named for his mother, long ago.

Rebecca went back inside. She noticed he only sipped his drink once or twice, as she dumped it down the drain. She scolded herself for giving him the instant iced tea, instead of making fresh brewed tea. She made a mental note to do so, if he ever came back for another visit. Then she sat with a cup of hot tea and poured over the pictures again. She liked the way the family in the pictures looked so happy together. Sifting through the photos, she found one taken inside the house. Rebecca lift it closer to her face. She knew it. There had been a ship on the mantel. She knew nothing about ships, but she tried to take careful measure of its size and shape as she could best tell from the picture.

"Jingle jingle. Jingle jingle."

"Hello."

"Hello, Miss Reynolds? My name is Larry Jacobson, Mr. Margatelli said he spoke to you about me?"

"Yes, He said that you and possibly a friend of yours might be interested in working for me."

"Yes, Ma'am."

"Great, just in time too, Tomorrow we have a large shipment of drywall arriving. Do you think you could start first thing in the morning, say eight o'clock."

"Yes Ma'am, we could."

"Okay, Great, the job pays twelve an hour and you're expected to do labor, which means help in carrying materials, but my brother will also expect you both to wield a hammer and do anything else he shows you how to do, does that sound okay."

"Yes Ma'am, it does."

"Alright, so then we need to know your hours."

"Well, we finish school at two-fifteen, so we can be there by two-thirty."

"Alright, how about two-thirty to six-thirty, during the week and a full day on Saturday."

"Sounds good."

"Wonderful, we'll see you tomorrow morning then."

"Thank you, Ma'am." He said excitedly and hung up the phone.

Thank you, thought Rebecca, as she too pushed the button to disconnect the call. Across the house, she could hear Robbie's radio blasting. She grabbed the pictures from the gritty surface of the freshly sanded countertops and went to find him.

"ROBBIE, ROBBIE." She caught his attention. "Guess what?"

"What!" Robbie turned down the radio.

"We now have part-time help, they start tomorrow." She said excitedly.

"Great that will help, good timing." He commented.

"And Look, Mr. Cavanaugh, George, she corrected herself, He came by and brought these." She handed him the photos, old ones with George's grandparents in them.

"That was nice, it answers some of the questions we had, doesn't it. Robbie studied some of the images. I wouldn't recommend the original siding, but we can get a newer product that looks just the same. Being right on the water with all the moisture and salt, I'd go with a simulated wood, it'll last longer."

"Okay, Yeah that was nice of him, he seemed very nice too, easy to talk to, but I couldn't believe that I had to hand him a stained plastic cup."

"Rebecca look round you; I doubt that he minded."

Rebecca looked around. They had made good progress on the house; all the walls and ceilings were torn down and new insulation was installed. Tomorrow they would begin putting up new dry wall. She had been assigned the kitchen counters and cabinets, to strip down and sand. She was almost done. Only the fine sanding was left to do. Then she could stain and polyurethane them.

"What would you like for dinner?" She asked her brother.

"I don't care as long as it's homemade, wait - steak and potatoes; that's what I'd like. No tomato sauce and no rice, just plain old, gut thudding, steak and potatoes."

Rebecca agreed. They could both use a good hearty meal. Steak and potatoes sounded perfect to her too.

Carl was miserable. All he could think about was a large grilled steak, a baked potato and a dark green salad. Beside it, a tall glass of frothy beer to wash it all down. He listened to the steak sizzle, as grease dripped from the meat onto the charcoals below. Heat burning his fingers as he ripped the potato open, slapping slabs of butter in it, then he placed a perfect daub of sour cream on top, sprinkling it with diced chives. On top of the dark leaf salad were mounds of croutons and bacon pieces, all smothered in an Italian dressing. Carl felt his taste buds jump to a standing ovation. Then he felt his stomach grumble in anticipation.

"Good Evening, Mr. Heartmeyer. Are you ready for your dinner?"

Carl wanted to get up and run, but the tubes and the wires and the guard at his front door wouldn't let him.

"Just relax, no surprises now, here it comes."

Carl listened to the sound of fluid being sucked down the tube. He hated feeling this pitiful. Unable to move, unable to see and unable to speak. Carl had replaced words for a snapping sign language, in order to speak with his nurse. One snap meant yes, two snaps, no, and three meant that he had to pee. Which happened a lot since he was plugged into a water bottle. Fortunately, a strategically placed plastic urine bottle was all that he needed. Although Carl hadn't entirely escaped the undignified catheter, at least, he hadn't had to shit in a cold steel bowl. In fact, he hadn't had to go at all.

"Good job, we're all done." He heard the smile in her voice. "After a couple more days of healing, the doctors will let you try to drink your nutrition shakes through a straw. Then all you'll have to do is prove to them that your bowels are still working, and they'll let you go home."

Home. He didn't know the meaning anymore.

"Here you go." She put the call button in his hand. "Buzz me, if you need anything, even if you just want to talk."

Was she crazy, he couldn't talk even if he wanted to. He wouldn't doubt it though that she had learned how to hold entire conversations by herself. Even managing to make her patients feel as if they were talking with her. He wished he could see her face. Her voice was kind, and he wagered her face was too.

"Good Evening, Miss Carson, how was your day." She said as Carl heard her play with one of the machines attached to him.

"I'm good, Thank you. How's our patient today." Julie asked.

Carl felt himself become woozy when the nurse wiggled the I.V.

needle in his vein. "Oh, you know, Mr. Heartmeyer, you can't shut him up."

"Ha, ha." Carl wanted to respond, but then he felt her squeeze his hand and he let his frustration release by squeezing back.

"I'll come and change that I.V. later." She patted his hand.

"Hi Carl." She placed her hand in his.

Carl waited for her to say something. They used the same system, except that with Julie, he squeezed her hand instead of snapping.

"Are you feeling better today." One squeeze.

"I'll bet you can't wait to get out of here." Another squeeze.

"They released me tonight, Randy's on his way to come get me. I'll bet you'll be glad to be rid of me." Two squeezes.

"I haven't been told anything or else I would tell you what I know."

"I'm sorry that I failed you, Carl." Two squeezes. "I made a lot of mistakes." Two squeezes. "Yes I did." Two squeezes. "I have to go." Two squeezes. "You take care." One squeeze. "Bye." She kissed the top of his hand.

Where was she going? He wasn't sure he could get through this without her. Carl felt a pang of fear. Fear of being completely alone. This whole thing had been a nightmare, and she was the only thing that had made it bearable. He wanted to scream. "Don't go" "Stay here with me." Or at the very least, "Please, take me with you."

Carl woke to voices in the room next door. Julie's was unmistakable, and the other one was Randy. Where was he? The last he remembered was being in the hospital. The nurse saying how nice the work looked. You couldn't tell he had been in an accident at all, she had told him. The feel of the room around him had been crisp and sterile. The smell of disinfectant was in the air. The cold, smooth feel of the hospital sheets. The rhythmic beep of the dripping I.V. All of this was gone.

Instead, Carl was in a slightly lumpy bed and covered with wool and polyester throws. The air smelt musty and stale. With his eyes still bandaged, Carl reached his foot to the floor, landing hard against the wood surface, the bed being much closer to the floor than the one in the hospital. Carl slowly edged his way, step by step, arms stretched out to guide him, toward the voices doing battle in the other room.

"I quit, Randy, I'm all through with this."

"Give it a day, besides you can't quit. The job isn't done yet."

"Have you looked at him? He's lucky to be alive, no thanks to me."

"I think you're being a little hard on yourself, besides you can't win them all."

"Yes I can. I do, or I did anyway."

"This was a tough one, Julie. You can't leave him, not when he needs you now more than ever."

"Look at me, do I look like I can finish this job, you need to get Tyrone or Bill."

"What he needs is you, Julie. I can get you some help, but who he really wants is you."

"I don't want to get him killed, Randy, I can't do this one right." I couldn't stay cold and distant. She thought. "I should have turned him over to someone else, long ago."

"Maybe you were a little closer than you should have been, but that wasn't a bad thing, you did your job well. You were up against a force, not an individual."

"Why does he need me now more than ever."

"Because the missions changed, it's become a cleanup job."

"For who, us or them."

"For everyone, it's turned into a mad race, and Davis is nowhere to be found."

Too close or not, she was in it to the end. "Get me Tyrone and I'll stay."

"That's a deal, stay on your good toes and let the others heal." Randy handed her a case. "I'll be back with reinforcement."

Julie opened her case, inside the sleek box was a black GLOCK 17, with a silencer and beside it was a modified M-4 rifle with silencer/flash suppressor. To one side of this, laid a laser sight and a night-vision scope. She was grateful now for the investment. Two boxes of ammunition were mounted to one corner. Julie picked up the pistol, inspected it and put it back down. She heard a bump behind her. As a reflex, she picked up the weapon and swung around to face the noise. With the gun pointed toward Carl, she knew she had been clumsy and slow. If it had been a real enemy, they both would be dead. The memory of the bullet slammed into her chest. Julie reached to rub out the memory and instead was met with the large stone. She placed her trusty friend back in the box and shut it.

"Carl, stand still and I'll help you to a chair."

"That's alright I can manage on my own." He stepped forward, almost falling when he banged into a coffee table.

"Don't be stubborn, let me help you." She reached out to grab his arm.

Carl pulled it away from her. "NO THANKS." He reached toward his eyes to pull off the bandages.

"NO, Carl, The doctor said not for at least another week."

Carl tugged on the bandages, disregarding her words. Then thought better of it. "What's wrong with them."

"Nothing too serious. The blows you received weakened the muscles, but the doctor is confident that if your eyes are allowed to rest and heal, that they'll recuperate and return to normal, but that hinges on no more strain." She took his arm again, this time he let her guide him.

Carl sat back in the recliner. "Where are we, Carl rubbed his chest, and why the hell does my chest hurt so damn bad."

Julie wasn't there when Carl was released, but she bet that he was released via the morgue. "Heartmeyer was probably killed."

"What are you talking about, Julie, there is no Heartmeyer, I was Heartmeyer."

"Not anymore. That pain you feel is probably from a defibrillator."

"What!" "Are you talking about those electrical pads that shock the heart."

Julie shook her head in the affirmative, though she knew he couldn't see her.

"They could have killed me."

"They did kill you, Carl, the defibrillator brought you back."

Julie stood watching Carl. He sat there, silent. He hadn't asked why, hadn't protested in anger, he hadn't reacted at all. A few minutes earlier he had been so angry, but now she couldn't detect a single emotion. She wondered if he had heard her and Randy's discussion. She had wanted to run away from Carl, to escape and evade her feelings for him and her guilt. She knew Randy was right she couldn't just leave. Leaving would change nothing. Trying to leave was wrong and she knew that trying to explain to Carl, why she needed to leave, would be impossible. At least, not without telling him that she loved him.

She had broken all her own rules. Especially, the most important one, the one that all others hinged from; professional distance. It required a detachment from herself and most important was the detachment from her client. No personal details and no long in-depth conversations shared sipping wine by firelight. It required concentration and discipline, both of which eluded her within fifty feet of Carl. The requisite indifference toward her client, which allowed her to keep her focus on everything going on around him. Instead, Julie found her focus on Carl. Her concentration broken by consuming thought after thought. Fine detail that should have been paid to sights and sounds had been replaced by obsession over details unknown; details about Carl's life, his family, Rebecca. Julie had broken every rule she had ever set for herself, and as a result, she almost got Carl, and herself killed. Julie hadn't been overreacting this morning with Randy, quite the contrary. She had been reacting. Reacting to her negligence and giving Carl a chance she had almost deprived him of. Julie wouldn't apologize for anything she said this morning, why should she, his feelings were irrelevant, it was his life that mattered.

CHAPTER THIRTY

Rebecca squinted and covered her eyes. She turned her body away from the window, only to have the realization shock her system, like an unexpected clap of thunder, that the day was well underway. Wow, she must be tired, just as the sound of thunder is a delayed reaction to a lightning strike. Rebecca's thoughts were the same to the sunlight. The sun, she couldn't believe it. She couldn't remember the last time she slept so long.

She sat up to find all the pictures George had brought her scattered across the bed. She picked them all up and placed them back in the envelope. Rebecca had slept; for one whole night, she had had no dreams, not a single one. No dreams of the cougar, no dreams of Carl and no dreams of far off remote places, places like mountains and forests and skies that go on forever. Rebecca was starting to wonder if her dreams were visions of heaven.

She looked at the clock on the floor to find it was ten. "Damn it." She said out loud. Ten o'clock, the two boys were supposed to be there at eight am. What kind of boss isn't there to greet their hired help on the first day, she scolded herself. She grabbed Carl's sweats and jacket from the floor and quickly pulled them on.

In the bathroom, she could hear people's voices outside. They had arrived anyway. She could be grateful for that. She pulled off her clothes and reached for the knob to turn the hot water on. Hooking her sweats on the wall, she turned toward the window to grab a washcloth off the rack, only to remember too late, that the window was wide open. There were no window treatments to obscure her or their view. Rebecca ducked.

Everyone was in the backyard, Robbie, the boys and the truck

373

driver of the flat bed, delivering the drywall. Rebecca knocked the sweats down to the floor and scrambled to get them on. She knew two things for sure; today she was going without a shower and tonight she was shopping for a blind. Rebecca dressed and then went back to the bathroom to wash her face and brush her teeth. She pulled her hair back into a ponytail. Looked into the mirror and convinced herself that she could do this. Then she went outside to greet her new help.

With a coffee cup in one hand, she hit Robbie with the other.

"Hey, what was that for." Robbie rubbed his arm.

"For not waking me up this morning."

"Well, I figured you could use the sleep."

"I could, but still." She had to admit she felt well rested for once, but she would have preferred to avoid that embarrassing moment. Maybe no one noticed her in the window. She shook the boys' hands, introducing herself. "Sorry I wasn't awake when you arrived."

"No big deal." Larry said, speaking for them both.

The truck driver handed Rebecca her copy of the delivery form. "Don't worry about giving me a tip, the view will suffice."

"Thanks." Rebecca folded her arms in front of her, spilling a little of her coffee, "But you weren't getting one."

He snapped his fingers, tilting his head at the same time, "I guess it was just my lucky day then." He climbed up into his truck, "Let me know if you need anything else, perhaps we can arrange a discount."

Robbie was laughing, and so was Larry, but Ryan was confused, "What did I miss?"

"Ha. Ha." Rebecca replied back to the driver. "Thanks for the load." She waved as he started up the truck and headed out of Ripley Road. She only regretted that he would be back, often. It was the best materials yard in the area.

"Ryan. Stop staring at me, wondering what you missed. I'm old enough to be your Mother."

"No you're not." Ryan answered.

"Well, I should be." Rebecca replied. "Careful carrying that up the stairs."

They had finished carrying in the last of the drywall. The living room was filled with stacks of the chalky white board. Rebecca closed the door behind them to block out the cold. It was starting to get nicer, but there was still a bite to the air. Rebecca grabbed a roll of plastic sheeting and a staple gun. Stapling it to a beam between the kitchen and living room. She was ready to start staining, but feared the white dust would stick to everything. Jingle, jingle.

"Hello."

"Hi Mom."

"Rachel! Hi, how are you? Wait, isn't today Saturday?'"

"Yeah, it is, but we were given two weekends off instead of a week for Easter break."

"That's right, so this is your second weekend then?"

"Yes."

"Did you guys get my package?"

"Yes, we did, thanks." Rachel sat silently on her end.

"What's wrong Rachel?" Rebecca was sure there was something. Silence... "Nothing." The thirteen-year old answered.

"Come on Rachel. I can tell that something's the matter."

"It's Tommy, He's not talking to me anymore."

"Why, Hon?"

"He says that every time he talks to me and David hears nothing from you, it makes him sad and Tommy doesn't want David to be sad."

"Oh, Honey, that isn't logical. You're kids, we're grown, there's a difference."

"How so, Mom?"

"Well, there just is." Rebecca had done it. She had given her daughter a bullshit answer, something she said she would never do. "Rachel, maybe there is no difference, but David knows that I'm working things out for myself right now. Maybe I am avoiding him. I'll call him." She gave in.

"Thanks Mom and thanks for the things."

"Rachel, wait."

"Yes Mom?"

"The pictures, did you get them?"

"Yeah, they're a little scary Mom, but I'm sure the place will come out great."

"Are they? Did all of you look at the wallpaper swatches? Uncle Robbie's working on the drywall now and I thought I could put it up before you guys get here. Or I can wait if you want to help me in June."

"Either way is okay, I liked the blue and Karen liked the yellow, so you can pick. Danny liked the sailboats. I have to go Mom, I've got to call Tommy. Remember you said you'd call David. Bye."

Rebecca heard a click, and wondered if she hadn't been set-up by two kids. It didn't matter. She was cornered now. Rebecca reached into her purse and pulled out the number. Ring...ring... ring, Maybe she'd get lucky and he'd be out working.

"Hello."

It was Anne, "Hello Anne, it's Rebecca."

"Rebecca!" She squealed.

Rebecca could hear Frank yelling in the background "Rebecca, how are you sweetheart, and how's that leg of yours doing."

"Tell Frank I'm fine, and my leg is all healed."

"Good, Good. Well I'm sorry to say that you missed David. He just left to get some supplies. What's your number dear, I'll tell him that you called."

Rebecca rattled off the number and said goodbye to Anne and Frank, finding out first how their house was coming along.

After hanging up, Rebecca exhaled, she was almost glad he wasn't home. She had no idea what she would have said to him, if he were. But then she was also sort of sad not to hear his comforting voice. Rebecca put on rubber gloves, opened the large can of stain and was smacked in the face with fumes. Then she went to the backdoor on the other side of the kitchen and opened it to let in, fresh air. Turning on her radio, Rebecca prepared to spend the rest of her day finishing her kitchen.

Rebecca heard a knock and was surprised to find someone standing in her back doorway. "Mr. Cavanaugh, George." She corrected herself, "Hi, she leaned out the door and looked at the stairs, "Did you come up those?" He smiled at her. "You shouldn't have, they're too dangerous."

"I saw a hibachi out there." He said in the manner of a defiant child.

"Yeah, well; I don't mind taking my own life in my hands. It's just other people's lives that I have a problem with."

"Why is that?"

"That's a long story."

"I don't mind, I have plenty of time." He told her as he took a seat.

"Maybe another day." answered Rebecca. He stood up. "I don't mean for you to leave, just that it's a complicated story."

"Aren't all long stories?" George relied.

"Yes, I suppose they are." She answered.

"I brought you something, actually it belongs with the desk. My father's chair, I had it fixed years ago, and never brought it back. I remembered it yesterday."

"Really, Thank you."

George went to the back door as if to get it. She hated to think of him determinedly carrying the thing up those stairs. "I can have one of the boys bring it up."

They both stepped out onto the landing, and she swore that it swayed.

"I see what you mean." George held onto the railing. "Young man, would you be kind enough to bring up the chair from my truck bed?"

"Yes, Sir."

"Thank you, Ryan." Rebecca yelled down.

"Thank you." George called on top of hers.

Ryan brought it to the living room and placed it with the desk.

"It's beautiful George, Thank you." Rebecca said as she touched it's wonderfully worn surfaces from years of use.

"I don't believe the two were designed to be a set, but they do look nice together." He commented.

"Yes they do, thank you." Rebecca smiled.

"You're welcome." He smiled at her. "I can see everyone is busy." He was afraid he would be in the way.

"Yes." She didn't want him to leave yet. "Would you like something to drink in the kitchen."

"Yes, I would, Thank you." He smiled just a little wider.

Rebecca's smile matched his. Entering the kitchen was rather a shock, the plastic kept more than dust out of the kitchen it also blocked the warmth. "It's pretty cold in here would you rather have a hot tea today."

"That would be great."

Rebecca placed a kettle on the stove and continued with her work. "So, how long have you lived here?" She knew nothing else to ask him.

"Here in this house? Only until I was nine. Here in Edgewater, I've lived my entire life. How about you Rebecca, where have you lived?"

"I grew up in Connecticut, but my husband was in the military, So we've moved around quite a bit."

"You haven't done that very much, have you?" George questioned.

Rebecca was confused.

George pointed to the woodwork. "Let me have one of those cloths."

"No, you're not dressed for this." She reprimanded him.

George reached down and snatched her cloth, dabbing it to his leg before she could snatch it back. "Now I am."

"You're crazy." She laughed.

He joined her, amused by her incredulous expression. "Scoot over, so I can teach you how to do this."

They both sat on the kitchen floor staining cabinets the rest of the afternoon. Each sharing what information they felt comfortable in sharing with the other.

He told her about moving out of this house when he was nine. He went live with his Aunt Eleanor, shortly after his mother had passed away. He lived there until he left for college. Then went to Duke, where he studied business, graduated and returned home. He explained how he created a company that designed and built obscure inventions. Adding that he retired a few years back, selling his company to another local corporation located here in Wilmington.

She told him of the things she had done and the places she had lived.

"I notice that there is a wedding band on your hand? Where is your husband stationed now?" George asked but was met with silence.

"Well, that is my long story." Rebecca kept her eyes on her task before her.

"Alright, How did you come to find this town and choose this house?" He asked her instead.

"Now that's an interesting story." Rebecca said excited to tell it. "I was in Rhode Island."

"Rhode Island? What were you doing in Rhode Island?" George was baffled.

"Well, I had driven there from Vermont." She explained.

"Vermont? Why were you in Vermont?" He asked, flat out confused.

"That was where I left my kids?" Rebecca answered.

"You have kids? And you left them?" He exclaimed, completely flabbergasted.

"Yes George, I have three kids, they're with my mother-in-law, who lives in Vermont." She stopped him before he could ask another question. "Let me tell my story."

"I'm sorry."

"As I told you, We lived in Tennessee. My mother-in-law offered to watch the children, while I took some time for myself and figured out where I wanted to finally, settle us down. But I couldn't decide. I went to Rhode Island to try it out, but it was so cold and it just felt wrong. Maybe because we had lived in Tennessee for so long. I don't know why. But while there, I went to the pier to go fishing with Philip, there was an art gallery there, where I saw a painting in a window. It was one of your Dad's paintings. The art dealer convinced me to come in and see some others, but the one in the window had a quality that the others didn't. But to me it painted a world that I thought I might belong in. The woman told me the painter had come from North Carolina. It seemed, as good a place as any, to start looking next. I drove down, and I ended up here. Talked to Jeffery McCandless about the house, which I had no idea was your Father's, until after I had made an offer on it and you accepted."

George was quiet. "What a freaky coincidence that I landed exactly here, huh. It sounds crazy, doesn't it George."

"I don't know Rebecca, Maybe not. Which painting was it?"

"The Dolphins." Rebecca answered.

George found it ironic that his father's final painting, the only painting that the man ever created, representing himself, was the one that Rebecca saw. The one that he almost decided not to place on Gallery. It has been six years, since that man had left him for good, six years that this house has stood vacant and alone. Seven offers were made on this house; the first six wanted to tear it down. Only Rebecca wanted to restore it back to life. Three children, he thought, he wanted to see this house become a home. Something it never had been for him.

George looked at her confused.

She came a long way to land here by coincidence. He wasn't sure if he even believed in coincidences, but he knew one thing. "I have to go." He told her.

"Did I say something wrong, George." Rebecca ran out the door after him.

"No, Sweetheart. It's late. I need to go home and get cleaned up." He opened his truck door.

"Okay, thanks for all your help." Rebecca checked her watch and waved goodbye toward the quickly retreating vehicle. George had his hand out the window waving and was gone as quickly as he had come.

❈❈❈

He picked up his cell phone and hit the speed dial.

"Hello." Barked the woman's stern voice.

George winced, pulling the phone away from his ear. "Put me through to Jeffery, please."

"Certainly, Mr. Cavanaugh."

"George, How are you?" Jeffery asked puzzled.

"Good, I need you to do something." George spoke quickly.

"Sure, Whatever you need." Jeffery was truly intrigued.

"Find me "The Dolphins" and get it back." George demanded.

"Where do you suppose I start looking?"

"Rhode Island." George answered.

"What part, George."

"For god's sake Jeffery, it's the smallest state in the country, it shouldn't be that hard."

"Okay."

"Wait, she said on a pier. That should narrow it for you."

"What, Huh, Who?" Jeffery missed something.

"Thanks." Click.

Carl was bored. He hadn't slept this much since he was in his cell. He wasn't sure if it was his body recovering that made him so lethargic or the complete silence that was boring him to death. Randy had done as he promised and within twenty-four hours Tyrone had come knocking down their door. Ever since, all Carl had smelt was the rank odor of spent carbon and cleaning fluid. He still didn't know where they were. Though it didn't matter, one safe house was probably the same as the next. Carl presumed there were others standing guard in the perimeter because periodically Tyrone's phone would ring and the occasional word would be spoken. By the sound of his voice and the weight of his walk, Carl assumed the man was enormous. He was baffled by the lack of words spoken between the large man and Julie. But no matter how curious he was, he wouldn't ask why.

He was still hurt by Julie's adamant decision to leave. As if everything they had been through together had meant nothing to her, and she could drop it all, him included, with less concern then dropping off her suits at the cleaners. Well, if she could be so cold and distant, then he could too.

Julie felt the rocks stoning her from both directions. She understood both of their anger, each of them mad at her for opposite reasons. She couldn't pretend that she hadn't screwed up. If she dared to look at Carl, he could see it in her eyes. It was the worst of betrayals to comrades in arms. He was quiet and distant. Surveying his odds. Trying to determine where he stood in a battle. She didn't blame him his reproach. It was well deserved. She broke the oath and allegiance, to defend above all else, her brother. She knew he was right. She was torn, if it came down to choosing between them, would she save Tyrone over Carl? Even she didn't know the answer to that one.

Julie could tell that Carl was getting restless. Pretty soon his agitation would exceed that of his anger and he would demand to know what their plan was. He would want to remove his bandages and hope to see again. They had been blessed so far with his recovery needs, causing him to sleep for days on end. But soon that would fade and with it would come a renewed energy for knowledge and a new determination to force a checkmate. What Carl didn't know was that our side had lost their queen, and it was General Davis' move. Only the General had EmNu-ed his golden stars with a subdued black paint, concealing himself. He was hiding somewhere; lurking in the darkness and waiting. The man had essentially disappeared, and they had no choice, but to wait for him to peak out from behind cover. She feared his next move, may be so stealth-full that they risked missing it, if they so much as stopped for a latrine break.

Julie was beginning to feel restless herself. "Did Randy say when he'd call." She asked the large man staring out the window.

"No, he just handed me the phone and said to dial *911 if there were a problem."

She clicked the last of the parts in place, and finished wiping off the GLOCK. Then she slid the magazine cartridge back into the stock, chambered a round and flipped the safety on. Holstering the gun, she announced that she would be right back. Stepping into the bathroom. Julie took a second to glance in the mirror, she was right, she was ready to retire. Ready to do it now, while she was still young enough to have a baby or two and still be able to play with her grandkids when they came along. Julie barely peed and then rinsed her hands before she joined the others, leaving the flush for next time around.

Swinging the door open, Julie caught sight of a glimmer. Her well rehearsed memory registered quickly, and her reflexes reacted. Instantly, her gun was in her hand, and the trigger had released with a loud bang. Before she fully understood what had happened, Julie saw Tyrone falling to the floor. With unrealized speed, she was fast assessing Carl's condition, wondering with horror what she had done. Instinct and training had failed her. She had shot Tyrone, her friend and her colleague. Behind the chair was the large man bleeding.

In his hand, was a knife, the glimmer was an all too real reality. Not merely a figment from another time, "Why."

"Money," he said. "He's marked for a wash out, Julie, if not me, then it would just be someone else." He choked on his next syllable. "I'm sorry."

"Me too." Both the hurt and scorn could be heard in her voice. Money had spoken louder than friendship. Julie could not conceive the thought. What was happening to her world?

"You're still a great shot." was the last thing she heard.

Julie could hear men's feet pounding the ground outside. Shit, she had forgotten to put the silencer back on after cleaning it. The result, an invitation to battle. "Oh god, Carl, they're coming." She turned to find Carl had pulled off the bandages completely. "No, Carl, No."

"It's okay, I can see fine."

She hoped that he could, but that wasn't the only problem. Ten men were about to come charging through that door. Julie fumbled through the dead man's pockets, searching one and then another, until she found it. Grabbing the phone, she yelled as she dialed *911. "Hide your face, Carl, hide your face, NOW." "DO IT, DO IT, NOW."

The door crashed open.

"STOP where you are, don't come an inch closer and put your weapons down."

With his tee shirt over his head, Carl had found Julie's M-4, had loaded the magazine and he too was pointing a weapon toward the men at the door. Clear vision or not, he knew the M-4, with the flick of a switch he had the safety off, with the flick of another, he had it set at automatic.

Someone was yelling through the phone. "What is it, what's wrong."

"I've killed Tyrone. I don't know if we're going to make it. I've killed Tyrone."

CHAPTER THIRTY-ONE

Pleased with herself, Rebecca stood in front of the mantle, admiring her latest find. Holding a photo, she compared the two. Rebecca was amazed at how similar the ship on the mantle and the ship in the picture appeared.

"Hi Robbie, What do you think?" She handed him the photograph.

"Yeah, pretty good, Where did you find it?"

"At a salvage barn, when I was looking for a bureau to go in the new bathroom."

"How much did they rob you, for it?

"What!" She said offended. Robbie stood there unflinching. "I paid fifteen."

"Hundred or dollars?" Robbie disliked her vagueness.

"Thousand. Dollars Robbie, what do you think." She wanted to laugh when he started to clutch his chest.

"Not bad. He choked out, How is the hunting going?"

"Not very good."

"Well, you can scratch the tub off your list, A guy at the materials yard told me of a house being torn down, but the only decent piece was the tub."

"Great, it's the most important piece anyway."

Robbie handed her the picture. "By the way the kitchen looks great."

"Thanks, What's next on my list."

"To help me finish up the walls and ceilings. so I can move on to the floors. But not tonight, I have a date." He smiled like a dog that stole a dinner roll when no one was looking.

"Oh Yeah, Who with?"

"Lily."

"Who's Lily?"

"You know her. The pretty girl, who works the register at the Chinese restaurant."

"Where are you taking her?"

"Actually, she asked me to go to a local nightclub."

"Really, Have a great time." She really hoped he did.

"Thanks, Rebecca. Feeling unsure if he should ask. "What happened to your new friend?"

"You mean George, I don't know. I think I might have said something wrong, offended him somehow." It wouldn't be the first time she lost a friend that way. She shook her head to Robbie, who then headed off to shower and change.

Rebecca struggled to lift her two new Adirondack chairs out of the back of her pickup.

"Here, let me help you with those." Larry lifted one end.

"Thank you, Larry. You're here late, it's what, seven already."

"Well, it's Friday."

"What does that mean? Shouldn't you be going out tonight?"

"I don't know, do you have a date tonight?" He asked.

"You're carrying my date." They placed it down and went to get the other.

"Can I stay and help?"

"If you'd like to. Why, did you and your girlfriend breakup?"

"We're fighting."

Right when they plopped the second chair on the ground. A horn came blasting from the back of the house. "Come on Larry, We're going to be late." A shout carried toward them.

Larry looked at Rebecca.

"Get a move on Kido, she's a'waitin'. See you tomorrow, Larry, Thanks for your help."

"I thought you were mad at me?" She heard Larry shout back.

"I was, now hurry up?" Allie called back. "Hi, Mrs. Reynolds."

"Hi Allie. You guys, drive careful out there."

"We will." She heard echo as they both pulled away.

Rebecca tried out her new chair. Plopped right down into it, flipped off her shoes and let her toes play in the sand. She felt the urge for a tea. Upon pouring a glass, she decided a spiked one might be even better. She returned to her chair with a blanket, library books and her iced tea. Finding no place to put her tea, Rebecca made a note to herself to cut a hole in the arm for a cup holder. But not tonight, tonight she was going to relax and enjoy herself. Good books, good drink, a good clear evening with a great sunset on the far horizon. What more could she ask for?

Rebecca glanced at the chair next to her. Don't go there, Rebecca. Don't go there - She told herself again. She tried not to, but the empty seat next her spoke louder than her own will. Could she ask for anything else? She knew that answer already. Her children for one, she missed them, but she knew they'd be home again soon. She glanced at the chair again, the one for Carl, her partner, her friend. Rebecca spoke to the sky above. "Have I asked for anything lately?" She questioned aloud, but she didn't dare speak the words.

❈❈❈

***He listened to her words. And wondered, what her next words would have been, if she had spoken them. He knew she could only be speaking to God as she sat there staring at the darkening sky around her. He looked at the sky too. Darkness approaching, he reached into his bag and pulled out his pair of night-vision goggles (NVG's) and waited. She sat there fragile and exposed. And for the first time in weeks, alone. She had no idea there were people, people like him, lurking and watching. Waiting to pounce if the moment were right. He feared tonight would be right.

They needed to find the General and end this whole mess. His whereabouts being unknown made her a viable target. Her being the only globally known link to the entire incident gave her intrinsic political value she knew nothing about. He didn't understand why Randy was so determined to keep Carl alive. Such sacrifices were standard protocol in their business. But it mattered not to him, because he too, was not going to allow Rebecca to be sacrificed for some political bullshit cause.

Unfortunately, it hadn't taken the General long to learn of the rescue. He and his dwindling men had been diligently searching for Carl ever since. He feared they were becoming desperate.

He felt a vibration and reached to answer it. "Yes."

"Our fears have been confirmed."

"Shit."

"We're assembling a crew to extract the package as we speak."

"Roger, Sir, Do you want me to ditto that here, Sir?"

"No, sit tight, but vigilant."

"Are you sure, Sir. It can be done clean and efficient, with no tell tale signs, except a bad headache."

"I know you're good son. That's why you're there. But let's try to keep that world as undisturbed as possible. Keep that option as a last resort."

"Yes Sir, Roger that. The Chinese have surfaced, Sir. They sicced Ling Chu on the brother. I believe only as a means to get closer. I can do that easy, Sir."

"You have your orders, over."

"Yes Sir, Out."

His orders. His orders were killing him. Watching her for months without being able to talk to her. Without being able to play with her how he used to. Standing so close to her that he could smell her subtle scent, and feel the warm energy she emitted. Intoxicating him as she stared him down.

He watched her through the glasses. She was exhausted. He watched as she sat there wrapped in a blanket, her head bobbing as she dozed every few minutes, while trying to read the words off the open book in her lap. He drank the last of his coffee, as he watched her body finally give up. He marveled at her tenacity and dedication. Working every minute of her day on fixing this house, as if its completion would make her world whole again. He wondered what was going on in that mind of hers.

Orders or no orders, he wouldn't leave her in a hard wooden chair freezing cold.

She woke to find that she was in her bed, only she last remembered being outside. She picked her book up off the bed to find it open to the last page she remembered reading. Her half drank tea sat on the floor beside the bed. She wanted to remember something, a dream perhaps, that she might have had. But she couldn't think what. A hazy memory swirled in her mind, a face and a voice, both familiar. Robbie's maybe. She couldn't place it. It was so dark, complete darkness and stars. She vaguely remembered stars. She remembered feeling tired, very tired. She could say that, whatever it was, a dream or a fantasy. She knew it felt safe.

Rebecca went outside to find the sun rising over the ocean. She heard a splash. Out in the water was the family of dolphins. The morning sky promised to be a beautiful day. Rebecca felt a chill breeze rush at her. She loved it here, but she knew she still needed to adjust to the openness. She couldn't shake the feeling of eyes watching her. With the wide ocean before her and the beach all around, she studied her surroundings. Rebecca noticed for the first time, there were no trees, no fences, no hedges or anything else she was used to having around her. She convinced herself that was the reason for her feeling naked.

Rebecca feeling energized, went to the kitchen, and dug out everything needed for a big breakfast and got started creating the fuel all the new men in her life needed. She flipped on the radio, flipped all the pancakes and then scanned the calendar hanging next to the phone. In two weeks, her household goods would arrive. They needed the floors done by then.

"Hey," He grunted, hello. "What are you looking at?" Robbie asked as he poured himself a coffee.

"Good morning, I'm checking out our schedule." She commented.

"No problem there, we're right on." He yawned stretching his arms above his head.

"Good, How did you're date go last night?"

"Good, I invited her over later, I hope you don't mind."

"No, Just for a visit or for dinner?"

"Dinner, If that's okay?"

"That's fine, It'll be nice to talk to a girl for a change." She answered to be polite, unsure how true her statement was, She preferred being around men, it was less complicating.

"Breakfast smells good." Robbie picked up a piece of bacon.

"The boys will be here any minute, I'm going to grab a shower, help yourselves."

Rebecca finished priming all the upstairs walls and sneaked through the noise and dust created by the two electric floor sanders, and the industrial vacuum, being used to finish the down stairs floors. Carrying her pail, she felt guilty leaving the others to the mess inside, as she stepped out into the bright sunshine to prime her chairs. Remembering the holes she wanted to cut, Rebecca returned with a jig saw and an extension cord. After finishing one, she stepped back to gauge the finished cut. Good enough, a little sanding would smooth the edge.

"What is the hole for?" She heard come from a voice behind her.

"I'm making a cup holder." She turned, tilting her head up high enough to see past the brim of the Stetson, to find Jeffery and a woman standing there. "Jeffery! How nice you made it out." He introduced her to his wife.

"We brought you a house warming gift." Amy handed it to her.

"How kind of you, Thank you."

Rebecca brought them inside to introduce them to her brother and the boys and then showed them around. Finishing the tour with the one completed room, the kitchen. She made it look as close to her kitchen in Tennessee as she could. Hoping it would help her and the kid's feel more at home. But she knew the rest of the house would be different.

"It's very pretty, Rebecca."

"Thank you." She offered them something to drink and then opened her gift.

"George always drinks it by the jug when we visit." She smiled at Rebecca.

"Thank you." She returned the smile. They had brought her an Ice tea set, with a recipe and ingredients.

"He just adores you, Rebecca." She told her.

"I couldn't believe my ears when he said that he'd been out to see you a couple of times. He hasn't left the house since he retired." Jeffery explained.

"It's like he'd become his father." Amy added.

"We can't tell you how happy we are to see this change in him." Jeffery commented.

Rebecca hated to disappoint them, "I really like George, but he hasn't been out to visit in over two weeks. I think I offended him somehow. I have a special knack for hurting people's feelings, it's not intentional."

"Don't be silly Rebecca. It isn't possible to offend George, his skin is thicker than a gator's." Jeffery exaggerated. "I'm sure he'll be out to visit sometime soon."

"Well, we'll let you get back to your work." Amy suggested movement to her husband by tugging his arm.

"I know it's short notice, but my brother has invited a friend to dinner tonight. Would you like to join us?"

Jeffery looked at the boss.

"We'd love to." Amy smiled. "What time."

"Six o'clock okay."

"Perfect." They both answered.

"Maybe you could convince George to come too."

"Or, I could give you his phone number, and you could call him." Jeffery replied.

"That would work." Rebecca gave him a pen and paper.

"See you tonight." She waved.

Rebecca was about to push her cell phone's "on" button when she heard it "Jingle, Jingle" in her hand. "Hello."

"Hello Rebecca."

"David! How are you."

"I'm good, how are you."

"Good."

Silence

"So, my mother said that you called?"

"Yes, I did." Rebecca felt a jolt of guilt.

"Why didn't you call back?"

She could ask why he hadn't called her sooner, but she knew she would be in the wrong. "I'm sorry, I should have."

"That's okay, Tommy confessed that He and Rachel guilt tripped you into calling."

"No, Well. Maybe a little." She had to admit.

"So how is your house project going?"

"You have to see it David, It's old, a fixer upper, but the view is incredible."

"I'm sure the house will be too."

"I hope so - it's getting there."

"So how are you holding up, Rebecca?" David asked softly.

"Me?" Rebecca didn't know how to answer that, she hadn't stopped working long enough to think about anything, never mind, ask herself how she is. "I'm okay."

"That's not really an answer Rebecca."

"It's not?" Maybe it wasn't, it was an easy answer. A; don't ask me because I don't know that answer, type of response. "I guess I don't know, David. I'm still working on it. How are you doing?"

"I'm throwing myself into work too. I know that I miss you and the kids. Every time that a calf or a colt was birthed. I so badly wanted you guys to see it. Every day, I hoped you would show up at my door."

David said nothing else. There was silence.

"I'm sorry."

"Don't apologize Rebecca. There is nothing for you to apologize for. My feelings don't need a response. I just wanted you to know I guess."

"Did I tell you that I have a family of dolphins that visit me."

"No, do you really?"

"Yup, I do. Some days they just swim by, but other days they stay and play in the water, jumping and splashing. Pretty neat huh."

"Yeah, pretty neat."

"You'll have to come see them, sometime."

"Maybe I will, well I have to get back to work now."

"Yeah, so do I."

"See you later Rebecca, I love you."

Rebecca's brain twirled, like a tornado and her heart imploded. She heard a buzz on the other end of the phone. David hadn't waited for her response, whether she would have responded back to him in the like, or maybe he knew she wouldn't have. "Good bye." Came out of her mouth too late, dazed, she pushed the button.

Looking down at the paper in her hand she waited a moment to gather her wits before she dialed George's number.

"Jingle, Jingle." "Oh God, She hoped it wasn't David calling back for her response. Even now, she didn't know what to say. "Hello."

"Hello Rebecca, how are you?"

"Hi George." She answered relieved.

"Hi, Are you alright?"

"Yes, I'm fine."

"I was wondering if today were a good day for me to visit."

"Yes, you don't have to call and ask, everyday is fine. Actually I was just going to call you."

"You were?"

"Yes, we're having a few people over for dinner and I wanted to know if you'd join us."

"That would be nice, what time?"

"Dinner is at six, but you can come by anytime you like."

"Thank you, I'll see you shortly, then. Goodbye."

"Bye."

"Hello." George entered the house to find it empty. "Hello." He called out again. He could see they had been busy. The living room walls and ceilings were all new and freshly painted. The floors were all sanded down and ready to be stained and shellacked. The desk and chair were removed from the room and the rug was missing too. The only thing in the room was sitting on the mantle. George picked it up to inspect it closer.

"Hi George."

She smiled at him, standing there in a dress and sandals. No longer the girl he knew covered in stain, paint and dust. She was pretty, he knew, but never really noticed before today. With her hair down and the cowboy hat removed, George stood shocked by the difference. But more shocked still by the likeness.

"Everything okay?"

"Yes, fine." He stood looking at the ship.

"Isn't it great, I took the picture with me, I think it's pretty close."

"It's exact." He corrected her.

"What? Really? Are you sure?" She couldn't believe it.

"You see this." George pointed to the name on the stern. "This is my grandmother's name shortened; Sarah Eleanor Cavanaugh. This is a replica of my grandfather's fishing vessel named "Sara Ella." "When I was little this was on my grandmother's mantle and I remember on stormy nights she would give me cookies and milk and she would rock me as she stared at this ship. I know that she was praying for his safe return." George stared at the ship. "God, my father hated the real one. He feared the ocean something terrible."

"You should keep it."

"No, it belongs right here." George placed it back on the mantle. "I can't believe you found it." He turned to look at her. But then he couldn't believe how much she reminded him of Isadora either.

"I can't either."

"You look very lovely today."

"Thank you." She smiled. She liked feeling feminine, something she hadn't felt in quite a while. "Want to help in the kitchen."

"Sure, I'm a whiz, just tell me what you want."

"On the menu is grilled steak and shrimp, garden salad, potato salad, and pasta salad. The last two are already done. Robbie was going to help with the shrimp, but he's running behind schedule. Do you know how to make it, because I don't? I wouldn't know where to start."

"Leave the rest of dinner to me." George ushered her to a stool. Then went to the refrigerator and pulled out a bottle of wine that he had placed there when he arrived. He asked where the glasses were and was surprised to find actual china in the cabinets. "I have missed a lot - haven't I."

"You have, I actually broke down and went shopping."

"I see that, and very decorative they are too." He held up the pottery plates with mosaic patterns on them. Then took down two glasses that matched the pottery. Pouring one for each of them.

"Do you like them?"

"Actually, I do." He found himself intrigued by them, as he is by her.

Robbie entered the kitchen. Clean, with wet hair and wearing freshly ironed clothes. "Hey, George," He shook the man's hand, "Great to see you."

"Like- wise." George returned.

Robbie asked if there were anything he could do before he picked up lily. The only thing she needed was a makeshift table to eat at tonight. Robbie set up a couple of sawhorses and placed a sheet of heavy plywood over them. Producing a dining table in the sand of the front yard. Then he headed off to gather his date announcing that he would return shortly.

"Knock, knock." George heard the rapping at the back door. He opened it to find Jeffery and Amy standing there with wide smiles on their faces. "What are you doing here?"

"Nice to see you too." Jeffery returned.

Amy darted him a stern look. "Rebecca invited us, where is she?"

"She's out front, setting the table." George pointed to the front door.

Amy joined her out front to find the table already set with the bright mosaic dinner place settings, set in ocean blues and greens. The tablecloth was made of evening blue silk, and the edges were fringed with dangling beads. The center of the table held a centerpiece of little blue flowers with white roses. In its center was placed a tall shimmering white, pillar candle. Surrounding this was small beaded votives containing matching shimmering mini pillars. "Oh Rebecca, your table is beautiful."

"Thank you." She was proud of it. It was feminine, yet had a grounded feel to it. Next to her place, she set a bowl filled with strips of folded paper. She had found a book at a local gift shop that was perfect for a night like tonight. It was filled with questions, silly to profound. Just the icebreaker she might need for easing the flow of conversation among strangers. Amy handed her a dessert she had made. It looked deliciously rich, full of butter, and an abhorrent amount of calories. She knew it would taste great. "Yum, this looks incredible, thank you." They both went back in to meet Lily and start enjoying their evening.

***He hated having to sit back and watch. At least her chair was facing him. He could watch her easily and hear every word spoken. She looked beautiful, but he sensed something was wrong with her. She was being polite, yet she was distant. She looked to be away in a far off world, somewhere else. He noticed the change in her after someone had mentioned that the blue flowers on the table were forget-me-nots. The old man must have noticed a change in her too, he thought, because he kept staring at her. Did the geezer really think he had a chance.

Watching Ling sit there eating and laughing made him angry. He should be there too. As a warning, if not an outright extinguisher to her and others like her. The only blessing on his side was that by now everyone knew what had gone down in Virginia. If they didn't want to end up a package at some coordinate, they all got his message, understanding that they best leave the girl alone.

He adjusted the piece in his ear.

"Rebecca, is that a wedding ring I see on your hand?"

The heartless Bitch. Why don't you just stab her in the chest, with that knife I know you have or better yet, shoot her, Ling.

"Lily..."

"That's okay Robbie. My husband passed away, Lily. I'm just not ready to take them off."

"I'm sorry."

No. you're not, you whore. He was surprised to see the look on the old man's face. Was it shock or something else, he couldn't decide.

The group became silent.

Jeffery broke the agonizing stillness by asking Robbie a question.

The two of them becoming engrossed in a conversation about the progress made on the house and what the plans were for the outside.

"Rebecca did you decide what you want on the front. I showed her a few plans." Robbie told Jeffery. "Rebecca - "

Everyone was staring at her.

"Did you choose which plan you liked?" Robbie asked again. Pointing to the front of the house.

"Yes, Yes I did. The one with the upper deck and the ground deck."

"That one is perfect. You'll lose a little of the front yard, but underneath it will still be usable, a storage shed, or something would work."

Jeffery remarked back and Ling and Amy became engaged in a discussion about decorating. He watched as George took Rebecca's hand. Watching him lean into her. Then Rebecca rose, picking up a serving tray of dishes and made her way to the stairs. George followed behind her with more plates. The others started to rise.

"We can handle it, sit, we'll be back." The old man told the others.

He adjusted the instrument to pick up the noises from the kitchen.

"I don't want to talk about it, George."

"How long has it been?"

"Eleven months."

Everything went silent. He moved to get a better angle through the NVG's. They were embracing in the kitchen. He better not be an old dog. He watched them return to the others, Rebecca with a plate and George with another bottle of wine.

He watched as the man poured her a large glass of the wine and a short one for himself. Then Rebecca passed out small plates. He presumed to be dessert. Rebecca lifted a bowl, he readjusted the instrument, "Take one Jeffery, and read it out loud. Everyone has to answer." Soon the group was laughing, arguing and then laughing again.

CHAPTER THIRTY-TWO

Julie was relieved to be stepping off the helicopter and back onto the solid familiar ground of the facility. Everything felt different, the buildings, the grounds, the world. The trees were green, the flowerbeds were alive with color and the air was fragrant and active with the sound of birds and the buzzing of bees. Julie felt refreshed by the expansive green lawns. They were a welcome change from the forested scenery they had spent their last months in.

She looked at Carl as he stepped off the Helicopter. He was wearing a special ops mask that allowed him to see clearly, but hid his identity. She was worried for him. He had said nothing the entire flight. He didn't question anything that had happened or asked why his face was covered. He still had said nothing about what had happened to him in the hospital. He was quiet and withdrawn and it was making her nervous.

Randy hopped off the helicopter last. Julie carried a feeling she couldn't shake. The feeling that something about Randy wasn't right. The feeling came to her, when he entered the safe house and told them, actually worked at convincing her, he was on her side. Granted, she wasn't going to put the gun down for anything, not until she was absolutely sure Carl was safe. But still, something was nagging at her and she couldn't figure out what it was. Tyrone. Randy had sent him to her. No, wait, she was the one who had asked for him. There was something. Something was bothering her. Something felt wrong.

"The apartment is just as you left it." Randy said.

Julie looked to him as he spoke, but neither she nor Carl said anything.

"Go home and rest, I'll sort this whole thing out." He said to both of them as he waved Tyrone's cell phone around, using it to point toward the stone and timber building that they call home, that she called home anyway. Carl probably called it his home away from home. She wouldn't blame him.

"Go on, he ordered, this is as good as done." He waved the cell phone again.

The phone. Why hadn't she noticed it before, it finally came to her, the call she placed to *911. The voice she had heard yelling through the phone wasn't Randy's. Julie was confused. If it weren't Randy, then how had he gotten there so quickly.

"How did you know to come help us, Randy?"

"What are you talking about."

"The phone call, it wasn't you on the other end."

"Those men who broke down your door, who else do you think called me."

That's what she was trying to figure out, and the only name coming to her was General Davis. "But those were Tyrone's men."

"No, Julie, those were my men."

But how could they be, she knew many of them. She knew they worked for Tyrone. Julie rubbed her head. Everything pointed the other way, but then why weren't they dead.

"You're tired Julie and confused, go home and rest."

Maybe he was right, she was tired, and she was confused, but not confused in the way he was suggesting. She was confused about loyalties. She was starting to wonder if any existed at all. She definitely was tired. She looked at Carl and knew that rest would elude her. Getting rest was the least of her worries. She had far more important things to deal with, before rest would come to her.

⚜ ⚜ ⚜

*** He felt the vibration inside his coat. He reached in to answer it.

"Yes."

"Hey, how is everything there."

"Fine, Sir."

"No incidences to speak of."

"Not even a hiccup, Sir."

"It went smooth. It got a little hairy when she got confused about whom she could trust, but it went smooth."

He said nothing.

"Hell, she even started questioning if she could trust me."

"Really."

"Yeah, he laughed, Everything is good, they're safe."

"That's good, Sir."

"I have a mission for you."

"Shoot."

"I have a package to be mailed at Destination, Delta Charlie- Tree, zero, zero, Fife- Golf, Romeo, Alpha, Nevada, Delta, Echo- Alpha, Victor, Echo- Style Bravo- over."

"Roger- over."

"Reinforcement ETA at 1500 hours- over- out."

"Roger- out."

He had told him before that he was good at his job, and the man was right, he was good. He wasn't fooling him. He knew the Major was playing both sides of the board. That board was a big playing field, and the Major was a strong player. It didn't mean that he was bad. It didn't mean that he was good. It just meant that he was smart. Politics was a dangerous game. And they were playing at high stakes politics.

He wasn't here for the game or the politics. He was here for Rebecca. He had his job to do like any other, but his main priority was to protect her. If anything happened to her while he was gone, there would be a high price to pay, indeed. The absolute highest. He read the mission again, if it were what he believed it to be, then soon she would be safe. He no longer would need to sit here and watch her, a bulldog clipped to a short chain, but the chain mattered nothing, he had fangs long enough to reach a million miles.

He read the cryptic script, package to be mailed, in other words stamped out, in Washington D.C., at 3005 Grande Ave. Style Bravo, he knew it to stand for Burglary. There were many styles used, some broad and some detailed. For example; Alpha meant assassinate, Hector meant homicide, Sierra meant suicide, Delta Hector stood for drug related homicide, Oscar meant over dose. The list went on and on. Changing occasionally as fashions come and go, but the basics remained the same.

That meant tonight he was supposed to stage it well enough to convince police, it was a burglary gone wrong. If it went as planned, then no one would question it as anything other, than an unfortunate event. He put away his Wilson Combat. The ballistics of the handgun and its thirty-six hundred-dollar price tag would destroy any belief that it was a random burglary. Instead he pulled out a cheap two-hundred-dollar handgun that anyone could purchase on the street, and he prepared himself mentally for the task at hand.

∗∗∗

Carl stepped into the apartment and felt some of the tension lift out of his body and at the same time, he could have sworn lead was filling it. It was so good to be back in this familiar, comforting setting that he didn't know what he wanted to do first. Make a cup of coffee, start a fire, look outside for his cougar, play a game with Julie or take a nap. He was leaning toward the nap, but he wouldn't want to climb into bed without showering. Although he felt almost incapable of carrying himself into the shower, he knew a shower would feel great. The only problem, he was afraid of what he might find in the bathroom mirror. Carl pulled the cover off his face and sat down on the sofa to rest. It was really too warm now for fires, he missed the ritual and the comfort it gave him. The lead feeling of over exhaustion was beginning to overtake him. Carl rose to open the sliding glass door.

"If you don't mind, I'd rather we left the door and the curtains closed." Julie said, trying not to be too obvious, in her attempt to get a good look at him. "Would you like a tea or coffee?"

"How bad is it."

"The coffee maker, I'll have to go see if there is mold growing in the pot after all this time." She began to walk quickly toward the kitchen.

"JULIE!" She stopped and looked at him. "Not the coffee maker, my face, how bad is it."

"It's not bad at all, Carl."

He could hear it hanging in the air, "But."

"But, it is different."

"How do you mean."

"I mean just that, you look different."

Carl ran over to the mirror by the door, the one he had used countless times to straighten his ties, he flicked on the light in the dark doorway, and forced himself to look at the reflection before him. His face looked perfectly normal, no disfigurement, no scars, no nothing. It was the perfectly normal face, of a stranger. Carl lifted his gauze wrapped hand and smashed the mirror.

"Are you okay." She ran over to him. He threw up his hands to keep her away. "It looks good." She said as she started picking up the broken mirror.

"Did they really beat me up that bad." He didn't think so.

"No, not that bad."

"Then why was the work so extensive, I don't look anything like myself."

Julie said nothing. She knew that was the point. Carl Reynolds was dead, Heartmeyer was dead, whoever he became now, would be free, disconnected from everything that had happened. She didn't want to be the one to tell him. He needed to figure it out for himself.

"But. What about my life."

She knew what he was thinking. He was thinking about Rebecca. Thinking about his kids. Thinking about the man he was and the life he once had. Thinking about the world that was connected to the old face.

"Is it gone? Can't I ever have it back?"

She didn't know what to tell him. She just didn't know. Didn't know any of the answers to the questions he had. She didn't know if his old life were over. She didn't know if he had to begin again. She did, however, know one thing. She was with him until the end: if that meant a day, a week or years. And God willing, if that meant, until death they do part.

***

***Dressed in black, from head to toe; he jimmied the lock and climbed the long winding stairs to the top. In the master bedroom, he found the sleeping figure, lying in the large bed. Taking out the gun, he pointed the weapon at the man's back. Unfortunately, shooting him in the back would be an unconvincing confrontation. He cleared his throat. The man sat up quickly.

"I've been expecting you, said General Davis. Tell your people that they may have won the battle, but I won the war."

At the very least, he deserved to hear the voice of the man who was about to kill him. "It's time, Sir, to go meet your God."

"My god is my penis."

Placing a pillow to the front of the weapon, he shot it.

Hanging on the bathroom door was the general's uniform, stars reflecting the moonlight coming in through the window. He reached into the jewelry box and grabbed all the high priced pieces, the ones he knew the General would have insured.

He searched the room, taking a few other pricey trinkets with him, he noticed that the man had everything neatly laid out, in advance preparation for his wife. He was grateful to him for having sent her away.

There were some things about his job that were unforgettable and some that were unforgivable. He was highly decorated and equally complimented. He was very good at his job, but he didn't always like it.

Scaling the backyard wall, he removed the mask once he knew for sure, he was safely, far enough away from the home. Pivoting onto the sidewalk, he removed his coat, and strolled away as if nothing had happened.

CHAPTER THIRTY-THREE

Rebecca took a bite of her sandwich as she turned the page of the biography she was reading about Cavanaugh, "A Man of Silent Words." Taking a sip of her tea, she placed it back into her new cup holder. Rebecca sat baffled by the words she read. "The son of a fisherman, Cavanaugh loved the ocean, as could be seen by his work later in life." Rebecca stared at the picture of his painting "The Dolphins" on the page before her.

"Taking a break?" George asked walking up from behind her.

"Lunch, want some?"

"No, thank you, what are you reading there?" He glanced over her shoulder to see the picture she was staring at.

"Want some Iced tea?"

"NO, thanks." He coughed.

"It's Amy's recipe."

"Well-maybe."

"Help yourself, it's in the fridge." Rebecca took another bite and then turned the page. "I hope you wore working clothes." She yelled back toward her friend.

"I did, If you would pull your nose away from that book a minute, you would see that I have." He lifted the book up, so he could see the front cover as he sat down in the chair next to her.

"Sorry George." She gave him a big smile. "How are you today?"

"Good, what are we working on this afternoon?"

"I'm wallpapering Danny's room."

"And Robbie?"

"He's finishing up the last of the floors."

"Great, That should be done in time before the movers come, then."

"Yes, in plenty of time." Rebecca was relieved. She knew that the day would be hard enough. She didn't want to worry about moving everything back and forth while finishing floors.

Rebecca threw the book down on the sand next to the other one.

"That book isn't worth your time Rebecca, it's rubbish. If you want to know whom my father was read that one." George pointed to his father's last novel "Which Way Towards Home." He sat down. "What is this?" He felt a tiny prick and reached around to pull something out from behind him.

"Sorry." She took it from him. "It's a chair throw, I work on it when I can't sleep at night." She held it up for him to see.

It was a small version of a quilt. White on the back but the front was full of color. It was covered with blues, greens, yellows and coral. A collage of dolphins and waves and sunshine and shells. It reminded him of his father's painting. He was becoming convinced that her coming here was no coincidence at all. Too many coincidences were starting to add up. She lost her spouse. She abandoned her children, and she was obviously artistic by looking at this cloth. What he was further coming to notice was that she had an ability to be distant, reminding him very much of his father.

"Do you want to help me upstairs." Rebecca stood holding her glass and an empty plate, staring down at George.

Upstairs, The walls were primed and the windows and trim were painted a sand color to match the wallpaper Danny had picked with sailboats covering it. "Interesting paper." George commented seeing a few strips started on one wall.

"You think so, Danny picked it from a group of swatches I sent him. I was kind of surprised he picked this one. It's sort of plain don't you think. It has no color really, beige with printed boats." She stood back from the walls trying to assess what the bigger picture would look like. "Maybe it would look better with wainscoting on the bottom half like the other room."

"Actually this room did have wainscoting a long time ago."

"Why was it taken down?"

"I don't know, it happened after I moved in with Aunt Eleanor, probably one of his private fits." She showed him how to smooth the paper with a wet rag and then handed it to him.

Back up on a chair she hung the next piece. "Which one was your room?"

George pointed to the other room. "This was the baby's room."

"The baby's?"

"Yes, my sister's room, I wasn't allowed into it." George said in a manner of fact.

"You weren't?" Rebecca questioned confused as to why a brother couldn't enter his own baby sister's room.

"I was young, six years old, but I remember her being sick. Even after she died, I was still not allowed to go into this room."

"What was she sick with?"

"Aunt Eleanor told me that she had small pox and that my mother managed to survive from it, just long enough to come down with cancer."

"I'm sorry, George."

"Don't be, I know my mother loved me." He said as he kept working. "There, how is that." He inspected the seam closely.

"Perfect." Rebecca answered.

George stared out the window. The view was amazing from the old window seat. He hoped Rebecca's children would have better memories from these rooms then he had had as a child. The only feelings he was left with, after all these years, were feelings of loneliness.

He looked out at the ocean that his grandfather loved, and his father abhorred. Closing his eyes, He willed himself to recall a memory of his mother, but none would come. George looked at the room around him. The presence of his father still lurked there. It wasn't a bad feeling, nor was it a comforting feeling. He recognized the tension he felt in the air. The same tension shared between himself and his father, his entire life.

He studied the splattered paint left on the wooden planks below his feet. George could identify which paint had been used with each of his father's paintings, as if the paintings were right there on the floor before him. When his father switched to painting, this room became his new place of isolation. Instead of behind his desk, he hid himself here. He wondered if the room had memories to hold. If perhaps, its memories were more vivid than his own.

George returned his gaze to the view outside. To the crashing of waves that were beating against the shore before him. He opened the window to let in the sound. Listening closely to the roar of the ocean tide. To the squawking of seagulls flying high in the sky. George remained still. Hoping his pain would subside. The pain he remembered of being a nine-year old boy. It had been fifty-one years since he had packed all of his things. Taking everything with him, his clothes and his toys. Everything with him, except for his home and his dad. George reached for his chest to clamp the open wound closed. Shutting everything out, as he had a long time ago. Wishing again, he was not forced to leave, by a man with whom he shared a name, but nothing more.

Rebecca returned, carrying glasses of tea, handing one to her friend as she took a seat. "What do you think, George?"

He took a sip but didn't face her. "It's good, thank you."

"No, not the tea, look at the paper I picked for this room." She held the paper up, rolled open in front of her, for him to see. "I want the girl's room to be pretty, like at Anne's house, they loved that room." She had found a paper with both blue and yellow flowers. "What do you think George?"

He looked at the paper and then at Rebecca. "I think it's nice. They'll love it." It was happy, and that made him happy.

Rebecca stood up and prepared to start working again. "Are you ready to start, George?" She asked as she unrolled the paper.

"Yes." He replied as he stepped on the dried paint. "When is Robbie striping these floors?"

"He isn't." Rebecca answered.

"He isn't! Why not?" He asked confused and a little irritated.

Rebecca looked at George, not sure if he were mad. "We decided to re-stain and Polyurethane them instead."

"Why not redo them, Rebecca? Look at them, they're covered in spattered paint."

"That's the point, George, That Paint is part of the Legacy of this house, we want to preserve it." Of all people, she thought he would understand that.

"Preserve it?" He didn't want it preserved. He wanted it cleaned up, erased. He wanted the house renewed. He wanted it lived in and loved in. Not preserved. The desk was one thing; the house would be nothing without it. The rug was his mother's. The ship belonged to his grandparent's. All were from before. But the paint, the paint represented everything wrong with this house. The death, the pain, the despair. The little boy rejected by his own father. "Preserve it? Why?"

"I don't understand, George, Your father was great. A novelist who people have mourned over and a painter, well, Look at his paintings. Have you seen his paintings?"

"Of course I have." Was she kidding, he knew each one inside out and upside down, if he had the skill; he could reproduce them from memory himself. "Great," He sneered. "The man was anything but great; an accomplished novelist, yes, an excellent artist, no question. But where it counted, as a father, he was a failure, worse yet, he never even tried. So take your reverence for the man, and throw it away, because he doesn't deserve it." George stormed out the door. Nothing he had to say would change her mind. It wasn't worth fighting about because he knew she would never understand.

He was so, angry. "What about the Journals, George?" She yelled out the window to the man retreating from her house. "Have you read them, What about the journals." He kept walking, rounding the house. It was no use he couldn't hear her.

Rebecca sat on the floor feeling the raised bumps of paint that his father spilt years earlier. She felt crushed. Crushed between a cold steel truck and a hard brick building. Her friend was in pain, and it killed her to see it, but she also couldn't deny that without his father, they would never have become friends. Besides, he didn't understand. "The dolphins" was more to her than some pretty picture. It called to her and brought her here. His pain reached out and grabbed her own. If only he could understand. But then... her too. She went to find the novel. "If she wanted to know who Cavanaugh was she should read it." He had said.

Rebecca sat reading the book. Determined that it held insight into George's life. She read it for meaning and double meaning and triple meaning. But she couldn't find any. It was just a very sad story about human loss. Lost joy, Lost love, Lost life. It pained her to read it, cutting into her own flesh wounds as she did.

She felt a presence come up behind her, casting a shadow all around her.

"Hi." He mustered a shameful greeting.

She looked up past the dark brim sheltering her eyes, "Hi, George."

"Oh, you're reading it."

"Yes," She didn't admit that she was on her third time around.

"Can I sit down?"

"Please, would you like some Iced tea?"

"Thanks, maybe later, I wanted to apologize for my behavior the other day."

She, put the book down, "That's okay."

"No, it's not, but thank you for tolerating my fit, maybe I'm more like my dad than I care to admit." He leaned back and stared out at the ocean.

She was quiet.

"Like his Dad." He had said. She looked down at the book. She had been looking for the boy in the story, not the man. "Dad," had she heard him correctly, did he really refer to his Father as Dad.

"Are you still angry at me?" He asked still staring out at the water.

"Angry? No, I'm not angry at you, I never was. I'm just trying to understand." She answered.

He picked up the book, flipping inside there was no library card, she had returned them and bought her own. The cover was dented, and the pages were dog-eared, he flipped through it; passages were highlighted. "I don't know if that is possible, I don't understand it all myself."

"He was very sad wasn't he." She looked at her friend, "And so were you."

"Yes." He answered, "I don't think I've ever recovered." He took his friend's hand. They sat watching the ocean. She was pleased when the dolphins came bobbing up to visit, stopping and playing in the cool ocean water. Splashing and flipping and twirling with ease. He watched her, her smile growing wide as they came nearer to shore, slapping their tails as if inviting her in.

She was content sitting there with her friend beside her. Happy to see her dolphins, she noticed when a warm breeze surrounded them and stayed. "Recovered." She repeated to herself. Rebecca wondered if she would ever be able to use that word. Like always, the dolphins would eventually leave, and the warm breeze had a tendency to leave with them. "Would you like to stay for dinner, George."

"Dinner?" He looked at his watch. "It's still early yet."

"I'm just planning ahead."

"I'd love to, Are you ready to get back to work. He asked her.

"Yes." She picked up the book, "Yes, I am."

He looked at his image in the mirror. Checking to be sure the silver piece of metal was positioned properly on his lapel. Randy thought about how to explain things to Carl. What options laid in store for him.

He felt a slight twinge as he held a ruler up to the silver rank.

There was no good or bad, right or wrong, or black and white when it came to politics. Like everything in life, it was made up of many varying shades of gray. When it came down to it, there were systems to be manipulated, secrets to be passed, and deals to be made. Everyone had had their role to play.

There were kings, and there were pawns. But it was the knights who ran the show, people like himself, and Yuri, and the budding, young Lieutenant. They were the sword and the soul behind every king's agenda. And God be damned, if they weren't going to have agendas of their own. He was no exception. Looking in the mirror, he attached the new shoulder boards to his dark blue jacket. The Lieutenant Colonel rank reflected back. He just hoped his full bird would be easier.

Carl heard a knock at the door. He heard Julie say hello and saw Randy come in wearing his uniform. It was the first time he had seen him wear it, since that day long ago, when he had first met him in the basement of the facility. Carl noticed the new rank on his shoulder. "How are you, Sir." He shook the man's hand.

"Good. You don't need to 'Sir' me. You're no longer in the military. Unless, you want to be."

"No thanks.'"

"Doesn't hurt to try."

"You're dressed for work, congratulations on your next rank, Randy."

"Thank you. Yes, I have to be getting back to D.C." Randy motioned to the kitchen table. Julie pulled out coffee cups for everyone, as the two men took their seats. "I wanted to come talk to you both before I left and I wanted to double check and make sure everyone was clear about they're choices."

"Carl, you understand that Carl Reynolds is dead. I think it would be easier if you left your old life behind and went on from here. But the decision is yours. You can create a new one or go back as someone else and try to reestablish your former life. But either way, Carl is dead and that's the way it has to stay."

"I understand."

"In that case, here is your new identity." He slid an envelope across the table toward Carl.

Inside he found a social security card, a birth certificate, and a driver's license. Inside was a brief profile of the man. He was a computer programmer, from California, had no family to speak of and was very much a loner. He had committed suicide.

"Suicide."

"As far as we could investigate, he was clean, he had depression issues, and he drank on top of it. As long as you don't start running for government office, no one should suspect you and he are not one and the same and no one should give a damn otherwise."

Carl read the name on the social security card. Alexander Dean Abbott; it was a rather average name. He didn't feel like an Alex, but he supposed it would grow on him. The last thing he pulled out of the bag was a stack of money. "What is this."

"Start up money, when you get where you want to be, open an account. It's only ten thousand it won't last you long. Give me your wallet." He started pulling out anything that was connected to Carl's old life. "Give me a plate, Julie." Randy pulled out a lighter and started burning his old social security card, his driver's license, his credit cards, his grocery courtesy cards, everything. The last thing he set flame to was Carl's picture of his family."

Carl wanted to scream as he sat there watching the photo curl and turn black.

"You can have Matt send Rebecca your old family photographs for the kids or you can burn them all. Even if you choose not to go back, you may not keep any of the photos. You are Alex Abbott. If you go back, you cannot discuss anything that has occurred. Even if, for some reason she knows you are you, you must make her understand that you are Alex Abbott. She must learn to act accordingly. I really would advise you not to go back, but the choice is yours."

Carl sat there blank faced.

"Do you understand the rules. It is for everyone's best interest, not just yours. I risked a lot keeping you alive. Everything must stay buried."

"I understand."

He hoped to God that he did. He turned to Julie. "Are you sure you still want to retire your handgun."

"I'm sure."

"I'm sorry to hear that, the company will miss you, I'll miss you." He said as he rose to leave. "Stay as long as you like, I advise you both to rest and think things through carefully. Matt will stay until he is needed back in D.C. Don't hesitate to send a message through to me if you need to. Oh, and I almost forgot, my brother-in-law, Kenny, would be glad to hire you on Alex. Think about it and let Matt know." He shook Alex's hand and hugged Julie. "Good luck to you both."

✺✺✺

He walked tall, carrying his rank proudly though the pentagon halls. He felt good knowing that he hadn't taken the easy way out, he hadn't sacrificed a deer merely for its antlers, for the prize that he wore on his chest. It had made the job harder, but it was worth the effort. For his soul, felt less stained and his sword, a little less bloody.

✺✺✺

Carl was on the balcony grilling burgers and corn on the cob. He had been thinking about all the things Randy had said for days now. He couldn't bring himself to a decision. He was having trouble, deciding which was the right and which was the wrong thing to do. No matter which direction, he argued with himself, no clear-cut answer would come to him. Julie was no help. She had remained quiet and distant since the day they had arrived. Always off, somewhere in the far reaches of her mind. He wouldn't be selfish and ask her to think about his problems, he knew she had enough issues of her own to figure out.

"How are things going, Julie?" Matt asked as she handed him a cola. "Is he talking yet?"

"No, not a damn word." It was killing her. She wanted to know what he was thinking about.

"Have you tried talking to him?"

"NO." She didn't dare, she didn't want to sway his decision. She certainly didn't trust herself to remain neutral.

"Why not?" He looked at her when she didn't answer. "You've fallen in love with him, haven't you?"

Wow, she had forgotten how bold youth could be. Either that or she had been playing the politically correct game for so long now that she forgot how to be honest. She wasn't sure how to answer him. She hadn't thought the "Love" question completely through. What she had thought through was the facts: she cared about him, she and he shared the same desires. A home, a family, a spouse to spend their life with. And the most obvious fact, they shared an attraction toward each other. But Love, she hadn't fully explored that concept. To be honest, she wasn't sure if she actually knew what love was. Did anyone?

Youths thought they knew everything. She had been there herself, at one time. It was why she had married Richard. She had thought that she knew him, that she had known herself, she had believed they were in love. It was only during these last years she spent aging that she had come to realize that she knew less and less.

She was starting to wonder if that was God's plan. Start us out thinking we know everything, then slowly, through a lifetime, teach us the truth, that we actually know nothing at all. Like the belief that we are born, we live and then die. Maybe we actually are born, spend a long time dying and then live. Love was somewhere in god's plan, but was it something you know or something you learn.

Julie knew it was something she didn't know, so it had to be something she would eventually learn. At least she hoped she would.

Maybe what Julie had thought was being selfless was actually being selfish. Maybe what she feared wasn't that she would sway him, but instead, what she feared was what he might have to say to her. That he wanted Rebecca more than her.

She looked at Matt. "I'll talk to him." She said, "I will."

Carl and Matt finished their game of chess with Carl announcing checkmate. "You've really improved, Matt, that was a good game."

"Thanks, Alex." Matt smiled as he put the last of the pieces into the drawer.

Then they grabbed a couple of beers from the fridge and went out onto the balcony to get some fresh air. Carl didn't know how much, of what had happened to him, that Matt actually knew. He didn't know what was safe to talk about.

"What do you think about your face, Alex." Matt asked.

That was one of the foremost questions in Carl's mind. The issue that his decision almost exclusively hinged upon, whether or not his family would know him. "What do you think?"

"Well, to be honest, at first glance you look like someone else, namely Alex. But then as we talked and we played chess and then when I watched you walk and do other things that are so you, I forgot that the face is different and I started to see you as you were. Which to be honest isn't all that dissimilar, once I think about it. Your eyes are exactly the same, so is your voice and the way you carry yourself."

"Really, do you think they would know me."

"I'm betting they would. At first glance, they may see Alex, but quickly, they would see Carl come shining through."

Carl hadn't realized before how observant Matt was. His carefree demeanor suggested otherwise. But then again his job had demanded it. Waiting on Randy, anticipating ours needs, he had missed seeing that trait in him, but he hadn't missed his kindness. Carrie's devotion and love shined straight through her son. He didn't want to miss raising his own children.

"Are you going to take the job."

"I haven't decided." He hadn't decided anything, until perhaps just now.

"Well, I think you'd be stupid not to."

"Why is that."

"He's great, you'd love working for him and the company pays good. Besides, what else are going to do?"

He had a point. His real background was destroyed and the new one was only partly true. He wasn't a programmer.

"My Uncle Kenny is all about loyalty, he'd pay you to go learn anything you want, just as long as you stay with him and the company. Think about it. I know that's where I'll end up eventually. I won't work for my Dad, but I will work for Kenny." Matt looked at his watch. "I have to go, I have a date with Emily." Alex looked confused. "She's home for the summer."

Was it summer already, it was still rather chilly here, especially in the morning.

Matt reached out his hand. "Call me anytime, Alex, I'll see you in a few days, if, I don't hear from you sooner."

Carl shook the young man's hand. "Okay, Thanks for the game." He picked up both their beer bottles and walked him to the door. He hadn't missed Matt's use of the name Alex, repeatedly. Randy had probably told him to use it frequently, thinking if he heard it a lot, that it would become a part of him. He didn't doubt that the concept was true. No matter what, it was going to take time.

He sat at the chessboard and pulled out all of the pieces. Setting up both sides of the board, he sat staring at both of the queens, glancing from one side to the other. He recalled the day he and Yuri sat here playing, noticing for the first time, that one side was real and the other myth. That day, everything had been so clear, reality was separate from fantasy, both as distinctive as the ivory and onyx squares of the board beneath. Only now, Reality could be the fantasy and fantasy the reality. It was up to him, he could flip the world around or choose to keep it as it was.

"A penny for your thoughts." Julie asked.

"It's not worth the penny."

"Let me decide that."

"There's two worlds, Carl pointed to both sides, only one is real and the other is a fantasy. Except now, I'm being told I can live in either one. Reality or Fantasy. You choose, Carl, whichever one you like. Excuse me, I mean, Alex. Are you following me, Julie."

"Yes, I'm following."

He wasn't sure that she was. "You see, the fantasy world, really means fake."

"But it can be, just as real." Julie insisted.

"But it can't, Julie, because I'll never forget the real one and what's more, I don't want to."

Julie sat still. She felt the entirety of his words stab into her heart. She felt him reach for her hand. She looked up and saw Carl, the man she met months ago, hurting for love, but not hers. Her love may have comforted him, but it didn't sustain him the way Rebecca's did. "For me, the fantasy has been more emotional and more caring, than any reality I've known."

She reached to him, clutching him, wishing she never had to let go.

He reached his hand to her face, gently wiping away the tears that ran down her cheek. Then he kissed her softly on the lips, a kiss that spoke of gentle love. The deepest love that friendship holds. As softly as he placed his lips to hers, he removed them, ever more gently. Then he embraced her. It was an embrace that whispered thank you, thank you for loving him, thank you for being his friend. Most importantly, it called out the thank you he knew not how to speak. Thank you for saving his life. "I don't know how to - "

She placed her hand over his mouth. "Please don't thank me for saving your life, because you've saved mine as well." She leaned in and gave him a kiss to remember her. A kiss that explained a lifetime of loving, to a man she would never be allowed to have. She drew away from him and for a moment she saw longing. In his longing came the answer, her answer to the circumstances he spoke of late that terrible night. For circumstance had no place in truth. Truth was solid and unchanging. It could not be pulled, it could not be swayed, it could not be altered by circumstance. Circumstance was a chosen view; a dream, and truth was truth. Julie understood what Carl was trying to tell her. Julie was a dream and Rebecca the truth. Although we love our dreams, the truth we hold dear. Carl was right, Julie deserved to be more than someone's dream. She longed to be someone's truth.

"Please answer me this though, because I don't think I could stand not ever knowing. What happened between us in the cave."

When he realized what she was asking, and that she had no memory of what happened either. He could not help, but to burst out laughing.

"Alex, it's not funny."

"Sorry." He tried to stop, but couldn't.

"Yes it is, you obviously have no memory of it either." She laughed lightly too.

"I don't know, but the jug was empty and we were both, nearly butt naked."

"The jug, Luke had warned me about drinking too much of the wine."

"He must have put something in it." They both agreed.

CHAPTER THIRTY-FOUR

The twenty-two year old boy stood in front of Rebecca with a clipboard in one hand and another hand stretched out toward her, with a pen in it for her to retrieve. He wanted her to sign the forms so they could both go on with their day. Rebecca wanted to sign it so she could go on with her life. It was finally over. That part of her life that had timed itself by the moves that they made. He handed her, her copy. She looked out the window as they climbed back into their truck. The movers were gone.

Rebecca looked at all the unopened boxes in the house. Stacked three high in some places. The corner of each box stated the room in which it belonged. Rebecca pulled out a knife and sliced one of the boxes open. It was filled with CD's and DVD's. The mounds of boxes felt monumental. She began to question her wisdom in asking the movers to place the boxes in their proper rooms, but to leave them unopened. No, she was right, her stress had released the moment they stepped out of her house.

She looked around at the furniture. A lot of it had to go. She no longer needed the thick bulky stuff, like the huge wooden couch and chairs. They had served them well over the years, but the time had come for their burial in the local dump. Rebecca concluded that it was as good a place to start as any. The furniture. Which pieces would stay and which would go. She made a list of all the ones to be dumped. Checking her watch. The boys could start on it when they got here.

Rebecca picked up her copy of the shipping log. Each box was numbered, and a description of the contents was on a line beside each one. Rebecca scanned the lines searching for her memories. She tried to find which numbered box they were in. Which box it was that held her life.

Held within it an ability to restore the failing images in her head. It wasn't listed. There was no listing for pictures, family photo's, snapshots, nothing. Maybe they weren't in a box all their own. Rebecca opened another box to find nick-knacks. Another one with blankets. One had coats and hats and mittens and umbrellas. She searched every living room box, nothing.

She moved onto the kitchen boxes. Opening one she found towels, Rebecca shoved them into a drawer. In another, she found pots. She clumsily threw them into a base cabinet. Another one was full of pans. She dinged and clanked and thumped them into the bottom of the stove. Two more contained glasses. Another one held tablecloths and potholders. She whirled onto the next. It held dishes. And more dishes. Canisters and spices. She cut furiously at the boxes with the knife. Unearthing plastic ware and utensils. The next held casserole plates and glass mixing bowls. She reached in again, pulling out something wrapped up.

Rebecca carefully unrolled the paper. Inside was her Mary statue, only it wasn't how she remembered. She studied the frail object, chipped and dirty, it looked old, much older than she remembered. Her head looked sad, with a flattened white nose, laying separate, severed from the body it had been glued to. Rebecca looked carefully at the pieces. There was no trace left, of there having been any glue, it had disintegrated, like her life. Like her memories. Like her sanity. All of it disintegrated.

Rebecca flew from the kitchen, knife in hand. Running down the hall. Stopping at the bathroom, she tore at the boxes, flinging the scale to the floor, she lifted the box and dumped it. Next she went to the bedroom. Dumping boxes of lamps and candleholders and books. Throwing candle jars and shoes. Nothing. Nothing at all, as if - she had made it all up.

Rebecca raced back to the living room, this time dislodging everything from its box. It had to be here somewhere. It had to be. Throwing videos and books, pillows and video games. There was not one article. Not one piece of anything. Not one -

"What the hell are you doing?" Robbie yelled, grabbing her hands, so she couldn't throw another object. The "welcome to our home" plaque dropped from her hand, thumping gently to the floor.

"Let go." She yelled back. Searching the room, scanning, "There has to be something. There just has to be." Robbie released her hand. Did she make it all up? Had she taken a turn off the bend, and not known it? "There's nothing Robbie." She stared at her rings. Had she bought them from some pawnshop? Was she crazy?

"What are you talking about?"

Her kids. Rebecca flew to the phone and dialed, Busy, busy, busy. She dialed again, Busy, busy, busy.

"What are you doing, Rebecca?" He stood in disbelief, staring at the insanity taking place before him. "REBECCA." His voiced ripped through the air.

She stared straight at him.

"What are you doing?" He asked her calmly.

"I'm calling my kids, I have to talk to my kids." She answered.

She was frantic. He could hear it, and he could see it. "Why, so you can scare them."

Rebecca put the phone down. "There's nothing Robbie." She said. "Not one picture, not one military plaque, not one piece of military equipment, no clothes, not even a damn sneaker that proves he existed. Nothing that would show we were married. That we shared a life together. "I have to call my kids. I have to Robbie. I have to know they're there." She picked up the phone and pushed the button.

Robbie grabbed the phone, then hugged his sister tight. "You don't have to Rebecca." He said. "I know the truth, I know Carl existed, I was there the day that you married him. It was the happiest day of your life." He felt her shudder. "I remember it, Becca. I know the truth." He felt the warm fluid soak into his shirt, as he gripped his baby sister to his chest. "I know." He reassured her again, pushing back the hair from her face. So many things he had let go unanswered. Like why people were chasing her in the dark, leaving her notes, making her run from her home. He thought it was all over. He hoped it was over.

Rebecca had cleaned up her mess. The living room was clean anyway. And organized now. The boys had finished dragging out the unwanted furniture. With Robbie, they had brought two truck bed loads to the dump. Rebecca placed the last of the pots in the cabinet below.

"I see the movers came."

He was smiling at her. Like he knew something, a secret, only for him. "They came this morning." She placed a dish in the cabinet. She was glad he hadn't seen her fit this morning. He was still smiling. "What?" She poured him a glass of tea.

"Nothing. Thanks." George answered taking the glass.

Thanks, She smiled, not Thank you, but thanks, she was rubbing off on him. He was smiling at her again. "What?" "You're smiling at me, but not at me."

"I am." He smiled again. "You remind me of someone that I have been thinking about lately."

"I do?"

"Her name is Isadora. I knew her a long time ago, at Duke."

"And?"

"That is all, we dated a while, I liked her very much."

"What Happened?"

"Nothing, she wanted to marry, I didn't. I didn't want the pain my Dad went through."

"Or the happiness?" Rebecca couldn't understand sacrificing happiness to avoid pain.

"No, not even that, not at so high a price." He regretted to admit.

"So, why are you thinking about her now."

"Actually, that is part of the reason I came to see you today." George reached to something on the back porch. Carrying it inside, he handed it to Rebecca. "A Thank You for the journals."

"You already thanked me for the journals."

"Now, I'm thanking you for making me read them."

"You are." She was so overjoyed to hear he was reading them. She couldn't imagine what it would be like to delve into twenty-five years of someone's thoughts and feelings. What it would reveal.

He nodded, "Open it."

She looked at the package. Covered in shell paper and tied up in a glittering ribbon and bow. It was pretty as is. She hated to disturb the wrappings. Carefully she untied the bow and unsealed the tape from the back. Sliding it out, she couldn't focus, her eyes had become blobs of blur. She picked up a dish rag and wiped her embarrassment away. "George, you can't give me this."

"Yes, I can, I just did." He was pleased with her affection for it. Taking it from her, he went to the living room and placed it on a nail above the mantel.

Rebecca gazed at the blue and green, the white and yellow and all the invisible glitter of the painting before her. She looked at the creatures, both happy and sad. At the house all around her and to the man standing next to her, her friend. "Thank you." She took his hand.

"I'm glad you love it, as I do."

She knew at that moment, that they were the dolphins, George and Rebecca, what an unlikely pair.

CHAPTER THIRTY-FIVE

David pulled his truck up to the pizza shop and stepped out. Stopping only to stretch his legs and purchase a local map, he headed toward the drugstore, but was distracted by the strong scent coming from the pizza parlor next door. He read the name on the pizza shop door, Margatelli's Pizzeria, not much of a ring to it, he thought. But it was straight forward enough, he supposed. The door was propped open by a wedge at the bottom. The line to the place flowed straight out the door, curving down the sidewalk. David assessed the long line and debated the wisdom of waiting. Passing the door, another whiff of the pizza assailed his nose. Placing his hand to his stomach, the grumble decided for him, David grumbled even louder placing himself at the end of the line. He hoped it taste as good as it smelled.

Looking around, David took in the sights, his view offering plenty to look at. It was hard to miss all the exposed skin of varying shades. He saw girls in bikinis and guys wearing long shorts. There was the distinctive sound of flip-flops, slapping against the heels of passing by feet. He heard laughing and yelling and cars honking long blasts and some short beeps. It was interesting to both watch and listen to. David also knew it was something he'd get bored of very soon.

To David's surprise the line had moved fast. David watched as the people retreated from the building, back out into the bright sunshine, with plates of pizza and cups filled high, with the sticky sweet fluid that rejuvenated their bodies. Inside the shop, he saw a television in the far top corner, the volume was low, but he could see the screen presenting a weather forecast. The weekend was promising to be mostly clear and sunny, high around eighty, with a possible shower or two on Sunday.

Finally, it was his turn. The round man behind the counter looked at David. "Not from around here and I gather that you're not here to soak up the rays either."

"Why would you guess that?"

"Well Son, the hat and boots gave you away, but I really doubt that you'll get much of a tan in those jeans."

"You caught me." David returned playfully.

"Funny though, I know a pretty little thing who comes here almost daily, who never fails to be wearing a black one of those." He pointed to David's dark brown hat.

"Rebecca?"

"Yeah, You know her?"

A woman popped her head out from behind the kitchen wall. She was just as round, as the man he was talking to, except she had grayer hair and was smiling and shaking her head vigorously as she eyed him over. She tossed the dough up towards the ceiling, quickly making the sign of the cross, as she murmured something towards the pizza dough falling back into her hands. "That woman needs to have her head examined. Between the kids and all those men of hers, it's a wonder she hasn't taken herself a vacation in a rubber room."

"MARIA."

"Don't Maria me, Anthony, I only have you and these pizzas to manage and it takes all of my patience, just to do that."

"Maria, She has the energy of a thirty-year old and she's driven."

"She's a saint, I say."

"No argument there." The man said, busily slicing up a pizza that a teenage boy brought out to the counter.

"She's a sweetheart, and she took that house when no one else would."

The man took David's money for his slice of pizza and cola.

"Abbey says that she has a sweet tooth too- for fudge." The woman said as she brought out another hot pizza pan.

David realized this was a small town atmosphere, even though it was a tourist beach town. He recognized the talk about the newcomer, as if it were his own town folk talking about his Rebecca. His Rebecca, He wondered what she meant by, All those men of hers.

"Could you tell me how to find her place."

"Sure thing, Go down to the end and turn right, then take the dirt and gravel road, follow it about a mile down. You won't miss it. It's the one with all the trucks in the back yard."

"Plus, the loud music, screaming children and the yelling men."

David rounded the bend to be met with blaring music and the loud pounding of hammers. He pulled the truck over to the side of the road and watched for a minute. He searched the ground for Rebecca, but didn't see her. Pulling the truck further forward, he parked it and got out. Surveying the lot again, he caught sight of someone cresting the roof. A man stood at the top, assessing the roof and then looked out toward the ocean or the front yard maybe.

David had to catch his balance. Leaning hard against the truck, when he glimpsed a bobbing black Stetson, jutting its way up and over the ridge of the house. She was standing there, on the roof, looking out to whatever it was they were viewing. Her figure was fully erect with both hands on her hips, emitting confidence and grace. She wore a bright-pink tee shirt and jean carpenter pants, with a hammer dangling from a loop at her hip. The nail bag was wrapped around her so many times he couldn't tell where one end started and the other one ended.

They resumed their work, finishing the ridge with the black asphalt shingles. For some reason, the radio was shut off, and David could hear her laughing at something the man next to her had said. He envied the camaraderie that the two so easily shared. David felt a pang of jealousy pull lightly at his heart. The whole time she was with him, he never saw such happiness in her, as he saw right now.

David saw the man pointing at him on the ground. David sensed a change in Rebecca's mood as she stood on the roof looking down at him. The smile fell away from her face, as she assessed him standing there at the end of the driveway. A second later it returned, her smile shining as bright as it had been just moments before. But to David it appeared slightly more restrained. Waving to him, she said something to the man next to her.

"Hey, come on up." Rebecca called down to him.

David went around the front of the house, stepped up onto the front deck and crossed over to the stairs leading up. Once he reached the top deck, Rebecca was there to meet him, standing at the base of the ladder leading to the roof. Behind her came the man. "All of those men of hers." He reheard the woman's voice in his mind. All he'd seen so far, was the one. A man, close to his own age, tall and lanky, with a smile and regard that clearly showed closeness between him and Rebecca.

Rebecca was surprised. He was here, standing before her. She didn't know if she should touch him, if she dared to hug him hello. Wearing his trademark jeans and white tee-shirt, Rebecca's stirrings came flooding back as she drank in the sight of him. Tanned and looking stronger than she remembered. His brown boots and hat made her smile, remembering the Virginia man she had met months earlier. Tender and kind, he was here, but why? He hadn't called or wrote, not that he needed to, but she was confused. Why come now. Then it came to her. She was confused no longer. He was a man of his word and tomorrow was June.

He didn't know if he should touch her. He wanted so badly to hug her, and hold her and ask how she was. The man standing next her was waiting there patient and calm. He wore a smile that beamed and sported a bronze tan, which matched his hair, highlighted by the sun. He heard the hammering of nails, realizing then that others were around.

"David, how are you?" She looked into his eyes; they appeared vacant and detached.

"Good, how are you?" He gave her a sliver of a smile and looked at the man next to her.

She stared at him. He was really there, She wanted to reach out and pinch him to make sure, or wait was it the other way around, was she supposed to pinch herself.

Both men stood there waiting.

Robbie broke the uncomfortable silence. "Hi, nice to meet you, he reached his hand out, "I'm Rob."

"David." She heard him return. Was it her imagination, or had the two men just engaged in a contest of strength, in the handshake before her. "Where are my manners, David, this is my brother Robbie, Robbie, this is David, you remember, I told you about him."

"Yes." Robbie answered. "Virginia right, I'll bet you could use a cold beer after that drive." Robbie left them and went into the house.

David felt sort of silly. Her brother, He was her brother, The Uncle Robbie that Tommy had told him about, but he looked nothing like her. He looked at Rebecca. She looked like she felt awkward. He reached out to touch her hand. "How are you?" He asked again.

"Good." She answered. His touch felt comfortable, rubbing his thumb across the top of her hand like he did back in Virginia.

He could tell she was good, she looked strong and healthy, with new muscles in her arms and sun in her skin. He wanted to hear more than, good, he wanted to hear details.

Robbie came back out with beers for himself and David. He had made Rebecca a tequila sunrise. She understood what the drink meant. He was telling her she needed to loosen up. He placed them down on the tempered glass tabletop, leading the others to take a seat.

They each took a seat under the large blue market umbrella. Rebecca was relieved to get a break from the beating sun. The roof had been hot, a large glass of water would have been better for her, but she knew her brother's choice in beverages had been right. She too felt the edginess in the air, they were all a bit uptight and a little alcohol would help to dispel the tension. She looked at the drink, ranging from yellow to red. She stirred it, mixing it into a mellowed orange, then lifted it and took a large gulp.

David looked around. The table set was comfortable. It was large enough for at least eight people, with padded chairs, in ocean color swirls. There was a propane grill and a wooden counter that covered an icebox in the corner. Looking down to the bottom deck there were lounges that matched. "Where are the kids?"

"They're in Vermont with my mother-in-law."

"Still." Tommy had been done with school for over a week.

"They start and end school later in the north."

He was confused. "The woman at the pizza shop said something about kids."

"You met Tony and Maria?" She smiled.

"They told me how to get here."

A lot more then that she was sure. "Jessica, a few houses down, has a couple of kids that are always visiting a lot." Speak of the devil. They heard a little voice calling.

"Rebecca," the five-year old yelled from the sand below, "Are they here yet."

"Not yet, Annabelle, two more weeks sweetie, and they'll be here." She answered that same question daily. "You want a popsicle?" Rebecca called down.

"Yes please." The little girl stood there.

"Well then, come up and get it, You know where it is."

David watched as she went to the outdoor icebox.

"Don't forget one for Petey." Rebecca added.

"He's napping."

"Why aren't you?" Rebecca asked.

"Because I'm a big girl. I don't need to take naps."

Rebecca knew she'd fall asleep an hour from now in one of the chaises below.

"Hey, you." Robbie interrupted, "You forgot to give me a hug hello."

"I already did." She wrapped her tiny arms around one of Robbie's arms.

"Well then, stop coming and going." He teased her. "You want to play me in a game of Race Car Derby." He asked the little girl. "I need the practice, I told Danny I'd beat him next time."

"I'll beat him too." Annabelle answered with red dye around her mouth.

"I don't know, Danny's pretty good."

"We better practice." She said in complete seriousness to Robbie, as she swallowed down the last of her popsicle.

"Who's your friend?" She walked over to David, stood two inches away and stared at him.

Rebecca introduced David to Annabelle.

"What's that?" The girl asked listening to something, there it was again.

Everyone could hear the noise now, The yipping and yapping from behind the house.

"I forgot." David said."Tommy insisted I bring Rachel a gift." He frowned, "I can take it back with me, if you don't want it." He added quickly.

Everyone went down stairs to the truck. David lifted a box out of the passenger side seat. In it was a puppy, too young to be from the collie, back in March. Its fur was rusty colored, with lots of wave to it. Its eyes were large, sad looking doe eyes. She loved it. "Oh." Rebecca said. Her heart melting at the sight of the puppy. Picking it up, she hugged it.

David was pleased. The smile on her face was worth all the strain he had felt up on the deck. It made him happy watching her expression glow, every time the puppy licked more of the salty sweat off her face.

Rebecca didn't want to put the puppy down, but the dancing and jumping child in front of her was in agony wanting to get her hands on its silky fur.

David pulled a bag out of the truck and produced a leash to clip to the puppies collar. "Here you go, hold on tight." He told the little girl. She ran away, over to the shaded sand under the house to play with the dog.

"Thank you." Rebecca looked at David. "The kids will love it."

"You're welcome." He picked up the bag of dog supplies. "I think it's a spaniel and golden retriever mix."

"He's beautiful." She picked up David's luggage and carried it upstairs.

Rebecca woke to the feel of David's arms around her. She shifted her weight and felt the pressure of his arm lift off of her. Pulling back the blankets she climbed out. Carefully raising her body, hoping not to disturb

David's sleep. Balancing her weight on the floor, Rebecca took a step forward, landing directly on a loose floorboard. The loud creak sounded through the room. Rebecca quickly turned to see if it woke David. Nothing. No flinch, No movement, No groan. She swiftly moved across the room grabbing her sweater as she made her escape. Closing the door behind her, it too released a squeal as the hinge complied with the door's motion.

Rebecca felt like a teenager again. Sneaking in at three o'clock in the morning, way after the midnight curfew. She smiled. Recalling Marie and her adventures. Out partying with boys, drinking more than they should and getting in more trouble than they should have to. Rebecca smirked and shook her head. Remembering the ritual of sneaking through her friend's home in the dark. Strategically skipping stairs on the climb to Marie's bedroom, avoiding large creaks like the one in her new bedroom floor. The difference. Then she was seventeen, faced only with the scolding wrath of angry parents. Now was different, now she was thirty-three and if caught, the only wrath she would have to face was her own inner turmoil.

She needed space, she needed coffee to counteract the wine from last night and she needed her thinking chair. Air to clear her head. The sight and sound of the ocean surf to calm her soul.

She opened the can that cured headaches and breathed in the aroma of the ground beans. Doling out the measurement, she closed the lid and flicked the switch. Across the room sat the pup. Staring at her through the door of the port-a-kennel. She reached down to touch its nose. He looked to her, like the burnt orange sky of sunset. She scanned her mind for a fitting name. None came to her. It was Rachel's decision anyhow, she reminded herself. Rebecca reached for the leash. Clipping it onto the collar, she pulled the large puppy out and quickly carried it out the back door, before it could pee on her. The scary sway of the back porch was gone, in its place was a firm new deck with stairs leading to the driveway below. Everything done, Robbie returned north, Back to a jam-packed schedule during peak construction time. She knew she'd never know how to thank him for all he had done.

Business done, they climbed back up.

Grabbing her coffee, Rebecca went down to her white Adirondack chair in the sand. With her she brought the colorful throw she had been working on. Finished, she would need to find something else to do in the dark hours of the night. She thought of the man lying in her bed. Had she been wrong, to say No last night. Rebecca sat debating with herself. Remembering the heat of his mouth, the sizzle of his hands and the pounding of her pulse. Could she still say that they might regret making love, Rebecca thought it through. There were few things that she regretted having not done in her life. She knew that couldn't be said for many of the things she had.

David - tender, loving, protective David. She loved him, but she somehow knew her love, wasn't enough. She remembered the concerned look of Pam and Daniel's eyes and she knew what was right. Making love to David would have been nice, but why make empty promises, and today in the daylight, she knew for sure they would have been empty.

Rebecca listened to the loud roar and crash of the waves against the shore. The water was rough today. She looked at the sky above, in the distance the sky held a looming darkness in its farthest reaches. She knew there was a storm approaching, making the child in her squeal with anticipation and excitement.

With a renewed cup of warm medicine, Rebecca stared out at the water from her perched view.

"Good Morning." David said as he reached his arms around her.

They felt good, strong and comfortable. She looked up to his face and he kissed her gentle and sweet. In his eyes, it showed, the bright blue ocean, calm and serene. His arms were the same. A strong reminder of March, yet to both, they felt temporary.

*** She may not have needed a man's arms around her, but she wanted them. He saw the joy in her having David's arms around her; watching her, she radiated. Her needs always were obvious. The heat of her, the fire in her eyes and sexual energy she emitted. He and everyone had felt it in her presence. She was secure, secure in her own femininity and in the knowledge of her own needs and desires. He envied David for receiving her love. He knew the truth, she was attracted to him, but she could never love a man who she knew would leave her feeling cold in the end. After the heat of loving her, he would always be off someplace living the lonely life of a special ops soldier, wading in the swamp of a jungle or trekking through the heat of some desert. He knew he loved it, probably more than he could ever love her. His heart hurt knowing that she knew that. He felt the heat of her desire and the glow of her admiration. But she couldn't love a man who would leave her embrace-less and cold in a bed all alone. As he spent his nights lurking in the forest, loving her coldly from a distance. He envied David and Carl for being the type of men to whom the love of a woman was enough. They both knew he wasn't one of those men. But for the first time in his life, Jordan looked at her and wished he were.

David watched as she played in the water. He had pleaded with her to come out, back to the deck with him, but the lure of the pounding waves were too strong.

In Rebecca, he saw his mustang, fierce and strong. She thrived on the challenge the sea presented her with on a daily basis. Ever threatening to throw at her its gales and knock her down with the thundering force of its waves hitting the shore. She loved it all. Each and every one of its varied moods. She glowed in the sunlight. Drinking in the rays and the calming peace that this salty world left behind, after it had hurled on her the best that it had to give.

Watching her fight the waves, like they were the cruelties of her life. She wasn't to prove herself strong, she already was. He had chosen to see the contradiction in her, as her weakness, and not the gift that she had to offer. Now he recognized his mistake. She hadn't given him strength by allowing him to care for her when they weathered that unforgiving blizzard. It was the mustang in her, the sometimes scared, but ever brave spirit that had given him the desire and courage to live again himself.

He wanted a woman to need his strength, and maybe during that low point in Rebecca's life, maybe she did get that from him. But, looking at her now, he knew he was seeing someone who only needed love and friendship. He knew he could give her that, but their worlds were far apart and he knew he would never be satisfied not being needed as the pillar of strength to his lover's world. That was something Rebecca would never need from him. She was a pillar all her own.

Like the mustang, when caged, she felt weak and scared. But when he sent it out to pasture, it was there in the open spaces, that the animal shined and was strong. Rebecca standing on the ocean shore was his mustang out to pasture... And he knew she was home.

❧

David climbed the ladder to the stable's hayloft. He reached into his jeans and took out a warm steel pocketknife and opened the long cool blade. Then he took his time. Taking great pains to carefully etch into the ceiling above where he and Rebecca had spent hours talking and holding.

Where he learned to love again.

He sat down and looked up at the perfectly carved heart that read David-N-Rebecca. He knew he would love her always and regretted only one thing. That he hadn't the added memory of her touch and scent and heat to put with his memories of loving her here, during those snowy afternoons. Where he wished time could have stood still.

David took the mustang from the stall and bridled him, but left the saddle. He grabbed the blanket Rebecca gave him and held it up for Ebony to smell. The horse snorted in the scent of Rebecca and he gently rubbed the horse's neck. The way he had watched Rebecca do it a hundred times that snowy week in March.

"She loves you, Ebony. She always will, but she's not coming back."

"We'll just keep her in our hearts together, okay boy."

He rubbed the horse's chest hard trying to end the pain in his own. Then he threw the blanket over the black horse's back and stepped up onto the fence to climb on. Ebony threw back his head and a breeze carried Rebecca's scent to the animal. David leaned down to the horse's head as Rebecca would and he whispered to him, "We can get through this, you and me, together."

Pam stood amazed as she watched David on the bareback of the mustang. "You sure you want to do that?" She called to him.

"Yeah."

"Wouldn't you prefer a saddle?"

"The saddle would make him feel caged."

"You going to be back for the picnic?"

He clicked his mouth and gently tapped the horse. "I wouldn't miss it." He yelled as he and Ebony streaked out toward the trees and to the pastures beyond.

An hour later Pam was surprised to see David headed back to the stables with ebony.

David put the blanket in his truck and spotted a woman who looked similar to Rebecca from behind. He approached her. Noticing that they looked a lot alike. Except she was probably a few years younger, than the spirited woman he had fallen in love with. "Love isn't less because you love another." He remembered her telling him one afternoon during that cold March month. Then David stepped forward and introduced himself to the young woman before him.

CHAPTER THIRTY-SIX

She sat in her Adirondack chair and placed her less than proper, southern iced tea in its cup holder. Although she had learned to make it for George, she couldn't stomach all the sugar, so instead, she took hers bitter without any at all. The sun was shining brightly. Rebecca shaded her eyes as she looked out to where the children were wading in the ocean waves. She made sure all three were head above water and then leaned her head back and closed her eyes.

She suddenly felt a presence by her side, but realized it was too large to be one of the children. Rebecca decided that it must be her familiar, charming old friend. "I just made you a fresh pitcher of Iced tea, George." She opened her eyes to find it wasn't George. Her heart lurched when it realized who was standing there; surprised to find a different charming old friend. "You're as stealth-full as always, I see." She smiled up at the unexpected man.

Danny came running protectively over to her and the girls were following quickly behind him. "It's okay, she yelled to them, This is a friend of mine." A few seconds later the children were all standing on the other side of her chair.

"How are you doing?" He said to the children.

Rebecca observed how he smiled and nodded to the children as he shook each one's hand. He still had that easy charm that instantly won people over. His smile and personable nature had always attracted her to him, her and every other woman on campus.

"You seem familiar to me." Rachel said to him.

"I went to school with your mother."

"Oh, okay." She seemed satisfied with his answer and smile.

"This is Jordan." Rebecca finally managed to spit out. Completely overwhelmed and struck off balance by the abrupt collision of her two worlds.

"Jeremy." He corrected her.

"It's okay guys, you can go back to your playing." Rebecca gently suggested.

He waved to them and they watched as the large puppy bounded along at their heels. "You make sure you keep an eye on Copper." She yelled behind them. Her mind raced back. "Do you remember that training exercise where that copperhead bite Young right in the seam of his ACU's, just above the boot."

"No, I don't."

"That might have been the semester before you started."

He was looking at her with that focus and intensity that he had. It was his power over her, some strong magnetic weapon. The way he could make her feel she was the only woman in the entire world. She remembered how women were drawn to him, men too for that matter.

"You back to the grind?" He motioned to the textbook on counseling techniques lying in the sand.

"Yes, I convinced the therapist down the street to bring me on board part-time while I work on my masters. I'm just taking initial interviews and histories." She told him, but felt that somehow he already knew all this. He stared at her.

"It's a start; I could go for some of that tea you spoke of."

Rebecca stood up.

Jordan didn't move.

She stood there inches from him, looking straight into his penetrating eyes. She refused to budge. She recognized instantly that he was up to his old tricks.

They lingered there for a moment or two longer and then he stepped back.

She led him onto the lower deck and to the stairs. "Jordan you should know me well enough by now, I'll never back down from your challenge."

They climbed the stairs to the top deck. He had been betting on her never backing down from him. Entering the living room, he looked around, he had wondered what the inside would look like. "You did a great job." It was cozy, warm and inviting, all the things he thought a home with her would be. "It was a big job."

So, it wasn't because of having no trees that had made her feel naked. It was him who was watching her all these months.

They stepped into the small kitchen, he leaned against the counter and watched her as she poured him a drink and filled her own glass with more ice.

"Was it you, Jordan, who I've felt watching me?"

There she goes again with Jordan. "Jeremy." He gently corrected. "Yes it was me, but many others also, both good and bad. Not to mention all your neighbors were a bit more than curious themselves." She said nothing. She wasn't even a bit surprised by what he had told her. She handed him the glass of ice tea. "Why was it that you always called me Jordan, or worse Mister Jordan."

"We were supposed to."

"That was a rule no one followed."

"It was a good rule, it maintained professional distance - something I desperately needed with you."

He watched her there, sipping at her tea as she leaned against the wall for support. She had let her hair grow out. She had always appeared pale and feminine to him, but now she seemed more delicate. No longer projecting that androgynous strength that being in a male dominated environment had created in her. Now fully female, she drew him to her with an even stronger allure, one he doubted she herself even knew she possessed.

He stood there staring at her and saying nothing in response to her admission. He must have known all along his effect upon her. She watched him and noticed he still commanded the air around him. Even without the uniform to expose the strength of his build, he still possessed the power to make her grip her surroundings to escape his force. "Why is it that you always called me Rebecca and never Miss Reynolds."

He noticed the smile fall away from her face. "Did that bother you."

"No, I liked it very much the way you said my name. But, I imagine that others must have noticed it too, demanding perhaps a little less respect."

He put the glass down on the counter and moved closer to her. "I'm sorry if you thought that. That was never my intention." He looked into her eyes and felt his body desire to be close to her. "To be honest, I liked getting close to you and flirting with you. The name Reynolds was an obstacle to that. It was another man's name. I didn't like being reminded all the time that you were married. I preferred to think of you simply as Rebecca."

He spoke her name in the same soft, seductive way with which he used to. "So, why did you decide to come see me now, Jordan."

"They couldn't force me to stay away from you anymore, Not now that they have taken me off this case. They've closed it Rebecca. You won't have the feel of watching eyes on you any longer." He longed for something he didn't dare hope for. For her to ask if he were staying or going. He wanted so badly for her to ask about him, his plans, but he knew if she asked about anyone, it would be Carl. He stood looking at her expectantly. Choose, he thought. He watched as she started to open her mouth, but then she closed it again, saying nothing. "What." He coaxed her.

"Do you know. I mean, can you tell me if he's ever coming back or-or is he really in Arlington?"

His heart sank, for once he had wanted to be wrong. He couldn't pretend any longer that her marriage had been what kept her from him. He had been right, she needed more than what he could give her, more than the arms of safety and protection, and more than mere passion, no matter how intense that passion was.

His silence was unexpected, he looked sad and she hoped she wasn't responsible, but somehow she knew that she had hurt him.

"I can't really say."

"Do you mean, you don't know or can't tell me?"

"Both."

"Did I say something wrong?" He looked directly at her, making her body beg for his. His eyes aching into her soul.

"I always wanted to know if given a choice, would you have chosen me over Carl." "Now I know."

She stood shocked by his remark, choice, there were never any choices, heat yes, careful distance, definitely. Everything else was unspoken. "Don't try and kid yourself or me Jordan. It was never a matter of whether you and I wanted each other. I think we both know the answer to that. It was always a question of whether I could have you, regardless of my marriage and Carl. And I think we both know that answer too. Even if; that obstacle as you say, wasn't there, if I had never been married. The answer still would have been the same."

"What about the other question."

"What's that?"

He reached out and placed one hand behind her head and pulled her to him. He locked his eyes to hers and flashed her his drop-dead smile before locking his mouth onto hers. She felt him easing away, when she knew she didn't want him to leave without her having kissed him back. She reached for his shirt and pulled him back toward her, she returned what he had given to her. She opened her eyes and felt her heart, her breath and her pulse all come to a dead stop. Staring intently at her, he had the most telling smile she had ever seen.

"It's not the full question, but it will suffice."

"Yes, it's pretty self-evident." She agreed.

He let go of her. "Goodbye Rebecca."

They had scorched each other, but now she felt cold. "Goodbye." She placed her hands into her pockets and felt the warm metal object. "Jeremy, Wait."

He turned back to look at her and saw a tear run down her cheek.

"Do I have something that belongs to you?" She handed him the small pocketknife.

"You kept it. I had this since the day I graduated from ranger school." He saw the tears streaming down her face now, Jeremy reached up and rubbed his thumb tenderly across her face. "Don't cry over a beast like that." She sucked in some air and he felt her shudder in his hands.

"I'm not, I'm so sorry - I'm sorry you killed a man for me."

"Don't Rebecca, don't be sorry." He looked at her with eyes the color of the sky on a stormy day. "I'd do it again, in an instant, if it meant keeping you safe."

He kissed her again, a bittersweet kiss. Not a kiss of passion, this time, it was a kiss that spoke of goodbyes. Jeremy opened her hand and placed the knife in her palm and closed her fingers around it. "Thank you." She memorized his stormy eyes. "Thank you for loving me that much." He smiled, the sadness dampening his charm only slightly. "You keep this to remember the love we did share and I'll keep the memories of what our love could have been." If I were capable of loving you the way Carl had, he thought.

He kissed her hand with the hard knife in it, then he turned and left her life just as stealth-fully as when he had been in it. But not before she saw him wipe a tear away from his own face as he walked away from her.

Rebecca placed the knife back in her pocket. Then she wrapped her arms around herself as far as she could, but it wouldn't calm the jabbing sensation that her heart was receiving. It wanted to run after Jeremy and ask him to stay, but she knew her heart would only be putting off the inevitable. It might be a week, a month or a year from now, but eventually he would leave and the pain would come anyway.

She walked to the front door and looked out toward the blue on the horizon. She knew she would never look at a stormy sky the same way again. She wondered if this pain would also return with each turn of the weather. Only time would tell.

She took her tea back outdoors and sat in her chair once more. She was no longer that person who held in all her emotions. The process of losing Carl had broken her of all that, not that she had much choice over it. She remembered the frustration he would feel, trying to pull out of her even the tiniest of emotions. But not now, she sat there allowing the fullness of her pain to flow from her. As she sat watching her children flirting with the ocean, she picked up the puppy, panting drools at her feet. She hugged it and let it lick away the salty tears from her face.

She sat there and looked out at the ocean. The pain began stabbing her harder, then those from earlier. She knew now the sensation of those who died from a broken heart. It felt unbearable and she hoped if she let herself feel it fully maybe it would pass quicker than if she fought it. It hit her the moment Jordan had walked out her door. As stealth-full with his words as he was his body. The pain came in the words he hadn't spoken. It was through the bitter joy of his offering himself to her that the truth became apparent. Her life had changed from that moment. There had never been a single day of flirting and standing too close to her, not a single day that she could recall where he hadn't asked her about Carl. Every day, except today. It was this knowledge that hurt like no other. A question; that needed no answer. As surely as Jeremy had taken himself out of her life by walking out that door. It was what went with him that hurt the most. Hope. The smallest bit of it she had had left.

Sitting there she felt the fullness of the empty chair waiting for her partner. Looking at it next to her, she was forced to finally accept that Carl was never coming back to her. She struggled to breathe in an ounce of air. Thick, hot and heavy it seemed to refuse to enter her lungs. Clutching her chest she felt it again. The realization; like the blade in her pocket, cold and hard. The cool blade inserted itself again. A constant ripping that wouldn't subside. Finally a large gulp of salty air reached her lungs biting sharp. She pulled the warm puppy to her chest, struggling to warm herself in the ninety-degree sun. Struggling to not fight it, she tried her best to allow her heart to mourn, staring out at the huge void before her.

Softening her gaze. She loved it here, staring out at the vast expanse of the ocean before her. It was massive. It could be so calm some days, like today. Yet, sometimes the wind could blow off it and give her a beating to remember. Other times it was graceful, bestowing on her a comforting breeze capable of healing all wounds. Since the very first time she saw the ocean as a small child, she had forever felt it's pull, beckoning to her to take up permanent residence by its side.

She had enjoyed every moment, fixing up this old place. She made friends in the process and looked forward to their visits. But through every minute, part of her had held onto the belief, that at sixty her and Carl would be sitting here watching their grandchildren. Just as she sat here right now, watching their own.

She watched the waves as they crashed against the shore. She listened to its comforting rhythm and knew it would be what gently lulled her to sleep at night. The ocean; was so many things to her now, like the men who had loved her. The gentle breeze that comforts as David had comforted her. The chaotic storm that sweeps in effects you for a moment and moves on, as Jordan had done for fleeting moments. But it is the constant, enduring tide that she loves the most. It is the tide that binds the marriage of the moon and the sun, orchestrating the beauty of the world around her. Pulling her, luring her, lulling her with its music and it was Carl who had been that for her.

The irony didn't escape her, the fact that Carl was the reason the others had been attracted to her. It was Carl who married the broken girl. It was his love that healed her and made her the woman the others had loved. It was Carl's love for her that helped her to grow into the confident woman, the love that allowed her to break out of the constraining shell she lived in and learn to fly. He encouraged that from her, even at the risk of losing her to someone like Jordan. It was also the sad and confused woman that his departure had left in its wake that had drawn David to her. It was her broken wing that he recognized and wanted to mend.

She looked at the empty chair next to her and longed for her best friend. He had taught her what love was, true love, by giving it to her. By loving her completely, all of her, her bad qualities as well as her good. It was now, when she no longer needed him, that she wanted him. Only she couldn't have him.

It was that irony and the irony of his loving her so deeply that made it possible for her to have the strength she needed to go on. She watched their children and knew that she would go on. She had had a love strong enough to last a lifetime. But it was that comfort that made her want him all the more, not less.

She knew she no longer needed his love. She knew she would always have that, even if she didn't have him. But it was through all of this that she came to understand how desperately she needed to love him back. And it was then, when the stabbing hit her once more, then that Rebecca no longer hoped for it to fade.

CHAPTER THIRTY-SEVEN

Rebecca heard a bump behind her and then a tinkling sound as a spoon banged against the inside of a glass. "Hi George, Thank you for the gift"You're welcome, they look really good in there."

"Yes, your mom had great taste." George had deliverymen bring her his mom's living room set. There were five pieces, all of it in the Queen Anne style, winged backed and tiger footed, two leather chairs, a couch and chair in royal blue, and a tapestry rocker, covered in blue birds and greenery. She loved them and she knew she probably never would have found something to match the rug as perfectly as they did. "You shouldn't have sent them, but I do love them, Thanks."

"Of course I should have, they were just collecting dust in my attic."

"Especially the rocker; I love the birds, thank you."

She was talking to him, but looking in the other direction. "That was my Grand Mum's, I'm glad you like it."

"I do."

She was sitting there, wrapped up in a blanket, staring out toward the public beach. "Rebecca are you alright? It's ninety degrees."

"Yes, I'm fine." She didn't want him to see her. She thought that she didn't care anymore, but realized that she still didn't like others seeing her pain.

The children walked by, calling hello to George, as they made their way to the house. He realized that Rachel had made lunch when they all sat at the table on the upper deck. "Rebecca what is going on here?"

"You wouldn't understand."

George was afraid he would understand all too well. Children being ignored, fending for themselves, Rebecca staring out at strangers. He understood far too well. It was his Father all over again. "What happened?" He crouched down in front of her.

She turned her head further away. But it was as far as she could turn it. She covered her face with the blanket wiping the flow from her eyes down her neck.

"What wouldn't I understand?"

"How I feel, you chose long ago not to know. You don't know. You can't understand, and you can't help. I just have to go through this alone."

Ouch, maybe she was right I don't know, and I can't understand. Those were his mistakes, and he was working on them. "You're wrong, I can help, maybe I did spare myself some types of hurt, but that alone, hurts very bad. I can help you, Rebecca, and you don't have to go through this alone. I won't let you and I won't let you become my father either."

Rebecca stared back out at the strangers playing in the water.

"REBECCA, Look at me." Her face was puffy, and her eyes were red and swollen. "And if you're going to stare at anything, stare at them, talk to them, hug them. You need them, and they certainly need you. I can tell you that."

Rebecca looked at George, her friend. She watched as a tear ran down his cheek. Was it a tear for her, a tear for himself or a tear for his father. She didn't know, but his pain was as real and as strong as her own. She could feel it. She grasped his hand to comfort him and to comfort her.

They both watched her children as they built a castle in the sand, all three yelling for Copper to leave it alone. The sun was starting to hit the horizon.

"Just imagine how my life might have been different, if I had had my Father and knew that he loved me." He smiled at her children. "Don't be my Father, Rebecca." He rose from Carl's chair. She guessed it was her friend's chair now. He leaned down, pushed aside her hair and he gently kissed her forehead. "Bye, Kiddo, I'll see you tomorrow."

"What? You're not staying for dinner."

He wished today of all days that he could. He said regretfully. "I can't, I have a date."

"You do?"

"With Isadora. I looked her up, she's widowed now, and she wants to see me."

"Wow." She smiled at her friend. "That's great."

"Yeah." He said. Her noticing now, how he was all spiffed up. Looking crisply clothed and smacking of elegant cologne.

"Bye, George." She let go of his hand.

He raised it high into the air, waving to the children. Yelling, "Bye, kids, see you tomorrow."

"Bye, George." They all yelled back.

Danny ran to catch George and give him a hug. He ran speeding back from the driveway with copper tight at his heels.

"Mom, Are you and George going together."

"What? Why would you ask that."

"Well, He visits a lot and I saw you, holding hands."

"No, sweetie, we're friends. Just very good friends."

"Oh." "Can we have dinner now." He asked, satisfied with her simple answer.

"Yeah, we can. Do you want to grill."

"Yeah, hotdogs?"

"Sure, Do you want to finish the castle first?"

"Nah."

"I'll help."

"Yeah! You don't mind?"

"No, I don't mind."

She stood up giving Danny a hug, before they both ran over to help the girls.

The sky was developing a rosy hue. Rebecca knew the sun would be going down soon. The castle was complete, but she would be surprised if any of it remained standing by tomorrow morning. It wasn't a great castle, but it was good. If Carl were here, it would have been great, huge and covered in turrets. She washed her hands in the approaching tide. The sand eroding away with the tow left her rings exposed. They were different, the luster appeared all gone. The band seemed to be made of brass now, not gold. Maybe it was a trick of her eye, but the message was clear. The time had come for saying good bye.

Rebecca took off the ring and held it in her hand. Grasping it tight one last time, she opened her fingers to find the tiny circle resting in her palm. Looking at it and to the water and then the sky around her. She turned to watch her children running up the stairs.

"Good bye, Carl." She flung the ring into the ocean. "I love you."

"I'll always love you."

"Always Remember that I Loved You."

Inside, Rebecca pulled hot dogs out of the fridge and went to the back porch to turn on the grill. Waiting outside was a large box. Dragging it in. She noticed, a postmark dated earlier today. It must have been sent same day delivery. The address read Mountain View Resort, from somewhere in Washington. Rebecca's heart raced. The green eyes of the cougar flashed in her mind.

She opened the box finding a note on top. "Thank you my friend, for giving me memories, make lovely ones with your children." That was it, no signature. She opened the box to find a checkered table.

Changed from their bathing suits, the children came running in for food. Faced with their mother struggling with the box, they helped her, each grabbing a leg and lifting up. Once it was standing on its own, Rebecca was sure she had seen it before. Sifting through the pictures in the envelope, she found it. A picture of the two Cavanaugh men, George's Father and Grandfather, sitting in the two leather chairs with the chess set between them. It had to be from George. She remembered him describing it months ago. She wanted to reprimand the grand-fatherly man. She lifted the board to find the interweaving C and R, Cavanaugh and Ripley. They brought the set to its place of honor between the two chairs. Then the four of them quickly made dinner, so they could play with the set, Rebecca trying her best to remember the rules. Awed by the pieces, the rules didn't matter. They'd make up their own for now and learn the real ones later.

CHAPTER THIRTY-EIGHT

Matt looked around at the people carrying bags on their shoulders, pulling behind them others that rested on wheels. They watched, as the large plane on the tarmac, roared forward, lifting gracefully off the ground and climbed skyward. The man next to him was finally going home. He was excited for him, but a little nervous too. The dim roar of the airport was interrupted by the call for Chicago flight 230 preparing to board. "Did you ever find out what the cougar vision meant?"

Carl looked at the boy, Uncertain if he could relate everything in the few minutes they had left. "No." He told Matt.

But in truth he thought it was all about survival. The ghastly experience of seeing the deer go down was a wakeup call to Carl. By watching a creature that doesn't feed on others die, Carl realized, that when it comes to surviving sometimes the innocent are the ones to pay the price. People like himself, his family and others, like Paul are sometimes brought down by predators. The cougar showed him which side of that struggle he would be on if he hesitated to trust his own instincts. Unlike the young deer that hesitated to run, Carl did what he had to do to survive. If taking down men who intended to prey on others, was what it took, then so be it. He wasn't proud of it, but he wouldn't lose any sleep over it either.

He'll never claim to understand why General Davis concocted his insane plan to start World War III. Nor does he suspect, will anyone else. Especially, since it is unlikely to come out that such an incident even occurred. No one will know, if it were fame and historical reference he was after, or just simply too many years of battle planning that pushed his gold stars a little too far. At any rate, the incident was over, and all Carl had left to do was to try to re-establish his life. He found himself more afraid of this, than anything else he has faced in the past year. Up until now, all he had to lose was his life. Now, something truly important was at risk, his happiness.

"I don't know if it is explainable." Carl answered.

"No, Maybe not." Matt agreed.

"Anyway, thanks for driving me to the airport. I'm glad that I got to meet you."

"Hey, No Goodbye's. You're going to be working for my Uncle, I'll see you around."

"Okay, So long, Matt. You take care of that smart little girl of yours."

"I will."

"You better, she could be your Rebecca."

"Oh she is, she is." Matt smirked.

"Flight 909 to Washington, D.C. is now boarding at gate twelve."

"There's my flight."

"Oh, hey, listen, before you run. Remember Ray, he's been assigned to pick you up in D.C. He'll drive you home, oh, and Julie said to buy a copy of The Washington Post at the airport. Take care Dude."

"You, too." Carl shook his hand.

Matt leaned in and gave him a brother-smack hug and then both turned and went their own way.

Carl was surprised that Ray wasn't at the terminal waiting for him. But then air flights seldom came in early. His had beaten its arrival time by fifteen minutes. Ray was probably off somewhere grabbing a bite to eat. Carl went to the newspaper stand and bought a Washington Post. Then he took a seat to wait for Ray.

The headline read: International Uproar Forces Tougher Nuclear Disarmament Agreements. Carl's attention was distracted by the television hanging in the terminal waiting area. "In the wake of the North Korean Nuclear Weapons Facility Disaster, today President Cartwright appointed Major General Harding, of the US Army, to represent the United States in the newly formed International Oversight Committee for the Elimination of Nuclear Tyranny. General Harding, along with representatives from forty-seven other nations, will be attending, what President Cartwright, described as the first of many scheduled meetings, prepared to draft tougher international disarmament laws. The first such meeting is scheduled for Monday in Hamburg, Germany.

In the wake of 1.5 million deaths, attributed to the explosion in

Hungnam, North Korea. President Cartwright has also appointed joint leadership to Colonel Bowers and Lieutenant Colonel Taylor for the assembly of U.S. Clean up and Assistance Teams. The teams were expected to be deployed as early as the middle of next week, to assistance with other U.S. Nuclear, Biological and Chemical teams already stationed in South Korea. International teams, from Russia, Japan, Germany and England were scheduled to arrive shortly after the U.S. Entourage. President Cartwright was taped earlier today as saying." They broke off to a clip of the president. He appeared slightly older looking to Carl then the night he was at the dinner. "It is a truly sad day, when millions of innocent people die needlessly. It is our responsibility as Leading International Nations to ensure that such atrocities never happen again. It is time for a united Korea to begin anew, my international colleagues, and I wish to aid Korea in her time of rebirth. Our heart and prayers go out to the people of Northern Korea."

Carl returned to the newspaper in his hands. As interesting as the article was he doubted that it was why Julie had wanted him to buy it. Carl flipped through the pages of the paper until he came to something that would trigger a bell. He realized what it was when he caught sight of the personals page. Scanning the short ads, Carl found the one he was looking for.

Invisible man-

Thanks for being a good friend. I'll never forget you.

Fortunately- Life does go on- Enjoy yours. I'll love you always.

Guardian Girl.

The long black stretch limousine inched its way up Ripley Road.

"Go slow." Carl urged.

"Yes, Sir. I'm going about as slow as I can." The driver answered back.

"Which one is it?" Carl asked tense and unsure.

"I was told the last one on the water, Sir."

Each inch that the car's wheels moved forward the tighter, the grip in Carl's stomach became. He knew not what to expect. Would they be there, would he recognize them, or would they recognize him? Would they want him back in their lives or would someone have replaced him. Only one house to go. "Oh, God, Carl could see a man coming down the back stairs. "Wait, Stop."

The driver stopped the car with a small jerk. "Yes, Sir, Would you prefer to go to the hotel?"

Car hesitated to answer, unsure of what to do. He watched the man climb into his car, and as he slowly drove past them, Carl noticed that the man was old enough to be Rebecca's Father.

"Sir."

"Yes, Ray."

"Would you like me to continue, or should I turn back around?"

"Let's continue."

Ray slowly halted the car at the end of the drive. "I'll get your bags, Sir."

"NO. Let's wait a moment, please."

"Alright, Sir."

"Do you see anyone, Ray?"

"No Sir, I don't."

There was a long pause where Carl stared expectantly out the tinted window of the stretch limousine, waiting and hoping to catch a glimpse of his family.

He pushed a button and heard the motor hum as the window opened, letting in the salt heavy breeze. It was a beautiful day, the sun up far past noon. The only sounds he could hear were those off in the distance, the caw of a seagull and the dampened sound of waves hitting against the shore.

An enthusiastic bark jolted Carl's gaze. It was close. Carl searched the landscape, catching a glimpse of the mound, moving cascades of fur cresting the dune, headed toward shore. Carl opened the door.

The driver stepped out and opened the trunk to get out his bags. "I'll pick you up at 7:00 am sharp, next Monday, Sir. DDAS is about forty minutes from here. Mr. Douglas said 8:00am sharp for the meeting."

"Yes, Ray, I remember. You don't need to pick me up." Carl protested.

"Orders are orders, Sir."

Carl wouldn't argue that. "Alright, I'll see you at seven am then."

"Sir."

"Yes, Ray."

"Would you like me to wait."

Carl thought he was reading his mind. "No, I'll be okay."

"I'll leave your bags on the back stairs, then."

"Thank you." Carl responded as he shook the man's hand and passed him a few bills for his time and patience.

Carl, dressed in his olive-drab suit, walked up the drive to see if his family was really there. To see if Rebecca would know him, still want him after a year of disappearing on them.

Carl looked at the house it was amazing. He looked at the view it was more amazing still. For on the water's edge was Rebecca. Dressed in a rose patterned sundress, kicking at the water. She looked twenty again, with her back to him and her long black hair whipping in the wind. The waves reached her, crashing against her legs. Carl watched as she reached down to pick something up. Almost to her now, remembering this from somewhere before. The image came rushing back of her picking up something golden in the sand. Only this time he was with her and in her hand was a ring.

When she stood up, there it was in her hand. She thought it was gone forever. But nonetheless, there it was in her hand, where it belonged.

When she stood up, she was there again. No longer twenty, but now older, with gray in her hair and a woman's figure, instead of a girl's. She was more beautiful than he remembered.

Looking up he was standing there. Not as a young soldier anymore, but as a grown businessman. Both tall and handsome with eyes glowing green like the cougar. Rebecca longed for this not to be a dream and if it were, she longed to remain dreaming forever.

"Hello." He said in an almost whisper.

Holding the ring up for him to see. She dared to break the spell by speaking back.

"It came back to me." She clutched the cold ring in her hand as she reached out to touch him. "And so did you."

Carl wrapped his arms around Rebecca and within seconds, Rachel, Karen and Danny's arms were wrapped tight too.

Walking hand in hand down the beach of their new home. It was then that Rebecca relaxed and let out a sigh, For home was by his side.

EPILOGUE

Four months later

Rebecca was happy. Things were beginning to feel normal again. Carl had returned. She knew in her heart that it was him, even though he insisted he wasn't. His mouth told her one thing, but his eyes told her another. He simply said, Hello. Stepping back into their lives as if he had never left. He offered no explanations and expected none in return. She told him the good things and left out the bad. He seemed satisfied with that. And she was satisfied too.

She had him and that was all that she needed. She knew that his heart carried a weight. A weight that perhaps one day would be lifted. The story of an old man revealed on his day of dying. And maybe too, she will tell him about the year she experienced without him, how she felt and how she wished on her breath that he would return. But for now, together was enough.

Flipping the burgers, Rebecca enjoyed the voices of her friends gabbing away, as she cooked for them, a last summer-fall meal, before they packed themselves away for the winter. Everyone sat bundled in sweaters. All feeling jubilant from beer and wine. She loved the voices and laughing, the sound of copper barking, the carrying sound of her children playing, the waves hitting shore, and the seagulls in the air. But most of all, she loved the feel of Carl's arms around her as she listened to it all.

"Carl, would you mind calling the kids to come eat."

"Who's Carl?" Amy asked confused.

"Did I say Carl?" She displayed no shame, but gave Alex a kiss that said, Sorry, "He's my deceased husband."

"She doesn't mean anything by it. He hugged her. I understand it takes time." He ran down the stairs.

"I'm sorry, Rebecca. I didn't know that was his name. I didn't think."

"It's okay. I don't talk about it much."

"Alex certainly is forgiving about it." Jeffery remarked.

"The kids have really taken to him, even calling him Dad already." Amy said.

"I think that it comes natural to them, he's so much like Carl."

Her friend wore a concerned frown. "But, he's not Carl."

"I know, You're right, he's not Carl. But he's as close to Carl as I'll ever find. And I really do love him for being Alex."

George looked at his friend and held Isadora's hand tighter. He saw the look in Rebecca's eyes. The same look his father had for his mother, and he knew. He knew that the lonely dolphin had returned home. He looked at Isadora, his lover and then back toward Rebecca, the friend his father had sent him. He felt the warm breeze that encircled him, lift away and drift back to the ocean from which it came.

He looked to the children playing with their father, listened to their laughs, his swinging them, teasing them that he would throw them into the freezing cold water. He watched the dog following tight to their heels. He looked to the sky on the far horizon. It's colorful pallet out there for everyone to see. Dancing the tango between day and night.

George was pleased with what he saw. For beyond the beauty, he saw the struggle. The struggle between the sun and moon. The struggle of life and the struggle of love. But most of all, he saw the struggle of faith. The faith to believe. The faith to hold on. The faith to keep living.

For the first time in sixty-two years, George felt content. Grateful even, for life had turned out good in the end.

ABOUT THE AUTHOR

Marianne A. McDonald lives in Goochland County, Virginia with her husband and children. She grew up in New England the youngest of six children. In 1989, she married a soldier and began experiencing a somewhat nomadic lifestyle before finally settling in Virginia.
"It's the Gentle Breeze that guides us" is her debut novel and although it is a work of fiction, it is also deeply personal to the author.
"I hope that you enjoy reading it as much as I enjoyed writing it." - Marianne

Please visit the author's website at http://www.marianneamcdonald.com to find information on other books by Marianne A. McDonald or to email her your thoughts or opinions of her work.

Also find her on Facebook:
Authors page: Marianne.a.mcdonald
Publishers Page: Marianne A. McDonald Books

www.ingramcontent.com/pod-product-compliance
Lightning Source LLC
Chambersburg PA
CBHW051432260626
47162CB00001B/65